LEGENDS OF A SHATTERED AGE

LEGEND OF TAKASHANIEL #2

RAMÓN TERRELL

LEGENDS OF A SHATTERED AGE
LEGEND OF TAKASHANIEL #2
RAMÓN TERRELL
Copyright © 2014 Ramon Terrell
Tal Publishing

ISBN: 978-0-9937236-9-8 (Paperback)

Edited by Mia Kleve & Vivian Caethe

Cover artwork by Martin Maceovic
Cover artwork revision by Nick Deligaris

Tal Publishing

ACKNOWLEDGMENTS

Every book takes a team to create. I'd like to thank my team:

Cat Lee, you have been amazing through the journeys of each book, and have always been there when I was in a pinch and needed help. You truly rock.

Flora Samuelson, you have been great with feedback as well as what you did and didn't like. Your honesty has helped this book become better.

Thank you, Rick Rhodes, for hopping in when I needed an extra set of eyes, and always cheering me on.

A very special thanks to Vivian Caethe for being the kind of tough editor that makes a writer stronger and better.

And also, a very special thanks to Mia Kleve. You're work has been great, and you've been a pleasure to work with.

1

The departing ship bobbed over the waves, fast diminishing toward the horizon.

Kita and Kenyatta had been down on the beach to look at the incoming wares, as they always did when a merchant ship arrived. But the higher import prices had quickly darkened what was usually a fun event of haggling and bargaining, so they left in short order. After hiking up what was more a hill than mountain at the back of the little town, they had engaged in a bit of sparring until the ship departed. Now from their position atop the barren hills of Rocky Point, Jamaica, the two friends looked from the unhappy clump of buyers on the beach to the merchant ship, *Salty Lady*, climbing over the rolling waves of the ocean headed northwest.

Kita whistled through his teeth, watching the departing ship bob over the waves, fast diminishing toward the horizon. "That captain rushed out of here like his life depended on it."

"Yeah, man." Kenyatta glanced down at the beach, and the unhappy shop owners who'd just paid a premium for goods they'd paid half as much for over many years. "You tink him lying about the ocean swallowing up ships at sea? Maybe an excuse for higher prices?"

"If not for the fear in his eyes and his urgency to be gone from here, I'd have thought so." Kita shook his head. "No. That man was afraid."

"What come out of the ocean to scare a sea captain?" Kenyatta asked. "Him look like he want to get out of the ocean forever, but in a hurry to get away from here at the same time. Never seen anyting like it."

Kita turned away from the ocean to look down at the town below. "Whether he's lying or not, it doesn't matter. Sumfest is in two days. The grounds are freshly tilled and smoothed, and those angry vendors will make plenty of profit like they do every year."

The mention of the annual summer festival nicknamed "sumfest", brought a smile to Kenyatta's face. He thought of the beach parties, the city streets packed with revelers, the straw hut taverns and eateries overflowing with jovial patrons talking loud and sipping rum. "Yeah, man. Dem carryin' in a few new artists this year. Maybe ..."

He trailed off when a sound, like an animal the size of a mountain taking in a deep breath, rolled over them. He looked out at the ocean to see a colossal wave rising several hundred feet from the beach. "Bombaclot ..."

"What now?" Kita asked, turning back.

Kenyatta never took his eyes off the ocean as he waved Kita over. "Impossible."

Kita's eyes widened. "What is *that*?"

The wave approached the shore, picking up speed and size.

"Ken ..." Kita cast Kenyatta a sidelong glance. "It's coming straight for land. *Fast*."

Kenyatta looked from the ocean to the throngs of people. Thatch-roofed huts filled with eating and drinking locals and visitors who'd come to perform at Sumfest. People socializing under towering coconut and palm trees, directly in the path of the still growing wave. "We've got to warn everyone. Now!"

"No time." Kita pointed out at sea.

They stared helplessly as the swell—now more than fifty feet high—raced toward the shore.

When revelers on the beach finally spotted the danger, shouts and panic ensued. People scrambled from homes and buildings; those beachside sprinting away from the shore. Some climbed onto the roofs of houses while others tried to climb trees or simply ran.

Kenyatta and Kita shouted at people to come towards them for higher ground, but to no effect. They might as well have been yelling from the other side of the world, for the distance and the roar of the predatory wave drowned out their voices.

Kenyatta clenched his fists in helpless frustration as the wave reached the beach and washed right over it. Shouts turned to screams, which were quickly silenced by the crashing water.

The two friends could do nothing but watch as huts were blasted apart as though made of stacked twigs. Some of the older, hardier trees withstood the flood while others snapped in half or were snatched out of the ground and washed inland to burst through the stone and wooden walls of homes and businesses.

Kenyatta and Kita looked on in horror, their eyes darting left and right as they took in the tragedy. The ocean itself rose up before their eyes and flowed over those buildings that managed to survive the first impact. People thrashed around in the rushing currents like ants in a stream. Some were lucky enough to wash upon high ground, while others collided with trees and buildings, or were pushed further into town and out of sight.

Then it stopped.

Kita's mouth worked silently as he watched in helplessness at the tragedy below. "How?" he finally managed. "How in the name of the Gods was that possible? Waves can't just leap out of the ocean. They don't raise up only in one spot, and settle back down like that."

Kenyatta didn't hear him. He just stared at the chaos which became a blur through the tears welling in his eyes. Rocky Point was a peninsula separated from the rest of the island by a clump of small bare mountains. In front of those mountains were a series of hills overlooking a town of colorful structures that brought the town to life.

Now that life was being crushed. Kenyatta looked out at the ocean. It washed completely over the town to crash at the base of the hills where he and Kita stood.

Like fingers sliding across the sand, the water retreated, leaving complete devastation in its wake. Homes and businesses lay in splinters. Trees, along with the dead and injured, lay strewn about the once-happy town like leaves after a windy day.

Kenyatta heard Kita's voice, and it sounded as though it wasn't the first time his friend had spoken.

"Ken," Kita placed a hand on his shoulder, "we've got to get down there and help the survivors. Another one might come in."

Kenyatta let out a ragged breath and nodded. "Yeah ... yeah, man."

2

Seung stood under the endless downpour of Inayo Falls. Cradled in the void of meditation, the roar of the falling water had long gone silent in her ears. And even though Seung hadn't traveled much in her life, she couldn't imagine a more beautiful and serene place could exist.

She drifted deeper into her standing meditation under the torrent. Eyes closed, standing erect, the young warrior held her hands in front of her heart, forefingers and thumbs pressed together, her remaining fingers curled inward.

When she sat directly on the earth, she felt a strong connection with it. From the rocks, to the tiny plants and shrubs, to the giant trees who whispered to each other through their network of roots in the ground. She could expand her awareness and feel the air, the sky, even connect with a nearby bird in flight.

She sometimes floated on her back in the lake at that base of the falls and let her awareness connect with the underwater plants, the moss, the fish. Today was one of her frequent, and more difficult, endeavors: to connect with the earth from a more challenging position.

Standing upon the lone boulder directly under the crashing

water, Seung stretched her awareness from her location to the shore. She felt the ever-unmoving presence of the earth. She rode the leaves that detached from the branches of trees and floated in the air.

Seung pulled her awareness back, then sent it into the water. She felt the presence of the moss at the floor of the lake. She felt the underwater plants, swaying with the lazy current. She felt the energy formed by the constantly moving water, and the presence of the beautiful gold, white, and red carp swimming along the bottom, pecking at moss.

She basked in her connection with the flowing water and its inhabitants, enjoying the quiet and tranquil depths of the lake.

Her body gave a sudden involuntary jerk. A huge and heavy presence appeared in the lake and pressed down on her. Seung's awareness recoiled, but the entity was everywhere. The force closed around her until it felt as though she was held fast in an unbreakable grip. Her brow twitched as she fought to hold on to herself. The force was so big, so powerful, she felt she would be absorbed in it if she faltered.

Anger, restlessness, resentment. Seung tried to move away, but the presence was there, filled with raw and primal emotion. She felt the sensation of being awoken from a fitful sleep to a destroyed home filled with enemies. Her home, destroyed, poisoned. The poison crept into her, filling her mind and body with pain and rage.

Seung's eyes popped open. She gasped, then doubled over in a fit of coughing when she inhaled some of the falling water. She slipped and fell off the boulder into the pond, and though she was awake from her meditation, the lingering connection remained. The anger turned to sorrow, then regret, then anger again. Was something in this pond trying to communicate with her?

She swam for the surface and inhaled a deep breath of air, coughing up the last bit of water that had made it to her windpipe. She made her way to the shore and dragged herself out of the pond. On hands and knees, she took several ragged breaths. *What was that?*

Seung pushed aside several locks of wet hair clinging to the side of her head and looked over her shoulder at the lake. *Was something in there?* She'd grown up swimming in that water and had never had such an experience. Such an enormous presence couldn't possibly live in that small body of water.

She climbed to her feet and walked to the shore, eyeing it as though it was a venomous animal. The sensation had already begun to fade, yet her curiosity hadn't. She dipped her toe in the water, then her foot. Nothing. Seung waded back into the water until she was waist-deep.

"Are you some kind of water spirit?" She glanced about her surroundings, then shook her head. "Talking to no one. I must look like an idiot." She waded in deeper until she was treading water, then floated on her back. She spread her arms out and felt her hair tickling her arms, as it drifted about her head like a cloud.

Watching a gray heron glide across the cloudless blue sky, she thought about the many times during her meditations when she'd felt a link with a nearby animal or bird, feeling their feelings, their contentment or fright, hunger, wariness. Seung blinked. *Is that what just happened?* The idea of something that large and powerful connecting with her nearly sent her swimming back for land. Instead she took a few calming breaths, then closed her eyes and opened herself again, carefully. Despite her caution, the images hit her hard again.

She fought to keep her fear in check and communicate with the presence. She sensed no evil, but whatever it was, it was unhappy. *What are you trying to tell me?*

If it heard her, it didn't respond, but continued to flood her with pain, anger, and frustration. It was like sharing a nightmare with another being. Death, sickness, rage. Scorched and poisoned lands filled with toxic chemicals from long ago.

Seung pushed through the bombardment. *Who are you? What are you trying to tell me?*

For a flicker of a moment the presence was fully aware of her, and she sensed disdain. She was the cause of its pain. She was the cause of its sickness. Not just her. All like her.

Seung struggled to remain calm under the accusations. *I've done nothing.* The presence pressed down on her with crushing force, and her body tensed. *Please, you're hurting me.* To her surprise, it responded.

"As you've hurt me."

It was like being spoken to by a mountain, so heavy and powerful was the voice. Countless images flashed through her mind, and she shook violently, unaware of the water splashing over her face, or that she was now below the surface. So many images. Too many to withstand.

Seung's eyes flew open. She looked around, surprised to find herself underwater, and half expecting to be attacked by some giant creature. Carp swam around her at a safe distance, eyeing her as they drifted by.

She worked her way to the surface and broke through with a long gasp of sweet air, and treaded in place, trying to get her bearings. She found the shore, several dozen feet away and realized she'd drifted to the middle of the pond. She swam hard and didn't stop until her feet touched the rocky bottom.

Seung splashed her way out of the water and bent over, placing her hands on her knees to catch her breath. She looked back at her peaceful retreat since childhood. Now it looked ominous.

"What in the name of the Gods?" Seung took a deep breath, and replayed the experience in her mind. She closed her eyes and saw the deep blue ocean, once vibrant and thriving now sick and dying. She saw fanged beasts with long necks and slitted eyes, frightful enough to stop her heart.

Snow drifted on the howling winds of an icy tundra, where a range of mountains stood watch over the frozen landscape.

Seung's shiver had nothing to do with the weather. "What did I connect with?" She hugged herself and continued to stare at the lake. "Do I even want to know?"

3

Seung took the long route home, passing through woods filled with maples, pines, oak, and red trees, inhaling the smell of the earth, moss, and tree sap. She closed her eyes and sighed allowing the song of the forest to ease her mind. With no small bit of apprehension from her experience at the lake, she tentatively opened herself to the environment.

All about the woods and leafy forest floor, squirrels scurried up and down the trees in play. A crow called overhead, and another answered. Then another. She extended her awareness further and touched the presence of a wolf resting at the base of a tall pine. It lifted its head and twitched its ears, alert to her presence. After a moment, it lowered its head and relaxed.

Seung smiled as she moved on, walking slower than usual as she practiced extending her awareness all around her. She felt the contentment of the trees, the bushes and shrubbery basking in the sunlight, the moss and lichen clinging to the trees.

She'd first stumbled on this ability as a child. Adults had told her it was her imagination, but it only grew stronger the more she practiced it. Over time, her ability to attune with nature grew stronger until it simply felt a natural part of who she was. That ability had been a comfort for a child who was different from everyone else.

The stray thought sent her fingers to the tips of her ears, and she quickly covered them with her hair. No one Seung had ever met had ears like hers. Where others rounded at the top, hers came to a point. Where others of her people had features only slightly angular, hers were sharper. Her eyebrows were more pointed, her jawline and cheekbones slightly longer. The people of Kyu Village, were used to her sharp features and melodious voice, but she hid her ears under her hair always. It was a deformity she never let anyone see.

Seung hopped over a fallen tree, then started uphill. The woods northwest of Kyu were her favorite place, aside from Inayo Falls. Trees with red, yellow, and orange leaves shone in the late afternoon light, a beautiful heralding of autumn's arrival. Seung closed her eyes and took a deep breath, letting it out in a contented hum.

She thought back to her encounter in the lake. She hadn't felt anything of that presence since retreating from the water. And the further she left it behind, the more the feelings dissolved to be replaced by the sweet and pungent smell of moss, the plants and flowers, the whispers of the trees, the bird chatter.

The possibility of something as large as what she'd felt living in that pond made Seung shudder. She shrugged the thought away. "Nothing lives in there but fish."

She reached the top of the incline and looked down on the village below, surrounded by woods alight with multicolored leaves. "The fiery puffs of fall," she murmured, and her round pink lips stretched into a smile.

THE HOMES of Kyu Village sat nestled against green, rolling hills, as though sitting upon huge wide stairs. Firmly packed dirt roads led through the middle of the village and branched off at various points at each level.

Seung inhaled the crisp fresh air of the breeze snaking its way down the hills. The wooden door to a home slid open and three children ran out, giggling and chasing each other. She looked up to see a fourth child peeking over the side of the gray tiled roof. The girl had a devious grin on her face as she cocked her arm back, a pine cone in her little hand as she took aim.

A woman with a large stuffed pack appeared from inside and yelled up at the child on the roof, then spotted Seung and bowed.

Despite her standing as the finest warrior in Kyu Village, Seung always felt undeserving of such reverence. She dipped into a small curtsy and bowed her head in turn, showing the elder woman equal respect.

The woman smiled and gathered up the children as the fourth boy climbed down from the roof. The woman looked past Seung with what seemed a concerned expression, then bowed her head once more, and herded the children up the path.

The deeper Seung moved into the village, the more populated it would become, so she paused to slide her hands through her hair to ensure it covered her ears.

To her surprise, however, few people populated the winding walkways. Those who were about, hurried from their homes up the hill toward the central pavilion. A tiny stab of fear pierced Seung's stomach. Irrational as it was, she couldn't help feeling that this was somehow connected to her experience at the falls. "Impossible," she told herself.

A man trotted down the hill in her direction, and when he spotted Seung, broke into a run.

Seung smiled at her best friend. "Tae Kim! What is it?"

"Good," Tae said, ignoring the question. Despite his having run from deeper in the village to find her, he still breathed easy. "You've saved me time."

Her eyebrows raised. "Oh?"

Tae Kim started back in the direction he'd come, Seung falling in step beside him as he said, "We have visitors."

Seung looked at him. "Why is that unusual?"

"They're from Ulleung Island off the eastern coast."

Seung felt the pit of her stomach go cold, though it was surely an absurd reaction. Why would this be connected to her experience? Yet somehow, deep down, she knew it was.

"You all right?" Tae asked.

Seung blinked. "Hm?"

"You know something I don't?" Tae asked, nodding at her clenched fists.

Seung glanced down at her fists and relaxed. "No. I was just thinking about something I saw near the falls."

Tae gave her a skeptical look. "As you say. They arrived here not long ago, and I was on my way to the falls to get you. Luckily, you're back earlier than usual. I spoke with several of them, but they aren't making much sense. They claim a giant wave rose high into the air and washed over the entire island..." he trailed off when Seung stopped. "What is it?"

"A wave washed over the whole island?"

Tae nodded. "That's what they say, but I don't see how it's possible. A wave powerful enough to wash over an entire island, even one as small as Ulleung, would arrive at our own shores. Kyu's not so far from the coast. Something that big would have reached us."

In the blink of an eye, Seung relived the horrible moments shared with her by the presence in the lake. "It could still be coming toward us."

"I sent scouts to the coast," Tae said. "One of them should return soon with a report."

They reached the central pavilion where it looked like all of Kyu was gathered. One of the village leaders stood on a raised platform, hands gesturing in the air as she spoke.

"... the warning of the unfortunate people who escaped the

fate of their beloved home, we have a chance to be prepared. Take only what you need and move to the Sun and Moon Temples. They are the highest point in the area."

"If an entire island was washed over," Seung said as she and Tae observed the uneasy crowd, "those people wouldn't have survived to reach us."

Tae nodded again. "I said as much. But they claim that they were out at sea on their fishing boat when it happened, and set a course straight for the mainland."

"They would have been riding high waves or drowning beneath them. This doesn't make sense."

"They claim the ocean settled immediately after Ulleung was destroyed." Tae shook his head. "I told you they weren't making much sense. I don't doubt that some tragedy has happened, but events like this can skew one's memory."

Seung closed her eyes. Images flashed through her mind of washed over islands and waves as tall as the towers in the cities from the Age of Technology. She saw endless destruction, felt the anger, the sickness, the resentment. And it all felt like it originated from the vision of a snowy tundra guarded by a glaring mountain range. She gasped. When she looked to her side, Tae was staring at her.

She looked at him, taking in his dark brown eyes, close-cropped black hair and high cheekbones.

He said nothing, but Seung knew that look. Tae wouldn't press, but it was obvious something was going on with her. She repressed a sigh of relief when one of Tae's scouts came trotting up the hill. The scout bowed to each of them, then delivered his report.

"Master Tae. The tide is normal and the ocean is calm. There's no indication that a tsunami or anything similar comes our way."

Tae Kim nodded. "Given the suddenness of that last one, better to keep watch. Tell the others to maintain their posts until nightfall. No need to send word unless something unusual happens."

Seung thought again of the vision of the mountain range in that harsh-looking snowy tundra. She felt a pulling from deep inside that seemed related to this place.

"... since you've returned, Seung."

Tae's voice interrupted her thoughts again and she blinked. "Hm?"

Her best friend sighed. "I said, you've been distracted since you've returned from Inayo. What's going on with you?"

Seung opened her mouth several times.

"Are you trying to tell me fish are drowning?"

Her teeth clicked when she shut her mouth. "Funny." She looked back to the raised platform, watching the announcements but not really listening. "I don't know how to describe what's on my mind without you thinking I've lost it."

He smirked. "We've known each other all our lives, Seung. You've always been weird." Tae chuckled and moved closer; Seung fought the impulse to ensure her hair was over her ears. "You're like my sister, girl. Do you really think I don't know why you style your hair that way? You probably think they're a flaw, but I think they're beautiful."

Seung felt a stab of alarm but she calmed. Tae was indeed like her brother. He would never tell anyone about her deformity. "How long have you known?"

"Since we were children and fell asleep camping in the woods."

Her lips parted in astonishment. "That was over twenty years ago," she whispered.

"Not my business. You always hide it. I respect that." He shrugged.

Seung smiled at her best friend. "Childhood cruelty managed to pass you by, didn't it?"

Tae winked at her. "I knew something was different about you when your voice started to sound like you were always singing. Trust me, when the other boys finally grew up, it became a rather attractive quality about you, even if it was unusual."

"We should talk with the refugees," Seung said, embarrassed. To her relief, Tae let the subject drop.

A woman stood and moved away from the main group as Seung and Tae approached. Seung gave a mental nod of approval at the woman's strong presence despite her petite stature.

"This is Mi-Suk," Tae said, indicating the woman.

Mi-Suk was half a head shorter than Seung, with somewhat tanned skin, indicating years of field work. A breeze ruffled her shoulder-length hair, and she ignored the stray strands that fell in front of her light brown eyes. She executed a precise bow. This one had a strong will.

"Master Tae Kim and Master Seung Yoon. I offer gratitude on behalf of my people and myself, for your warm welcome. It has been...hard."

Seung returned the bow and said, "I cannot imagine what you've been through, Mi-Suk. We are sorry for the loss of your loved ones and your home."

The other woman pressed her lips together and gave a curt nod. "Thank you. All that is left of Ulleung is what you see here?" She half turned and waved out a hand to indicate the other refugees.

The haggard group stood silently, staring straight ahead. Their clothes and hair were soiled and tangled, patches of sand stuck here and there to their bodies. With an effort, Seung kept the emotion from her face and her voice. "We are happy to help you rebuild your lives here, or anywhere you wish."

Mi-Suk nodded again with a forced smile. "The people of Kyu are kind. Have you come to speak with me about what happened?"

"I have."

Mi-Suk spread her hands. "That won't take long, for there is little to say. I normally work the fields and harvest the vegetables and roots. Today I was asked to help on the fishing boats, and I was excited for the change in routine."

And that invitation saved your life, Seung thought.

"We set out at dawn, and were out for half the day. Once our barrels were filled with fish, we set out for home. We were in sight of Ulleung when we heard a sound as if the ocean itself drew a deep breath. Only a moment later the giant wave rose and fell. Not a mile away. Maybe not half that distance."

"How can that be possible?" Tae Kim asked. "That close, your boat surely would have been caught in the wave."

Staring at the ground, Mi-Suk clenched her jaw. "We saw what we saw, and that was a giant wave rising high above the tallest buildings in the great cities, and crashing down on our home. No one ..." She sniffed and took a deep breath, then squared her shoulders and looked at Seung and Tae. "There were no survivors. All we could do was sit in the water and watch the island die. Three fishing boats carrying the twenty four of us are what's left of Ulleung."

"I'm sorry for asking you to relive that horror," Seung said.

"We will relive that horror for many days to come," the other woman said. "But if I may offer this in exchange for your kindness, and that it may save your beautiful home, I do it gladly."

Seung felt the tug in the pit of her stomach again, urging her toward some distant frozen land she'd rather not visit, but knew she must. "Kyu Village is your home for as long as you wish it. Please extend our condolences to the rest of your people."

Lips still pressed together, Mi-Suk responded with another precise bow.

"She's a strong one," Tae said, when the woman was out of earshot. "She grieves in silence while comforting those who grieve openly. If there are any half as tough as her, Kyu will be all the better for it."

Seung was only half listening as her mind played through

what the woman had said: giant waves washing over islands, a huge presence that felt like it was the size of the ocean, or was the ocean itself. She felt the tug in the pit of her stomach grow stronger, and she looked to the northeast.

"You see something I don't?" Tae asked.

"No ... but yes." Seung unconsciously placed a hand to her stomach. "Whatever answers there are to this, they're that way."

"And you know this how?"

She shook her head. "I just know."

"Of course." Tae stared in the same direction as Seung. "Since we were kids, I learned not to ignore your intuition. Is this one of those times?"

When she nodded, he gave her a sidelong glance. "Sometimes I think you listen to the trees, the ground, or even the air, Seung. You sure you're even human?"

Though the comment was meant in jest, Seung felt a stab of uncertainty at the question. She thought about the times she'd tried to tell her friends or older family members of the things she could feel, how she could hear the trees speaking to each other, and feel the mood of the forest. "Such a fanciful imagination, you have," was the usual response.

"I don't know," Seung answered before she caught herself and joined in with Tae's quiet laughter.

"Sometimes I think you're serious when you talk like that, my friend." He looked over his shoulder at the assembly, where the speaker had stepped down and the crowd was beginning to disburse. "Looks like talk is over. Come. There's much work to be done in case this mysterious tsunami comes our way."

"You must do it without me," Seung replied, looking to the northeast again. "I have to..." *Have to what? Chase after an hallucination? A nervous feeling in my stomach?*

Tae frowned at her. "That feeling you have?" He shook his head. "Intuition or not, Seung. How is it possible you know this? And what could you do about it alone? Our best action would be to ensure we're on high ground and prepare for the potential flood."

"You've known me my whole life, my friend," Seung said. "I can't explain how I know this, or even how I'll deal with it, but I know that remaining here is not the right thing for me." She faced her best friend and placed her hands on his shoulders. "Kyu looks to you, Tae Kim. Do your part as I do mine."

Tae nodded past her. "You would do your part there? In some distant place you've never been?"

"I would," Seung replied. "I can say no more than to ask you to trust me."

He shook his head, but pulled her into a tight hug. "If you were anyone else, I would've written you off long ago."

"But I'm not," Seung replied, fighting back the images in her mind to fully share this moment with her dearest friend. This moment which could well be their last, for she had no doubts this journey would be filled with danger.

"You go to pack immediately, then? Will you at least wait till tomorrow, or are you to set off now?" He sighed at Seung's guilty grin. "Of course you wouldn't wait till tomorrow." He wrapped her in another hug, then kissed her on the cheek. "Be well and be safe. And don't make me come looking for you."

"Thank you, dear Tae. And you as well."

She took a side trail toward her home, feeling Tae Kim's eyes on her back. She stepped around the side of a house and leaned against the wall. The pulling in her stomach was stronger than ever, as though confirming she'd made the right choice. "But where am I going?" she thought aloud. The pull inside her once again made her look to the northeast. Something was waiting for her, and she doubted she'd like what she found. She took a deep breath to steady her nerves.

"Very well."

4

Kenyatta set his jaw as he helped a woman pull yet another partially buried body from the mud.

"I tink dis the last one," she said. "Gods be merciful I *hope* it's the last one."

Gods. Two years earlier Kenyatta had seen the power of the Gods brought to bear through mortals. Thoughts of that battle at Takashaniel sent his thoughts speeding back to the fateful day when a wall of darkness washed over the fields of the great tower. Hundreds of demons had descended on the fields of the Tower of Balance; Takashaniel. He, alongside Kita and three warriors from Japan, had battled the endless horde to their physical and mental limits.

The Children of the Gene. That was what Iel, the guardian of Takashaniel, had called them. Within Kenyatta, Kita, and the three Japanese warriors, existed a gene given by the Daunyans—the true name of the Gods—that quickened only when an irritant entered this plane of existence; an irritant such as a demon.

"Don't go lettin' ya faith be shaken, bwoy," the woman said, mistaking Kenyatta's silence. "Da Gods be merciful even in tragedy. Dem get us through dis."

Kenyatta smiled at her. The Gods gave them the free will to choose their lives and live with the consequences and triumphs that resulted. Including tragedies like this. Humans were no more exempt from mass death due to natural forces any more than the animals they share the world with.

Having no words to offer, Kenyatta nodded his head and placed a gentle hand on her shoulder. He stood and looked around. Splintered huts, trees snapped like twigs, collapsed houses and fallen businesses. All of Rocky Point was destroyed. Not a single house or building had been spared from the fury of the ocean when it hammered down on the place. Kenyatta replayed the moment before the waves hit. He remembered the ominous sound of a tremendous inhalation as the waves rose up into the sky.

"Demons," he murmured.

"I'd struggle to believe every demon we battled at Takashaniel combined could manage this," Kita said as he climbed up from the remains of a fallen house. He glanced at the lady Kenyatta had been helping, but she was already off to help more injured survivors. "It would take a tremendous amount of power to reap this much destruction."

"You heard that sound as the ocean raise up before the town, ya?" Kenyatta glared at the open sea. "Ain't nothing got power to create something like dat, man. What else could it be?"

Kita looked out at the ocean as well, but offered no answer. "I heard people wondering what could have caused it. Maybe an earthquake in the ocean. All they have are guesses."

"You don't believe it any more than I do," Kenyatta replied. "Tsunamis wash in from the ocean, not raise straight up out da water to crash down on top of you." He ran a hand through his twisted locks. "Demons, man. Or one really powerful one."

"So, what then?" Kita asked. "We go back to Takashaniel to find answers?"

"I don't know," Kenyatta replied. "I feel like we don't have time for dat, but we need answers." He turned away from the ocean to face Kita. "Der is a man who come from a long line of people called nature readers. We could try him."

"Nature readers?" Kita frowned. "That's an...odd title."

"Me grandfather know dis man. Him talk all the time about how da man help him with his garden because dem friends. Grandpa say him a little on the grumpy side at times, but a good man. Maybe he knows something."

Kita looked around at the ruin that had been Rocky Point. "Other than helping everyone get to higher ground, I don't think there's anything else we can do here."

After asking around for more than an hour, they finally found the man on other side of the hills, walking in the midst of traumatized survivors. Though slender, there was a strength to the man despite his advanced years. He moved with a sure step, studying the ground, touching trees, whether fallen or not. He seemed to pay closer attention to any place where water collected.

"Seems really concerned," Kita said dryly.

"Everyone do what they can," Kenyatta replied. "He seeks answers in his way."

"By going out for a casual stroll in the midst of a disaster?"

In answer, Kenyatta pointed as the man dipped his hand in a large puddle of water and closed his eyes. He stood and gave an irritated shake of his head.

"Ya find someting, old man?" Kenyatta asked.

"Ya parents raise you better than to address an elder as 'old man,' bwoy?" came the retort.

"I apologize," Kenyatta said. "Can we help you?"

"I don't know what you tinkin' you can do to help me."

Kenyatta stepped forward. "Please forgive me my lost manners on this terrible day. I'm Kenyatta Ihe, and dis me friend, Kita Sepata."

The man rubbed his chin. "Ihe. Only one family in Jamaica wit dat name."

"You were friends with me grandpa," Kenyatta said.

The older man thought on that for a moment, then his face lit with recognition. "Barry. Such a long time ago, my friend leave dis world."

"When I was no more than a handful of years old," Kenyatta said, his voice taking on an uncharacteristically serious tone.

Kita gave him a pat on the shoulder before offering his hand to the older man. "Nice to meet you, sir."

Kenyatta didn't miss the muscles clench in the old man's forearm as he accepted Kita's hand.

"Looks like the foreigner got more manners than you, bwoy," he said to Kenyatta. "Name's Malimokuru." He looked around at the ruins of the little town. "I need get out to the ocean if I'm to find out what's going on."

"I'd think that's the last place to be," Kita replied.

Malimokuru made a helpless gesture. "I'm a nature reader. I can't know anyting about the sea until I'm out in it, dippin' my hand in it, feelin' the water and everyting livin' in it. It's the only way."

Kenyatta waved a hand in the direction of the beach. "So you can dip your toes in over there and be done with it, ya?"

Malimokuru shook his bald head. "Nah, man. Doesn't work that way. You bite the tip of a piece of food, you don't get all the flavor hiding deeper in. I need get out in the ocean and dip my hand in.

Kenyatta sighed. "Then let's get out dere while the water's calm and hope we don't get swallowed up in another tsunami." He spared Kita a quick warning glance, and his friend nodded. If this was indeed the work of some major demon, they would be virtually helpless out in the ocean. But they were just as helpless here as well, and Kenyatta had a feeling that the last flood was a warning.

A woman turned down the street toward them, her arms laden with blankets. The woman—somewhat impatiently—approached when he waved her over. "We're trying to help," he said to the woman. You know who's organizing?"

"On my way there now," the woman said, holding up the blankets.

"Tell everyone to get to high ground as soon as they can," Kenyatta replied

The woman nodded. "Yeah, man. People already on the move." She looked from him to the others. "We could use some extra hands, ya know. Lotta people injured and in shock."

"We're on our way to do our part now," Kenyatta assured her.

They reached the docks and found a boat that would have been small under the best of conditions, but looked a great deal smaller given the recent event.

Kita looked at the boat, then out at the ocean. "Oh yeah. That looks safe."

Kenyatta let out a nervous chuckle. "Yeah, man."

"The swell that come crashin' over Rocky Point can flip dis boat or a ship ten times its size." Malimokuru climbed into the little rowboat and moved to the front. "Quit wastin' time and get in."

"I suppose we rowin' then?" Kenyatta said as he and Kita climbed aboard.

"You see extra oars?" Malimokuru replied.

At the nature reader's insistence, they rowed for a couple hours until Jamaica was little more than an outline on the horizon.

Kenyatta and Kita pulled the oars aboard and the trio sat in silence for a time. Kenyatta leaned back on his elbows and shared a look with Kita as they watched Malimokuru. The nature reader sat cross-legged with his eyes closed for a time. While the older man appeared to meditate, Kenyatta's thoughts drifted back to the horrors of the day, and considered what abysmal monster might be behind them. He was about to speak his thoughts on it when, without a word, Malimokuru leaned to the side of the boat and dipped his hand into the water. After a few moments, he immersed his arm in above the elbow.

Kita drummed his fingers on his lap in the ensuing silence, gazing out at the surrounding infinite blue sea. "Water seems calm enough. Maybe whatever happened was an anomaly that just passed through."

"Maybe," Kenyatta said. "Let's hope so—"

With a wide-eyed gasp, Malimokuru snatched his arm out of the water and fell back against the other side of the boat. The sudden movement was so harsh, the younger men had to hold on to the sides of the boat to stop it from capsizing.

"What happened?" Kita asked. "What's going on? Did something attack you?"

"No ... It can't be possible," he said between breaths. "Someting so big, so primal."

"Whatcha on about, den?" Kenyatta asked. He looked over his shoulder towards Jamaica and licked his lips.

Malimokuru's eyes were wide with fear. "Fish, large and small, are swimming away. Sharks, bottom-dwellers, anyting livin in the ocean that can move, is fleeing."

"From what?" Kita asked.

The nature reader pointed a trembling finger toward Jamaica. "Dat tsunami wasn't natural, man. Someting big force the waves up in the sky and bring em crashing down. Someting big and powerful. A primal force like nothing I've ever felt."

Kenyatta stared into Kita's eyes as Malimokuru spoke. Demons. Or a major demon. What else could summon such a destructive force? "How much time we have?"

The old man sat staring at the floor of the boat, but looking much farther away. "I don't know. It was too much. If I'd maintained the connection any longer I might have gone insane. It was like a mountain roaring in my mind. There was no focus to it, man. Just a kind of frustrated rage, like it's mad at everyting and nothing at the same time."

"I don't understand," Kita said.

"I can't explain any better," Malimokuru replied. "I just know anyone back home better get to high ground and hope it's enough."

"Enough?" Kenyatta and Kita asked in unison.

Malimokuru nodded. "What I felt was enough to swallow Jamaica whole."

"It's under us?" Kita asked, and he and Kenyatta looked over the side of the boat.

"No ... I don't know. It was a presence. Like another mind touching mine, or I touched it. I don't think it knew I was there, and I'm glad it didn't." He looked toward the island again. "What I felt was limitless rage heading in the direction of our home."

Kenyatta snatched up his oar. "We need to get back now."

"We're safer out here," Kita said.

"We can warn ..."

Malimokuru shook his head sadly. "Best we can do is get close enough to witness the destruction. You want that?"

"I'm not gonna sit here and not try," Kenyatta snapped. He snatched up his oar, lifting his as well, and they rowed with all their strength back toward Jamaica. After an hour of nonstop rowing, they took a break, then resumed. Despite pushing themselves to their limits of endurance, to the anxious trio, it felt as if the boat hardly moved.

"Land," Malimokuru finally called.

Kenyatta looked over his shoulder, relieved to see Jamaica still there waiting for them. They might still have time to warn as many people as possible to get to high ground...

His hope shattered with what sounded like a huge intake of air.

5

"What ... the hell was that?" Malimokuru whispered. "Sound like da whole world just inhaled."

"No." Kenyatta leaned over the front of the small rowboat, staring in horror at his beloved home."

"What's your problem?" Malimokuru asked, following Kenyatta's gaze. "I don't see nothin' ..." he trailed off, his mouth hanging open, at the sight of the ocean rising between them and the island.

"Not again," Kita said.

"Dis what happen before?" Malimokuru breathed.

"No," Kenyatta said, watching as the wave continued to rise, casting a shadow over the little rowboat and its insignificant burden. "Nothing like dis."

"Impossible," Malimokuru said. "No act of nature work like dis. No wave just rise up out the ocean like that."

"Demons," Kenyatta breathed.

Malimokuru frowned. "What?"

Kenyatta didn't answer, but stared in helplessness as the enormous wave rose and leaned toward Jamaica.

"By the Gods," Kita said. "Not everyone would have gotten to high ground by now. *Is* there a high enough ground?"

Kenyatta barely heard the question as he watched the hand of the ocean slap down on his beloved home. Even from their distant position, he heard the crash of the huge wave. Unbidden images of screaming people being washed away into the ocean flooded his mind. Trees snatched out of the ground like weeds. Collapsing houses, exploding walls, mudslides, endless destruction. A chill shot down his spine despite the heat of the cloudless day, on the cruelly placid water upon which they floated.

Then it ended. The giant wave slid back into the ocean and disappeared as if it had never been. In the space where Rocky Point and the rest of Jamaica had been, was bare ocean.

Malimokuru leaned forward and squinted into the distance. "There's nothing left. The land, people, trees, everything."

The veins in Kita's arms bulged under his tight grip on the oar. "It's just ... gone. Everything ... gone." He looked at Kenyatta, who sat staring at the place Jamaica had been. He gave his best friend's shoulder a squeeze. "We need to get back. Pray to the Gods there are survivors."

Kenyatta silently picked up his oar, and he and Kita rowed on.

None of them were ready for what they found. Backs to their destination, Kenyatta and Kita followed the nature reader's directions as they made for home. Or rather, where home had been. When they heard Malimokuru swear an oath under his breath, they stopped.

The entire island hadn't been swallowed by the ocean, but a large part of it had. Kenyatta peered into the distance and saw only the highest mountains, and the hills at their base, remained. "How, in the name of the Daunyans, someting like dis happen?"

Kita glanced at his friend. It was a rhetorical question, of course, for he knew Kenyatta had already made up his mind. It could be nothing other than a powerful demon, or many of them. Kita wasn't so sure. In all their battles two years ago, not once had they seen a demon wield such a force. Perhaps a more powerful demon had escaped the abyss to this dimension?

They rowed on, and soon the rowboat bumped aside bits of flotsam from moored ships, wooden debris from destroyed homes, snapped trees. And more.

Kenyatta clenched his jaw as the first body floated by, face down in the water. Then another, and another. After he lost count of how many they passed among the wreckage, tears welled in his eyes to provide a blurry curtain of relief.

Malimokuru looked over the side of the boat. Soil and debris churned up by the catastrophe made it difficult to make out the remains of buildings and structures which would be sitting below the surface like an oceanic tomb.

Shouting pierced their collective sorrow, and Malimokuru pointed in the direction of the voices. "Survivors," he said.

Dozens of people sat on floating debris in an endless carpet of destruction, some frantically waving at the trio, while others sat despondent, not even bothering to look up.

"Dem can't be all that's left," Kenyatta said in disbelief. They turned the boat toward the survivors, and Malimokuru guided them through the maze of wreckage.

"If there's survivors here," Kita said, "there may be more on the other side. It's a big island and many people lived in the hills and mountains. Word had already spread to get to high ground after the first wave hit."

"Oh ho!" Malimokuru called out to four people sitting astride the long trunk of a coconut tree. "Our tiny boat can't hold many. We'll take the youngest and eldest aboard. There's more that survived. All of us will get to land together."

"Thank you," one of the survivors said. "She looked into Kenyatta's eyes with a mixture of gratitude and shock. "The ocean raise up and come for us. It just pound down on everyting. What could we have done to bring such wrath of the Gods down on us?"

"Not the Gods," Kenyatta said under his breath.

They continued on, and though their craft couldn't begin to hold a fraction of the survivors they encountered, they used the tough giant leaves from floating tropical trees to form ropes. Anything flat and strong enough was used as makeshift oars. The strongest of the survivors rowed toward land while others aboard flat planks and tree trunks held onto the ropes to stay linked together.

Kenyatta took heart at the sight of the floating city trailing in their wake as they accumulated more and more survivors along the way. It didn't make the sight of the floating human and animal bodies any easier to bear, but people had survived.

One of the three men they'd brought aboard along with the woman who'd thanked them earlier, insisted on taking a shift, and Kenyatta and Kita rested at the back of the boat.

Kita looked out at the endless destruction and shook his head in disbelief. He opened his mouth several times to speak, but not words came.

"Yeah, man," Kenyatta said.

Kita watched his best friend staring out at the surrounding devastation, his hand clenching his oar. Kenyatta's life had been one major loss after another since he was old enough to remember. One of those losses, his grandfather, was the reason he and Kita had grown up together as brothers. Kita thought about how Kenyatta's feisty grandfather had died at the hands of a group of thugs.

Mateo Sepata, Kita's father, had heard the gunshot. Like a crack of thunder, it was a sound from another time, another era. Guns were from the Age of Technology. A relic revered by some as proof of humanity's former greatness and ingenuity, reviled by others as a symbol of why the Gods had cast them down, destroyed their technology and all knowledge of how to create it.

Kita's father had gone to help, despite his mother's insistence he stay with the family. Mateo had returned with a silently weeping boy Kita's own age. Over the years, Kenyatta would sometimes open up about the vague memories he'd had of his parents before they'd died. They had entrusted Kenyatta's care to his grandfather who, at the end of his own life, had entrusted the boy to a stranger with a good heart.

"Me grampa good at seeing a person's soul," Kenyatta had once said.

Kita sighed. Both parents and a grandfather, lost to him before his eighth birthday. Kenyatta's older sister, Taliah was his only surviving blood relative.

Kita leaned over. "I...I think we need to talk to your sister as soon as we can."

Eyes downcast, Kenyatta nodded absently. His twisted locks fell over his face, obscuring his despair.

After several more hours and more than a hundred survivors collected, they reached land with a gentle enough slope to climb. All but Malimokuru climbed out of the boat. Kenyatta and Kita each offered a hand to help the older man, who waved them off.

As soon as the nature reader's feet touched the water, he screamed and fell into a fit of convulsions as though being electrocuted.

One of the survivors closest to the nature reader grabbed him when he collapsed. Kita sloshed over to them and helped pull Malimokuru's limp body out of the water.

Kenyatta climbed out of the water and helped pull Malimokuru onto dry land.

The man who'd helped Kita placed his ear over Malimokuru's mouth. "He's breathing."

There was a collective sigh of relief.

The woman who'd ridden aboard their boat knelt beside the unconscious man, her light brown eyes going from Malimokuru to the others. "I'm startin' to think it's the ocean itself, want to kill us." She ran her hand over the nature reader's bald head.

Malimokuru groaned, and his eyes slowly creaked open. He

looked at the woman leaning over him and offered a strained smile. "Dis what an old man gotta do to get attention from tha ladies, ya?"

The woman snorted, but still held his head in her hands. "Dirty old man."

"What happened?" Kita asked when Malimokuru looked up.

He groaned again, but didn't try to sit up. Kenyatta glanced from him to the woman cradling his old head in her hands and hid his smirk.

"Angry," Malimokuru said in a cracked voice. "It's very angry."

"What?" Kenyatta looked at Kita, who shrugged. "What's angry?"

Malimokuru mumbled incoherently, then fell unconscious.

6

L and and sea, back and forth. Kenyatta and Kita rowed out into the ocean in search of survivors until the sun dipped below the horizon. Each time, they returned with dozens of people aboard floating trees and planks.

Despite Kenyatta's insistence on going back out after sunset, there was no moon to light the night sky, and so he'd finally relented.

Kenyatta returned to see that Malimokuru had awoken. The nature reader led them further uphill where the survivors had set up camp.

His face alight in the glow of the campfire, Kenyatta sat with his knees drawn up to his chest, his arms wrapped around them. He looked up through the trees at the stars, which gazed indifferently back at him.

"We helped save a lot of people today," Kita said.

Kenyatta nodded with half-hearted smile at his friend's attempt to lift his spirits. All he could think about, however, was finding the demon responsible—no matter how powerful—and exacting retribution for himself, the survivors, and the fallen. It wouldn't take the pain away, wouldn't mend the wounds caused by the loss of most of his homeland and the deaths of many friends and strangers alike. He would do it anyway, though, even if the only logical reason was to prevent the fiend from killing again.

That stray thought sent his thoughts speeding a world away, to another island he'd once visited. In that brief moment, he thought about the woman he'd met two years ago on his trek to defend Takashaniel. He prayed to the Gods this fate hadn't befallen her home.

"I don't know what it was," Malimokuru said, startling Kenyatta out of his daydream. "But it's the biggest thing me ever encounter. Like feelin' the anger of a mountain bearin' down on you."

"Maybe you hallucinate da whole ting, ole man," one of the other men said.

Malimokuru responded to that statement with a sidelong glare. "Been at dis longer than you been alive, bwoy. Think whatcha will, but ya know nothing 'bout da world." He swept his hand in the air to encompass the sky.

"Since before the Age of Technology, humans well on dem way to disconnecting with the world; our intuition, connection with the earth, everyting. Even more than two hundred years later, most of us still tink we know more than we do."

The man fidgeted, obviously uncomfortable, but Malimokuru held his gaze the whole time he spoke. "Ignore the forces of nature to your own demise, bwoy."

"What was it, then?" Kita asked. "You said it felt like an angry mountain."

"Better if it *was* a mountain," Malimokuru said. "They don't move. Whatever dis was, it felt big as a mountain. A confused and angry mountain."

Kenyatta frowned at that. How could a demon be confused about anything? They existed only to destroy. He saw Kita look at him from the corner of his eye, and knew what his friend was thinking. Despite Kenyatta's suspicions, Kita was still skeptical of the nature of whatever being caused the destruction.

Long after the others curled up to sleep around the campfire, Kenyatta sat staring at the stars. He fed the diminishing flames, and they roared to life again. The crackle of the newly energized fire was comforting in a way, yet as he stared into the fire, at the glowing embers within, anger burned just as hot within him.

Malimokuru knew nothing of the existence of demons, yet he believed it was some huge sentient being that had caused this catastrophe. Kita wasn't so quick to assume it was a denizen of the abyss, though he hadn't ruled it out, either. That confused the angry warrior.

Kenyatta's face tightened as he glared at the crackling fire. Demon or not, he would find it.

"THERE AREN'T enough boats to get everyone off the island."

Kenyatta opened his eyes at the sound of Kita's voice, the smell of cooking meat reaching his nose shortly after. He sat up and stretched.

The sole woman of the group roasted some sort of small animal over the crackling fire. Beside it sat a pot, steam rising from the contents inside.

How had he slept so hard? Normally it took no more than the crunch of a leaf, or sensing movement nearby to have him awake and on his feet.

"You were up late and it was an emotionally draining day," Kita said in response to his perplexed look. He crouched beside Kenyatta. "I would have woken you up when the food was ready."

Kenyatta stood and stretched again, reaching his hands toward the sky with a contented groan.

"There's talk of making for Carrabisha," Kita said. "Word has it that the other side of Jamaica wasn't hit as hard, and most of the ships are intact."

"Some good news at least," Kenyatta said. "Dem carryin' folks away now?"

"Since first light," Kita replied. "One ship is on its way around to us. Three ships have already departed for Carrabisha. We hope they'll return with more."

"We need to be on that boat," Malimokuru said. The man looked haunted.

Kenyatta looked him over. "Dis something to do with what happen yesterday?"

Malimokuru took a deep breath and blew it out in a whistle. "Me dreams last night could be called nightmares. Whatever touch me yesterday," he ran a hand over his head, "it's not done."

"You still don't know what it was?" Kita asked.

"No. But it showed me a primal anger like nothing I feel before. What it did yesterday could have been worse."

Kenyatta's eyes widened. "Whatcha mean, worse? It nearly wash over the whole island."

"It could have done just that, what I'm tellin' ya." Malimokuru stood and brushed the dirt off his baggy brown pants. "And I'm tellin' ya, it's not done. Whatever dis ting is, it's sitting in a seething fury. Through the jumble of thoughts and emotions I got a glimpse of its mind, and where it lives. Jamaica wasn't a target, but a location where its rage played out."

"I got other suspicions," Kenyatta muttered, ignoring Kita's warning look. What good was keeping demons a secret when humans would know soon enough? They'd helped defend Takashaniel two years ago, and the one who'd summoned that terrible hoard of fiends had been thwarted, but not defeated. The one named Brit, some inhuman being powerful enough to summon the most powerful demons in the abyss was still around somewhere.

And now two enormous and unnatural waves destroy most of

his beloved homeland, killing countless people and leaving civilization on one whole side of the island in total ruin. Kenyatta held no doubts that only a demon could be capable of such wanton destruction.

Malimokuru's voice broke through Kenyatta's dark thoughts. "Through dat horrible link I hope I never experience again, I get a glimpse of someplace frozen. Frozen ground, mountains, air. I see snowstorms and a range of mountains look like dem starin' down at you. I get the impression dis ting live in those mountains."

"Then we go," Kenyatta said.

"Just like that?" Kita replied. "Go where? There's a lot of cold places, Ken. And even more mountains." He turned to Malimokuru. "Unless that thing gave you directions, how do we know which miserable, freezing cold place to go to?"

"I'm a nature reader, bwoy. I read nature. I touch the ground and feel the mood of the trees and plants. And if another living animal is willing, I can link with their mind and feel what they feel."

"Which is why you say you felt rage and confusion," Kita said. "But you said it was primal. What do you mean by that? Frustration is a human emotion, isn't it? How can it be primal?"

Malimokuru held up his hands in a shrug. "I never encounter anyting like it. All I can say is dat it's intelligent, powerful, and huge. Through the link I know it lives far from here."

"How far?" Kenyatta asked. He instinctively reached for his swords before realizing they weren't there. He felt naked without the trusted blades. They'd seen him through many a battle, cut apart many a demon. Now they were part of an ever-growing list of personal loss."

"Askata," Malimokuru said.

Kita's eyes went wide. "That's half the world away. You're telling us that something that lives on the northwest lands of

Nomar, in the frozen tundra of Askata, can deal this kind of destruction from there?"

Malimokuru nodded. "I'm also tellin' ya that it's not over. Whatever it is, it'll strike again. I got the feeling it was in some sort of lucid state. Maybe why it cause all this destruction."

It's a demon. That's why it cause all this destruction. Kenyatta wished the thing would appear now, that he could unleash his fury on the abysmal creature. "If whatcha say is true, we need get on the next ship."

"You mean like that one?" Kita pointed toward the western horizon where a ship just came into view.

Kenyatta looked around the camp at the worn-out survivors. Some had heard the conversation and also looked to the west. The camp quickly came alive as news of the approaching ship spread. Many fell to their knees in thanks to the Gods, while others scrambled about to gather what provisions they'd scavenged from the wreckage.

"Doesn't look like as many people today as when we first get here," Kenyatta said.

"A lot of them continued up into the hills," Kita said. "Many don't intend to leave."

Kenyatta nodded. "Dis is home. Better to die in ya homeland than in some foreign place, or on the way there."

If not for the need to find the cause of this tragedy and put an end to it, Kenyatta might have done the same. He wondered how many had escaped death and were, even now, hiking over the forested hills and through the mountains to reach the other side of the island.

The sun was halfway across the cloudy sky when Kenyatta, Kita, and Malimokuru finally boarded the *Leaping Rhonda*, a charming ship that transported three dozen survivors to their new home.

Kenyatta leaned on the port side rail and gazed out at the sea. He arched his back, feeling the phantom weight of his lost swords. Those weapons, enchanted by the guardian of Takashaniel, were now lying somewhere on the ocean floor.

He drummed his fingers on the rail. Without their weapons he and Kita were helpless against even the weakest of fiends. It would be like cutting water. A demon could heal from the most grievous of wounds dealt by a conventional blade.

The sound of wooden planks creaking announced Kita's approach. "The captain says we should reach Carrabisha in three days." He leaned on the rail beside Kenyatta and looked out at the sparkling blue sea. "Maybe four, depending on the wind." He smirked. "I wanted to ask him how the ship came to have the name *Leaping Rhonda*, but I decided against it."

Kenyatta knew it was an attempt to lighten his mood, but it hung too heavily on him.

Silence stretched between them for a time before Kita spoke again. "I know there's nothing I can say, my friend. But we'll find out what's behind this and do something about it."

"You don't believe it was a demon."

Kita thought on that. "I don't know what to believe. Malimokuru's experience speaks of something different than what we've experienced demons to be capable of. Could be some kind of elemental, maybe? We've seen a lot of strange things, these past two years."

"Yeah, man," Kenyatta said. "Monsters never seen in the world. The most powerful race of demons in the five hells." He shook his head. "Stuff of nightmares."

"Malimokuru says this is going to happen again. It could happen in the same place, and that what remains of ... the island, will be completely washed over. I'm sorry," he said when Kenyatta's jaw clenched. "I didn't want to bring it up, but I figured you'd want to know."

"Yeah, man. I'll keep it in mind when I'm cutting the monster responsible into tiny pieces to send back to the abyss."

"And what will you do if it's not a demon? What Malimokuru described doesn't sound like one. What then?"

Kenyatta had no answer. "Let's just ... deal with it when the time comes, ya? We got plenty else to worry about."

"Like that?"

Kenyatta looked in the direction Kita pointed and swore. In the rapidly failing sunlight, three figures climbed over the rail at the ship's bow. One turned slitted green eyes on him, and Kenyatta reached over his shoulder for a sword that wasn't there.

7

S eung raced across the countryside astride her black stallion, Swiftspirit. The crisp wind in her face was a welcome relief from the troubles on her mind. Her departure from Kyu had not been without objection. Some felt she was shirking her responsibilities to the village, while others were simply baffled at why she would leave at such a time. It hurt all the more that Seung had no definite answers to those questions.

But Tae had been there. Ever faithful and loyal to the end, Tae Kim had helped her assuage the villagers' concerns, displaying a confidence in the urgency of her errand that she herself didn't fully possess.

Soon, what little sunlight remained disappeared behind a canopy of dark clouds rolling in across the sky. A raindrop spattered on her nose, then another in her eye. She flinched and wiped her face.

Seung had barely enough time to grumble at the prospect of rain when the sky opened. In minutes she and her mount were soaked.

"*Jikuh!*" she swore. Beneath her, Swiftspirit blew out through his nostrils and shook his head.

Seung took stock of her surroundings. Little more than a scattering of trees and ankle high grass stood on either side of the road. She patted the stallion on the neck. "No shelter to be had, my friend. We must push on."

Swiftspirit whinnied and shook his head. He tried to speed up from a canter to a full gallop, but she kept him in check. Seung smiled at the back of the black horse's head. He always knew what she wanted, as though he understood her words. Still, with the now poor visibility and wet terrain, she couldn't risk giving the horse his head.

Thunder rumbled in the sky, followed by light flickering inside the clouds. "No shelter," Seung said again, and leaned low in the saddle. Thunder sounded again, much louder this time, and the following streak of lighting lit the surroundings. From the corner of her eye, Seung thought she saw a figure pacing her. *Wolves.*

Thunder and lightning again, and again she saw a figure from the corner of her eye, pacing the galloping stallion. When Seung saw the figure again, she reflexively reached behind her back to feel for her weapon, *Vyirayoi*. Nothing on two legs should be able to pace Swiftspirit's gallop. She kept her eyes forward and senses open. Yet another innate ability that made her different. On this rainy night with lightning streaking the sky and ominous figures pacing her, Seung was glad to have it.

She urged Swiftspirit into a slow run. This time, when the lightening flashed she saw not one, but two figures just off the side of the trail. She leaned forward and spoke into the horse's ear. *"Dene miru kima oi."* The stallion snorted in response as she loosely tied the reins to the horn of the saddle.

Seung placed her hands on either side of the horn and lifted herself up. Supported only by her hands, she curled her body and planted her feet on the seat. Lightning fractured the darkness again, and the two figures were closer.

Seung leapt straight into the air and whipped *Vyirayoi* from its strap on her back. Using momentum from years of wielding the weapon, she swung the halved shaft about and snapped it together as one.

She whirled the long-shafted weapon around and over her head, turning a circle to land in a crouch on the wet gravel road.

Her pursuers were on her the instant she landed. Only the rain beating on the attackers alerted her to where they were in the darkness. She ducked and sidestepped, kicked out and spun *Vyirayoi*, attempting to catch them with one of the two flat curved blades at each end.

Every tactic she tried missed the mark. Her attackers simply flowed around her every move. The rain intensified as though the very elements aligned against her. It roared in her ears and pounding on her as though dumped from an enormous bucket.

Several bolts of lightning flashed in the sky, and in that flickering light, Seung saw two hulking *things* stalking around her in a circle. Their bodies looked to be composed of water, and where their faces should have been were only two yellow slits glaring at her; through her

The creature on the right lunged, and she feinted a retreat. She quickly reversed the motion and turned inside its reach. She spun into a crouch and whipped *Vyirayoi* around with the motion. The blade passed right through the creature's watery leg. The lack of physical resistance set her off balance, and Seung had to roll sideways to get away from a possible counterattack.

No sooner had she planted her feet and turned, when water creatures were on her. She skittered backward, striking out with her weapon at each step. The blades dealt no damage, but did manage to knock their swinging limbs apart long enough for her to keep her distance while they re-formed.

Through the roaring deluge she heard, then felt, the rapid triple thud of hooves pounding the road. Though she worried for her brave companion's safety, she dared not take her eyes off of her attackers for even an instant.

Solely focused on her, the water creatures were either oblivious of Swiftspirit's approach, or didn't care. The stallion never slowed. He ran headlong into the creatures and blasted them apart in an explosion of water.

Seung wasted no time. She sprinted down the road, hoping Swiftspirit wouldn't be attacked. She looked over her shoulder, but saw nothing of the water creatures. When the sound of pounding hooves grew louder, she twisted the shaft of *Vyirayoi*, splitting it in half, then strapping it across her back.

Swiftspirit came around to her right. Seung leapt toward him, planted her hands, and sprang herself up and into the saddle. As soon as he felt her settle on his back, the stallion surged forward. Seung lowered herself in the saddle and spoke into his ear, urging him to slow down. The gravel road was fairly even, but she wouldn't risk her loyal friend snapping an ankle in a hole hidden by a puddle of water.

She glanced over her shoulder again, but still saw no sign of her inhuman attackers. She divided her focus between her surroundings and the road. She let Swiftspirit pick his path, but since her night vision was easily a match for any horse, she also kept careful watch for any other hidden dangers.

As the night stretched on, only the rain continued to assault her. Seung snarled up at the sky through her limp, wet hair, plastered to her face and the side of her head.

Time passed at a crawl as the rain beat down on rider and mount. The chill of the night crept into her riding clothes like a serpent, coiling around her midsection with an icy squeeze.

Seung considered how long she'd been riding, and figured Little Seoul couldn't be much farther away. Normally she enjoyed the half day's ride to the city. Now it was a race against the cold wetness creeping into her bones, and whatever those things were that she'd left behind on the road.

When she heard Swiftspirit's shod hooves clip-clopping with

his every stride, she breathed a sigh of relief. Well-kept roads meant civilization was near.

The welcome sight of torchlit buildings soon came into view. Seung had to force herself not to give Swiftspirit his head and let the stallion sprint the final distance to sanctuary.

As with most cities created before the End of Technology, there was no wall encircling Little Seoul. As she glanced at the dark silhouettes of the many buildings and homes sprawled before her, Seung wondered how big an undertaking it would be to enclose such a massive place. Many of the ancient kingdoms before the Age of Technology had protective walls surrounding castles and palaces.

She slowed Swiftspirit to a canter, then a trot as she neared the perimeter fields. Blazing light from torch poles lit the last quarter mile to the city entrance. Seung slowed her equine companion to a walk, allowing their eyes to adjust to the light.

A towering gate made of stone came into view as she crossed into the light. Four red columns held up a large tiled roof of the same color. The structure stood between four stone guard towers, each spaced every fifty feet to the right and left.

Seung eyed the towers. Archers were no doubt watching her from the two nearest structures; she could practically feel the arrows trained on her.

The call to halt came when she and Swiftspirit were within shouting distance.

"State your name and business."

"Seung Yoon, from Kyu Village. I'm traveling north and east, and seek warm and dry refuge here in Little Seoul."

The next question came nearly on top of her last words. "At night? In such heavy rain and thunder?"

Seung clenched her teeth, then took a deep breath. "Would that I could control the elements, I would have arrived at your fair city under the warmth of the sun."

"Yet you come under the cloak of night and rain."

She eyed the gate and the dry space underneath its roof. "Soaked, cold, and in dire need of a hot bath to warm my bones. And to dry my dear friend who has borne me as a burden all this way."

Silence was the only response for many heartbeats. Beneath her, Swiftspirit tossed his head, a clear indication of irritation from the disciplined horse.

"If there is more to discuss," Seung called out, "can we do it under a dry structure that my companion and I might find some relief from this downpour?"

"What companion?" came the reply. "I see only you. Does someone else wait in the dark beyond the torchlight?"

She sighed. "I was referring to myself and my horse, upon whom I'm sitting. The rain has soaked him as thoroughly as me."

"Beasts of burden are not companions, but tools for our use. Come, and stop under the Gate of Welcome."

Seung bit back her retort and did as instructed. Once underneath the roof, Swiftspirit blew out through his nostrils and shook himself as soon as she dismounted. Seung shielded her face and gave the stallion a good-natured shove. "My four-legged gentleman." The horse blew out through his nostrils again. "I know," she said, rubbing the flat of his head. "You'll be warm and dry for a night, and then we'll be on our way."

"They are obedient animals," a man's voice said from behind, "but that beast cannot understand your words. Are you of fragile mind to speak to it such?"

Seung side-eyed the speaker, a man—more boy than man—who looked to have seen less than twenty years of life. She noted his lifted chin, brash tone, and squared shoulders. This one had something to prove. His companion, older and clearly smarter, sighed and favored her with an apologetic look. He must be under some sort of punishment to have to work with this idiot.

"Has Little Seoul's manner of greeting visitors changed since my last visit?" Seung asked. "I seem to remember feeling more welcome."

"Did you arrive under the cover of night and in the rain?" The younger guard waved a hand out at the unrelenting downpour.

"Urgent business required an immediate departure from my village. I assure you, I've not enjoyed being soaked."

"What business?"

Seung kept her features neutral. "My own."

The man-boy looked her up and down. "Because of your suspicious conditions of arrival, I'll need to search you."

Seung wondered why the older man hadn't spoken yet. Surely he knew this was absurd.

The older guard hid his smile behind his hand and cleared his throat. "I don't think ... that will be necessary."

"I'm in command here," the younger guard said.

"For training purposes, no?" He bowed to Seung. "My apologies for the rude welcome. I am Sun Pak, and this is my ... superior, Bong Jin. There have been odd happenings of late, which has the city on guard."

Seung arched an eyebrow. "What happenings?"

"None that concern you," Bong Jin said.

She ignored him. "Have there been attacks? Raiders?" Such was not uncommon since the End of Technology. It seemed no matter what momentous event befell the world, humans would find a way to make their lives more difficult.

The random thought made Seung frown. Had she just thought of humans as something apart from herself? In the brief moment she considered it, such thoughts had been subtly creeping into her mind with every year that passed; but why? She pushed the question aside for later.

"You speak as though you have some knowledge of this," Bong Jin said. "Maybe we should speak to you more ..."

"It was a guess, most perceptive leader guard," Seung said.

Beside the fuming young guard, Sun Pak stifled his laughter with a cough.

Bong Jin looked from Seung to the other guard and back. "Perhaps I should turn you away."

"On what grounds?" Seung asked angrily, her patience fading.

"Refusal to cooperate."

"With what?"

"I *said* that we were to search you for—"

"You don't want to do that," Seung interrupted. She leveled her hard gaze directly into the boy's eyes, hoping he would heed the warning. She didn't need any trouble here, not so early in her errand.

"You see my weapon clearly. I've come alone, wet and cold, and seek shelter for a night or two."

Bong Jin stared at her and she saw trepidation in his eyes, though he tried to hide it with his too stiff posture.

Sun Pak stepped forward. "My young comrade, here, cannot take chances, but I assure you there will be no search of your person, Miss ..."

"Yoon Seung," she replied in the traditional manner of surname before given name. She offered a slight bow.

Sun Pak returned the gesture while Bong Jin balled his fists. The more experienced guard placed a hand on Jin's shoulder and gave a squeeze. The young man turned an incredulous look on him, but relaxed a bit.

"New responsibilities of this magnitude must be taken seriously," Pak said. "I'm sure you would agree?"

Seung nodded. "Surely."

Sun Pak turned to his younger *superior.* "I'm sure our visitor poses no threat other than to cause the wooden floors to warp under the water pouring off of her and her horse companion. My advice is to allow her entrance."

"If something happens, it will be under my watch," Bong Jin replied.

"Under my guidance," Sun Pak countered. "If it makes you feel better, I will escort her through the gates to find accommodations." He turned to Seung. "If it pleases you, of course."

"My thanks," Seung replied with another bow.

Sun Pak smiled as Bong Jin tipped his head, spun on his heel, and returned to his post.

"Apologies on behalf of my commanding officer," Sun Pak said once the young man was out of earshot. "He is new to authority and I fear he rather enjoys it."

"Not a problem," Seung replied.

"I doubt you need an escort from me," he continued, "but if you're unsure where to find lodging, I can recommend."

"I'd rather know about these strange happenings you referred to," Seung said.

They moved along an avenue where the buildings had longer awnings which provided shelter from the downpour.

"You would likely think me an insane old man," came the cautious reply.

Seung realized his features had been obscured in the dim lighting of the entry gate, but now she took a closer look. Age lines mapped a weathered face and strong jaw. His bushy eyebrows—which matched his salt and pepper gray hair—knitted together above eyes that had seen too much.

"I'll keep an open mind," she said.

Sun Pak gave a curt nod. "There have been reports of strange creatures that look to be made of water lurking in the wild. Hulking things the height of a tall man stalk the night, mostly out there," he jabbed a thumb over his shoulder. "I'd thought it was nonsense till I saw ... something ... myself. They're mostly seen at night near ponds or running streams in town."

"Near a large water source," Seung mused.

The old soldier nodded. "The bigger ones don't come into the city, for a mercy."

"Bigger ones?"

"We've been lucky. These things have only come at night when most are asleep. They haven't attacked, but they don't look friendly either. The big ones,"—Sun Pak looked around as though expecting one of the monsters to creep from around a corner—"I saw one with my own eyes, stalking around just outside the torchlight of the field you crossed. I swear on my honor, that the thing was over ten feet tall and half that wide."

"Were they ... did they have slitted yellow eyes?"

Sun Pak nodded. "So you've seen them."

"I was attacked by two on the road here."

Sun Pak looked at her in surprise as they stopped under a sloped awning.

"My weapon didn't work on them," she indicated *Vyirayoi* strapped across her back. "The blades just passed through. My companion, here, dealt the blow that defeated them."

"Oh?" Sun Pak's bushy eyebrows rose, and Seung thought of two hairy spiders climbing toward his hairline.

She gave Swiftspirit a pat on the neck and the black stallion whickered and nudged her with his nose. "I'd dismounted while he was still running. He crashed into the water creatures and they came apart. We didn't stay long enough to see if they re-formed."

"Smart lady," Sun Pak replied. He smiled at the muscular stallion. "With a loyal and courageous friend. A trained warhorse is rare to come by. Only the elite warrior class have them."

"Not a warhorse," Seung replied. "Only a friend who would protect me as I would him."

Sun Pak looked doubtful at that, but shrugged and pointed down the street. "The Nightingale's Roost is that way. Just turn right at the corner and it's at the end of the next block. Can't miss it. They have steaming hot baths to melt the ice from your bones. They also have a Fire Room where you can more quickly dry your sodden gear and clothes."

"Perfect," Seung replied.

The old guard bowed. "They'll have accommodations for

your companion as well. The stable hand will have him dry, fed, and spoiled by the time you're ready to depart."

"My thanks, Officer Sun Pak," Seung said. "You've saved me a lot of time trying to remember this city at night."

He nodded and turned to leave. "I feel compelled to suggest you travel by day, if possible. They've only ever been seen at night."

Seung led Swiftspirit across the street and turned right at the corner. As Sun Pak had said, the Nightingale's Roost was in sight at the end of the block. She gave Swiftspirit a pat on the neck again.

Day or night, it mattered little. She appreciated Sun Pak's warning, but something deep inside told her that whatever waited for her in this journey, would be far worse than this night.

S eung's dreams were haunted by monsters made of water, and an enormous presence pulling her down into the depths of the ocean. She tossed and turned in her bed, causing the blankets to wrap around and bind her. The sensation fueled her dreams; the monsters wrapped around her, bound her arms and legs in an inescapable grip. She opened her mouth to scream, and water flooded in.

Seung jolted upright and fought the covers off. She sat on the bed, her hair disheveled from her unconscious struggles. She took a moment to slow her breathing, then looked around the room.

Sunlight glowed around the edges of the thick purple curtains beside the room's solitary table and chair.

Her chest rose and fell with every heaving breath, and she closed her eyes and urged her nerves to calm. When she opened her eyes again, Seung realized that she had a tight grip on *Vyirayoi*, which leaned against the wall beside her bed. She released the weapon and scooted to the edge of the bed, where she sat in silence for a time. The dreams had been so vivid and real, it took her a moment to realize she was drenched in cold sweat and not ocean water.

"Whatever this thing is, I need to get to it before it drives me crazy."

She rested her forehead in the palm of her hand and closed her eyes again. Her conversation with the old soldier left Seung with an anxious feeling in the pit of her stomach to accompany the pull toward the snowy lands northeast. *This keeps up and there won't be any room in my stomach for food.*

She stood and stretched, then changed out of her night-clothes into a pair of pale green trousers and a woven long-sleeved top. After washing her face in the washbasin, she sat on the bed and combed her hair, wincing as she tore through the knots formed due to her restless sleep.

Once her raven black hair was straightened, she spread it around the sides of her face before tying it back into a loose ponytail. As always, she tapped the tips of her ears to ensure her hair covered them. Satisfied, Seung grabbed her travel pack and made for the door.

She stepped outside the Nightingale's Roost and took in the surroundings. Little Seoul was much the same as the last time she'd visited. The buildings stood so tall it hardly seemed possible that humans could've erected them. Moss and ivy covered many of the taller structures, while smaller and more manageable buildings were still maintained.

Her stomach gave a long grumble, reminding her that she hadn't had a meal since her snack on the road the night before. She took a moment to get her bearings, then started west toward the Hunger District. The hard stone street had no give beneath her sandaled feet, and Seung wondered if every big city from the Age of Technology had such hard surfaces. Unlike smaller towns and cities built after the End of Technology, the enormous cities the village elders spoke of had roads like this one, lined with spiderweb cracks and holes, but many times harder than any cobblestone or brick she'd ever seen.

She eyed the colored lines stretching endlessly along the stone ground. Tae Kim had once told her of the time he'd traveled across the sea to Japan, where he'd met a woman with more knowledge of the ancient times than any other person he'd ever known. "Carriages that moved without being pulled by man or animal," Seung thought aloud as she navigated the streets filled with residents milling about. "And these lines were some kind of guide to keep them from hitting each other."

It all seemed strange to her. Although she'd seen the occasional rusted metal skeletons of such horseless carriages with their strange flattened black wheels, much smaller than the wooden ones of today. Her stomach groaned again, and she placed a hand over it.

Seung smelled the Hunger District well before she reached it, and so did her stomach, for it groaned all the harder. The smell of fresh baked pastries and grilling meat wafted out of the windows of bakeries and cafes. Though it all smelled enticing, Seung had a mind for something that wouldn't sit heavily in her stomach.

She continued down the avenue until she reached a shop that smelled of baked bread. She smiled at the sound of thin metal figurines jingling as she opened the door. The aroma of fresh pastries, breads, and meat pies hit her in full, and she suddenly wanted to eat everything in the shop.

"Well!" A man appeared from the back of the shop and stood behind the counter. He offered a generous smile beneath round blue eyes and sandy blond hair that marked him as a foreigner. "Lucky you are, my lady," he said in a heavily accented version of the common tongue of her homeland. "You've come into the best bakery in all of the Hunger District. How may this humble baker serve you?"

Seung frowned, then laughed. "Humble baker of the best bakery in the Hunger District, hmm?"

The man offered an exaggerated bow. "How else might I entice you to my goods?"

Seung pointed at a roll the shape of a waning moon. "What is this?"

"Quite possibly the most delicious, flaky, crescent pastry to ever grace your lovely pallet, my lady. That one is filled with tiny slices of cinnamon-spiced apples and baked to pure perfection."

Seung's stomach growled in anticipation, and she offered a crinkled smile when the baker chuckled. "I'll have one."

"Excellent choice, my lady."

The crescent was indeed flaky and delicious, and the filling was not only just of apples with the cinnamon spice he spoke of, but also a creamy sauce that tasted of apples as well. "Mmm," Seung looked at the display of warm pastries, wondering if all of these were as good as the one she'd just had. "You're a slim man, good baker. If all of your goods are as tasty as this one, I can't imagine how you fit through the door."

"Please," the man said, "my name is Gilles. And after so many years, my nose no longer smells them for food rather than quality."

"Gi ... lles," Seung tilted her head. "Is that a name of power? It has a good sound."

Gilles puffed out his chest in a caricature of pride. "A name of power indeed, my fair lady. Why, my name means none other than Shield of Goatskin."

Seung clamped her lips together and bit her tongue.

Gilles stared at her a moment longer, then broke into laughter.

At that, Seung laughed as well. "I'll have another," she said, once their mirth subsided. "And a bit of information, if you have it."

The baker whose name translated as Shield of Goatskin served her another crescent. "The first is easily done. The second, I shall try."

"I travel north and west," Seung said. "I've need of a map."

"A travel master," Gilles held up a finger, "that's who you're looking for." He pointed past her. "When you so hesitantly leave my irresistible bakery, you will head toward the end of the street whence you came and turn right. At the next avenue, you will turn left. Once you're midway down the avenue you'll come to a place on the right simply named, the Travel Master. A short walk.

Seung thanked Gilles and followed his directions straight for the shop. As the 'humble' baker had said, the Travel Master was indeed a short walk away. Licking the last few crumbs from her fingers, she entered the shop and looked around in awe.

Maps and illustrations covered every wall. They covered the floor and occupied every bit of available table space. Some were hand painted, some drawn, and some, although faded with time, looked as real as the places they depicted.

"Good day," said a young voice, and Seung turned to see a boy who looked to have seen no more than seven years smiling at her. He offered a bow, and Seung bent slightly at the waist in kind.

"Are you the owner of this fine shop?" Seung asked with a smile.

The boy giggled. "I'm too young for that. But grandma is old, like you." He leaned toward her. "But you're prettier. This is her shop."

Seung opened and closed her mouth. "I see."

"How lovely, the harsh bluntness of a child," said another voice, and Seung saw a woman appear from the back room of the shop. Though her mostly gray hair and occasional wrinkles told of many years passed, her smile, quickness of step, and the shine of her eyes, were youthful. She walked around the counter and stood beside the boy. "How may this,"—she bounced her fist on top of the boy's head—"*old* woman serve you?"

Seung chuckled. "I'm in need of a map for the way from Little Seoul through Pyon, and across the sea to Nomar."

"Nomar ..." The woman moved past Seung and made straight

for a rolled up piece of parchment on one of the endless shelves in her shop. "Of all the places to adventure to, it's always you young warrior types who pick the most insane ones." She waved for Seung to follow her to the front counter.

"As a travel master, it is my duty to warn you that the quickest path to Nomar is also the most dangerous. You would travel by ship across the Siren Straight."—she pointed to Pyon—"a two to three day trek." She moved her finger along the map toward a body of water separating the two lands. "Fill your ears with something to muffle their wails, lest you be driven mad, and thus overboard to your death. Of course, that's assuming you find a captain crazy enough to take you."

"Would that there was another option," Seung said.

"Of course." The older woman waved a dismissive hand. "Your journey is important, and your time short, hmm? You must take the shortest path, no matter the danger. Never heard *that* before." She tightly rolled the map, then tied it in the middle with a piece of string.

Many a traveler has stopped through my shop and spoken of this faraway place. "If you reach Nomar, know that it is a place many times larger than this land. It is filled with wonders and horrors equally foreign. If you travel alone, be swift, and do not to stop in the forests at night. There are things in the world forgotten by the ages, but dangerous all the same."

The travel master's last words lingered in Seung's mind every distracted step to the stables boarding Swiftspirit. She felt the tug deep in her belly; insistent and clear. Her goal ultimately lay to the distant northeast. But first, she must travel north and slightly west to Pyon. She just wished she knew what lay in wait between her and the harsh snowy lands of her destination.

9

The first sailor to die saved their lives. The unfortunate man's machete passed through the creature's watery body much as if he'd sliced through an actual body of water. The monster had ignored what should have been a grievous wound, and swatted the sailor overboard.

"Weapons won't work," a crew member beside Kita said. "How do we get these things off the ship?"

Kita watched as the two monsters stalked toward them, yellow slits for eyes boring through him. "Try blunt objects!"

"Get to the kitchen!" the captain ordered several of his men. "Bring as many pans as you can spare. Better'n nothin'."

"Aye."

One of the monsters sprang forward just as the men hurried belowdecks. It caught a sailor who was too slow to get out of the way, and shoved its liquid hand into his mouth.

The captain cursed. "Damn ting's drowning him." He reached for his sword out of reflex, then released it and used the only weapon he had; his fist. The punch went through the watery head with a splash, but the captain may as well have been punching a pond. The creature was stunned for only an instant before it grabbed him by the head and lifted him off his feet.

Kenyatta searched the deck for anything large enough to combat the monsters, but found little of use.

"Watch it!" Kita shouted.

Kenyatta instinctively rolled backward without looking. Saltwater sprayed him from the splash where he'd been standing. He came to his feet and saw that the monster had swung an elongated limb down with enough force to splinter the wooden panels.

Kita shot past Kenyatta with a hand in loops of rigging and swung it into the monster's head. The water creature's head exploded in a splash of saltwater, and it stumbled sideways. Kita used the momentum from the swing and brought the heavy rope around again.

Seeing his friend's success, Kenyatta got to his feet and found more coiled rigging. He rushed to Kita's aid, and together they beat the monster back even as it struggled to re-form its head.

The sailors were quick to follow suit, and two others went for the second monster, who'd drowned the poor sailor, now sprawled on deck while the captain struggled to free his face from its grip.

Soon they had the water monsters on the defensive, beating them back toward the rails just as the men who'd gone below resurfaced with arms full of cast iron pans. They distributed the makeshift weapons and the two groups battered the creatures with heavy blows that staggered and disfigured them.

From the corner of his eye, Kita saw what looked like a spout of water shooting toward him, and he ducked. The stream flew over his head and into the side of another sailor. He heard the crack even before the poor man cried out and curled sideways over his broken ribs.

Another stream came at Kita, but this time he swung the

rigging at it. The watery stream shattered into a splash and fell harmlessly to the deck.

Kita wiped the salty water from his face and saw that a third monster had attacked.

"Two more!" Kenyatta shouted. He ducked just in time to avoid a swinging claw larger than his head. Once again, he used momentum and the weight of the rope to bring it around in another heavy swing. The force of the blow blasted most of the monster into a shower of saltwater, and it simply collapsed into nothingness. Panting, he surveyed the ship. What should have been only one more of the monsters was now three.

"Dammit," Kita growled. "Three more! Starboard side!"

Kenyatta looked to that direction as three new monsters climbed over the rail. "Yeah, man. This could be a problem." He hefted the rigging and ran toward the closest monster. "If all dem need is the ocean to take form, we better figure something out quick."

"Like what?" Kita swung the rope again, barely catching the monster as it hopped backward. "Start a fire?" He rolled sideways, barely avoiding an elongated limb. He swung with all his might and the heavy rigging dashed the monster into a shower of saltwater.

"Step back, bwoy."

Behind Kita, Malimokuru crouched with his hand in a pouch they'd never seen before. He whipped his hand out and spread a layer of strange colored sand over the monster. The old man spoke words in a language Kenyatta didn't understand but sounded like an incantation. The sand lit into countless tiny flames. Though steam rose from its body, the monster gave no indication that it felt any pain. It reached for Malimokuru with an oversized hand, then fell to the deck and splashed apart. Several nearby sailors yelped and hopped over the watery remains as it slid across the deck.

Malimokuru was already on the move. He doused monster

after monster with the sand, uttering the same incantation each time.

"Not bad," Kita said in admiration.

Kenyatta nodded his agreement. The man might be quite a bit older, but he moved with the speed and dexterity of someone many years his junior.

The nature reader continued his assault, spraying monster after monster with his strange sands until the deck was once again populated only by panting sailors.

Kenyatta and Kita went to the captain, who was still on his hands and knees retching up saltwater. He offered the man a hand, but the proud captain waved him off and climbed to his feet.

"Close call, ya?" He went into another fit of coughing, then wiped his mouth. "Can't think of a worse way for a captain to die than drowning. Especially while still aboard his own ship, ya know." The men shared an uneasy chuckle until the captain coughed again. "Wouldn't have minded having ya man over der a little earlier in dis fight."

Kita looked over his shoulder at Malimokuru, who was speaking to one of the sailors. "Nor would I."

The sailor who'd been talking to Malimokuru jogged over and saluted the captain. "Skippah. Old man ovah der ask permission to spread a thin layer of sand around tha whole ship. Him say it protect ..."

"Tell him spread whatever he want, if it keep dem tings off me ship."

"Aye, Skippah."

"Ya know anyting 'bout dat man ya travel wit?" the captain asked them.

"Apparently not," Kenyatta replied. "Never seen him do anyting like that before."

"Well I don't know what dem tings were, coming aboard me

ship, but I'm thankful the man is here. Otherwise we'd all be rottin' at the bottom of the ocean."

"Is that common among nature readers?" Kita asked as they watched the captain thank Malimokuru.

"Never seen anyting like it," Kenyatta replied. "But then, never really seen a nature reader in action, either."

After shaking the hand of every grateful crew member, Malimokuru joined the two friends.

He offered no conversation, just leaned on the rail for a time and stared out at what remained of the failing daylight. "Water elementals," he finally said.

"What?" Kenyatta and Kita said in unison.

"Ya heard me right," the old man said. "Never thought they were real. Just some folktale dem talk about when ya train to be a nature reader. Good thing I pay attention, ya?"

"I never hear of a nature reader with magic sand," Kenyatta said.

Malimokuru ran a hand over the pouch strapped to his waist. "Unless you travel every corner of the world, there's a lot more out there than ya know." He gave them an appraising look. "But I'm tellin' you someting you already know,"

"What makes you say that?" Kita asked.

Malimokuru snorted and looked back out the ocean. The sun disappeared below the western horizon, and the golden glow on the sea began to fade with the last of the light. "Dem look wary of me until they realize I save their lives." He nodded his head in the direction of the sailors, milling about while stealing nervous glances about the ship and over the rails.

"You two weren't fazed. Surprised, but unfazed. You two seen magic before."

"Yeah, man," Kenyatta admitted. "We have, though nothing like what you do."

Malimokuru stepped away from the rail. "I would hear more about it. We got plenty of time before we reach Carrabisha."

"Nice admission," Kita said as the old man stalked off and began distributing the sand along the perimeter of the ship.

"Why lie?" Kenyatta replied. "He ain't stupid."

"So you plan on telling him everything about two years ago? Nobody knows about the existence of Takashaniel. You go on telling him about a hidden tower that maintains a barrier between this dimension and the demon world, he'll think we're insane."

"I doubt it," Kenyatta said. "Besides, if him tink we crazy, what does it matter? When we get to Carrabisha, we continue on. With or without him."

"He's the reason we know where to go," Kita reminded.

Kenyatta had no rebuttal for that. "He knew what those things were when we didn't. Demons aren't much of a stretch beyond that."

"Which brings us back to the point of everything that's happened," Kita said. "You still think it was a powerful demon, or demons, that caused all this? I'm no expert on demons or monsters spawned from the elements, but I doubt they cooperate in such a manner."

Kenyatta's features darkened. "Elemental, demon, whatever. We find it. We put it down."

Kita watched his best friend's mood darken by the moment. "Hey there." He grabbed Kenyatta's shoulder. "Careful with that."

"With what?"

"Revenge," Kita said. "It's a sweet poison."

"We stop what happen to me homeland from happening anywhere else, man."

Kita looked into his friend's dark brown eyes, made darker by the last glow of the fading sunset. "As long as that's the reason."

Kenyatta stared back into his friend's eyes. No matter the reason, the result would be the same. Whatever destroyed his homeland and mercilessly killed so many would be brought down. He needed Kita, his brother, by his side, but he would do it alone if he had to.

He looked out at the sea, or where the sea would be, for now all was dark except for the stars that began to light the infinite sky. "Yeah, man."

S wiftspirit's hooves pounded the dirt and gravel road as he thundered across the landscape. Seung rode low in the saddle, her shimmering black hair blowing out behind her head and revealing her pointed ears. If she encountered anyone, surely they'd be hard-pressed to notice her deformity as she sped past.

Loathe to have waited till the next day, Seung had to remind herself of her fight the night she'd reached Little Seoul, and the warnings of both the old guard, Sun Pak, and the travel master. In the end, she'd decided to wait till the next day in hopes that the water monsters only appeared at night.

From dawn till midday, there had been no encounter, for which she was thankful. She hoped she could reach a town of some sort, or even a farm or village. The thought of fighting those things alone with a weapon that did no harm to them was undesirable.

Tree branches laden with yellow, orange, and golden leaves were like streaks of flame in her periphery as she sped across the countryside. The air, crisp and fresh from the previous night's rain carried the scent of pollen and damp earth.

Seung allowed her mind to wander. If she survived whatever

confrontation awaited her in the snowy lands, she would find out more about her heritage. It was time. Surely whatever intuition was guiding her in the direction of her quest would help when it was time to discover the secrets of her unusual nature. Whatever the situation, she could no longer live not knowing who or what she was.

Despite the daunting prospects and her own trepidation, it raised her spirits. Perhaps a village elder could point her in the direction of someone who knew her family.

Maybe Tae Kim would accompany her wherever she needed to go to learn about herself. If ever there was someone she wanted by her side for such an adventure, it was her dearest friend. Her lips twitched. Well ... there was another.

She thought of the mysterious duo who'd shown up at Kyu Village that fateful night, two years ago. Monsters, like nothing she or any others had seen before, had attacked in numbers. They likely wouldn't have won the day if not for the appearance of those two amazing warriors.

Her face flushed at the thought of how the darker one—Keyatta, she thought his name was—had looked at her. What was he doing now? He lived on a huge island, from what he'd told her. Both of them were islanders, and she hoped they'd been spared the same fate that had befallen the people of Ulleung Island. Her face hardened. All the more reason to reach her destination as quickly as possible.

The shadows of the trees and surrounding low growth began their retreat to the east as the sun began its descent toward the west. The air chilled, and clouds rolled in to hasten the arrival of night.

Seung let out a sigh when she first noticed that the air grew heavy with dampness. The normally welcome freshness of the smell of rain now dampened her mood along with everything else.

When the first raindrop spattered on her hand, Seung glared up at the sky.

"*Jikuh!*" she swore. "The Gods Themselves must be aligned against me." Beneath her, Swiftspirit gave a disgruntled wicker.

"I know, my friend." She gave the horse a friendly pat on the neck. "We'll not repeat the events of two nights ago."

Seung kept the stallion at a speedy but manageable pace. She rode as long as she dared, squinting against the heavy droplets stinging her face until the rain finally became too intense. She pulled Swiftspirit to a halt and led him to the edge of the road and dismounted. Rain dripped from her nose and ran down her face as she knelt and touched the ground, then closed her eyes.

The trees were enjoying the nourishing rain. She felt her way through the network of roots and fungi that connected the countless trees and allowed them to communicate with one another. After some time, she noticed what felt like a circular pattern to the communication, and focused on that.

Seung stood and grinned. "This way, my friend."

She led Swiftspirit through the trees, doing her best to navigate around bushes and shrubs, feeling for holes in the ground that her companion might not notice. They moved deeper into the woods. Leafy branches intersected overhead as though the trees reached to embrace each other. The leaves of the intertwined branches formed a beautiful multicolored shelter. Under different circumstances, Seung would have basked in the beauty of these woods.

The day darkened under the ceiling of rainclouds, and the canopy of foliage overhead made the woods darker still. Despite this, Seung had little trouble navigating through the towering oaks, maples, alders and pines. She led Swiftspirit around shrubs with white and pink flowers, which swayed as she passed, their slim green leaves dragging along her legs like long caressing fingers.

I see well at night, she thought. *I've got this singsong voice. And I hear better than anyone I've ever known.* She touched the tip of her ear. *Probably due to these.*

Seung snorted under her breath. At times like this, she wondered if her differences might be some sort of strange heritage rather than birth anomalies or a deformation.

Tree trunks covered in bright green moss became more frequent, as well as the sweet smell of wet earth and plant life. The steady drum of raindrops penetrated the leafy canopy to spill onto the ground and foliage below. Seung drew a deep breath and blew it out with a contented hum.

Sometime later she gave a cry of triumph at the sight of the little clearing she'd discovered through listening to communication between the trees. She looked around in amazement as she and Swiftspirit stepped into it.

Only patches of grass and wildflowers populated the glade, as though human hands had swept the area clean. She looked up at the leafy canopy; almost no rain made its way to the ground, here.

Swiftspirit blew out through his nostrils and gave himself a shake, spraying Seung with more than a bit of water.

"Hey!" Seung shielded her face with her forearm until the onslaught was finished, then glared at the stallion before giggling at the sight of the disheveled gear strapped to the animal.

"That was quite rude, my friend." Despite the admonishment, Seung smiled at her companion and gave him a pat on the neck.

Despite having little hope of finding anything dry enough to burn, Seung made several trips around the perimeter of the camp found enough to build a nice pile.

After relieving Swiftspirit of the saddle and gear, she fished a box of tinder out of one of the saddlebags and soon had a camp-fire burning.

She hung the gear from the low branches of a nearby tree and removed Swiftspirit's reins. While the stallion grazed, Seung settled in front of the fire with a piece of dried meat with some root vegetables.

The presence that had connected with her at Inayo Falls filled her thoughts as she snacked on the tough dried meat. How could it live in such a harsh environment as the snowy tundra she had come to suspect were the lands of Askata? The village teachers spoke of the freezing lands as beautiful, yet hospitable only in some parts, and only at certain times of the year. Most of the land was an unforgiving tundra of endless dangers.

She finished her meal, closed her eyes, and leaned back on her elbows to enjoy the heat of the crackling fire on her face.

"Doesn't *she know what woods these are?*" Joscel asked using the *whisper*, an innate ability of their people in which the speaker's words were carried on the wind, and only into the ears of the intended recipient.

With more than passing interest, the four figures watched as the woman, barely more than a child to them, sat in front of a campfire with more trust in her animal companion than any human would have.

The girl stroked her right ear as if she was unsure what it was or why it was attached to the side of her head.

"*Apparently not,*" Ikara replied.

Joscel grinned. "*She will find out soon enough. Should be fun to watch.*"

"*That attitude won't do,*" said Immendiel. Both males bowed their heads in obeisance.

Tinnoviel, the fourth of the group *whispered,* "*What would you have us do?*" Upon Immendiel's look of surprise he continued, "*You are the best tracker in all of Yathienel, and have patrolled these woods more than any other. In this, I defer to your judgement.*" He nodded in the direction of the girl lounging in front of the fire. *"Is she a threat?"*

Immendiel didn't think so. Her connection to these woods was stronger than all but the Daunya Master himself. *"Watch, for now, and when the opportunity presents itself, we will speak with her."*

Tinnoviel arched an eyebrow. *"Reveal ourselves?"*

Immendiel never took her eyes off the young woman who looked as though she was uncertain of the very skin she lived in. It was written all over her mannerisms and habits, the way she felt the surroundings around her with little more than a child's ability. *"She shares our heritage."* She looked up into Tinnoviel's green eyes. *"Do you not find her interesting? Wouldn't you like to know more?"*

"At the risk of revealing ourselves to her?" Tinnoviel continued to stare at the lounging figure, illuminated by the golden glow of the crackling campfire. *"She obviously lives as a human. We are not to reveal ourselves to them."*

Immendiel nodded. *"True. But look at the way she rubs her ears. Runs her fingers along her face. It's as though she doesn't know who or what she is, but hungers to."*

Tinnoviel pursed his lips. *"As you said. We will watch. If the opportunity presents itself, we will see."*

Seung let out a long, contented sigh, basking in the music of the rumbling campfire, its warmth draping around her in a blanket of tranquility. The blanket fell away at a nervous wicker from Swiftspirit.

Seung was quick into a crouch, *Vyirayoi* in hand. A dozen feet away, Swiftspirit tossed his head and whickered again.

The sound of giggling bobbed along in the darkness of the surrounding tree line, childlike, but without the innocence. Seung turned her back to the fire, and allowed her eyes to adjust to the darkness while still keeping the fire in her peripheral vision.

Her body tensed when she heard it again: giggling that sounded as if a score of children had surrounded her, playing a game she knew she wouldn't like. Left, right, overhead, giggling all around. The young warrior held firm, eyes darting in every direction.

In the corner of the camp, Swiftspirit tossed his head again. What could be out there to agitate the normally stoic horse? Feeling uneasy, herself, Seung called to her equine companion, speaking in the language she somehow knew, yet didn't know where she'd learned it. Swiftspirit whickered again, but settled down, the whites of his eyes visible as he looked around.

The tittering floated on the air and pranced about the camp, passing behind her like a sigh across the back of her neck. Seung gave an involuntary shudder. She scanned the campsite in every direction, but still found nothing.

The campfire darkened and the yellow flames shifted from bright yellow to orange. Seung frowned at the oddity, then her eyes widened as the fire shift to red, then purple, then blue.

The trees, once a hospitable refuge from the rain, now looked more like looming sentries, their branches forming long fingers snaking their way towards her.

What's happening?

The woods went silent, not a cricket or frog or grasshopper sang. Even the occasional raindrops penetrating the leafy canopy were mysteriously silent, as though muted. The darkness beyond the campsite grew black as pitch. On the other side of the fire, Seung saw Swiftspirit whinny, but she heard nothing.

Seung's heart beat faster, her eyes darting this way and that as she searched for...what?

Another giggle, followed by another behind her again. When she spun around, she found nothing. No matter which way she turned, the laughter was always behind her.

"Who's there?" Seung demanded. "Enough with your games."

Again, more snickering from every direction. A small stab of apprehension cut through Seung's irritation. *I should be gone from this place.* Seung barely finished the thought when she saw it.

The campfire shifted back to yellow and the flames leapt for the nighttime stars. It quickly settled to its normal height, and a tiny winged figure danced along the very tips of the flames. With every rise and fall of the fire, so, too, did the humanoid figure leap and drop.

Seung froze, not trusting her eyes. The little figure dancing atop the flames—seeming part of the flames themselves—was like nothing she'd ever seen. Entranced, she studied the dancing figure, trying to determine if it was in fact, part of the fire.

The fire roared and rose higher than should have been possible, and the figure became more distinct. It danced to the edge of the flames and leaned forward, standing tiptoe on one foot while its other leg stretched out behind it. It spread wings of fire toward the sky and performed a beautiful pirouette. Then it placed a tiny hand in front of its face and blew a kiss of yellow ashes.

It was the most beautiful sight Seung had ever witnessed, as the golden ashes turned blue, then red, and then faded away. The winged dancer spread its arms as though welcoming an embrace, then disappeared back into the flames.

Seung blinked, dumbfounded. "I've seen some strange things," she said under her breath, "but this ..."

The tittering returned, and tiny voices floated on the wind, coming from every direction, echoes and whispers of playful mischief and childlike wonder.

Look at the human so tall and fair
Days she spends combing that shimmering hair
Those round pink lips,
That in-between face
Those magical hips

She moves with "near" grace.

THE TAUNTS CAME from everywhere at once, leaving Seung in a daze. Through the sudden fog in her mind, she realized everything was okay. Perhaps she was just being overanxious because of traveling on her own. Yes, that was it. She was just overreacting to nothing more than her imagination. She should just sit down in front of the fire and be at ease.

Then another thought occurred to her. All of her heavy, wet clothes were more of a burden than she'd realized. How had she worn them all this time? She should strip off these heavy clothes. She had never before noticed how bothersome all of this was. Especially her coin purse.

And her shoes, so annoying they were! Even the clip that she wore in her hair felt ridiculous. Surely her hair was not so unmanageable that she needed such an unnecessary bauble. The only thing she need wear was her undergarments. They were light and easily manageable, not heavy and cumbersome. Yes, she would remove every article of clothing save her undergarments, and how much faster, then, would she travel? In fact, why wear anything? Surely even her undergarments were a hindrance too.

Seung looked over at Swiftspirit, still casting about nervously. Why had she brought him along in the first place? He was nothing more than a convenience. How much faster her journey would be if she left the animal and made her own way, quickly, and without the burden of useless supplies weighing her down.

Seung reached for the first button on her jacket, then hesitated. She frowned, then shook her head. What in the name of *Nakiya* was she doing? And who was *Nakiya*?

She shook her head again. Her thoughts were a fuzzy, jumbled mess. As she fought to clear her mind, she felt a subtle resistance, as though she were pushing against some befuddling presence in her mind. Seung focused on that sensation and attacked it. She had been about to strip naked and stalk out into the night without Swiftspirit, wearing nothing more than her skin.

She gritted her teeth as she fought back against whatever it was that clouded her mind. Something or someone was toying with her. But how could they enter her mind in such a way?

"I've got your little game, whoever you are," she whispered. In a louder voice, she said, "Will you come out and face me directly, or continue to cower in the forest and send me stupid suggestions that I'll never heed?"

Her response came in the form of another round of whispers and giggling floating through the air. Behind her the campfire roared again, and when she turned, something slammed into her back. She cried out and spun to see an acorn lying on the ground. Even as she stared at it, the acorn disappeared in a puff of blue smoke.

Seung tried to settle her hammering heart as she scanned the area in vain. She needed to leave this place, but in which direction? Whatever was out there seemed to be everywhere. She heard giggling from behind, this time close. Instead of spinning to face it, she kicked out.

Seung smiled in satisfaction when her foot connected with something and the giggling came to an abrupt halt. *"Ah hee hee hee—ugh!"*

When she turned, Seung's mouth fell open. A golden silhouette of a tiny, transparent humanoid creature slowly and deliberately picked itself up from the ground. It turned to face her and spread its butterfly-like wings.

Seung couldn't believe her eyes. *What is that?* she thought.

The little humanoid beat its wings and hopped into the air. With a giggle that sounded anything but friendly, it darted towards her. Seung watched as the winged creature zigzagged in front of her, then felt herself suddenly and painfully struck by an unseen force that propelled her backward through the air. She hit the ground and tumbled in a cloud of dust and flailing limbs, then crashed into a nearby tree.

With an effort, Seung tried to lift herself up, but her body felt heavy as a log. She gritted her teeth through the dizziness as waves of pain shot through her. She held a hand to her forehead and closed her eyes.

After a moment, Seung managed to open her eyes and steady her vision. She looked across the camp where the little winged figure danced through the air. It made its way toward her, dancing and somersaulting, skipping through the flames of the campfire as it made its way closer.

Seung groaned and lifted herself up to her elbows. With what little strength she had left, she scooted backward until her back was against the tree.

The little winged creature landed on her upraised knee, tilted its head as it dipped into a curtsy, then disappeared in puff of pink sparks.

IF SOUNDS COULD BE SEEN, they would have been a blur. Once Seung found consciousness again, her first instinct was to leap to her feet. But the throbbing in her head and the pain in her upper back meant that she could neither leap, nor move with any surety.

Unable to summon any strength to her limbs, she kept her eyes closed and lay still. Voices spoke over her, and though she understood none of the words, part of her knew it was the same mysterious tongue that occasionally sprang unbidden from her mouth.

Both male and female, the voices were melodic and beautiful. Was this what she sounded like to others?

"Quenaril a n'toindelil emphita noe ma putonde a sudile? Selunde kamsa de tiseo a meia de na'eahase?"

"Doa na tinde mo. Samada misekeo da quese, ne ide sikeo samada sahamida."

The speakers went silent, but Seung forced herself to remain still. When the silence stretched longer she gathered what strength she had, then snapped her eyes open. Her visitors were gone.

She climbed to her feet a bit too quickly and her head swirled in protest. She stumbled sideways on wobbly legs and leaned on a nearby tree for support. With one hand clutching the side of her head, she looked about. There was no sign that anyone had been there.

Great, she thought. Surely they would have relieved her of her supplies and either tried to take Swiftspirit, or chased him away. A nearby sparrow chirped, and on the other side of the campsite, another answered.

Seung squinted and raised a hand to shield her eyes. Morning. How long had she slept? A day? Two? She looked across the campsite where Swiftspirit stood not far from the last place she'd seen him, apparently relaxed and looking at her with his ears perked up in her direction.

Her relief was complete when she noticed her travel pack and gear lying in the same place she'd left them, seemingly untouched.

What in the name of the Gods has happened to me? She pushed away from the tree and nearly fell over when a wave of pain shot through her head. She braced herself on the tree again and waited for the dizziness to subside.

After several moments of deep steady breaths, Seung carefully stepped away from the tree and made her way to one of her saddlebags. She retrieved a waterskin and splashed crisp cool water over her face, and felt instantly revived.

Seung waited a few moments to ensure her head was steady

enough, then went about cleaning up the campsite and saddling Swiftspirit. It was a slow affair, but she managed to get it done.

She patted Swiftspirit on the neck and grabbed the reins. She took one last look around the campsite, which seemed to look back at her, as innocent as nature itself.

Seung glared at all of it and none of it, then led the stallion back through the woods toward the road.

11

"Shall we continue to watch her?" Joscel asked in his normal voice, the use of the *whisper* unnecessary as the woman disappeared into the foliage, and out of earshot.

"No," Tinnoviel answered. "The road she travels runs parallel to the Wood, but it will veer. As long as she remains on the road, she will be a safe distance from us. They do not see or hear well enough to be a concern."

"But she is *manuile*," Immendiel said.

"Only partially."

The tracker glanced sidelong at Tinnoviel. Even without consideration of his tremendous skill, the warrior was bigger than most males in the wood; nearly the stature of a human warrior. "You don't think she possesses enough of our attributes to feel the existence of our home, do you? Even by accident?"

Tinnoviel considered the question. "She was born and raised among humans, that much is obvious. Whomever her parents are, they taught her some of our ways from an early age, but they are no more than familial habits or odd quirks about herself that she likely doesn't understand."

Joscel and Ikara nodded, a look of pity crossing their features.

Immendiel frowned at the smug pair. "I've seen a formidable human or two. Your 'superiority' may well get you in trouble one day."

Ikara choked back his laughter. "A human? Their senses and reflexes are as dull as their minds."

"You ever see one catch a fairy off guard?" Tinnoviel asked. The reminder of the woman who'd kicked the little sprite fluttering behind her silenced the other two.

"Stranded between two worlds from birth," Immendiel said, staring absently in the direction the woman had gone.

Tinnoviel glanced at the tracker. She, too, had a look of sympathy for the young woman, but it wasn't from a place of arrogance, as most of their people felt toward humans. "Time to return to the Lady Seiyun and give our report."

Immendiel nodded in deference. "You think this will interest her?"

The warrior waved his hand in the direction the woman had gone. "When was the last time you saw one like her?"

Again, Immendiel nodded.

One by one, the group fell away from their perch and leapt from branch to branch, moving through the woods without a sound. Tinnoviel took one last glance over his shoulder at the empty campsite, then dropped away.

SEUNG URGED Swiftspirit into a trot and immediately regretted it when her head started pounding in sync with the stallion's every step.

She slowed him down and took another draw from her waterskin. For a mercy, the clouds finally moved on and the golden glow of early morning greeted her.

She took a deep breath and filled her lungs with fresh morning air. The crisp, cool water along with the warm sun on her face made Seung's head feel better. She navigated Swiftspirit around puddles and soft wet road. From the looks of the clear, blue sky and white clouds, the soaked earth was the only indication that there had been a storm the previous day.

That stray thought took her back to last night, and the source of the throbs in her head. As a child, adults had told stories of magical creatures in the woods; mischievous little beings who were best left alone. She imagined every child in every village heard similar stories, but she'd never imagined them to be true. Seung thought back to her encounter last night, that little humanoid being dancing in the top of the flames, spreading tiny wings of fire and blowing kisses of colorful ashes. And then there had been the devious giggling, and her apparent mistake at kicking ... whatever it was.

Seung gently rubbed her head again. Creatures made of water creeping around in the rainy night. Tiny creatures capable of launching her across a campsite without even touching her. She gave her surroundings a wary glance. Whatever was out there, she wanted no part of it again.

Birdsong and chirping insects penetrated her dark thoughts, drawing a smile to Seung's face. She wanted to let her head fall back, but knew that would start it spinning again. She settled for closing her eyes and imagining herself soaring with the eagles above, playing with the squirrels running along the bases of the trees, climbing and jumping and teasing each other.

Further back in the woods she spotted a few deer grazing. They raised their heads to look in her direction, mouths moving sideways as they chewed the tender wet grass.

She grinned at the curious animals, and despite her aching head and the mysterious creatures she'd encountered, she soon found herself in a fine mood. She reached into one of her saddlebags and drew out a carrot, then, with a pat on Swiftspirit's powerful neck, leaned forward and presented the treat. The horse promptly slipped it out of her hand and began crunching.

Occasionally she passed travelers, asking of news from the north and how the people were faring. As anticipated, more than a few people had learned of the fate of Ulleung, and word had traveled north along the coast and reached Pyon quicker than expected.

"Cities along the coast have been fortifying and making preparations to evacuate at the slightest hint of a storm," a woman told her. She waved her hand up and down the road to encompass the many horse-drawn trailers and carriages. "Many of us are merchants who travel to every city or town north and south. Some talk of moving trade more inland. That's where I'm going."

"Is there a town or city nearby?" Seung asked. She pulled out her map. "According to this, I should have come to the beginnings of a city, here."

The woman looked at the map and shrugged. "Either your map is very old, or just incorrect. We came from that direction and passed no city."

She frowned at the area Seung pointed to. "Come to think of it, when we passed through that spot, I remember my mind feeling foggy. All I wanted was to get us through as fast as we could. Once we was several miles down the road from it, the feeling went away. Maybe the area's haunted." She glanced about, then leaned in closer. "You might think me the fool for saying it, but I've heard tales of strange creatures walking the day and night. Shadows with wavy swords for arms, creatures that look to be made of moss, with long teeth, claws, and glowing eyes."

It would indeed have sounded ridiculous if Seung hadn't had her most recent experiences. "My thanks for your time," Seung said, bowing her head. "Take care. The road is no less dangerous ahead."

"Have a care for yourself as well, young lady," the woman

replied. "I can't imagine a pretty one such as you traveling the
road by yourself."—she glanced at *Vyirayoi*, the weapon halved
and strapped across her lower back—"but then, you look like you
know your way around that thing."

As the day wore on, the road became crowded with travelers.
Whether on horseback, guiding oxen-powered trailers and
wagons, or on foot, it looked as though an entire city was on
the move.

Seung thought she might replenish her supplies without
having to stop in town, but to her disappointment few had food
and water for sale.

Several hours after her conversation with the merchant,
Seung felt the strange head fog she had spoken of. The further
she went, the more intense it became. She thought again about
her encounter in the woods, and wondered if some curse affected
the area.

She snorted at the ridiculousness of the thought. "Must be
something in the air. Maybe a concentration of toxic plant or
something." She spoke the words, but a tiny part of her believed
otherwise.

A trail came into view that led off the main road. Seung
stopped and peered down the path, and saw a walled village. She
unfolded her map and frowned at the spot where she should be.
Nothing marked a civilization here.

"Why didn't the travel master list this one?" From the corner
of her eye, she saw people staring at her with puzzled expressions. Did they know something she didn't, or was it the same
thing that had caused the fog in her mind? She hoped it wasn't
some airborne toxin. If so, it was already too late. How disgraceful
it would be to leave her home on a fool's errand and die, or lose
her mind, on the side of a road.

She shrugged. *Too late now.* "Maybe someone there will have
answers."

She guided Swiftspirit onto the trail, and the fog in her head intensified with every step. She nervously looked about, but there was no sign of anything causing it; no toxic plants she was familiar with, no smoke or fumes she saw or smelled.

The closer they drew to the outer wall, the more restless Swiftspirit grew. She leaned forward and gave him a pat on the neck. "You feel it, too?" The stallion tossed his head in response.

The solid iron gate guarding the entrance felt far too imposing for a village not far from a well-traveled road. Perhaps they had problems with large predators or bandits.

The echo of her knocks brought no answer. A creeping uneasiness settled in her stomach, but Seung needed to replenish her food and water. She touched her forehead. Her headache had all but gone, but now this cursed head fog replaced it.

She stared up at the unfriendly barrier. Perhaps this was a sleepy town, and no one had yet come to man the gates. That seemed unlikely, for it was already nearing midday.

With more than a little trepidation, Seung touched the heavy metal bar on the gate. She didn't know what she'd expected to happen, but when nothing did, she slipped her hand under the bar and lifted. It resisted her efforts. She frowned. The bar didn't feel heavy, rather, it felt as though some invisible force was holding it down against her efforts.

More mischief from those little creeps. Seung frowned in defiance and tugged with all her strength. She nearly hopped out of her skin when a jolt of some strange energy shot through her.

"What in the name of the Gods was that?" she whispered, rubbing her hand. It hadn't hurt, but it was unexpected.

As she stood there glaring at the metal bar, it fell away and the gate creaked open. Seung had *Vyirayoi* in her hand before the bar hit the ground. She stared into the opening, not able to see more than a few feet inside.

With a great deal of hesitation overruled by the need to

replenish for the road and shake off this terrible head fog, she led Swiftspirit just inside and stopped to look around. Her spirits fell.

Dilapidated buildings leaned against one another as though in a stupor. Rotted wooden shacks and rusted metal poles and beams lay strewn about streets and sidewalks. Plant overgrowth pushed out of broken windows and splintered walls and doors.

Weeds as tall as a small child inhabited the many cracks in the unkempt streets. Not a soul roamed this forgotten place, not even the usual scavengers that typically inhabited an abandoned dwelling.

Swiftspirit gave a nervous whicker and tossed his head. Seung glanced at the stallion. The whites of his wide eyes practically shined as the stallion looked around wildly their surroundings.

"Right again, my friend," she said, remembering the night before. She turned back toward the gate when she heard what sounded like a whimpering child.

Seung half turned and looked over her shoulder. The street was still empty. An uneasiness crept into the nape of her neck and traveled down her spine. She heard the sound again, so faint she barely made it out.

She waited quietly for it again, but nothing. After several more heartbeats of silence and her instincts nagging her to leave, she turned away. Again came the whimpering.

Seung stepped away from the gate and moved down the street. "Someone there?" she called out. "Do you need help?" Her instincts screamed at her to leave this place, but Seung couldn't abandon a child if it was in danger. She heard the sound again, a high-pitched whimper that could only be a child. She moved in the direction of the sound, eyes scanning everything, *Vyirayoi* in a tight grip. The whimpering sound led her to a broken-down deli.

The stench of rotted fish attacked her nose before she got close. *How long has this place been abandoned?* The wasted food seemed weeks old, but the village looked to have been abandoned long before then.

Seung tied the reigns to the saddle and whispered into Swift-spirit's ear. As with every time she spoke using the language innate yet alien to her, the stallion appeared to understand. Despite the horse's obvious agitation, he stood vigil outside the shop.

The smell of rotting sea life was overwhelming, and Seung fought to not gag.

She heard the whimper again, only a few feet away behind a display counter. When she slipped around she saw ... nothing.

Seung frowned. She had clearly heard the sound coming from just behind this disgusting counter, but there was nothing there except some large dust balls and fish entrails sprawled about the floor.

She started to draw herself upright, but froze when she caught a different smell.

Seung glanced about with her eyes, but saw nothing. Finally, her patience played out. She spun and simultaneously whipped *Vyirayoi* around to a defensive angle.

A large green hand slipped past the shaft of the weapon and caught her by the neck. A second hand rammed the shaft of *Vyirayoi* against her chest.

"You look forrr something you cannn't finnnd?" The gurgling voice sent a wave of panic through her body. The arm attached to the massive hand was green and covered in scales, while moss-like hair grew between the scaly plates.

Seung looked up from to the patch of orange moss-like hair on its chest, to a long thick neck supporting a head covered in hanging green moss. Bulging yellow eyes looked hungrily into hers.

Seung shoved down her initial panic and released the shaft of her weapon with one hand. She attacked every pressure point she knew with rapid punches and knife-hand strikes. She might have been assaulting a piece of moss-covered wood for all the effect it had.

It yanked her closer to its face with such strength, Seung thought her neck would snap. Little black spots filled the corners of her narrowing vision as her air was increasingly cut off. She gripped the shaft of *Vyirayoi* with both hands again and used every ounce of strength remaining to her to push back. If she lost consciousness she was dead.

Seung kicked the beast in the groin to no effect. She curled her legs and snapped her left foot out and to the side, once, twice, thrice, in rapid succession. The kicks would have broken a human's ribs three times over, but had no effect on her inhuman adversary.

She struck it in the midsection with the butt of her hand, kicked and punched, jabbed and chopped, but it was like fighting a tree.

Thin green lips drew back to reveal a mouth filled with jagged knife-like teeth. Its lips continued to curl back, revealing more and more teeth, until half of its face was a huge mouth that could swallow her whole!

Wide-eyed and her heart hammering in her chest, Seung struck its wrist repeatedly. She had to break its hold before it snapped her neck.

Blackish green sludge oozed from its mouth, flowing between row upon row of teeth like scum slithering between the rocks of a running stream. The teeth elongated, and Seung thought perhaps being swallowed whole would be preferable.

It lifted her into the air and leaned its head back, giving her a clear view of all those teeth, and the gaping blackness beyond.

She squirmed in its vice-like grip, but it easily held her aloft, one hand clamped around her neck, the other holding the shaft of her weapon still pressed against her chest.

Seung's face tightened with effort as she struggled to break free. *I will not die like this!*

She'd barely finished the thought when they were suddenly falling. They tumbled across the wooden floor while Seung continued to beat at its hand, but still the green monster didn't release her neck. It held onto her even as it climbed to its feet. She managed to look around the green creature to see Swiftspirit, just inside the rundown shop, snorting and stamping the ground.

With the orange and green mossy beast distracted by her equine companion, Seung took advantage of the loosened grip. She held her weapon with both hands and rotated the shaft.

She ignored the pain of the shaft sliding down her chest and stomach, and forced her arms to the right as she spun the weapon.

Seung finally managed to shift *Vyirayoi* just far enough to the right that one of the blades spun around and bit down into the monster's shoulder. It grunted—much less of a reaction than she'd hoped for—and she used that tiny instant to pull back. The blade sliced down its arm, and she immediately thrust forward again, driving the sharp tip into its face.

Whether in pain or anger, the monster had opened its huge maw again. Seung quickly snatched the weapon back, then drove the blade straight into its mouth. That got a reaction, and the mossy brute finally released her.

Swiftspirit whinnied and charged again. At the last instant, when the stallion reared up on his hind legs to strike, the monster reached out and grabbed hold of his neck. Swiftspirit let out a horrible scream that Seung had never heard before.

Tears spilled from her eyes at seeing her beloved companion about to die. Then the grief gave way to rage, and with it, strength. Seung swung her arm around and up, and stabbed the monster in the side of the neck. She pulled the blade free, then drove it into the monster's head with everything she had. The creature gurgled loudly and let both of them go. Swiftspirit staggered backwards and coughed. Then he straightened and shook his head, snorting.

"No," Seung said, reading the loyal stallion's intention. "*Malei!*" Swiftspirit snorted in displeasure, but backed off.

She moved toward the moss-covered creature, its hand clamped over the yawning gash in the side of its head.

When it struggled to rise, Seung exploded into action. The monster reached out to grab her again, but was now far too slow for the prepared warrior. Seung ducked under its arm, and, while crouched, drove her blade into its foot. Continuing the motion, she curled into a ball, and used the shaft to vault herself up and kick the monster under the chin.

She held onto the weapon and her momentum pulled the blade free. Midair and upside down, Seung turned her body and bent her legs, bringing herself upright again. As her body turned, she swung *Vyirayoi* around and cut a diagonal slash across the creature's face as she descended.

It dumbly reached out to grab her weapon just as Seung landed, but she was faster. *Vyirayoi* whirled in her hands and severed half of the monster's arm. It staggered away, making another pained, gurgling sound. Seung spun *Vyirayoi* around and down, and one of the blades sheared right through the monster's right leg at the knee. Despite what should have been a grievous wound, the beast still lurched forward and tried to bite at her.

Seung hopped backward out of reach, and got a good look at the monster. Whatever the thing was, the loss of two limbs seemed to concern it little. For several heartbeats, they stared at one another, green blood seeping from the disgusting thing's bleeding stumps, Seung standing ready, *Vyirayoi* tucked under her arm.

The mossy horror let out a shrill scream and clawed its way toward her. It was a clumsy, lumbering effort, and Seung easily kept out of reach long enough to remove its remaining arm. When it fell forward, she leapt on its back, spun *Vyirayoi* over her head, and brought the blades down on its unprotected neck. Steel passed through flesh and bone, and a green head—mouth still agape displaying those awful jagged teeth—hit the floor with a thump. Green blood seeped from the fatal wound like sap from a tree as the headless body slumped to the floor.

The grisly sight would have been enough to inspire nightmares, yet Seung fell back in horror when a black mist flowed out of the stump. What looked like an evil face made of black smoke opened its mouth and let out an airy wail, then dissipated.

What in the name of the Gods? Seung hopped off and circled around the headless monster, her back pressed to the wall. When she reached Swiftspirit, she grabbed the reins and led him out.

Seung had barely set foot outside the cramped battleground when she heard the whimpering again. "Only a fool is twice the victim," she muttered, scanning the area.

When she turned toward the village entrance, she heard the childlike voice again, but this time, the whimpering sounded like taunting. The sound made hairs on the back of her neck stand on end.

Seung had barely swung into the saddle when Swiftspirit broke for the gate. The stallion surely felt as she did about this horrible place, so she gave him his head. Swiftspirit stretched out into a full run, but despite the horse's speed, they drew no closer to the gates.

What have I wandered into? Seung thought. No matter how fast the horse ran, the gates fled just as quickly until she finally pulled him to a stop and looked around. There must be another exit, but even if she found one, would she encounter the same problem?

Something moved in her peripheral vision. Seung turned in the saddle to see a hulking green monster much like the one she had just killed. It stalked lazily out of a house a short way down the street, seeming not at all concerned that she might flee.

Seung dismounted and tied the reins to the saddle. She glared at the lumbering horror and snatched *Vyirayoi* from her back.

Without a word, Seung started toward the monster. She'd just snapped *Vyirayoi's* shaft together when another green brute appeared from a house across the street, then another from farther down.

A fourth moss-covered horror crept out of a tattered inn. Seung thought about how much effort it took to kill the first one as she looked from left to right, before and behind her.

Surrounded.

12

"I'll be fine to never sail the ocean again," Kita said.

Beside him, Kenyatta waved to get Malimokuru's attention as he walked down the ramp from the ship. The old nature reader had done his job well. His mysterious sands had indeed been an effective deterrent to any more of the monsters he'd called water elementals.

"Yeah, man," Kenyatta replied. "If ole man over there wasn't on the boat, we might be lying at the bottom of the sea. And without our weapons enchanted by Mira, we practically helpless."

Kita chewed his lip at that comment. "You still think those things were demons even though he said they were elementals?"

Kenyatta leaned back against the rail and propped his elbows up. "Maybe, maybe not. But I feel my chances better if I got my swords. What happen two years ago ain't over, man. We send all dem fiends back to the abyss, but we see nothing of the one who summon them."

Kita gazed out at the sparkling blue ocean. The golden light cast on it by the sun made it ominous in its tranquility, given the creatures they'd fought the night before.

"Wanna know what I think?" When Kenyatta looked at him, he continued. "I think those things were what the nature reader said they were. I think we're dealing with some kind of being that controls water, and that it might not be a demon. Maybe the situation *is* connected to the demons." He shrugged. "Just a guess."

"If it's not a demon," Kenyatta replied, "what makes you think der's a connection?"

Kita drummed his fingers on the rail. "Whatever Malimokuru linked with in the ocean. He said it was primal, fitful, maybe angry. Aside from anger, those aren't your typical attributes for a demon. You know that as well as I do. They like to be in the thick of the destruction they cause. I think it would have tried to destroy the old man's mind as soon as he connected with it."

Kenyatta thought on that. It made sense, even if it complicated the situation. If they were dealing with some sort of sentient being from this world, why would it cause such destruction, and what was the source of its unrest? More questions, no answers.

"Here's someting I'm not used to seeing," Malimokuru said.

"What's that?" Kita asked.

"Young men tinking. You look like you're in pain from it."

Kita chuckled, but turned a concerned look on Kenyatta when his friend didn't join in.

Malimokuru moved in front of him and peered into his eyes. "Careful, man."

"Whatcha mean wit dat?" Kenyatta asked.

"You can only hold anger and hate for so long before it's holdin' you."

Kenyatta turned an incredulous look on the nature reader. "The destruction of our home and countless people don't bother you so much?"

Malimokuru pressed his lips together in a wrinkled line. "I've buried more friends and family than years you've been alive, bwoy. Ya lose enough people in ya life to one circumstance or another, life gets a little more perspective." He started away from the pier and the two younger men fell in step on either side of him.

"So, what?" Kenyatta said. "You just go numb and don't feel anyting anymore? Just ... move on?"

"Ya go through the emotions," Malimokuru replied. "Ya grieve, get angry, feel whatcha gotta feel. But you move past it, bwoy. It's different for everyone, but what you holdin' on to,"—he shook his head—"you gotta let it go. Feel the pain, even the anger. But work past it. If you travel thousands of miles on vengeance alone, it'll have fed well on you by the time you get to your enemy. You'll be hollowed out and dead inside when it's all done."

"So we just let it go?" Kenyatta asked. "Put it in the past. Move on. Be happy."

"Skull so thick he doesn't hear what I'm sayin'," Malimokuru muttered, then spoke louder. "I'm saying get to dis ting, whatever it is, and stop it from destroying anything else. But don't let the hate blind you. You don't even know what you're lookin' for, and it might or might not be what you think it is."

From the corner of his eye, Kenyatta saw Kita's eyes widen, but when he gave him a questioning look, his friend gave a subtle shake of his head. Later, then.

"Our good captain give me enough coin for a room at an inn and a meal, with a little left over for provisions. Man was grateful for our help."

"You mean your help," Kita said. "You're the one that saved us all."

"Yeah man," Malimokuru said. "I was being nice. You were quite useless, but you hold em off long enough for me to get topside."

"Pfft." Kenyatta rolled his eyes. "Ole man take half the night to hobble up and help."

Malimokuru snarled. "Rude, young fool."

"I'LL NEVER STOPPED BEING AMAZED at how fast word travels," Kita said. The trio walked the newly fortified avenues of Carrabisha, where street merchants sold their wares from wagons that could be packed up and rolled away in mere minutes.

Stucco buildings with tiled roofs, whispers from a long ago broken age, already well maintained in the coastal island city, were now outfitted with heavy wooden shutters that could be closed and locked.

Cart vendors called out their wares at the edges of the bustling streets; every one of those carts positioned at a street corner.

"Yeah man," Kenyatta said. He took a deep breath. The crisp coastal air had that hint of salt in it that he so loved; fondly, yet painfully, reminding him of home. "Dis place got the look of one doing business as usual with an eye out for disaster."

Even as he said it, Kenyatta noticed more than a few locals casting glances toward the ocean. The refugees were easy to spot, for they looked even more wary of the beach.

"I'll feel better getting off dis island," Malimokuru said. "Or any island."

"No argument here," Kita replied.

Malimokuru stopped walking. "Midday is still a while off. We can buy horses and ride to the northern tip of Carrabisha—All Saints Bay. We sell the horses and catch the next boat out to Moriana Bay, southeastern-most tip of Nomar. We get far enough inland not to worry about some wave washing over our heads, and we figure it out from there."

Kenyatta shrugged. "Fine with me. But we go nowhere until we got weapons, first."

Malimokuru looked as though he wanted to argue, but let it go. A blade might not work on a water elemental, but it worked fine on a pirate, and plenty of those roamed the seas.

"We can get this done faster if we split up," Kita said. He turned to Malimokuru. "You know how to pick out a horse?"

Malimokuru stared at him. "Nah, man. I'm just a...*nature* reader."

"Ah," Kita said. "Of course. We'll find weapons and buy provisions, and meet you at the edge of town, north. Deal?"

Malimokuru grunted. "Yeah, man. Let's get dis finished and be outta here. I won't sleep right till we're on the mainland."

The sun was halfway between the eastern horizon and midday by the time Kenyatta and Kita acquired weapons and provisions.

Kenyatta looked his new sword over for what must have been the tenth time. "Of all the gaudy "weapons" we've seen, dis the only one that's not a showpiece belonging over a fireplace. And he only had one."

"Not many people fight with two swords, Ken," Kita said. "And I didn't make out much better." He gave his staff a whirl. "The wood is sturdy, but heavy and stiff. Nothing like the staff I had before."

"And like dis ting,"—Kenyatta held up his sword—"is nothing that'll banish a demon. We come across any demons, we'll be running more than fighting."

Kita sighed. "Think you can contact Taliah? Maybe she can get us to Takashaniel so Mira or Iel can put the charge on these."

"Nah, man," Kenyatta replied. He peered up the road to see a figure leaning against a post with three horses hitched to it. "I've tried several times since we set out to get here. She's not feelin' me."

"You can't connect with her?" Kita asked, concern in his voice.

"She's not connecting with me," Kenyatta said. "I don't have that kinda power. I focus my thoughts on her, and she pick up on it. She tell me it's a combination of her abilities, and us being siblings. But the communication part of it is kinda one way."

"Too bad," Kita said. "She could have just transported us to the region we're going to."

Kenyatta glanced at Kita. "Before we get to the old man up der, what was on your mind that had your eyes 'bout to pop outta your head?"

Kita's face lit up. "Can't believe I forgot." He grabbed Kenyatta's arm and stopped. Further up the road, Malimokuru had started to untie the horses. When he saw them stop, he dropped the reins and went back to leaning against the post.

"Better make it quick," Kenyatta said, chuckling. "Ole man gonna leave us."

"There's no question those things on the ship weren't demons," Kita said, "and I don't think whatever caused the tsunamis is a demon either."

Kenyatta sighed. "We've been through this already ..."

"What did you feel when the waves came? And when those things climbed aboard the ship?"

Kenyatta frowned. "What do you mean?"

"What did you feel?" Kita pressed. "Think about it."

"I ..." Kenyatta's frown deepened, then his eyes widened when it dawned on him. "Nothing." He turned a thoughtful expression on Kita. "I felt ... nothing.

Kita slapped him on the chest with the back of his hand. "And if any of them had been demons ..."

"We'd have felt the gene burning inside us. That's the only time it awakens."

"Exactly," Kita replied. They started walking again. "I can't believe you forgot that."

"And you didn't just remember it today?" Kenyatta replied.

Kita grinned. "Don't change the subject. My point is, we can rule demons out."

"That just adds more questions," Kenyatta said.

"But at least we have one answer."

Malimokuru began unhitching the horses once they were

near. "Glad ya had a nice conversation," he said as they packed the provisions and gear.

"Anyone happen to tell you how long it takes to ride from here to the northern port?" Kenyatta asked.

"Afraid so," Malimokuru said. "Gonna take a little longer than I thought."

Kenyatta felt his spirits sink. "How much longer?"

"At a steady canter for half a day, it'll take four days."

Kenyatta laughed in resignation.

Despite the unexpected length of the journey, luck was with them. They encountered no danger on the road, and kept the horses at a steady, but manageable, canter, enabling the animals to continue for longer distances. They reached All Saints Bay well after midday.

It might have been arguable whether it was good luck or not that they'd made it to the docks before the last of the ships had set sail, but the timing was good nonetheless.

The smell of fish and salty air, typical to any wharf, was lost on Kenyatta and Kita as the duo eyed the moored ships, bobbing up and down with the flow of the rippling ocean.

"Can't wait to get on one of those," Kita said dryly.

Kenyatta slung his pack over his shoulder. "More boats."

Malimokuru joined them outside the stable. "Got good coin for the horses." He turned a self-satisfied smile on them. "We're in good shape."

"We appreciate everyting you've done to help us, nature reader," Kenyatta said.

Malimokuru tipped his head. "Ya welcome, bwoy."

Luck traveled with them, this day, for they managed to bargain for cheaper fare in exchange for Kenyatta and Kita to help crew the ship.

"Hopefully no more incidents," Kenyatta said as he and Kita watched Malimokuru walk the perimeter of the ship, spreading a layer of sand as he went.

"That'd be nice," Kita said. "Hopefully when we get to the mainland, the old man will ..."

Kenyatta looked at him. "What?"

The word had barely left his lips when Kenyatta felt it. He swore an oath as his hand went to the hilt of his sword, for deep within his very being, the gene of the Daunyans quickened.

13

"Now you feel it." Kita said.

"Same as you," Kenyatta replied. He scanned the shadowy deck in the waning daylight. The crew moved about, manning the ship as it rocked back and forth to the rhythm of the ocean. "I got a bad feelin' about this."

"Because we don't have weapons able to banish whatever it is, and we're out in the open water?" Kita asked. "Why would you be concerned?"

The first mate spotted them and his brow knotted with irritation. "What's with you two? The deal was for extra hands on deck, not hands on weapons." He took a step back. "You're not planning to make trouble, are you?"

"Tell everyone to be on guard," Kita said. "We can't explain it, but something's out there ..."

Suddenly, the ship rocked violently toward the starboard side. All about the deck, sailors cried out and dove for the nearest handhold.

One of the deckhands wailed as he slid toward the rail. A crew member grabbed one of the man's waving hands, but he couldn't hold on, and sailor continued his downward slide.

The poor man hit the rail with enough force to flip him head over heels over the side. His screams faded as he fell away into the waiting darkness.

Over that same side, four long, milky white appendages slinked out of the darkened ocean and wrapped around the rail. The appendages flexed and continued to slowly pull the ship over.

Kenyatta and Kita managed to grab hold of the shrouds connected to the mainmast. They could only watch as several more sailors and a deckhand went tumbling toward the rails. The men rolled silently, hit the side, and went over.

Kenyatta heard the splashes then the cries for help, barely audible over the roar of the ocean. The calls turned to screams, then silence.

The white appendages pulled the ship further sideways until everyone hung suspended in the air, their only lifeline being the strength of their grip.

"Oh, no." Kita pointed past Kenyatta. "I don't think our old friend can hold out much longer."

Kenyatta strained to look over his shoulder. Feet dangling beneath him, one of Malimokuru's hands slipped free. Now hanging from one hand, the nature reader grunted, and swung his legs back and forth, then let go.

"Auck," the old man cried out when he hit the deck.

"What da hell him do that for?" Kenyatta said, watching in horror as the nature reader slid toward the four appendages.

Malimokuru reached into the pouch at his waist, then flung a handful of sand at the tentacles. He shouted a single word, "*Amacit!*"

The sands lit into silver sparks that showered over the appendages. The finger-like tentacles sizzled, and acrid smoke slithered into the air. They let go of the rails and slipped back into the water.

The ship rocked violently upright at the sudden release.

Kenyatta and Kita wrapped their legs around the shrouds as the ship swayed back in the opposite direction. Below, Malimokuru had still been sliding downward. When the tentacles let go and it rocked back, he slid to a stop, then started to roll toward the opposite rail.

"This is gonna get bad real fast," Kita said when four unburned appendages appeared on the port side of the ship and grabbed the rails. This time, several sailors rushed to the side and began hacking at it with cutlasses or any nearby object that could be used as a weapon.

Four more appendages slinked up from the ocean to swat at the sailors, one wrapping around a victim and lifting him up and overboard. The man hollered and tried to cut at the tentacle, but it dropped into the water and both were gone.

Kenyatta and Kita dropped to the deck just as eight appendages appeared on the starboard side.

"How big is that thing?" Kita said.

"Too big," Kenyatta replied. "I'll get the other side. You go help them." He pointed at the sailors still trying to break the tentacles' hold on the rail.

They split up. Kita's staff was a blur as he beat back the tentacles, whacking one after another, forcing them to release their hold.

The ship creaked ominously as Kenyatta sprinted across the deck. He drew his sword and sliced through one of the thick tentacles. From this close, he saw they were each as large around as his body, with the undersides lined with suction cups. Several giant squids? Surely there was no such thing as a *kraken*.

He got his answer when he severed one of the tentacles. Not only did the other three shudder in what seemed like pain, but the four to Kenyatta's right also flinched. He heard triumphant howls on the other side of the ship and saw that the tentacles had reacted on that side as well.

Kenyatta shook his head. The sailors didn't understand what

that meant. "Not good at all," he muttered. He held his sword, ready as he watched the seven tentacles waving in the air before him, just out of reach beyond the rail.

Malimokuru groaned as he climbed to his feet. Kenyatta stole a glance at the old man, impressed with his durability despite his advanced years.

The appendages reached for the rails again, and Kenyatta went into action. He severed another one and it fell flopping to the deck, black liquid oozing onto the paneled wood. He never stopped moving, his sword a blur in his hands. He managed to cut several more of the milky white tentacles before they all recoiled again. Beneath the ship, the water rippled.

"Good job, bwoy," Malimokuru said. He reached into his pouch for another handful of that strange sand. "You're hurting them."

"It," Kenyatta said.

"What?" Malimokuru frowned at him, then looked at the waving tentacles. "Whatcha on about with dat 'it,' talk?"

Kenyatta didn't answer. He knew the nature reader understood his meaning from the trepidation in his voice. He kept his attention on the tentacles waving in front of him as if trying to decide what to do. They drew back, then moved farther apart and swatted the deck. Barrels shattered and parts of the deck splintered under the weight of the blows.

Two tentacles wrapped around the bowsprit and pulled. The ship dipped forward and screaming sailors tumbled toward the fore.

Kenyatta grabbed hold of the rail and waited for the tentacles to come closer. Around him, the ugly things swatted the ship, breaking wood apart and snapping rigging. One of the smaller sails detached and blew away.

He let go of the rail and slid down the deck just as another tentacle slithered out of the ocean and wrapped around the foremast. It flexed, and the wood creaked in protest. Kenyatta curled his legs, and pushed off from the leaning deck. He drew his sword back as he fell, waiting till the last instant, then drove it into the giant tentacle as he hit. This one was more than twice as wide as his body, and though the blade bit deep, it didn't go all the way through.

The gene of the Daunyans burning within him, Kenyatta easily swung his legs to create momentum, then dislodged the sword as he lifted into the air. He twisted midair and landed on top of the tentacle. The skin on the thing was somewhat soft and slimy, and his feet slipped out from under him.

"Bombaclot!" Kenyatta fell flat on his back, but was quick to reverse the grip on his sword and stab down just as he slid over. The tentacles spasmed as the sword sank to the hilt into rubbery flesh. Kenyatta held onto the sword and lifted himself up. He swung his leg over and straddled it, keeping one hand firmly on the hilt.

Below, the ship bucked upright again when the appendage at the fore released the bowsprit. He heard the others shouting up at him, but his concentration was on not slipping off.

The tentacle moved away from the ship, and Kenyatta swore under his breath as he rode it out and over the dark, rippling water. "Bad idea, man."

By now the sun had dipped below the horizon, and the moon shone bright in the cloudless sky. Small solace that it was, Kenyatta was grateful to be able to see. But what he saw brought him little comfort. Three smaller tentacles were racing toward him.

No matter how loudly Kita shouted for him to let go, Kenyatta either didn't hear, or didn't heed his words. Across the deck, Malimokuru also shouted similar—if admonishing—words, but the ever-stubborn Kenyatta rode the gigantic tentacle even as it unwrapped from the mast and drifted out to sea, and likely his friend's imminent death.

His helplessness lit a fire inside him, and Kita turned his rage upon the smaller appendages still assaulting the ship. He whirled his staff and brought it down on another of the milky white things even as it slapped at a sailor who barely dove aside. Kita hit it with such force, there was a loud crack, and the thing flopped on the deck, then lifted into the air, hanging limp from the afflicted area.

Back and forth Kita went, swatting and breaking any tentacles that came too near. The gene of the Daunyans burned inside him, a warning that whatever this thing was, it wasn't native to this plane of existence. This was a demon, and a big one.

He wished he'd had his old staff with the blade at the end. He could have sliced these things apart as Kenyatta had done.

The stray thought about his friend, now out at sea with whatever these things were, set his blood burning again. He roared and spun his staff over his head, then brought it around his body. He hit another tentacle with enough force that it folded over his staff before dropping to the deck. Below the ship, the water rippled more violently.

"What the hell are these things? Or is this one big thing I don't want to see?" He looked out at the moonlit ocean, barely able to make out the figure of the giant appendage. Somewhere on that thing, Kenyatta clung to it. Or had he already fallen into the ocean? Kita had to trust his friend. They'd been through too much together for it to end with him being devoured by some giant squid. "You've gotten out of some tight spots, buddy. I hope you've got a plan."

Kita knew even as he said the words that Kenyatta, ever resourceful, likely had no plan.

"SHOULDA HAD A PLAN FOR DIS," Kenyatta said as he watched helplessly as several of the smaller appendages—having abandoned the ship—now speeding toward him.

He looked down at the giant tentacle on which he sat. "Ugh." He took a deep breath, then with both hands on the hilt of his embedded sword, pulled it toward him. The sword sliced through the rubbery, slimy flesh, and Kenyatta again had to hold on as it shuddered. He looked up. The smaller tentacles were almost on him.

Kenyatta pulled the sword free and reached into the gaping wound. He gritted his teeth through the revulsion as thick black goo oozed out of the gash and covered his hand.

"Don't tink about it," Kenyatta said to himself as he pushed through soft tissue to grab hold of cartilage and bone. "Just don't think about it."

He waited till the finger-like tentacles were just in reach, and whipped his sword outward. A length of appendage longer than he was tall fell away. The stump wavered for a moment, then crashed back into the sea.

The other tentacles twitched and moved away, and the one upon which Kenyatta sat waved and bucked. He drove his sword into the wound again, and held tight to the hilt and his grip inside the deep gash. As soon as it stopped, the smaller white appendages attacked again.

Kenyatta tried to fend them off, but his giant slimy perch continued to wave and twitch. It was all he could do not to simply slip off.

One missed swipe of his sword earned him a painful slap from behind. Stars lit his vision, but he held on. Another tentacle came in, and he waited till the last moment, then sliced it across its width. The nearly halved tentacle hung by little more than a patch of skin.

He didn't wait for another fit of bucking this time, but yanked the sword free and stabbed it again, then again. On the third stab, the tentacle reared upright, and Kenyatta left the blade embedded and held on.

"No different than climbing a tree, now," Kenyatta growled. "A slimy disgusting tree." He tightened his grip on the wound and drew his sword free again as the smaller appendages came in. He fought them off and managed to sever another one, when a spout of water erupted from below.

Kenyatta gritted his teeth against the pain of saltwater stinging his skin as it sprayed him like a geyser. When finally stopped, Kenyatta opened his eyes, relieved it hadn't stripped the skin off of him. Then he looked down. Dozens of feet below, the sea roiled.

"And dis how I die." Kenyatta drove the sword into the giant tentacle, tightened his legs around it as best he could, and waited. The tentacle began to sink into the ocean.

Once he was just above the water, Kenyatta held his breath.

14

Vyirayoi was a blur in Seung's hands as she whipped it over her head, around her back, whirled it vertically from the left side of her body to the right. Outside the cramped space of the fish shop, she was deadly, but her enemies showed no pain upon injury or even dismemberment. And there were at least a ten of them.

"Now I know why this place was abandoned." Seung spun the weapon and brought it down and under her arm. One of the bladed ends sliced deep into the side of a green brute to her right. Knowing it wouldn't react to the injury, she dropped to one knee and pulled the weapon free. Seung continued the motion and drove the other blade into a lunging monster behind her.

The flat, curved blade stabbed into its scaly moss-covered midsection. With the shaft tucked under her arm as a brace, Seung threw all her weight into turning her body, and wrenched the blade free.

Both of the disgusting creatures continued forward as she knew they would, and she kept spinning. Both ends of her weapon sliced into the green brutes again, cutting them in half.

Seung planted her feet and reversed her turn. She whirled

the blade horizontally as she moved. The blades kept the monsters at bay until she could ready herself. She took a quick glance to the side and spotted Swiftspirit. The stallion bucked and kicked out with his rear hooves, catching one of the mossy creatures square in the chest. Despite the size of the hulking beast, the kick still knocked it backwards.

She moved closer to her equine companion. Despite the fierceness of the powerful stallion, nothing he could do would kill these things. "We fight together, my friend."

Seung gave herself the length of her weapon plus a foot or two more away from the horse to allow herself room to move. She continued to use sweeping and vertical attacks. The green horrors had a reach as long as her weapon, but her strategy kept their slashing claws away.

Instead of grabbing for her, one monster simply lunged in with a bite. She cried out at the sight of those teeth, longer than her fingers, inside a gaping maw that could have swallowed her head whole. She spun to the right of the biting monster.

The creature had fully committed to the lunging bite, and couldn't recover fast enough. Seung brought *Vyirayoi* around with her spinning body and brought one of the blades down on the monster's exposed neck. She kept the weapon turning even as the head bounced on the ground, and whirled it around to sever a reaching arm.

Ignoring the rotted stench of green ichor that splattered over her, Seung kept moving. Despite having its limb severed, the monster slapped at her with its remaining claw. Seung ducked, but not quick enough. The giant scaly hand grazed the side of her head and shoulder, and sent her spinning to the ground.

Seung fought through the throbbing pain and dizziness, and swung her weapon in an outward arc as soon as she hit the ground. The reflexive maneuver saved her. *Vyirayoi* bit through tough scale and mossy hide and severed the pursuing brute's leg below the knee.

Seung scramble to her feet on wobbly knees while blinking back the fuzziness in her vision. If the thing had hit her fully, she'd have been knocked unconscious.

She took a deep breath and blew it out. Despite having felled several of these things, there were still more than half a dozen, and there was no telling if there were more that might be drawn to the commotion. It hardly mattered, she realized. Her head was pounding, her shoulder ached, and her movements were slowing.

Behind her, Swiftspirit's pained scream sent her heart into a flutter. He leapt alongside her and kicked out at a pursuing monster. The black stallion had a cut in his shoulder the length of her foreleg.

Seung screamed and went into a flurry. She leapt into a spin and brought the weapon around as she turned. One of the blades sliced cleanly through the neck of a lumbering monster. She jumped straight up and kicked it in the chest before the headless body began to fall. The kick was meant to propel herself away, rather than the dead beast. She glided backwards and into one of the two monsters pursuing Swiftspirit.

She flew toward it, weapon leading, and the flat curved blade bit into her target's lower back. Seung tucked the shaft in her underarm, hooked her arm around it at her elbow, and pulled upward with all her strength.

The blade sliced up from the monster's lower back all the way through scale and bone, and out through its shoulder. As if too stubborn or dumb to die, the brute stumbled after the stallion, but Seung wasn't finished. She whipped the weapon around and severed one of its legs.

The monster finally fell to the ground and struggled futilely to rise as green lifeblood flowed from its body.

Her fury played out, Seung stumbled sideways but steadied herself. The pounding in her head intensified, and her legs could barely support her. *Vyirayoi* suddenly felt many times heavier in her grasp, and she could barely bring it to bear against the monsters.

She fended them off, but her movements were increasingly slow and sloppy. One creature slipped inside her defense and dealt her a slash across her hip, then slapped her arm when she staggered.

The strength of the blow knocked her a dozen feet to the side, and *Vyirayoi* flew from her grasp. Pain exploded through her body as she rolled over gravel and rocks.

Seung lay on her side, eyes barely open. She had failed her people and her parents' legacy. She would die, not defending her village or saving her people, but in an abandoned and forgotten village filled with monsters that would feed on her corpse. The last thing she heard as her heart sank, was Swiftspirit's angry roar, and a bellow in a language she did not know, yet was oddly familiar.

TINNOVIEL'S HUNCHES were never wrong, and today was no exception. The enchantments placed upon the nearby village would deter any human, but would they work on one who shared the bloodline of his people?

He got his answer long before he reached the wooden gate. With hearing sharper than any human, Tinnoviel heard the fighting as he ran down the trail through the trees. He arrived at the village gate and immediately saw that the magic had been engaged. Only someone with the blood of the Wood in their veins could have activated it. He flipped open the locking bar and pulled the gate open.

The stench of urchas assaulted his nose as soon as he stepped through. He sprinted down the gravel path. Several dozen feet away, the woman's black stallion bucked and kicked, while an urcha slapped the woman into the air. She hit the ground hard and tumbled in a cloud of dust.

When she didn't move, Tinnoviel reached over his shoulder and drew his weapon. Crafted from the bark of the kakaya tree, the flat, fan-like blade's cutting edge wasn't honed to slice, but it was strong.

He launched it in an overhand throw. The weapon spun end over end and struck the pursuing urcha in the side of the head.

The tip of the wooden blade bit into the side of its head, and the creature staggered sideways. Tinnoviel was there just as the blade fell away. He pounded the lumbering savage with such precision and brutal grace, the creature couldn't begin to understand its fate even as it died on its feet.

The warrior left the urcha on the ground a broken and bleeding mess, and went to the horse's aid. The animal had taken several injuries that would need treating, lest they become infected.

Tinnoviel's weapon was nearly invisible, so fast was it in his hand. Urcha did not feel pain, and severed limbs could be reattached. Worst still, severed limbs left undisturbed would eventually grow into another full-bodied urcha, in time.

Tinnoviel left the two urchas the horse had been fighting in much the same condition as the first.

He rushed to the woman's side and tried to rouse her. From the corner of his eye, he saw more urchas approaching. The village was overrun with the things. Perhaps this time the Lady Seiyun would finally heed his advice and once and for all figure out a way to safely destroy this place.

When the woman didn't wake, he lifted her into his arms. "Dumada!" he called to the horse. The stallion snorted and galloped toward him. He draped the woman over the horse's withers, then leapt into the saddle. "Ryika!" The horse launched into a full run straight for the gate. Tinnoviel looked back to see the lumbering urchas stomping after them. Dumb as they were, the mossy brutes knew there was no escape from this place, and they expected to taste the flesh of their prey soon enough.

Tinnoviel faced forward, called out a word of command, and waved his hand. With the spell now dismissed, the village exit grew closer.

The stallion reached the gates in short order, and Tinnoviel hopped out of the saddle. He opened the heavy wooden gate and the horse trotted through. Tinnoviel took one last look to see more than two dozen urchas running toward him, sharp-toothed maws agape and salivating. Having realized the spell was lifted, they were running faster, not only for their prey, but escape.

He slammed the gate shut, replaced the bar, and uttered the command to reset the spell. He felt the magic tingle in his body as the wards settled back in place. Tinnoviel grinned at the thought of the likely shrieking urcha, clawing their way to the gate in crazed rage, yet drawing no closer.

His grin disappeared when he heard moaning behind him. He looked back to see the woman lift her head just long enough to look at him, then she fell unconscious again.

15

Seung opened her eyes to dawn glowing through a window that looked to have been carved from the inside of a tree with an expert hand. She gingerly touched the side of her head. Her mind felt clouded, her memory fragmented.

She slowly turned her head and saw that she lay on her back in a bed with the perfect balance of soft and firm. As she lay there, waiting for her mind to gather itself, Seung thought she might never want to climb out of it.

Her memories finally started to reassemble themselves, and she remembered battling ugly green monsters alongside Swiftspirit.

She sat up in alarm and her head spun. Seung gasped at the terrible pain hammering her head, but still tried to rise.

A gentle yet firm hand pressed her back down and Seung relented, not having the strength to resist anyway. She took a deep breath and looked to her right.

Standing a few paces from her bed was possibly the most beautiful woman Seung had ever seen. She couldn't have been more than five feet tall, but every inch of her was regal. Her long silky hair was so black, it had a tint of blue, and was a striking contrast to her smooth, brown skin. She wore a silken robe depicting a crane standing in tall grass on the lower left side and an eagle gliding far to the upper right side, just below a bright orange sun. Almond-shaped green eyes looked down on her with a warmth that Seung found instantly comforting.

"Be at rest," the woman said. Her voice was the sound of the forest, the clouds above, and open fields of shimmering grass. It was like listening to the song of nature. "Swiftspirit is fine, but it is you who have worried us. Rest."

Seung nodded and let out a contented sigh. Out of a lifetime of habit, she reached up with barely enough energy to adjust her hair to the sides of her face. After a moment, she turned her head again and looked directly into those shiny green eyes, finding them harder to gaze into than the first time. "How do you know his name?" Her voice sounded so weak, even to her own ears. "Did I talk in my sleep?"

The smaller woman—who looked little older than Seung—responded with a warm smile. "You have said little more than mumbling and moaning during your slumber. He would have died fighting beside you, you know. You have a brave and loyal friend, *haloren*."

"Who?" Seung asked, her face screwed in confusion.

"Ssshhh," the woman soothed in that melodic voice. "Too many questions for now. All will be answered when you awake again. Rest."

Before she could think of a response, the woman passed her hand over Seung's face and hummed. Seung closed her eyes and slept.

———

SEUNG AWOKE some time later to the pitter-patter of rain tapping the leaves of trees and plants, and the roof of her warm accommodations. A breeze passed through the window and stirred her hair. She closed her eyes and forced herself to push the sheets back.

The gentle touch of the cool wet air was soothing against her bare skin ... Her *skin!* She quickly pulled the sheets back up to her neck and, after an alarmed glance around the room, peeked under the covers. She was completely naked! A sudden feeling of violation crept into her thoughts and her mind began conjuring scenarios of people she knew nothing about undressing her.

The door opened, and in stepped a woman possessed of a similar beauty as the first one. Though not as regal or possessing an air of power about her that the first woman had, she still exuded grace.

Like the first woman, she looked young yet older at the same time. It was like looking upon a wise young woman. Seung found herself staring at her host, trying to puzzle out the mystery in her features.

Sparkling green, almond-shaped eyes looked down on her with kindness. The woman's sharp, angular features were like nothing Seung had ever seen. Even the way the woman stood, so perfectly still, yet vibrant and alive, was seemingly inhuman yet somehow ... familiar. And her ears. Seung couldn't stop herself from staring at the other woman's ears, for they ended at a pointed tip, just like her own. But unlike Seung, this woman made no effort to hide them.

Upon seeing the flushed face of her houseguest, the young woman gave a polite bow followed by a disarming smile. "Be at ease *quyo*. I alone undressed you and cleaned your body. I assure you it was necessary to keep you from succumbing to the bacteria of your wound."

The kindness and warmth of her melodic voice eased Seung a bit, and she responded with a curt nod in thanks, unconsciously adjusting her hair over her ears.

The woman watched this in puzzlement. "Your clothes and gear have been treated and will be returned to you. For now, we offer you this." She went to a door to the left of the room and produced a silver dress.

Seung's eyes widened at the exquisiteness of the garment. She touched the material. The fabric felt it was as if it was woven from air. It was so light and smooth, even silk felt rough by comparison.

She looked up at her host. "I doubt I'm delicate enough to don such an exotic dress." She looked down at the garment. "Nor should I even touch it with these rough hands that have held nothing but weapons and ..." Seung trailed off at the woman's smile. "I ... thank you for this kind gift."

The woman nodded and turned her back so that Seung could slip into the dress in privacy. Once finished, she moved to the far side of the room from her host, who was now gazing out the bedroom window at the rain. "The material is so light I still feel like I'm wearing nothing."

"You will become accustomed to it. All of our clothing is crafted from the same plant: The *Yiko*."

"I can't believe this is made from a plant," Seung responded in wonder. "It's so light, and the colors so vibrant."

"There are many things in this world that exist outside of your imagination," the woman said. "The *Yiko* is but one."

Seung looked at her, puzzled. She had the distinct impression that when this woman said "your," she was speaking in plural.

The woman turned back to Seung, and the warrior from Kyu found herself transfixed by a gaze heavy with the weight of knowledge and experience.

Seung's eyes betrayed her sense of decorum, and she looked at the woman's ears again. Ears deformed just like her own. Was it in fact a deformation, or something else? She unconsciously reached up to touch her left ear, which drew a smile from the other woman.

"Those are one of the main attractions human men had for us, you know."

Seung opened and closed her mouth several times not knowing what to do or how to respond. Her warrior instincts told her to be on guard, but she couldn't deny the gentleness of the two women she had encountered so far. "*Human* men? What other kind are there?"

The other woman regarded her as an adult would a child, yet the expression was somehow not condescending. "There are others. You will understand more after you remember. If you choose to, that is. For now, we must prepare you for your meeting with the Lady."

"No," Seung shook her head as the woman moved for the door. "I'm going to need a little more to go on than that. You've yet to tell me your name, where I am, and why I'm here. And remember what? And what's a *quyo*? You called me that."

The woman responded with a patient smile and an upraised hand. "All of your questions will be answered soon."

"I don't have time for soon, no matter how quickly that comes. I was on an extremely important errand and cannot be delayed any longer than need be—"

"There is time," the woman interrupted. "We are aware of your errand and will help you if you wish. For now, we must prepare you for your audience with the Lady."

"Audience with the Lady," Seung repeated dryly.

"The Lady of the Wood," the other woman answered. "And please forgive my rudeness. My name is Alaquenia." She gave a half bow that Seung returned. "If you would please follow me, I will take you to a place where you may bathe and break your fast."

Food and a bath. Then I have to get moving. "Thank you," Seung replied. They left the house that Seung came to realize was not much larger than the room she'd slept in, and followed a path coated with fine gravel that crunched beneath their sandaled feet.

Seung's eyes were in constant motion as she took in every

detail of her surroundings. From what she could tell, they were in the heart of a forest. She looked up and her lips parted in amazement. The towering trees formed a canopy high above which sheltered them from the rain she could still hear pouring in sheets.

"How do the smaller plants survive without sunlight?" Seung asked absently as she craned her head this way and that, marveling at the sights around her.

"Why do you believe they do not receive sunlight?" came the innocent reply.

Seung frowned. "All these trees? They block out the rain, the sky, everything. If rain can't penetrate them, I doubt much sunlight would."

Alaquenia smiled again. "I envy you the many discoveries you're soon to experience. Today we have no desire to receive the rain, so the trees shelter us from it. Only the plants receive the water if they wish."

"Ah." Seung sighed, lines forming on her forehead. "Of course."

"Our home and lifestyles will seem odd to you, but hopefully you will become comfortable in time."

"I appreciate that, but I don't have time to visit." *Nor become a crazy recluse.* "I must be gone as soon as possible."

Alaquenia turned that worldly gaze on her. "Disquiet and urgency. The plague of human youth. You must unlearn these tendencies."

Seung sighed again. Was this woman out of her mind? "And why would I do that? I'm *human*, aren't I? And what of you? You keep referring to humans apart from yourself. Am I to believe you are something other?"

"If you were more in tune with your nature you wouldn't need to ask that question." There was regret in Alaquenia's voice. "But that isn't for me to answer. Reserve your questions for the Lady. She best knows how to aid you in your condition."

"My condition?" Seung asked with a bit of heat in her voice.

"Come, please." Alaquenia led her down another path lined with pink and yellow flowers and plants with giant leaves like the ears of an elephant. "After you've bathed, I will take you for your visit with the Lady."

"Who is this Lady you keep talking about?" Seung asked. "Or am I not supposed to ask that question either?"

For the first time since Seung had been in her presence, the other woman took on a serious expression. "She is the Lady of the Wood. Wisest of us all. She has kept our civilization safe, and is the wisdom and mother of our land. Nature itself knows the name Seiyun, for she has been a friend to nature long before most of the People were born. She is all that we are, and it is an honor for you to meet her."

Seung didn't know what to make if it. Alaquenia's words sounded positively insane, yet the woman seemed of sound mind.

They stopped at a large pond fed by a wide towering waterfall. Clouds of white mist floated in the air where the falls met the crystalline water below. A bouquet of boulders gathered at the base of the falls, as well as along the edges of the pond. Phosphorescent green and purple plants, with leaves like needles or beckoning fans, glowed along the shore.

Redwood trees with trunks wider around than her house back in Kyu towered high above, their tops piercing the forest canopy. It was an effort to keep her mouth from falling open again as Seung turned a circle, marveling at the profusion of colors. Plants large and small, trees she recognized, while most she did not, stood around the pond as though gathered in communion.

Alaquenia's melodious voice drew Seung from her awe. "I will leave you to bathe. Normally there would be no time constraint placed upon your enjoyment, but we mustn't keep the Lady waiting. As you've said, you have not the time. I will bring your change of clothes upon my return." She indicated the pond with an open hand. "Please, enjoy."

Seung saw her host's visage had softened once again. "Thank you. I won't be long. Is there anything for me to bathe with? Soap, of some kind?"

"That would pollute the water and make it unsuitable to drink for our forest friends." Alaquenia walked to a tree covered in a strange orange moss. She gently removed a handful, and offered it to Seung.

"This is moss from the *Okaya* tree. It isn't really moss, but there is no other word for it in your tongue. It's as thin as the hair that grows on your arms. Once you dip it into the water, it will soften and become a thick lather, similar to your soap. You'll find it soothing to the skin."

"Thank you." The moss felt coarse in her hands. It reminded Seung of coconut shavings she'd tried when a foreign trader bearing exotic fruits had come to her village. Her mind was still in a fog, and the strangeness of this forest made it even more difficult to cobble her thoughts together.

Alaquenia placed a comforting hand on her shoulder and looked into her eyes. "All will become clear. For now, enjoy your bath."

With one last smile, Alaquenia turned down another pathway, and left a bewildered Seung standing at the shore of the pond with a handful of orange moss.

16

S eung ran her hand along her arm in an attempt to hold onto the bliss invoked by her bath with the orange moss Alaquenia called *okaya*. Her mind felt clearer, and her skin felt renewed and refreshed. She practically tingled with energy.

Despite her suspicions of Alaquenia's sanity, she was the only person Seung knew. Now she was alone, swimming in a waterfall-fed pond in the middle of a forest with no sense of where she was and no weapons.

No weapons! Seung's heart fluttered. In her head-fog, and overwhelming wonder at her surroundings, her instincts must have gone dormant. She felt naked without *Vyirayoi* strapped to her back. What had happened to it? Had her mysterious savior left it back in that awful village?

Seung sat at the base of a lakeside tree, her nerves jittery despite the feather-like golden leaves swaying overhead as though seeking to caress. She closed her eyes, cleared her mind, and forced herself to settle. To anyone else she would seem asleep or meditating, but it was more than that; a kind of sleep she couldn't define, yet no one she'd ever met could understand.

She opened her eyes and saw to her surprise that there were, indeed, others who lived in this forest. Seung had thought Alaquenia and the other woman she'd seen at her bedside were just two recluses living in the forest, perhaps driven mad by their own seclusion. Nothing could have been further from the truth.

Though she hadn't seen many people pass by, the occasional person did walk the paths along or near the pond. They seemed unsurprised by Seung's presence, which indicated to her that this must be a community of sorts. They all moved with the same inner grace as her host, though to differing degrees. Perhaps due to personality?

Seung watched the inhabitants as they went about, some sitting in meditation much like herself, while others gathered in quiet conversation. Animals walked freely across, and even along, the many pathways that snaked in and out of the trees. Not for the first time since Alaquenia had left her here, Seung wondered if she was having some sort of grand fever dream.

A man passed close enough for Seung to see that he had the same angular features she saw on Alaquenia.

He noticed her sitting by the tree and tipped his head in greeting. His eyes moved about her face as he took in her features, and his smile twitched. "*Oyada yun, melada. Misei.*"

Seung responded with a half-smile and tipped her head in turn. It was all she trusted herself to do, given the shock that she actually understood the man's words. "Good day to you, lovely lady," she whispered. "How do I understand this?"

She watched him move on, noticing his graceful gait, the image of his angular cheek and jawbones, and sharp-pointed eyebrows burned into her mind. But it was his melodic voice and pointed ears that made Seung both excited and apprehensive. He possessed the same kind of voice the people of Kyu always noted about her. What did this all mean?

"You've come far for someone who has so far yet to go."

The gentle voice jarred Seung from her daydreams, and she sprang to her feet.

A man, in pale blue robes made of the same material that Seung wore—yet somehow even more luminous—smiled affectionately at her. "My apologies for startling you, but the Lady Seiyun would see you, if you please."

"If I please?" Seung offered a crinkled smile. "So formal. I'll just need to dress. I'm also hoping to run into the person who saved Swiftspirit and me.

"Worry not," the man said. "Your savior has been made aware that you've awakened. You will meet him." The man then offered a slight bow. "I am DaunyaSai. Welcome to Yathienel."

"I ... Seung," she stammered. "My name is Seung Yoon." Her brow crinkled as she tried out that last word. "Ya ... thienel? I thought this place was called the Wood."

"That is similar to what you would call a nickname." DaunyaSai held out a hand toward one of the many pathways spider-webbing the forest. How did anyone not get lost in here? "You must have many questions."

"That's a modest way to put it. My mind struggles to keep up with all of this."

The wooded path ended in a huge open space with three running streams crisscrossing it. Though mostly clear, the occasional animal both small and large strolled casually alongside the two-legged residents of the forest.

Seung's mouth fell open. Deer walked among these people as though it were nothing unusual. They crouched low to drink from streams, grazed, and even sat on the ground. To see such trust from the normally skittish animals, surrounded by people milling about, was unbelievable.

"The Lady Seiyun has the answers you seek. Come." The man named DaunyaSai led her to the biggest tree Seung had ever seen. The base of the massive thing was larger around than her entire village.

"What in the name of the Gods is that? How can a tree be this big?"

"This is a So'orya," DaunyaSai replied. "The largest species of tree in the world. Many of us build our homes upon its great branches." He turned to her. "I understand you've no reason to, but I am going to ask you to trust me."

Seung looked into his eyes. She felt tiny under his kind, yet powerful gaze. "What are you going to do?"

"Take you to see Seiyun," came the answer. "Please. Grab my hand and don't let go. You will be startled, but I assure you all is fine."

For some reason she couldn't understand, Seung *did* trust him. She took his hand, and DaunyaSai turned back to the tree. He offered nothing more than a wink, and they lifted into the air.

Seung let out a yelp and clutched his hand. He didn't seem to mind that she might be crushing it, but Seung had no intention of letting go.

"Almost there," he said in that gentle voice.

Their swift assent brought them to a balcony where DaunyaSai guided them over the side, and onto the platform.

Seung doubled over and gasped. "How—what in the name of the Gods did—how did you—"

DaunyaSai smiled. "Come."

He led her to a set of gleaming double doors carved with designs so intricate, Seung couldn't imagine how long they had taken to craft. On either side of the doors stood two armed guards. They showed no indication they knew Seung was there, but each bowed to DaunyaSai with an obvious deep respect.

"Here we are," DaunyaSai said. "The Lady's private rooms."

The guards opened the doors, and as she and DaunyaSai passed, each offered Seung a sharp nod.

The room was as large as Seung's house. Who needed this much space? Hanging on the wall nearest her was one of several giant tapestries. This one depicted a person with pointed ears and golden colored skin. He was suspended in the air, legs hanging relaxed, toes pointed downward. Beautiful silver wings extended up and out above his head.

Seung studied the face. The inhabitants of this place called Yathienel had sharp, angular features, yet this person's features were sharper still. It was as though the people of this forest were molded from his image.

From his scalp to just below his chest hung a shining black braid. The rest flowed freely down to the back of his knees. Seung's eyes drifted to his hands. The thumbs, forefingers, and middle fingers of both hands touched, and his palms were half facing each other and half facing outward. In the middle shone a brilliant golden light. Such power and grace emanated from the tapestry that Seung felt compelled to kneel before it.

"That is Quel'yar."

A melodious voice pulled Seung from her entrancement, and she turned, her breath caught. Regarding her with an expression somewhere between curious and hesitant was the same woman who had been at her bedside when first Seung had awoken.

Now able to get a good look at her, Seung was struck by the simple power the woman radiated. Strength beyond the physical wafted from her, seeped from her pores. It glowed from her eyes, the same glowing green that must be inherent in the people of this wooded land. This was a woman who carried the weight of responsibility of an entire people on her shoulders.

"I give you the Lady Seiyun, Queen Mother of the people of Yathienel." DaunyaSai indicated Seung with an open hand. My Lady Seiyun. I give you Seung Yoon." He cleared his throat. "Please forgive me, Miss Seung Yoon, but I've not acquired your homeland or title."

"I ..." Seung blinked at him. "My homeland is here, Korea. Though I come from the south, a village named Kyu. I've not a fancy title that might impress, but I am a senior member of our village warrior band."

Seiyun watched her through it all, those shimmering green

eyes hard, but not unkind. Seung held the gaze with much effort. Never had she met so formidable a person.

After several tense heartbeats, Seiyun nodded in some kind of silent confirmation and broke eye contact. She turned back to the tapestry. "Interesting that you've found Quel'yar before the others."

"Quel'yar?" Seung tried the name out.

The Lady smiled as a mother would to a child. "The Mystic, as He is called. It is to Quel'yar that the clerics pray for guidance. Any use of magic attained through mystical studies are derived from Quel'yar."

Seung looked at DaunyaSai, thinking of their recent ascension to the palace. He gave a subtle nod of his head.

Seiyun glanced from one to the other, her expression impressed. "Personally escorted by the Daunya Master himself. You've been afforded a great honor, young lady."

"Daunya Master?" Seung thought she felt her head-fog returning.

"Forgive me," Seiyun replied. "This is all new to you."

They followed Seiyun to the far wall opposite the one holding the depiction of Quel'yar. Another tapestry of equal size and stunning beauty hung before them. This person was distinctly female, but with the same delicate, sharp angled features and pointed ears as the other. Her luminous black hair spiraled around her lithe form, spreading as though a breeze gently stirred the strands.

The corner of her mouth slanted in a half smile. *A knowing smile*, Seung thought as she stared at figure's eyes. Those eyes spoke of omnipotence, as though a mere painting saw deep into her soul. The woman held her arms out wide as though to embrace the viewer, yet her body leaned away.

"This is Se'lir, The Lady continued. "In matters of love, Quel'-yar's sister, Se'lir holds sway." The Lady of the Wood looked reverently upon the depiction of the deity. "Whether it be love of one's mate, homeland, people, country, or craft, in these things it is to Se'lir that we pray."

Seung found that she shared Seiyun's awe of the figure. Though only an artistic depiction, Seung thought she felt a presence within it, like the painting captured the actual essence of the person.

"Se'lir, residing in the province of love, knows our hearts best," Seiyun continued. "That is why some call Her the Goddess of the Heart. Mostly, humans think of her as such."

"Goddess?" Seung's eyebrows knitted together. "I've never heard of anything like this." She looked from Seiyun to DaunyaSai and offered a polite bow. "Please excuse me if this seems rude, but you aren't the first person to refer to humans as though they're separate from everyone here. I admit that the people of this place look different, but not human?"

Seiyun's responding nod said that she'd been expecting the question. "Do we look that different to you? Do we seem so foreign that you feel no familiarity, here?"

Seung opened and closed her mouth several times, unable to come up with an answer that didn't sound insane. She touched the tip of her left ear and Seiyun's eyes sparkled above her amused smile.

"You know of only part of your lineage, Seung; your human lineage. Fate has seen fit for you to finally learn of your other heritage. That of the Elfinestraya."

"Elfin...what?" Seung shook her head. "There aren't any others that live on this world but humans. You would have me believe you're more than a different looking race of humans?"

"Indeed." Seiyun moved away, and Seung followed. "In your language, we would be called elves. The name elf is a derivative of the ancient word elfinestraya which means the Star People. When first our two peoples met, hundreds of thousands of years ago, humans looked upon us as gods. When we attempted to explain that we were no more heavenly than they, humans then believed that we were from some other world among the stars, and their reverence for us did not lessen."

Seiyun chuckled helplessly. "It didn't help that the translation literally is a description of our people. We who dance under the stars; The Star People, in the human tongue. elfinestraya, in our language."

"For generations, our two peoples lived harmoniously. We exchanged gifts of fruits and vegetables as well as some of our crafts that were considered to be of value among their culture. Gold and jewels, even animals were brought to us as a show of friendship."

Seung thought she heard a bit of disapproval in Seiyun voice at that.

"Not wanting to offend, we accepted these animal gifts. After leaving their company, we would travel a distance, explaining to the animals when and where they would be set free, and why they had been captured."

"You're able to communicate with animals?" Seung asked incredulously. "How is that possible?"

"It is a trait you should possess," Seiyun replied, and Seung thought of her relationship with Swiftspirit. Did her horse companion truly understand her words?

"Your earliest ancestors," Seiyun continued, "were able to do the same, at least on a rudimentary level."

They took a path winding between massive branches extending from the floor of the courtyard through to the ceiling. Birds nested throughout the branches yet Seung saw no sign of the mess birds typically made. *Someone must clean this place constantly.*

"There was a culture among the early humans who were connected to the earth in ways similar to us. They were highly intuitive and lived in societal structures much like our own. We openly traded and intermingled, teaching and guiding them, and in turn, they shared their knowledge with us as well."

"They were unable to enter reverie as we do, but they were capable of separating their spirit from their bodies almost at will, an ability that our people do not possess. What impressed us the most was their ability to closely mimic our language without possessing all of the necessary vocal cords. We found this most intriguing and it further closed the cultural gap between us."

Seung had been taught the history of humanity during and after the Age of Technology, and had never heard any of this. She'd even learned a bit about the ancient age before then, and nothing of these elfinestraya were mentioned. It was a lot to accept. "Who were these people?"

The Lady took on a distant look before answering. "They lived in many places around the world, from the great continent of Khem to the tropical islands, and even the lands you know as the fabled Atlantis and Lemuria. The latter was affectionately referred to as Mu. Alas, the land of Mu was doomed to destruction by forces outside its people's control, and those who survived were scattered across the world."

A shadow passed over Seiyun's features. "Thousands of years passed and the people of Mu were lost to each other. As humans changed, so did our relations with them. They developed an insatiable taste for blood and flesh. They fashioned trading systems using items they considered of value. We foresaw what these changes meant and became more ... conservative in our interactions.

"Their hearts succumbed to the diseases of fear and jealousy, and they began to create weapons that grew more and more destructive." Seiyun's regretful sigh punctuated her words. "Time passed more quickly, speeding toward what is now history to you; the Age of Technology.

"During this age, humans lived much shorter lives than their predecessors, and with a shorter lifespan, came a shorter historical memory between generations. We came to realize that it took a mere three to four generations before our relationships with a family or community began to fade away.

A sorrowful expression overcame The Lady's angular features. "With the passing of time, humans became more aggressive, more ambitious, and more mistrusting of each other. We knew that if humans fought and killed one another, there was no place for us in their world.

"With great regret we were forced to sever ties. We withdrew deep into the forests and enacted enchantments upon our lands to keep them hidden. We became one of the many legends of an age long past; fictional beings in campfire stories to be shared among a people who had otherwise forgotten us. Thus have we lived for centuries, and more."

They came to an open balcony overlooking yet another waterfall, even more beautiful than the one Seung had bathed under. The Lady of the Wood turned toward Seung while still gazing at the waterfall. She spoke absently, her melodic voice a dirge rekindling the death of an ancient unity.

"Since our withdrawal from the human world, we've watched closely the events which have taken place over a millennia. Every step humans perceived as progress was in fact, a step away from their true nature. Humans began to fly in machines and move from place to place in horseless carriages. They no longer saw other forms of life as equal, but beneath them."

It was a sad story that rang true. "You must hate us for what we've done," Seung said.

"No more than ourselves for standing aside and allowing a young species to hurt itself and those around it," Seiyun replied. She studied the young warrior, mostly taking in her facial features.

The scrutiny was uncomfortable, but Seung endured it. She'd been looked at as an anomaly her whole life, though it was rarely more than curiosity.

"You've felt out of place for most of your life, have you not?

You only partially fit in, and as you grew older, you found your features had begun to change, that you looked different. You even found your voice was unlike any other person you knew."

They came to a balcony overlooking yet another waterfall. Seung's eyes widened. The size of these roaring falls eclipsed anything she'd ever seen. She had to crane her neck back just to see the top. It even dwarfed her beloved Inayo Falls back home.

"You were born from a rare love," Seiyun continued. "The differences your parents had were beyond appearance, yet they forged a life together that was unshakable and enviable to all who knew them."

That drew Seung's attention from the falls. "You knew my parents?"

Seiyun's expression grew distant, and Seung thought she saw a hint of sorrow. "I knew them, but it was *their* parents who I knew well. You see, your parents were young and adventurous, not caring for rules and why they were put in place." The Lady's smile was still sad, but there was fondness in her eyes. "Of course, they inherited such attributes from your grandparents."

"What do mean?" Seung asked, not knowing where all this was going.

"Your mother, Lariena, was willful and mischievous. She found the rules of this land to be restrictive and unfair. Ever did she disguise herself and sneak away to find adventure amongst humans."

Seiyun's gaze drifted into a faraway place where only memories existed. "Your father was never completely comfortable here or in the human world because of his place between the two peoples. Humans looked at him strangely because he was so different. His melodious voice and non-humanlike tendencies made him uncomfortable around that part of his heritage."

"He found life with us easier, as he was more accepted. But he was still different, and treated so. It's one of our flaws. We tend to be an exclusive people, even toward those who share part of our heritage. Your father, Derian, never felt comfortable enough to live among either of his two peoples."

Seung shook her head. "What are you saying? That I'm an ... an *elf*?"

"Not entirely," Seiyun answered. Your mother was Yathieneli, of the People of the Wood. Both her parents were of elven descent. You father's mother was an elf, but his father was human. Even during the height of human and elven interaction, rarely did we couple with them. When such relations did come about, which is inevitable when two groups intermingle, we were quick to discourage such a life."

"Because humans are beneath you?" Seung asked, barely containing her accusation.

Seiyun's glance at her made Seung feel small and childish. She opened her mouth to apologize, but the Lady looked away. "We are not without our faults, and ego is an unfortunate one we share with humans. Humans once lived well beyond a hundred years, but today, a human is lucky to see a century of life, and in such time they become frail and longing for their spiritual ascension."

The elven queen's tone grew wistful once more. "Our people live many centuries, some reaching a thousand years. Such a relationship would be difficult cope with. Imagine falling in love and watching your mate age before your eyes, over the short span of a century."

"Humans grow old and delicate, less vibrant and energetic after only three quarters of a that. You, on the other hand, will have barely reached adulthood after your first hundred years of life. Your human mate would pass from this world after a mere eighty or ninety years if you are lucky. Yet you would live on, alone with the happy memories, but also the memory of watching your beloved age and die before your eyes while you only become stronger. It's a painful experience."

The way this woman spoke sounded personal. Seung stole a

glance at the elven woman, statuesque as she stood gazing out at the falls. She started to ask, but thought better of it. "I don't mean to be without respect, Lady Seiyun, but I don't know what to think. You tell me that my bloodline belongs to an ancient race of beings who share this world with humans, yet I know nothing about them.

"It's true that I've never felt normal. The older I've gotten the more different I became. I'd always thought my voice just some anomaly, my ears some strange deformity. I never knew my parents and was raised by my aunt, who always spoke highly of them and told me that my questions would be answered when I was ready. You've given me answers, but how can any of this be possible? My dad being half human and half a people called elves? And my mother supposedly a full-blooded elf? Why was I never told?"

"Your parents wanted a human life for you. Unlike your father, when you were born you looked human. So, despite our objections, they chose to leave Yathienel and seek village life among accepting people. They found such a life, for a time."

The Lady's voice took on a grim tone. "We of the Wood knew that living in the human world was, by its very nature, dangerous, and we take special interest in every child. Your mother was willful. She wouldn't listen to me or her own mother when we told her that you would change with age.

"We asked your mother's sister to remain close to your parents, and to watch over you. For a time, your family lived a nomadic lifestyle. When people began to notice that no one in your family aged over the years, your parents relocated. Eventually they met the end of their physical lives in a great battle defending the village you lived a large part of your life in. I suspect both of them knew it was their time."

Seiyun wiped tears from the corner of her eyes. "They left you in the care of your aunt, who adored you. Meilura raised you as her own and altered your childhood memories to suit that of a human child, until you were ready to learn the truth of who you are."

Seung held her head, trying to organize her swirling thoughts. It was too much to take. Too much to accept. She'd always wondered why parts of her memory felt shrouded in a fog, but this?

"I could never get a straight answer out of Aunt Lili," Seung said. "'When the time is right, you will learn everything.'" She looked at Seiyun. "That's what she always told me."

Seiyun nodded. "Meilura ... or Aunt Lili, as you know her, is a wise woman. I could have trusted no other to properly look after you should the unfortunate have come to pass."

Seung felt the subtle tug in the pit of her stomach and looked to the northwest.

Seiyun followed her gaze. "Your *Mayuil* returns."

Seung turned an uncomprehending look on the elven woman. "There is no word in the human tongue for it," Seiyun explained. "Think of it as a ... task intuition. It saddens me to say this, but time rapidly approaches for you to move on. She turned and swept out of the balcony. "Fortunate that the Daunyans brought you to us. Recklessly heeding a *Mayuil* can be fatal."

Seung's heart fluttered. "Fatal?"

"Come."

17

K enyatta heard the crash and felt the crush when he hit the water. He forced his eyes open, and gazed into the silent depths. To his surprise, he felt no burn in his eyes from the salt-water, and his sight was far better than he'd expected in the darkness of the ocean. *The gene of the Daunyans,* he thought, for what else could it be?

Clinging to his sword and tightening his handhold in the wound he'd created in the huge appendage, Kenyatta rode it down. The descent was fast and he began to worry that the pressure might kill him, but the gene of the Daunyans burning inside must be protecting him.

The tentacle snaked its way ever downward, the ocean growing darker the deeper he descended. When it came to an abrupt halt, Kenyatta's sense of alarm grew. He must be near whatever was attached to this huge thing.

The tentacle lazily moved sideways, other tentacles of varying size swaying around it. A mass of the appendages were clustered together like a bed of snakes, and as he drew near, they parted.

Bubbles exploded from his mouth when Kenyatta nearly

cried out in terror. *By the Gods.* A red eye twice his sized turned its infernal glare upon the islander. The tentacles retreated and the gigantic horror was revealed.

Two crimson eyes glared at him above a mass of writhing tentacles. Below those tentacles, endless rows of hooked teeth snapped in anticipation.

Kenyatta wanted to close his eyes against the horrible sight; just gazing upon the thing felt as though it would drive him mad.

A flicker of black specks flowed across the whites of its eyes, and the gene inside Kenyatta flared as if in response. This was either a great demon, or a monster inhabited by one. He didn't know how he knew it, but he did.

The monstrous creature opened a mouth that could swallow a hundred of him. Its roar was deep and horrifying in spite of being underwater. Kenyatta clenched his teeth and forced himself to keep his eyes open.

After the beast played out its rage, Kenyatta reversed his grip on the sword and pulled it free, then drove it into the wound again and twisted.

The great monster bellowed again, and Kenyatta struck again. The gene was obviously prolonging his ability to hold his breath, but it wasn't indefinite. He needed to kill this thing, somehow, or get it to send him back to the surface.

He struck again and again, then sliced open any smaller tentacles that came too close. The monster waved its wounded appendage in an attempt to dislodge him, but Kenyatta held on. If he let go, he was surely dead.

The enormous tentacle suddenly sped away. Kenyatta said a silent prayer to the Daunyans as he held on, hoping he didn't explode from the pressure of his rapid ascent.

The night air was cool against his skin, but Kenyatta hardly noticed as he clung to the waving appendage, his twisted locks smacking his face and shoulders as it shook violently to dislodge him. It swung downward. When Kenyatta saw the ocean rushing to meet him, he squeezed his eyes shut and braced himself.

The tentacle slapped him against the surface of the water. The impact felt like being hit across his body with a giant paddle, but still Kenyatta held on. The tentacle lifted high into the air, then sank downward again.

"*Booooombaaaaaaacloooooot.*" The ocean rushed toward him again, and Kenyatta gritted his teeth. The water smacked against him as the tentacle broke through the surface and rushed down, like an arrow shot through the air.

Kenyatta opened his eyes, but kept them squinted against the rushing water. The giant head came into view again, but its attention seemed divided. Was it still battling the ship above?

It settled its evil gaze over Kenyatta again, and he felt he might simply shatter under the weight of so much powerful hatred. The tentacle sped toward it, and the monster turned its full attention toward him and opened its humongous maw. Was this the whole of the beast, or only the head? Kenyatta forced that horrifying question out of his mind.

The tentacles over its mouth waved in his direction, the smaller ones—still as large as Kenyatta's body—writhed in anticipation.

Kenyatta clenched the hilt of his sword as he sped toward what was surely his doom. The head twitched, then half turned away. The tentacle on which he clung slowed down, and without thinking about what he was doing, Kenyatta launched himself away. Downward.

With strength augmented many times over from the God gene burning inside, Kenyatta streaked through the water like a bolt, sword leading, straight for the great beast's eye.

With a sickening squish, the sword—and Kenyatta—plunged into the eye in an explosion of soft tissue and fluid that clouded the water.

Fighting back his revulsion, Kenyatta grabbed a handful of torn veins and held on as the giant head reared back. He clamped his eyes shut through an even louder roar, then drew his sword back and stabbed. The tip of the blade bit through soft tissue as a knife through butter, and Kenyatta wasted no time in ravaging the ruined area.

What looked like black smoke began to seep from the wound. Kenyatta cried out, bubbles spewing from his mouth again at the sight of what looked like a screaming face in the smoke.

His lungs starting to burn for air again, Kenyatta pulled himself out of the destroyed cavity where the monster's eye had been. The tentacled horror went into a frenzy. If there was a body attached to this thing, it wasn't visible, to which Kenyatta was thankful. He looked about at the dozens of tentacles writhing in agony. If he launched himself toward the surface from here, he might be snatched up by one of those things.

From the corner of his eye, Kenyatta spotted a small figure speeding toward the mass of tentacles and gaping maw. From the horrific bellow of the monster, followed by a cloud fluid, Kenyatta guessed it must have plunged into the other eye.

Kita. Kenyatta wanted to go to his friend, but his lungs were on fire. He reversed his grip on his sword and drove it into the side of the beast's head. He tucked his feet in and braced against it, then pushed away with all his strength.

Kenyatta kept his body straight and rigid as he sliced through the water. With lungs on fire, it took great effort to not succumb to the natural reaction of opening his mouth to breathe.

The moonlit surface rushed down to meet him and he burst through, high into the air with a great wheezing gasp.

So high did he fly from the surface that he saw the ship sitting in the now calm waters, little more than twenty feet away. Somewhere nearby, he heard something else breaking the surface. Kenyatta clenched his sword, expecting another attack, when he heard a wheezing gasp much like his own.

He had just enough time during his descent to see that it was Kita who had broken free. A couple dozen feet apart, they passed each other as one fell and the other rose.

Kenyatta plunged back into the water and immediately cast about. He saw no threat but the faint outline of waving tentacles, slowly falling away into the darkness.

He swam for the surface and called out until he heard Kita's voice. He swam in the direction of his friend's voice and found Kita treading water. They wasted no time in greeting, and swam for the ship.

Sailors leaned out over the rails looking out at the moonlit sea for any signs of survival of their comrades. Someone cried out and a light shined in their direction. Sailors pointed and shouted, and it looked as though half the ship came to that side and began yelling encouragement to the two warriors.

The sailors cheered them on with waving hands, beckoning them toward the ship. Ropes were dropped along the side of the ship, and Kenyatta and Kita each grabbed one and were hauled up.

"I can't believe you went down there, man!" Kenyatta said. He accepted an offered hand to climb aboard.

"You thought I was gonna let you have all the fun?" Kita replied. "But I do admit, if I'd known that thing was what waited down there, you'd have been on your own."

The captain pushed through the crowd of sailors, Malimokuru in tow. "What was it? Whatcha find down in the depths?"

Kita wiped his face. "Nothing you want to even imagine. I recommend getting this ship moving."

Kenyatta saw the hesitance on the captain's face. "You try to hold out for any other survivor overboard?" When the other man nodded, Kenyatta pressed his lips together and placed a friendly hand on his shoulder. "What we see down there was big enough to split this ship in two and eat it. I don't think anyone out there survive, man, but we help you any way we can."

"You tellin' me you could see underwater at night? Impossible."

"You see the size of some of dem tentacles?" Malimokuru said. "How big a body ya think dem things belong to?"

The blood drained from the captain's face at that reminder. "One last round of lookin', and we go. But I don't like leavin' any of me crew."

"We'll help, whatever your decision," Kita said.

"What tha hell ya fools see down there?" Malimokuru asked once the captain was out of earshot.

"Something huge and beyond terrifying," Kenyatta replied.

Kita nodded in agreement. "It was enough to make me never want to dip my toe in a puddle ever again."

"You think dat was what cause the tsunamis?" Malimokuru asked.

Kenyatta recalled the sight of the horrific monster and it was enough to have him curled up in a ball on the deck. He forced himself through the memory and recalled the sight of that black cloud with the wailing face seeping from the grievous wound he'd dealt it. "It would make sense," he finally said. "I can't think of anything worse than what we saw."

"It was the stuff of nightmares." Kita looked out the darkness beyond the ship rail. The normally soothing song of the ocean now sounded like the friendly call of a predator, waiting just out of sight.

After assessing the damage, the captain used the time it took to make repairs to the ship rigging to set lookouts for their lost comrades.

Kenyatta and Kita shared a look. Given what they had just fought, both knew it unlikely the lost crew members had survived.

Once the crew had fixed as much damage as was possible,

they began the solemn business of preparing for departure and facing the fact that their crew members were gone. Several men on each side still kept watch, holding on to the slim possibility of spotting someone out at sea. They found no one. Finally the beaten ship and its shaken crew were on the move.

If there was such thing as good fortune, it found them. Through the rest of the night, nothing more than the occasional swell challenged the ship and its crew. The three companions felt the collective relief of the men when the lookout called down from crow's nest. "Land!"

Men rushed to the rails, desperate for a glimpse.

"No hint of any danger," Kita said. "Maybe that thing was the cause of all this after all."

"Yeah man," Kenyatta said. He gave Kita a knowing look when Malimokuru wasn't watching. A look that said he no longer felt the burn of the gene of the Daunyans inside. He could hardly wait to set his feet on solid land as he and the others waited for the ship to finish docking. On either side of him, Kita and Malimokuru stood at the rail, similarly anxious to disembark.

Many sailors remained aboard with their captain to assist in repairs while others set off to shop for supplies.

Sailors were a hardy bunch, more comfortable out at sea than on land. This crew, however, had seen its fill of the ocean for a time. To a man, everyone cast wary glances at the sea.

"Dare we hope this thing is already done?" Kita asked. They stood next to the pier overlooking the ocean, watching as Malimokuru stepped into the water to his ankles and closed his eyes. "Maybe you should keep trying to contact Taliah," he suggested.

The mention of his sister again sent Kenyatta's thoughts back to everything they'd gone through two years ago. Battle after battle, endless hordes of demons, a tower that balanced the negative and positive energies of the world, and served as a barrier between this world and the abyss. The guardian of the tower, Iel, had explained it all, but Kenyatta still had a hard time wrapping his mind around it.

He started to respond that maybe he should keep trying, when they heard a choked cry of shock.

At the edge of the beach, Malimokuru collapsed.

18

Kenyatta and Kita ran to the fallen nature reader and together, gently lifted him out of the water. His chin, covered in gray stubble from lack of shaving, bounced as he mumbled. "... long time ago. We're sorry. Hundreds of years. Better now. Please. Forgive ..."

Kenyatta and Kita shared a worried look.

"Why do I have a sinking feeling?" Kita asked as they lay Malimokuru on his back and crouched over him." The old nature reader mumbled for another few moments before falling silent.

Kenyatta watched his chest rise and fall as he lay unconscious in the sand. "Same reason I do. Killin' that thing in the ocean was too easy."

Kita sighed at his friend's sarcasm. "Of course."

Kenyatta rubbed the back of his neck and looked out at the waves. "Too good to be true that we kill that thing and this is all done."

Kita chewed his bottom lip. "Maybe the Gods figure we haven't suffered enough just yet. Gotta keep going."

"Careful, man," Kenyatta said. "You want dat gene in your body to stay dormant when a demon come callin'?"

Kita snorted. "You think the Daunyans would really take it away because of something I said?"

Kenyatta raised his eyebrows. "You wanna take the chance? And speaking of demons, you see that face in the black mist that come from the monster?"

Kita went pale. "Yes. What in the five hells was it? I've never seen anything like that before, and hope never to again." He looked down at the still unconscious Malimokuru, then around ensure that no one was nearby.

"It reminded me of the battle at Takashaniel. Whenever we banished a demon back to the abyss, something similar happened. Remember?"

"How could I forget," Kenyatta said. "I don't know what's worse, that demons might be able to possess a body in this dimension, or that there are actually other things in the depths of the ocean like what we fought. That gigantic horror down there wasn't a demon, man."

Kita stared at Kenyatta as he digested that ominous thought.

"The world's an old place, bwoy." Malimokuru opened his eyes and turned a weary but smug expression first on Kenyatta, then Kita. "Far older than humankind. Things you don't want to think about live in the deep places in the world."

Kita ran a hand over his head and chuckled nervously. "So that collapse and babbling was an act? Why?"

Malimokuru lifted himself onto his elbows. He waved an impatient hand for the young men to help him to his feet. "Not an act. I touch the water to see if I feel anything like last time. When I get no connection, I step in with both feet."

Kenyatta and Kita stared at him. "You thought that wise?" Kita said.

Malimokuru shrugged. "Not anymore. You don't stop makin' mistakes no matter how old you get."

"So I'm guessin' you were attacked by the same thing as before?" Kenyatta asked.

Malimokuru was silent as they started hiking across the sandy beach toward the former resort city of Coral. Once named Cape Coral of the formerly named state of Florida, the city had been a beautiful destination during the Age of Technology. Now it was simply Coral, oceanside city of Fleria.

Communities and business sectors had been separated by countless canals in what was a wealthy city. After more than two hundred years of neglect, many of those barriers had eroded and fallen back into the ocean.

Coral was still beautiful, but more wild. Tape grass and sago pondweed thrived beneath the surface of the water, while cattails, sawgrass, and many other species of plants grew in a tangle nearly everywhere.

The smell of the ocean mingled with that of muddy water and a variety of animal denizens large and small.

Soon they came to a frequently traveled pathway and veered out of the tall grass, thankful not to have encountered any reptilian predators that no doubt lay concealed in the foliage.

His nerves steady again, Malimokuru stared thoughtfully out at the path in front of them. Kenyatta thought the nature reader didn't intend to answer the question, when he finally spoke. "Not an attack, really."

Kenyatta frowned at him. "Whatcha mean, not really? We see you collapse in the water back there, but it wasn't an attack?"

Malimokuru rolled his eyes. "Think, bwoy. If an elephant seal lay on you, ya might be dead, but that don't make it an attack."

"Did it apologize, then?" Kita asked. He chuckled until the nature reader gave him a look. "Sorry."

Malimokuru shook his head at them. "Whatever dis ting is, it's enormous, powerful, and less than happy. Especially with humans."

"Why would it be mad at humans?" Kenyatta asked. "I'm not understanding all this."

"We didn't have a lengthy conversation," Malimokuru said.

"You try getting information outta something that make you feel like you be blasted apart every time it speaks. Best way I can describe it, it speak in my mind, and I feel like my mind wants to break apart."

"And that's not an attack?" Kenyatta asked.

"If it want to attack me, I be long dead," Malimokuru said. The grave tone of the man's voice left no room for debate.

They turned north at the hard road of cracked and broken stone present in every city dating from the Age of Technology. Ahead and behind, locals and foreigners traveled the painted road.

Kenyatta watched the passersby as they lazily went about their day. Perhaps word hadn't traveled this far yet.

They stopped a man carrying a basket of tropical vegetables and fruit not unlike what grew in Jamaica. The sight of yet another reminder of the fate of his homeland made Kenyatta's heart ache.

"Ho there, friend!" Kita waved at the man. "Might we ask how far we are from the nearest place to buy food and sturdy mounts?"

The man turned his sun-darkened face toward them and jerked his head down the road. "Not far. Another half hour and you'll find food and lodging." He looked them over. "I'm guessing you're another batch of refugees from the islands."

So word *had* beaten them here. Kenyatta looked over his shoulder at the seemingly carefree people walking along the road. Maybe they didn't think the disaster would reach this far.

"You'd best go a little farther than these outer towns," the man continued, "unless you want to pay a premium. Vendors can smell a newcomer a mile away, if you get my meaning."

He tucked the basket under his arm and pointed northwest. "You'll not find horses around these canal communities, but if you go farther inland, that way, the stables'll start to show up."

As the local had said, they soon came upon the first shops on the outskirts of town. They pressed on for another couple hours, each silently wanting to be as far from the ocean as possible.

"Before we do anything else," Malimokuru said, "I need a drink down my throat and food in my belly."

"How about there?" Kita pointed at a building styled like a big wooden hut with a thatched roof. A sign mounted on the front of the hut said Cap'n Anna's. "Let's see what Cap'n Anna has to eat."

As it turned out, Cap'n Anna's was a hopping eatery filled with benches and round tables. Serving men and women moved about the establishment, while locals gossiped about whatever concerned the people here. They overheard many a conversation about the refugees from Jamaica and more than a few sympathetic glances flicked in their direction.

Their serving woman finally arrived with a fellow server in tow and delivered plates of fresh fruit and grilled meats. Kenyatta inhaled the aroma and his stomach grumbled in anticipation.

"You mind a question?" Kita asked the woman.

She slid a few stray locks of dark brown hair away from her face. "What's that?"

"Is there any news?" Kita said. "Anything about the ocean, land; anything strange going on? We're traveling north, then west. Anything we should know about?"

The serving woman tilted her head in thought, the stray locks falling back over her face. "You're lucky right now. We're not in hurricane season, so there's that." She cast an apologetic look over Kenyatta and Malimokuru, but the older man gave a friendly shrug.

"Hmm. Other than the usual highway bandits and predators out there, not much else to worry about." She opened her mouth to say more, when a tall, hooded figure stepped through the door and moved to the bar.

"Well ... there's them." She covertly jabbed a thumb at the figure who stood to one side of the bar, leaning in to speak to the bartender.

"Trouble?" Kenyatta asked.

"Not exactly," came the reply. "But they're a mysterious lot. We don't get many of them here, but occasionally they show up. No one knows where they live, they don't talk to anyone, and they're always covered up, head to toe, no matter how hot and humid it is."

"Maybe dem like privacy," Kenyatta said.

She smiled at him. "You're accent's cute. And maybe that's so, but you ever seen anyone that tall?" She glanced over her shoulder. "Closer to eight feet than seven."

"It's not strange to be tall," Kita said.

"They're all that tall," the woman said, then she shrugged. "Anyway, that's all I have. Everyone gives those people their space, and I recommend you do the same. They haven't caused any trouble, but it don't mean they *aren't* trouble."

Kenyatta watched the figure towering over the bar. Nearby patrons were in a wary silence, and the entire establishment had gone from an energetic babble to a subdued murmur. When the tall man, or woman, received their drink, they drained the mug and left as quietly as they had arrived.

"That was ... interesting," Kita said.

"Yeah, man." Kenyatta looked at Malimokuru. "You were quiet through all of that. Whatcha about?"

"Listening, bwoy."

A thought occurred to Kenyatta while he scrutinized the nature reader. "Eh, man. You hear everything we say back on the beach, ya?"

Malimokuru gave a noncommittal shrug.

Kenyatta glanced at Kita and their eyes met. Kita looked back to Malimokuru.

"Ya must think we crazy, talking 'bout demons and the like," Kenyatta ventured. "Or maybe we was just playing with your head to see if you listenin' to us."

Malimokuru regarded him with an expression a parent might

give to a child who was obviously lying, and doing a bad job of it. "Listen, bwoy ..." He quickly scanned the eatery. The other patrons had returned to their chatter, but he lowered his voice anyway. "I been in this world a long time. You think I been a nature reader as long as I have and not see things to make a person's hair fall out?"

Malimokuru frowned at the space in front of his feet, then the puffy white clouds drifting overhead. "The Age of Technology brought some good, but it also brought a lot of horror with it. When that age ended, things wake up in the world from long sleep. I don't know where it come from, but I one time seen something that look like it climbed straight outta hell. I only seen something like that once, and it was enough."

Kenyatta wondered how the old man survived such an encounter. Perhaps more of that strange sand he used. "Sounds like we got a lot to talk about. Maybe once we're on the road, ya? Got a lotta miles ahead of us, sounds like."

Malimokuru nodded. "That's another thing. When me connect with it again, I get a clearer glimpse of the place I saw in the first connection. I'm not sure if it meant for me to see it, but I did. Snowy tundra, white mountains, and snowstorms."

Kita spread his hands. "There's more than a few places that fit that description."

"Yeah, man," Malimokuru said. "But I told you before. I know dem mountains. And they're in the frozen lands of Askata. Whatever cause this destruction rules dem mountains. And I get the feeling it'll bring a wrath down on us like something from the Gods if we anger it."

19

Seung perused the endless rows of books in Seiyun's private study that seemed like it was anything but. Some of the books were as thin as the side of her hand, while others were tomes that looked like they weighed more than the person reading them.

She exited the rows and entered another section of the massive "private" study that had independent walls, each displaying a tapestry with majestic figures woven into the fabric similar to the ones in Seiyun's room.

Seung stopped in front of a beautiful piece depicting a male figure standing with his body facing partially away from the viewer. His long, powerful limbs were smooth with lean muscle, and his pale orange eyes peered out of the portrait, as if peering into the soul of the viewer.

His skin was as black and shiny as polished onyx, yet from the crown of his smooth, hairless head to the tips of his toes, glowed a multi layered purple, blue, and white aura. His ears, though not as long and pointed as that of the people of this land—Seung still couldn't bring herself to think of them as elves instead of humans with abnormalities—were still elongated with somewhat of a pointed tip. The hand farthest from the viewer hung at his side, while the closest arm was bent at the elbow. A glowing white flame hovered above his palm.

The figure wore a simple white garment, connected at the left shoulder while the right arm and chest were bare. Although white, the garment radiated a multicolored hue which was perceptible only upon close scrutiny. The sound of the Lady Seiyun's voice broke Seung's trance.

"Eons ago before time existed, Amayilah, the Daunyan of Creation, sang life into existence. The whole of creation was, then, one beautiful indistinguishable cloud-like mass of infinite consciousness.

"It was then that Her twin brother, Omalah,"—Seiyun indicated the figure in the tapestry—"individualized the consciousness. From within the mass of amorphous and androgynous life, Omalah breathed our spirits into being and refined our essence."

Seung stared at the piece of art as the other woman spoke. The magnificence and power emanating from the tapestry grew more overwhelming and humbling the longer she looked at it.

Hesitantly, Seung pulled her gaze from the Daunyan of Spirit to look upon a woman bearing a striking resemblance to Omalah. Her face was identical to his, but softer and more feminine. She appeared to be hovering in mid-air, her legs hanging slightly bent. Her face was soft and kind, and her full lips stretched into a subtle smile. A silver cloud sparkled in the middle of her cupped hands. This could be none other than Amayilah, Daunyan of Creation. Seung was amazed to see that within the pearly white garment Amayilah wore, was what looked to be humans. She leaned closer and squinted. Humans, or human-like beings, as well as every other living creature in all of their various histories in the world. It was too overwhelming to study for long, yet Seung didn't want to look away.

"Amayilah, Daunyan of Creation," The Lady said.

Seung gazed at the ethereal figure. Like Her brother, Amayilah was not an elf. "Amayilah." As soon as the sound left her lips, a feeling of serenity and contentment washed over Seung. She felt more alive, invigorated.

"Looks like someone has an affinity with Amayilah," Seiyun remarked."

Seung wrenched her gaze from the tapestry to look at Seiyun. The Lady shared a grin with DaunyaSai, who was leaning in the doorway.

"Unsurprising news," the Daunya Master said. He stepped into the room and stopped beside Seung. "There is something powerful deep inside you; a tiny spark that has not yet been lit."

"Sounds like the childhood stories my aunt used to tell me," Seung replied.

DaunyaSai responded with a half grin. "Indeed."

Seung looked at him. "Are all ... elves, so mysterious when they talk?"

DaunyaSai's soft laughter drifted through the room. "Only when we apply great effort to seem exotic." He looked into her eyes for several uncomfortable heartbeats. "You will one day amaze yourself, Kiluriel."

"Who?" Seung frowned. "What's a *Kiluriel*?"

"It is your name," DaunyaSai replied. "You're elven name and, thus, your first name."

"I've never heard it before now."

"For good reason," Seiyun said. "Reasons I may one day explain to you. But as you've said, and I now agree, there isn't time." She turned an expectant look on DaunyaSai.

The Daunya Master bowed respectfully. "I've chosen those whom I feel will best aid her, and who will most benefit from the task."

Seung looked from one to the other. "This doesn't have anything to do with me, right?"

"DaunyaSai has selected five companions to accompany you," the Lady said.

"I didn't ask for ..." she trailed off at the other woman's arched eyebrow. "Um," she cleared her throat. "With respect, Lady Seiyun, I've undertaken this task alone. I wish to endanger as few lives as possible."

"As admirable as it is ill-advised," the Lady replied. "So much like your father in this."

"Lariena wasn't much different," DaunyaSai added.

Seung forced down her irritation at being a sidebar in the conversation, but it must have shown in her face.

"Patience," Seiyun said. "I understand the urgency of your quest. I've come to know what's at stake, more than you realize. Without help, you'll not survive to see your task completed."

Seung felt a stab of defiance at that. "May I ask why you believe so?"

"You do well to hide your youthful irritation," Seiyun replied.

Seung's eyebrow twitched. Was that sarcasm or not?

"I believe this," The elven queen continued, "because of many years lived, and because my dear friend here, has insight into the nature of what awaits you in the frozen lands of Estufel."

"Es ... tufel?" Seung shook her head. "I don't know this place."

"Humans know it as Askata. We know it by its older name, since before the Age of Technology when it was known as Alaska. You must trust me—trust him," she indicated the Daunya Master standing with his hands clasped behind his back. "You don't truly comprehend the enormity of what awaits you."

Seung wanted to argue, but she remembered the presence that had overwhelmed her in the lake back home at Inayo Falls. And that was just a connection through a body of water. What could be so powerful to do that?

"Come." Seiyun turned away. "I've a few more tapestries to show you before your companions arrive.

They moved to three freestanding walls. Like the others, they were five feet wide and stood from floor to ceiling. The first was a young diminutive female, not quite a woman. A shimmering brown dress, the same color as her hair, clung to her body. Seung frowned and leaned closer, then her eyes widened when she realized that the dress *was* her hair.

The female's youthful face held a fierce wisdom that belied the appearance of what should be a girl having seen no more than thirteen or fourteen years of life. Her playful smile was infectious, as was the joyful energy wafting right off the cloth. It looked as though the artist had captured her in dance, holding a carved flute in a delicate hand. Her pearly skin glowed with an inner luminance that should have been impossible to portray in a mere piece of art.

"Nakiya," Seiyun said. "The playful one. She is known as the Daunyan Child, the Redeemer."

Seung tried to place the girl's features, but failed. She looked like a combination of The Twins of Creation—as Seiyun had called Omalah and Amayilah—as well as Se'lir and Quel'yar. It was as though each of their features were combined in this girl. "Whose child?" Seung pointed absently in the direction of the other four tapestries. "She favors them all.

"She is the child of Omalah, and Se'lir," Seiyun replied. "It is because of this, that She is the closest to us than any of the other Daunyans. It is She who protects us while still allowing us to experience the positive and negative of this world. It is to the Daunyan Child, The Redeemer, that we pray when we need strength and courage in this life of trials."

"I can see it," Seung said, mystified. "That playful, childish look is on the surface, but there's a strength not easy to miss."

DaunyaSai nodded. "It is said that when one is at their darkest hour, when hope seems farthest away, Her flute and cheerful laughter can be heard."

They moved to the next tapestry depicting an intimidating male figure. He stood facing the observer, one hand with fingers curled like a claw facing upward. Further scrutinizing the art, Seung noticed that each finger of the clawed hand was different.

A lightning bolt encircled the forefinger, while the middle finger looked to be covered by a raging windstorm. Raging waters covered the finger next to the middle, and the smallest finger was covered in blue flame. The thumb looked like an eruption of earth.

"This," the Daunya Master said, "is Boraka, the Destroyer. Each of His fingers represents the elements of nature, whose destructive force is guided by His hand."

The Daunyan of Destruction looked to be not very tall, but his torso was wide with rock-like muscle. His legs, while short, were thick, solid, and could have been made of muscle chiseled from granite. A long, black beard grew from his chin nearly to his waist.

Like the other tapestries, the woven canvas seemed to hold some bit of the actual figure it depicted. The presence of the God felt as if it shook her soul. It was like a mountain trying to condense itself into a humanoid form. Not a mountain, the entire world. A million worlds.

"If He's a God," Seung whispered, "how could He be destructive?"

"Through destruction emerges life," DaunyaSai answered. "When the forest burns the soil is revitalized, and that fresh nutrient rich soil feeds new life, which in turn feeds other life. In the cycle of physical life on this world, destruction must exist."

They moved to the last tapestry. "Unlike the heavens, in this dimension in which we live, there must be balance between negative and positive." He indicated a cloaked figure that would tower over the observer even if the tapestry wasn't so long.

"In the presence of mighty Oberon, the energy of Boraka is tempered."

Seung could only stare in amazement at the figure on the wall. Oberon, the Daunyan of Balance, stood gazing down on her. His cloak, black as pitch, swirled around him like a mist. His smooth, inky black hair flowed behind his head, and his appearance continuously shifted in a subtle manner. One moment, he looked like a pale-skinned elf with longer pointed ears, the next, his skin gradually darkened to fair, brown, dark, then the same ink black color as his hair. Seung found him more intimidating than Boraka.

"There is no form Oberon cannot assume," said DaunyaSai. "He is everything and anything, and is known to all in many different forms."

Seung hugged herself. "I hate to admit it, but he frightens me. At the same time, I feel drawn to Him. As though He would understand me more than the others would." She threw a nervous glance at the other tapestries.

DaunyaSai and Seiyun gazed up at the mighty figure. "You needn't worry about offending the Gods," the Daunya Master said. "They are Gods, after all, and not subject to the temperamental pettiness of mortals."

"Good to know," Seung whispered.

A polite knock on the door drew their attention, and they turned as it creaked open. "My Lady Seiyun," the guard said. "They've arrived."

20

S eung watched a group of five enter the study. As each person stepped through the door, the warrior from Kyu finally accepted that these people were not humans. Seiyun and Daun-yaSai didn't seem human either, but seeing this group broke down the last of her skepticism.

Two of the three females looked to have seen little more than thirteen or fourteen years of life. One of the girls offered a bright smile. Seung's mouth twitched in an awkward response. The girl stood barely five feet tall. Her close cropped hair reminded Seung of freshly forged steel, a beautiful contrast with her golden-brown skin. She offered a wink that promised playful mischief.

The second girl was half a head taller than the first, with hair of a similar color, but more a blend of white and silver. Instead of a smile, Seung received a thinly veiled scowl in greeting. "Any brains behind that dull stare?" the girl asked. One of the males cleared his throat, and the girl looked down and grumbled at her feet.

Seung watched the girl pass. Why the unprovoked hostility?

The third female looked somewhat close to Seung's age, though perhaps several years older. When she turned her brown-eyed gaze on Seung, it felt as though the woman were peering into her soul.

Seung looked away. Never had she felt so exposed. When she looked back, the woman was in the midst of a graceful curtsy to the Lady Seiyun. Seung watched the exchange. Though the Lady of the Wood was queen to these people, her relationship to the one called DaunyaSai seemed closer to equals. This woman looked as though she ranked only one step below that.

Seiyun addressed her. "Kiluriel Seung Yoon Sen'Mora, meet your companions."

The hostile girl snickered. "That's a lot of names," she whispered from the side of her mouth to the other girl. "And two of them are hard on the ears."

Seiyun arched an eyebrow, and the girl dipped her head apologetically. "Tikena Mojin will lend her passion and courage to your quest," the Lady continued, "and hopefully acquire manners along the way." Tikena's cheeks darkened. Seiyun opened her hand toward the other girl. "This young lady is Nuviel Titika. May your darkest days ahead be brightened by her light."

Nuviel offered a deep curtsy first to Seiyun, then a less formal one to Seung. "Pleased to meet you, pretty lady."

Seung's smile crinkled. "And I you."

"Some of the trials awaiting you are surely beyond the reach and power of a sword," Seiyun continued. "Daunya Apprentice Yurin Kei Daunyana will bring the might of the Daunyans against your enemies."

The older woman inclined her head and fixed Seung with a brown-eyed gaze that held the warrior of Kyu Village paralyzed. Surrounding her brown irises was a yellow ring that pulsated like a heartbeat. Seung willed herself to break contact and at least blink, but she was helpless under that powerful, yet offhand, stare.

What must have been only a heartbeat or two of that gaze felt like an eternity, but Seung finally blinked and looked away. She caught herself from stumbling forward, and held back her gasp. She looked at the woman named Yurin Kei Daunyana and wondered who or what in the world she was.

"The skills of a tracker are invaluable," the Lady of the Wood declared, "yet on a journey such as yours, you'll need something more. Alurien MerTana, Ranger of Yathienel, shall guide your path and fight beside you.

Alurien MerTana stepped forward and bowed. Seung's lips parted as she stared in amazement at the elven male. Perhaps it was because she was so self-conscious about her own ears, but she noticed his were longer than any she'd seen in this place so far. The tips peeked through the silky black hair which fell past his shoulders. He wore a charcoal-colored tunic beneath what looked to be a vest. Four thin wide strips of heavy blue and black cloth, front and back, hung from the top of the garment to his ankles. His wide-legged flowing pants were the same color as the strips of the vest, and were long enough to cover his feet.

"A pleasure, Kiluriel Seung Yoon Sen'Mora." The elf's baritone voice, though still melodious, caught Seung off guard.

She looked into his blue eyes and inclined her head. The stern elf's face was tattooed with long solid blue stripes dotted with white that flowed from beneath his eyes to meet at the tip of his chin. "A pleasure I return, Alurien Mer'Tana."

Alurien returned the nod, and even that small gesture was precise. For the last seven years of her life, Seung had led the warriors of Kyu as their best. There was no enemy, man or beast, that she'd faced down with so much as a flinch. Yet the hardness in this elf's eyes made him almost as difficult to look at as the Daunya Apprentice. If he was pleased or not at being selected for this mission, he didn't show it.

"Lastly," Seiyun said, "I present to you the Daunya Warrior, Tinnoviel Nai SaunyaLi."

The elven warrior stepped forward and bowed deeply to the

Lady, then executed a precise bow to Seung—one warrior to another. She returned the gesture and studied his face. He looked vaguely familiar, and Seung guessed he must be the one who'd saved her life and brought her here.

"These five warriors were personally selected by Master DaunyaSai himself," Seiyun continued. "Their expertise, resilience, and loyalty will be most valuable to you in the days to come. Across land and sea, you will travel to places rarely glimpsed by our people. Today and forevermore it will be known that you six companions fought on the behalf of Yathienel with the blessings of the Daunyans." With the grace of a queen, Seiyun spread her arms. "I declare you The Companions of the Seven." May you look after each other and keep one another safe against the dangers ahead."

THE LADY OF THE WOOD, alongside DaunyaSai, escorted the six companions out of her rooms and along the brilliantly ornate halls that seemed too vast to have been built along the branches of a tree. Seung reminded herself that the trunk of the tree was larger than her entire village, which seemed equally impossible to grasp, yet made the size of this structure more conceivable.

"From the moment you arrived in Yathienel, I've spoken with Master DaunyaSai at length," Seiyun said. "For several years we've sensed the ever growing presence of *Nyersh*." At Seung's uncomprehending expression, she clarified, "demons, as you would call them. They are entering our plane of existence in growing numbers, and I'll soon be forced to call a meeting of the Council concerning these recent events. It will be difficult to sway them into action without proof. That is why it is my hope that you six will return in time and attend the Council with me. Your personal accounts will be invaluable." She looked to DaunyaSai, who bowed his head to Seiyun and spoke.

"Something monumental is happening. An enormous mass of dark energy is gathering far away in the southeast. I suspect there's a focused presence of demonic energy increasing near Takashaniel."

Taka what? Seung thought.

"The Tower of Balance," DaunyaSai clarified as though reading her thoughts. "I've not the time to detail its history now, but it was created not only as a focal point of balance between the positive and the negative forces of this dimension, but also as a barrier, or gateway, to other dimensions."

The grim expressions of her new traveling companions spoke clearly of the seriousness of DaunyaSai's claim. "I cannot tell you what you will encounter at sea, but in this ever-changing world, there are things from the depths that swim closer to the surface. If the weather is favorable, you should reach the new lands within twelve days. Be warned, monsters from the ancient world preceding the humans' Age of Technology are awakening. Demon hybrids, humans and beasts inhabited by fiends from the upper abyss, roam the lands. You'll be tested in ways I cannot foresee."

The Lady kissed each of them on the forehead, the taller companions bending to receive her blessing. "Once you leave, I'll not see you again until your return." Seung thought she detected a hint of sorrow mixed with pride in the elven queen's voice. "Be strong and be safe. And may the blessings of the Daunyans and Yathienel be with you."

With those final words, the companions left the Queen of the Elfinestrayans and the Daunya Master. No sooner had they rounded a corner out of earshot of the queen, than Seung heard a grumbling insult hurled her way.

"Sent on a mission in the stinking wake of *N'thresha!*" The elf girl practically spat the last word. "Would that I could just die than suffer this disgrace."

Seung clenched her jaw. The word was unknown to her, but there was no doubt it was an insult.

"You would consider an errand handed to you by the Lady herself a disgrace?" It was Tinnoviel Nai SaunyaLi who spoke.

"The 'honor' of this errand is sullied by the presence of this ... *Nyet'alo*," she flung her hand in Seung's direction, "this *N'thresha* whose human stink will lead every beast and demon from miles around to descend on us."

Nuviel gasped. "Tikena, that's rude ..."

"Then perhaps you should withdraw," Tinnoviel replied. "Though I am unsure if the Lady Seiyun will be able to find a replacement as low as the rest of us to complete this dishonorable task."

Tikena had no response for that.

Seung glanced sidelong at the girl. They'd met for the first time less than half an hour ago, yet this little elf hated her with the passion of a lifelong enemy. "I'm sure there will be plenty to deal with that'll keep us all occupied."

Tikena glared up at her. "No amount of help we give you can change the filth that flows through your veins, *Nyet'alo*. Find what honor you can on this trip, and maybe Oberon's gaze will find you ..."

"Enough, Tikena." He'd spoken softly, but the weight behind Tinnoviel's words cowed the young elf. He cast her a stern look, then his expression softened, and he placed a hand on her shoulder and gave it a squeeze.

They came to a balcony overlooking a vast open air courtyard, where hundreds of elves congregated and partook of the food and drink that filled the long banquet tables. Sparks of light flickered inside the multicolored haze drifting about the courtyard. Tiny sprites darted here and there, some landing on the glasses or tables where elves ate and drank, while others landed on their shoulders, or hovered between them.

Seung stared warily at the little light-filled beings. "I seem to remember encountering something like those little glowing things before. They were less than friendly."

Behind her Tikena muttered something contemptuous, but Seung ignored the hostile little elf.

Tinnoviel cleared his throat behind the back of his fist. "Um, they can be ... difficult to outsiders. Humans travel the roads that pass this forest. We have safety wards in place to deter them without their knowledge, but if on the unlikely occasion any wander too close, the sprites"—he cleared his throat again —"well, they 'convince' the wanderers to wander back out of the forest. Sometimes relieved of their possessions and ... any spare garments they might be wearing as well."

Seung narrowed her eyes. "I seem to remember something like that as well. Fortunately, I still retain my gear, garments, and dignity."

The Daunya Warrior nodded. "A combination of your elfinestrayan blood and strength of will." He looked down at the mingling elves of the Wood. "Please, friends. Partake of the food and festivities. This will be our last night of comfort and joy be to be had for many days to come."

The others filed out until only Seung, Tinnoviel, and Alurien remained. "Are you not coming, *Insei*?"

Seung glanced at the ranger. Though she hadn't heard that word before, she knew it meant "old friend".

"Later," Tinnoviel said. "Please, go. I'll join you all soon."

The ranger gave a curt nod to Tinnoviel, then to Seung, and left.

For a while they said nothing, and Tinnoviel left Seung wrapped in her own thoughts. "I ... I want to thank you for saving my life." She turned to face him. "Thank you for saving my and Swiftspirit's life, and bringing us here."

Tinnoviel nodded. "Those words came with some difficulty, hmm?"

"I'm ... not used to being saved by anyone."

"Because it's usually you who are doing the rescuing." His sharp elven features were quite handsome when he offered her a half smile. Seung felt her cheeks burning. "We all face a time when we are in need of help from another," he continued. "Perhaps one day, you'll save me."

Seung looked down at the gathering. "This is still more than I can believe. I'm surrounded by a truth I can't deny. I see myself reflected in all of you."

"But it's a lot to accept. I understand. There is a lot for you to learn, not only about our people—*your* people—but about yourself, your lineage. You come from a powerful line, Kiluriel."

"Kiluriel," Seung repeated. "That name is familiar and foreign to me at the same time."

"Would you prefer I address you by your human name?"

"I honestly don't know."

"Then tell me when you do. As I told the others, I recommend you eat and drink, and be at ease. We leave before dawn."

The Daunya Warrior left her on the balcony with her thoughts. Demons? Hybrid demons? Monsters from the old world? How was she to believe any of this? Then she remembered her fight on the road to Little Seoul. Those creatures made of water were like nothing she'd ever seen. And the entity that had assaulted her mind at Inayo. Now this. She looked out at the gathering of elves.

Elves. She'd never heard of them, yet she was part of them. If Seiyun, this Lady of the Wood, was to be believed, only a quarter of her bloodline was human.

"Too many questions," Seung murmured. "If for no other reason than to get answers, I must survive this."

21

Kenyatta woke from a sleep filled with demons destroying towns and villages, burning cities to the ground. At one point, he was back at Takashaniel, alone against an endless horde of demons sweeping over his head in a giant wave that crashed into the Tower of Balance. The barrier shattered, and the denizens of the abyss flooded into the world and set it ablaze.

He sat at the corner of his bed, sweat trailing down the center of his back. "By all the Gods, let that dream not be prophetic," he whispered.

Kita stirred in the room's other bed. "Hmm? You say something?"

"Nah, man. Well, yeah. Bad dream."

"About Takashaniel?"

Kenyatta looked across the room at him.

With only his head visible from the covers, Kita rolled over and looked at Kenyatta. "It was about Takashaniel, wasn't it?"

"You can't tell me you had the same dream, man. That's not possible."

"Maybe it was more than a dream." He unwrapped himself and swung his legs over the side of the bed. "We battled hundreds of fiends and never once laid eyes on the one who summoned them. I doubt he's given up. Maybe it's the gene of the Daunyans giving us these dreams as a sign of what might happen if we don't find him."

Kenyatta took a deep breath and blew it out. "I got a feeling everything that's happened is connected to that. I just wish I could confirm it with Taliah."

"I'd also like to get her to infuse our weapons with Daunyanic power like our lost ones." Kita moved to the closet and slipped on his pants and tunic. "We were lucky with that thing in the ocean. It seemed like it was only possessed by some sort of evil spirit. I have a feeling that if that thing had been an actual demon, we wouldn't be here talking about it."

Kenyatta ran a hand through his twisted shoulder-length locks. "Yeah, man."

They knocked on Malimokuru's door, then went downstairs to the common room when the nature reader didn't answer. They found him at a table with a steaming bowl of stew.

"Thought you two wouldn't be awake till tomorrow," the old man said. He blew on a spoonful of what looked like root vegetables and beans, then shoveled it into his mouth. "Sit down. I told them to bring out two bowls when dem see two foolish bwoys come sit with me."

Kita chuckled. "Thanks."

The trio mostly ate in silence, likely due to a mutual understanding that they needed to be on the road as soon as possible.

"While you two slept," Malimokuru said, pointing his wooden spoon at them. "I go out and replenish my sands. You're lucky you got me with you, with all dem demons stalking about." He waved an impatient hand when Kenyatta and Kita glanced around at the mention of demons.

"Nobody's listenin' to us"—He leaned forward—"but we do need to figure out how to get your weapons workin' against dem fiends. I can't banish them all on my own, ya know."

"How do you know ..." Kita trailed off at Malimokuru's bored expression. "Uh, never mind."

Their gear and supplies replenished, stomachs full, and horses acquired, the trio rode out of the city of Coral. The hard, cracked roadways of the former age gave way to dirt roads, that again turned into the hard roads from an age more than two centuries gone.

The horses' shod hooves clip-clopped on the hard surface, and Kenyatta couldn't hold back his grin when they turned uphill on what the Malimokuru called an "onramp".

"You find in the giant cities from days past," the nature reader said, "that there's many things like dis, called 'freeways.' It's a term back from the Age of Technology. Horseless carriages by the millions used these."

As unbelievable as it all sounded, the evidence was everywhere. They navigated between the rusted-out carcasses of the horseless carriages Malimokuru referred to, some small, some unbelievably large. All had black wheels, were once round but now flat and rotted. They were made out of a strange material that wasn't wood, yet Malimokuru assured them these strange contraptions moved many times faster than the swiftest horse.

They pushed their mounts at a quick pace while the sun was still low in the sky, and eased up with the approach of midday. Fleria was much the same as the islanders' homelands: hot, humid, and tropical.

When they stopped to rest their mounts, Malimokuru schooled them in the history of the Age of Technology. Humans built what he called airplanes, that flew higher in the skies than any bird. He told them of other machines that flew so high, they left this world and entered the part of the sky that was present at night. A place called space, where the stars lived.

Kenyatta and Kita listened politely through it all. They'd already seen much in their lives most would consider impossible, but the old man's claims seemed even more implausible.

Under the shade of a palm tree, Kenyatta and Kita gathered around as Malimokuru unrolled his map. "We're here." He pointed at an artery that extended north from Coral and arced west.

Kita chewed his lip as studied the map, then looked up at the wide freeway stretching as far as he could see. "This is the fastest route despite being littered with all these horseless carriages. But when night falls, we should get off and take the dirt trails."

"Why would we do that?" Malimokuru asked.

"Because," Kenyatta said, "it's good to give the horses a break from dis hard stone, and things come with the night you don't want climbin' out at you from something close." He pointed at the rusted carcasses up and down the road. "All around us."

Kita nodded. "Since you already know about demons, you should also know there's a kind made of shadow. They don't move in the light, but if you're in a dark forest, daytime or not, they can attack. As soon as night falls, they could materialize out here. The worst thing that could happen is them coming out with us surrounded by these carriages and little room to maneuver."

Malimokuru swallowed. "Then we best get moving."

They did, though they dared not push the horses too hard in the punishing humidity. Once their shadows elongated in their flight to the east, the three riders guided their horses off the raised freeway, and onto the smaller dirt roads.

The sun had barely disappeared beneath the western horizon when the first shadow demon materialized. Kenyatta gripped his sword when he felt the gene within him come awake.

The two warriors suddenly moved to ride side by side, and Malimokuru gave them a questioning look. The answer came soon enough when Kita ducked under a sword that swung out of the darkness from the side of the road. Another came at Kenyatta, and he ducked the attack and rolled from the saddle. He snatched his sword free at the same time his feet touched the ground, and he crouched, silently waiting.

Having similarly dismounted, Kita landed nearby while Malimokuru pulled his mount up and wheeled it around.

"We should keep moving ..." the nature reader started to say.

"They'll cut our horses down if we do," Kita said over his shoulder. He'd barely spoken the last word when the attack came in full.

Kalistyi. That was what Iel had called them. Seven shadow demons converged on them in the last light of dusk, their arms wavering like mist as they transformed from arms to swords.

The two warriors launched into action.

Kenyatta made quick work of the first kalistyi, beating away both of its sword arms and lopping off its head. He spun and dipped to one knee, driving his sword through one side of the demon and out the other. The featureless black head fell to the ground along with the two halves of its body.

Immediately dozens of small tendrils slithered from the wounds and connected with the severed body parts.

Kenyatta was already on the move, cutting apart another, while Kita beat two shadow demons down until they were no more than amorphous blobs on the ground. As soon as he relented to fight back another attack, the defeated fiends began to reform.

"Dis gonna go on forever, man!" Kenyatta sidestepped a stabbing sword arm and severed it. The demon staggered back, and he cut it apart before it could offer any semblance of a defense. His instincts screamed at him, and he ducked. A sword flashed over his head, and Kenyatta spun and stabbed straight out. His sword punched through the midsection of the kalistyi behind him. With speed his adversary couldn't hope to match, Kenyatta pulled the blade free and cut it in half at the waist.

Kita leapt upward and tucked in his knees. Two blades that would have disemboweled him passed harmlessly underneath, and he brought his staff around his back and down. The end of the staff connected with the top of the demon's head and sent it sprawling to the ground. As soon as Kita's feet touched the earth, he hammered the shadow demon several more times. Heeding his own battle-forged instincts, Kita spun his staff and his body around to deflect the sword-arms of two more attackers from behind. "We can't keep this up. Malimokuru!"

"A little longer, bwoy," the nature reader yelled.

"Sure thing," Kita muttered. He ducked another swipe at his head, at the same time sweeping the attacker off his feet. He brought that end of his staff around to deflect another sword, then thrust the other end down into the fallen demon's head. He felt the staff punch through the fiend's head and hit the ground underneath. He yanked the staff out of the ruined head, and whipped it up and into the crotch of the kalistyi he'd just blocked.

If the fiend had been human, it would have been out of the fight. But this was no human. The force of the attack had little more effect than knocking it off balance. But Kita was no ordinary human warrior, either. That small window of time the demon stumbled was enough for him to spin his staff over his head and slam one end into the side of his enemy's head.

The featureless head snapped sideways with a loud crack. Kita tightened his grip, spun his body, and brought the staff around the other direction. He hit the fiend so hard it flew off its feet.

The kalistyi hit the ground hard, but quickly rolled to its feet and charged. It had gone only a few steps when a spray of yellow sand fell over it. Kita heard Malimokuru shout a word, and the demon burst into glowing yellow flames.

The demon screeched—the first sign of any true damage inflicted—and in the span of a few heartbeats, it dropped to the ground and began to evaporate.

The two warriors weren't the only ones to take note of this turn of events. The other shadow demons broke off the attack and regarded the nature reader. Kenyatta realized that move had made Malimokuru quite vulnerable.

The Jamaican warrior went on the offense, cutting apart any kalistyi within reach as he quickly made his way closer to the nature reader.

"Whatcha doin', man?" Malimokuru demanded. He tossed a small handful of sand over Kenyatta's shoulder and into the face of a pursuing demon. With a word, it ignited.

"Keepin' you safe, man," Kenyatta said.

"Seems like I'm more saving you two," Malimokuru countered.

"And dem know it," Kenyatta said. He parried a descending blade, stepped around and turned. He brought the sword around and down through the over-extended sword-arm. The kalistyi hardly noticed it had lost its limb, and continued to fight until Malimokuru tossed sand onto its back and lit it afire.

"I think I see whatcha mean, bwoy," Malimokuru said. A group of shadow demons were slowly converging on them. The nature reader stole a glance over his shoulder. The daylight was almost gone. "There's not enough moon in the sky to see them when the flames go out."

Several more demons materialized to replace those destroyed, and all were focused on Malimokuru. Kita beat a brutal path to reach them, and he and Kenyatta defended the nature reader on each side.

"Any sign of our horses?" Kita asked. There wasn't much hope in his tone.

"No," Malimokuru said. "Dem bolt as soon as you left the saddle."

Kenyatta cut apart two more demons and severed the head of a third while the first two reassembled themselves. "How much of that sand ya got?"

"Lucky for you, as long as I've got some of the original from Shaldun, I can mix it. Not as powerful, but it does the job."

"Shal-what?" Kenyatta ducked another attack. From the corner of his eye, he saw a shadow demon lift off the ground from Kita's position and crash into three more.

"Later," Malimokuru said. "But if dem keep coming, we'll be in a bad way real quick."

"Then we need make a breakaway now," Kenyatta said. "We'll move back and get them in a cluster, then you roast 'em all."

"No," Kita yelled. "Keep at least one of them here!"

"Why?" Kenyatta and Malimokuru asked in unison.

"As long as one is nearby, we can easily pace your horse."

Kenyatta would have snapped his fingers in excitement if he wasn't occupied with not being cut down from every side.

"Ya crazy, man," Malimokuru said. "Ya not keepin' up with a runnin' horse."

"Just do it and keep at least one alive," Kenyatta said. "We'll worry about the rest."

They worked their way backward, all the while Malimokuru prepared himself, grumbling about young fools.

"Now," Kenyatta shouted. He and Kita beat back their immediate opponents and retreated. Malimokuru sent two large handfuls of sands flying into the mass of what must have been twenty kalistyi. The demons hadn't gathered together in a neat little huddle as they'd hoped, but he spread both hands out wide to encompass those in front, and most on the sides.

"*AFREETUMINOS!*"

The word vibrated deep in his chest, and the nature reader fought to hold himself together while unleashing such raw power. This time, instead of simply catching fire, the shadow demons erupted in blue flames that spread to any within reach. The flames flared with a life of their own, and the demons flailed in agony.

Kenyatta nearly cried out. That wasn't the same word he'd heard the nature reader use before, and the power behind his voice sounded like it came from something ten times his size.

When Malimokuru turned his horse and sent it speeding down the trail, he and Kita broke off and followed.

Those few kalistyi that escaped the fate of the others gave chase. With the gene of the Daunyans burning inside them, the two warriors easily caught up to and paced Malimokuru's mount. The trio ran on, the nature reader's horse hardly needing encouragement to keep running.

"I can't see anymore," Malimokuru shouted over the horse's thundering hoofs.

"I'll take the lead," Kita said, and Kenyatta fell back to watch the rear.

"And what good is that?" Malimokuru said. "You act like you see in the dark, bwoy."

"We can," Kita replied.

"We got a lot to talk about," Malimokuru muttered.

Kenyatta looked over his shoulder. Far in the distance, the last kalistyi disappeared around the bend as they outpaced it. He remembered the first time he and Kita had nearly perished, battling a number of them in a dark forest a year ago. The fiends had come on relentlessly. Why weren't they doing so now? He got his answer when Malimokuru shouted with relief.

"Thank the Gods. Lights up ahead!"

Kenyatta ran to the side to peer around the running horse. Hundreds of torchlights signified the nightlife of a nearby town.

"Tarrow's Field," Malimokuru said.

22

The innkeeper had looked at them oddly when the late arriving trio asked for a room with either three beds, or two beds and an extra set of blankets. They hardly cared which. After the events that sent them fleeing into Tarrow's Field, no one intended to sleep in a room alone.

Malimokuru sat cross-legged in a corner, eyes closed, four pouches of sand in his lap. "Ya gonna stand by that window all night, man?" he asked, his eyes still closed.

Kenyatta peered out at the torchlit town from his place beside the window. So far, he'd seen no sign the demons had followed them, but it wasn't an impossibility. They were shadow demons, after all, and night was one big shadow, so to speak. "I don't see you sleepin' either."

"Somebody's gotta fortify these sands to keep you two alive, ya?"

Kenyatta snorted, though he didn't refute the point no matter how much it grated on him.

"I think it's a safe bet that none of us are getting any sleep tonight," Kita said. He sat in a chair on the other side of the room from Malimokuru, inspecting his staff. "I've no plans to wake up in the next life because a demon murdered me in my sleep."

"That's what confuse me," Kenyatta said. "At any time, dem things could do just that, but never have."

Kita nodded in agreement. "Demons exist to destroy and cause chaos. Why the discretion?"

"Brit." Kenyatta looked over his shoulder. "It's Brit."

Malimokuru had been humming softly through the conversation. Finished, he secured the sands and slowly uncurled his legs with a groan. "What's this Brit, you're talkin' bout?"

"The reason dem shadows attack us out on the road," Kenyatta said. "He summon hundreds of fiends more than two years ago. Me and Kita, and three other warriors battled the horde and stopped him."

"A horde of hundreds?" Malimokuru looked skeptical. "You mean for me to believe five of you swingin' sticks and knives around manage to hold back a horde of demons? Demons?"

Kita looked up from his staff. "Sticks ... and knives. All right, then."

"The Children of the Gene," Kenyatta said, resuming his post. "The Gods select a small number of humans to be born with the gene. It's dormant until a demon is nearby, or enough powerful ones break into this dimension. When it's active, we're stronger, faster, more dexterous. We see better, too. It's why we could have outrun your horse."

"Hmm." Malimokuru strapped one bag of sand to his waist and stowed the other in his travel pack. "During my training as a nature reader, dem tell stories about something like this. Humans gliding through the air, bringing the wrath of the heavens down on creatures from the abysmal realms. I was young at the time, and believe it all. Then me grow up and figure it was just stories to scare us. Now I seen my first demon." He shuddered. "Horrifying."

"There's a problem," Kita said. "He'd leaned his staff against the wall and now studied the map. "There doesn't look to be any civilization between here and the next major city."

Kenyatta looked at him. "I don't like the sound of that; campin' out in the wild wit dem shadows stalkin' about."

"At this point, I'd say it's a gamble," Kita replied. "When was the last time we were attacked since Takashaniel?"

Kenyatta glanced at Malimokuru. It still felt weird speaking about it in front of anyone, despite the nature reader's own experiences and their recent run-in with the kalistyi. "Fair point. But the last several days got me thinkin' it's only gonna get worse."

Kita shrugged. "No choice about it. We've been awake all night, and dawn is almost here. Why don't you two replenish our supplies."

"Whatcha thinking?" Kenyatta asked.

"I'm going to find a tavern and see if there's any towns or cities that aren't on this map."

KITA WAS SURPRISED to learn that Tarrow's Field was home to eight taverns, twice as many as was typical for a town that size. His first three attempts yielded little more than gossip and attempts to swindle him. Every third person he talked to was the "best guide in town," and he found no one willing to share information about the best route going northwest without being bought a drink or three, or being outright hired.

He finally came into a bit of luck in a tavern named The Kicker's Club.

Kita stood outside the tavern, staring at the sign and considering the kind of clientele he could expect to encounter, given the name of the establishment. In the end, he shrugged. "What other options do I have?"

As soon as he entered the tavern, the smell of spilled beer and roasting meat rushed to his nose and fought with the clamor for his attention. Men and women of equal rowdiness filled the place, shouting to be heard over the din.

A sturdy woman in an apron carried an oval tray over her head as she passed through the clumps of patrons, excusing herself to the sober, and shoving aside the inebriated.

Kita felt the floor vibrate from the constant loudness as he navigated the crowd. After more than a few collisions with drunken patrons and deflecting careless elbows from animated conversations, he finally reached the bar and ordered a wheat beer.

The bartender poured the beer and slid it down the counter with practiced precision. The mug slid to a perfect stop in front of Kita, and he grabbed the foaming mug and found a wall to lean against. He took a long draw, studying the crowd over the rim.

After many unsuccessful conversations and some wasted coin, he finally got a name: Grizzled Bear. The instructions had been to simply look for a huge boulder of a man with a black and white beard and a matching shock of hair.

So far, no one fit the description. Then he noticed a gathering of cheering patrons around a table. A thick arm raised in the air and he saw the steak-like hand attached to it, holding some sort of painted tile. The arm went back down with a raucous slam that sounded above the steady cacophony of the tavern. Some in the crowd shouted in victory while others groaned. Money changed hands, and some of the onlookers left.

In between the passing bodies, Kita thought he caught a glimpse of black hair streaked with gray, and decided to have a look. As he passed through the crowd, the noise at the table grew loud enough to drown out everything else.

Four men—one fitting the description Kita had been given— sat at a square table, each holding a row of colored tiles with circles indented into them. Each tile had a different number of circles arranged in a different pattern. Mostly, the men placed the tiles on the table, connecting them to long rows of other tiles.

Occasionally someone would thump a tile down with more force, causing the table to rattle and the tiles to shift in a jumble.

"Better get rid o' that Big Five, Jax," rumbled the man who could be none other than Grizzled Bear. Kita chuckled. The man looked exactly like the type of rugged outdoorsman one would expect to find in a rowdy establishment such as this. From the dingy brown animal-hide pants, to the scruffy coat and thick beard, and the reeking of ale and infrequent baths, he personified the place. Still, there was a likable quality about the man.

After several more rounds, the burly man raised his right hand high over his head while studying the tiles in his left. The other players braced themselves just as that huge hand descended. The big man slammed the tile piece down on the table with a loud crash, and Kita felt the floor vibrate again.

The other men at the table recoiled with a groan as the rest of the tiles bounced in the air and fell disheveled on the table.

"Bones!" Grizzled Bear grinned at each of the other three players in turn, then reached to the side of the table and slid a stack of copper and silver coins toward himself. "Don't know why you keep tryin', but I'll take yer money all the same."

"You can't always win, Bear," one of the losers said as he shoved his chair away from the table and stood. "I figured out how you play, and I'm beatin' you next time.

"Just make sure yer bringin' that fat purse o' yers. As many times as you fellers come back to beat me, I'll never have to hunt again!"

A hunter as well, Kita thought as he watched the three griping players leave the table.

"And what're you lookin' fer over there, young feller?" the man bellowed, jerking his chin in Kita's direction. "You thinkin' I'm not seein' you standin' over there watchin' me take them fools' money away? What do you want with me, then?"

Kita took that as an invitation and moved to stand at the table, opposite the loud patron. With a nod from the man, he took a seat.

"I'm just passing through and this place looked like it was worth a visit." He glanced cheerfully around the common room. "You must come here to play pretty often, then?"

The man didn't bother to hide his skepticism. "Yeah, I'm sure yer curious about how much I play, here. You don't look like no one who needs help huntin' anything, and yer not from these parts. So I'm thinkin' yer needing a guide." He held his hand up with the back of his fingers facing Kita, and flicked them toward himself. "Out with it, little man. Let's have it."

23

Seung found her new companions at a bench, partaking of what was most certainly a meatless meal. Her stomach grumbled at the sight and smells all the same. She approached the table with a bit of hesitance. This group had been tasked by their queen to accompany her, but that didn't mean they wanted to be friends, or even liked her. Other than the cheerful Nuviel Titika, no one had been exactly warm. There was Tinnoviel, the man who'd saved her, but though he was polite, he didn't seem particularly friendly either.

Nuviel spotted her measured approach and stretched her little arm high in the air. With the most dramatic side to side wave Seung had ever seen, the young elf beckoned her over. "Come. Eat before the food is gone!"

Seung grinned with amusement as Nuviel shifted sideways to make room between herself and the solemn ranger. "May I?" she asked, and Alurien indicated the empty space with an open hand. "Thank you." She started to say something more, but couldn't think of anything that wouldn't sound like nervous small talk. She lifted a plate from the stack between the large platters of fruit, vegetables, roots, and giant steaming bowls of soup.

The food was surprisingly filling and packed with so many pronounced flavors, Seung found herself reaching for more. During her second helping, she studied her new companions.

Tinnoviel and Yurin exchanged perhaps a dozen or two words, but everyone ate in relative silence despite the surrounding merriment. Tikena sat apart, further down the table. As soon as Seung looked in her direction, the little elf caught her and scowled.

"Why in the name of all the Gods does that girl hate me so much?" Seung muttered under her breath.

Alurien swallowed a bite of some kind of glowing green vegetable. "Does it matter?"

The response startled her, for she had more or less been thinking aloud, and the ranger had ignored her up till now. "I suppose not, but it would be good to at least understand."

"What would you do with such a revelation?" It was Yurin Kei Daunyana who spoke. Her voice was deep for a female, but each word sounded like a note plucked from a harp. The air practically sang her words.

"Perhaps I could fix the problem," Seung replied.

Yurin looked down the table where Tikena sat concentrating intensely on her food. "Some are cut deeper by tolerance than a sword." She turned her mesmerizing gaze on Seung. "You are correct to want to understand the problem." She returned to her meal.

Spoon halfway to her mouth, Seung waited, but the Daunya Apprentice said no more. *Thanks so much,* she thought. The other woman glanced up at her and arched an eyebrow.

The festivities were to continue well into the night, but the group had a long journey ahead, and took their leave. A young elven boy who looked no older than twelve years—Seung found it impossible to tell with these people—came to inform them their gear awaited them at the pasture. Seung, however, should stop by the carver to obtain her weapon.

"We will wait for you at the pasture," Tinnoviel said.

"In the morning?" Seung asked.

The Daunya Warrior gave her a quizzical look. "We go now."

"Now?" Seung looked around at the darkened woods and the stars peeking through the leafy canopy. "Wouldn't it be better to begin out journey at first light?"

"We see just as well in the dark," Tinnoviel said, "and the magic of Yathienel is rejuvenating. Best we take advantage of this and travel through the night in these woods. We and our mounts will still be fresh with energy at dawn."

The elf's words added to the mountain of questions Seung already had, but if true, she welcomed the advantage even if she didn't share it.

As she followed the boy, Seung inhaled the many sweet smells of the forest. So many flowers, plants, and trees she didn't recognize. A plant with long stems and pink bulbs emitted a most pleasant sweet smell, while a group of yellow and purple flowers smelled similar to the fragrant lilacs which grew near her beloved Inayo Falls, but with a hint of citrus. She closed her eyes and took a deep breath.

They came to a fork in the trail, and the boy pointed her down the path that led to the carver's shop. After he left, Seung closed her eyes again and allowed the energy of this place called Yathienel to settle over her. Tinnoviel's words were true. The forest spoke to her; touched her soul.

The Carver Shop sat in the middle of a thick knot of trees and shrubs, easily missed if one paid no attention. As soon as she stepped through the door, Seung spotted a white-haired elf bent over a large piece of light brown tree bark. She bowed upon entering the establishment, and the elf stopped his work and bowed in turn.

"If it pleases you," he said without preamble, "after speaking with the Lady Seiyun about your mission I took the liberty of enhancing your weapon." He went to the back of his shop and returned with the double edged long-shafted weapon she had used in countless battles and skirmishes against man and beast. Where the sharp curved steel blades had been, were now blades made from what looked like the same bark he had been working on when she'd entered.

The carver held up a hand in the face of her growing horror. "Please allow me to speak before you protest, young warrior."

"I am listening, Master Carver," Seung replied, forcing politeness into her voice.

"We use the shed bark of the strongest tree in the world: the kakaya. It can stop a blade, and can be honed to a sharp edge. It is what all of we, the people of the Wood use for our weapons and the structures we build."

Seung stared the weapon. Her beautiful steel blades were gone. Jaw clenched shut, she stared at a weapon that was now foreign to her.

"I only ask that you try it here. If you are dissatisfied, I can easily return it to its former state without delaying your departure more than half an hour. But I have worked with the kakaya for most of my life; more than two hundred eighty years."

Seung hardly registered that last bit, so stunned was she. A smithy would never so alter a person's weapon without their consent. A warrior's weapon was as personal as their clothes. Was this some kind of elven tradition?

"This weapon," the carver continued, "was designed for you in your human homeland by a master smith. It was quite formidable in that state, but the true essence of the weapon was not fully realized."

Seung blinked. *Vyirayoi* had been forged by not only a master smith, but the best in the region. There was no equal to it in all of her homeland.

"The metal was strong and thin," he said, "but the wood and bark from the *Kakaya* tree is far stronger, and can be formed into almost anything." He tapped the part where the steel blade had been. "This will not cut like steel," he swiped his hand sideways in a chopping motion, "but its strike is equally devastating, and the tip is still sharp enough to pierce." He bounced it in his hand, then offered it to her.

"It's much lighter now, and in time you will wield it in such a way as you would never have thought possible. For now, I will fit it with these weights." He withdrew from a shelf four long slender wooden rods no wider than a twig, but when he tossed one to her, it felt impossibly heavy for its size.

After watching him attach the other three, she handed him back the fourth, which he attached. They were barely visible, and when Seung gave *Vyirayoi* a practice whirl, she found they did nothing to distract or hamper her movements.

"When you have the time, practice without the weights. You will find your movements faster and more dexterous." He watched as she inspected the altered weapon. "I don't take lightly that your survival depends on its effectiveness. With those weighs attached, you'll find no difference in heft from its former condition. Once you've mastered it without the weights, you will find yourself quite formidable. And with those words in mind, do you wish me to return your weapon to its previous state?"

Seung wanted to be angry at the man, but the more she flipped *Vyirayoi* around her wrist, spun it, took test swipes, she found the carver's words to be true. She gave a polite bow. "As you said, my survival depends on the effectiveness of my weapon. I wish you hadn't altered it without my consent, Master Carver, but I can't deny the truth in your claims."

The carver returned the bow. "Had there been more time, and the need not so great, I would have consulted you first. In time, you will come to see the value in what I have done. I hope you'll find a way to forgive my actions.

"One more thing, young warrior," the carver said as she was turning to leave. "I've been told there are things in the world that no earthly blade can conquer. You will find this weapon equal to the task."

Seung regarded him with a quizzical expression. "Thank you again ... Master Carver."

"I am not the one to thank for that enhancement. Such is outside my province. That is the work of the Daunya Master."

Another surprise. What were they expecting her to encounter in her travels? What did they know that she didn't?

She arrived at the pasture to see her companions waiting. Their horses had no reigns, no saddles, and no extra gear. Each elf had a pack strapped to their back and nothing more.

Tikena read the bewilderment in her face and sneered. "We don't need hunks of animal skin strapped to our friends in order to stay astride, and it's only fair that since they carry us as a burden on their backs, we carry our packs on our own."

She regarded Swiftspirit with an exaggerated smile. The stallion swung his head in Seung's direction, ears pointed forward.

"But worry not, oh savior of the world," Tikena declared, "for your companion is hobbled with all the fine trappings of a skilled *human* rider."

Contrasted with the elves' mounts, free of gear, the sight of Swiftspirit fitted with saddle and saddlebags, a pack strapped across his rump, left her mortified. As if to further her embarrassment, the reins in his mouth jingled softly as he shook his head and blew out through his nostrils. It may as well have been a bell echoing in a quiet audience hall.

Tinnoviel's mouth twitched, but he hid it by frowning at Tikena as Seung defiantly strode up to her longtime companion. "I'm sure it will not take you long at all to adapt to our ways, should you choose," he said in an attempt to be amicable.

Seung nearly rolled her eyes, but appreciated the gesture. "Right. I'm ready when you are."

The five elves leapt astride their mounts with ease. Seung, feeling quite the lumbering ox, put one foot in the stirrup and swung into the saddle. She clenched her jaw and ignored the others as she grabbed hold of the jingling reigns.

"We travel northeast," Alurien MerTana said, thankfully breaking the silence. "The fishing town of Najin is a three day ride. The best way to reach it will take us through the open plains and over a range of mountains, known to our people as the Inyuns."

Nuviel guided her horse beside Seung. "Don't be so grim. Sure, we'll face monsters of every kind, and maybe even a demon or two. But it'll be an adventure."

Seung frowned at her. "Who said anything about battling a demon? You surely aren't trying to tell me they exist."

"Not so long ago you didn't know *we* existed." Nuviel smiled broadly, her eyes playful and fierce. "There is evil in the world you can't imagine, friend." She placed a hand over her heart. "Whether I win or lose my battle with the darkness, it will never touch my heart. The Daunyans hold us."

"How old are you?" Seung asked, as they guided started into the trees.

"Old enough, I think." Nuviel pursed her lips, one finger pressed against her cheek. "Yes, old enough. They wouldn't have let me come with you all if I were too young."

Seung's eyelids drooped until they were halfway closed.

Nuviel tilted her head. "Are you tired already?"

Seung let out a sigh. "In a manner of speaking."

24

"I still say you're not tellin' me the whole story!" Bear threw up his hands and pretended to walk away in disgust. Kenyatta and Malimokuru stood to one side and watched in amusement as Kita tried to convince the man to guide them through the Mord, a patch of heavily wooded swamp that stretched between Tarrow's Field and the Redlands. From there, it would be three days, four at the most, before they reached Phoenix.

"I been a resident o' Tarrow's Field for most of my life, and know the surrounding hills and fields better'n any." He snatched the map out of Kita's hand and shook it. "I drew this map and had it duplicated. People from all around use this doggone thing fer huntin' and travelin' the area without dyin'. I also made sure everyone knows that The Mord is a death trap. Every manner of animal and creature a man could wish not to encounter lives in there."

"You want me to take you into that hellish swamp and out the other side? When I said I knew about the place, I wasn't lyin'. That's why I don't wanna go back in. There's more'n crocs and large dogs in that place."

"Large dogs?" Malimokuru asked, doubtful. "No dog of any kind lives in a swamp, much less like the one you describin' to us."

Grizzled Bear snorted and spat on the ground.

Malimokuru closed his eyes in revulsion.

"Ain't no kinda dogs yer used to seeing, I'm tellin' ya! Them's the kinda dogs that grow as high as a man's waist, and with fangs the length of yer hand. Don't take but one of them things to make a believer outta ya. If you live, that is. And the Stingarm is worst of all." He leaned forward as he spoke, and Kenyatta sniggered at the man's theatrics.

"If that thing comes for you, best to just put yer head between yer legs and kiss yer arse—"

"Name your price to guide us through," Kita interrupted, "and for your trouble getting back, plus all supplies needed." He pulled a gold piece and a handful of silvers out of his pouch.

Grizzled Bear's eyes widened at the sight of the money, and the three companions thought they might roll out of his head and land in the puddle of drool that was no doubt collecting at the man's feet.

The big man stared at the large sum of money for a moment as if weighing the risk, then leaned back and shook his head, thick beard sliding left to right across his barrel chest. "Nope. Can't do it. Not sure if there's enough money to make me want to go sloshin' through that swamp."

Kita pocketed the money, which drew a pained look on the guide's face. "Then I guess we'll have to find someone else willing to take us through. We were told that you're the best, but I'm sure we can find another capable guide in your stead."

"I'd like to see you try," Bear roared.

Kenyatta knew Kita had the man. In the short amount of time since they'd met, Kenyatta knew Grizzled Bear's pride was bigger than his appetite for money.

"Bah! But you'll just get yerselves killed letting anyone else walk you through that place. Then ole Bear'll have yer deaths on his conscience for the rest of his life. You ain't gonna have me losing sleep behind yer foolhardiness. Get yer stuff together and pack light. Only the threads on yer backs and the food in yer sacks." He spat on the ground again, much to Malimokuru's "delight".

"I'll meet you at the front gates a couple hours before dawn, tomorrow. We need to get a good start. I don't want there to even be a chance that night catches us in that bubbling cauldron of hell." He stomped away.

After a few steps, he called over his shoulder. "You might wanna stop by the local herb shop and ask for Sasha's Milk. It's good fer fightin' fever dreams and malaria and the like. You'll find other stuff to help you out when yer babblin' from some swamp disease or another." At that, the burly hunter continued on his way, spitting and cursing out the side of his mouth.

———

THE FOLLOWING MORNING, the three companions found their guide waiting at the designated location, grumbling to himself as he readied his gear.

"Got some special oils here that are the stink of a swamp skitter; ugly, foul-tasting little rodent." He held up a jar of yellowish liquid. "Grows about as high as your knee and stinks to all hell." The big man laughed and spat, bringing a disgusted snort from Malimokuru.

"Why would we want to smell like some foul-smelling swamp rat?" Kita asked.

"Didn't you hear me? I said they's foul *tasting,* too. Few predators will eat the durned things. They secrete some kinda nasty oil through their skin that keeps 'em warm, but also smells and tastes terrible. Mostly, it just sticks in yer mouth and throat and you taste it for days later. Not too many things'll eat it, unless they are near to starving. Even then, I think I might rather starve." The burly hunter smacked his lips in distaste. "Anything that smells this stuff'll mostly likely avoid us." He slipped the jar of swamp skitter oil into his sack and shouldered it. "We'll put that stuff on right before we enter. No use stinkin' longer'n we have to, eh?" He gave an exaggerated wink and the nature reader just leaned his head back and rolled his eyes, causing Kenyatta to snicker under his breath.

"Before we go, there's something we should tell you." Kita walked closer to the man as he spoke. "We're hunted by things you may never have heard of before. Creatures that look to be made from shadow have been pursuing us for days. We have very little at our disposal to eliminate them. If you travel with us, more than the dangers of the swamp may lay in wait."

Kita looked Grizzled Bear in the eye. "I'm serious, here. These things can come out of the shadows and are quiet and deadly. If you wish, you could lead us part of the way in. We've already bought one of your valuable maps. We'll still pay you handsomely for your help and we understand if you choose not to trek through the swamps all the way with us."

Grizzled Bear discharged a bit of spittle as he half snorted half laughed at the suggestion. Malimokuru clenched his downturned lips together. "Bah. You'd be making me out for a coward if yer thinkin' I'd just leave ya to that stinkin' swamp. I'll be there with you every step through, and if them shadow whatever-you-call 'ems come a-runnin', me and ole Hack here"—he held up a large axe—"will come 'a thumpin'." Another exaggerated wink.

Kenyatta laughed.

"Creative name for that savage tool at your hip," Malimokuru grumbled.

"You a funny man," Kenyatta said. "Just watch ya back in der. Dem tings not to joke about, ya know."

Bear eyed the islander, and then looked at Kita. "Be careful in the swamp because the shadow monsters are dangerous," Kita translated, eyeing his friend.

Kenyatta looked from Kita to Grizzled Bear. "What?"

DESPITE THE ABSENCE of a town between Tarrow's Field and the Mord, Grizzled Bear had insisted they leave Malimokuru's horse housed, and walk, as it was only a couple hours away. It made sense, given what the guide had told them about the place; a swamp filled with monsters was no place for a horse.

"I been a guide and a hunter for more'n thirty-five years. I seen and heard things these last ten years that'd make yer hair unravel and stand on end, young feller." He jerked his bearded chin at Kenyatta, who grinned politely.

Kenyatta noticed Kita looking at him. His best friend had been shooting concerned looks his way ever since the destruction of his homeland.

Grizzled Bear misinterpreted Kenyatta's mood and gave him a pat on the back. "No need being so concerned, young man. You look like you know how to use that there weapon, and you got your friend. And don't forget about ole Grizzled Bear." He gave the axe strapped to his hip a little pat. "Got more'n a few miles on this baby right here."

"You were talkin' bout things you see over the years?" Kenyatta said.

"Yeah that." Bear looked ahead at a distant wall of trees that must be the border to the Mord. "I seen monsters never heard of before, things flying across the sky that no man has a name for. There's still books around from the Age of Technology, but ain't seen the likes of any of the stuff been stalking the world nowadays."

"Many things sleep in the deep places in the world," Malimokuru said. "Even in the height of technology, centuries ago, we still never explore every inch of the world. Things sleep inside the world since before humans was more than scattered tribes livin' with the land instead of against it."

Grizzled Bear eyed the nature reader. "Not sure what yer meanin' by that last bit, but I'm believing you about stuff wakin' up. Don't know why it's now, but it is."

The group hiked through a mostly barren patch of land, with only the occasional rodent or a pack of coyotes trotting by in the distance. The sun had barely risen halfway between the eastern horizon and directly overhead when the first hints of the day's heat arrived.

"Some say the world's a more dangerous place than back then," Grizzled Bear continued. "I say it's just different. From what the history tellers say, I'll take what we got now. This ole axe has done well to keep me from gettin' eaten alive. Some of the stuff them history tellers talk about from hunnerds o' years ago ..." Bear shook his head. "Glad I'm not livin' in those days, if what they say is true. I'll even take the strange folk walkin' around, too."

Kenyatta, Kita, and Malimokuru shared a look. "What ... strange folk is that?" Kenyatta asked.

"You'd think me crazy if'n I told ya," Bear replied.

"We're open-minded," Kita said.

Grizzled Bear shrugged. "Every summer, these tall folk come through town, never speakin' to anybody. They wear these cloaks that cover them from head to toe, and yer lucky if you see a bare hand stickin' out. If there's more than one, they stay to themselves, but whatever the case, they never talk to anyone. And did I mention they's tall? I seen a man"—he frowned—"or at least I assume it was a man, who had to have been closer to eight feet tall than seven. Never seen any of 'em shorter'n seven feet tall, and I seen more'n a few with my own eyes, mind you."

In the distant sky, carrion crows circled high above what was surely some misfortune. Kenyatta looked ahead at the now not-so-distant swamp, wondering what lay in wait for them. The prospect of encountering kalistyi in there was not a desirable one.

"And then there's this guy I met once," Bear said. "Nearly scared the lunch outta me, pardon me sayin'."

Kenyatta snapped out of his thoughts. "Whatcha on about? What man?"

"Was about to tell you if you'd clam up and let me. I was on my way home from huntin', a good day, too. Took down a deer. Enough fresh meat to go for the rest of the season ..."

"When you met who?" Kita interrupted.

"Mph." Grizzled Bear curled his upper lip at them. "Don't appreciate a good hunt, I'm guessin'. Yeah, so I'm luggin' this hefty sack of meat and furs back to town, left the rest out in the wild, you know. Scavengers and all. So I'm bringin' food and furs back, and I see this solitary man standin' about a half mile outta town."

Grizzled Bear gave his head a shake. "Normally, you see fellers hangin' about like that, they're wantin' to rob you. But this guy was by himself. By himself out in the hot sun, I might add, still as a statue. Anybody out in the hot sun like that for no reason, can't be up to no good, and he's right in my path."

"So I got my axe ready. But when I get close, he never even turned to face me. Just started askin' questions about what life was like in these parts, where I'm from, and what it's like to hunt the way I do. Weirdest man I ever met. I imagine if I met a feller who wasn't human, he'd be askin' questions like this guy. He was tall, too, but not like them other weird folk. Had long hair, black as night. Skin had some strange sorta inner red glow, like he was on fire from the inside." Bear gave them a sidelong glance. "Told ya, you'd think me crazy."

Kita snorted. "Not at all. We've ... seen a few unusual things in our travels as well."

The sun was directly overhead when they reached the Mord, and Bear stopped to shrug out of his travel pack. "That's it."

A wall of trees spanned as far as they could see in either direction. So dense was it that they could see little more than a few feet inside.

Kenyatta and Kita looked at each other and then again at the fortress of foliage before them. The trees, vines, shrubs, and prickly bushes stretched as far as they could see in either direction.

"How far does this swamp stretch?" Kita asked.

"Ha. Don't even bother thinking about that," Grizzled Bear said as he sifted through his pack. "You want to add days to your trip, we'll go that way." He chuckled at the responding groan, and pulled out a small animal skin pouch. "All right, then. Time to start stinkin'."

"You already do," Malimokuru muttered, resignedly pouring some of the contents into his hand and applying it to himself.

The scent hit Kenyatta's nose immediately, and it screamed in protest. "Ugh. How could anything smell worse than a skunk? Dis is one foul smell."

"I never smell something so terrible," Malimokuru agreed.

"You're the nature reader," Kita said, his voice nasal from pinching his nose. "You've never heard of a swamp skitter before?"

"No," Malimokuru almost gasped. "And there are plenty other things in dis world I never seen. It's called livin', bwoy. You keep doing it, and you keep learnin'."

Grizzled Bear laughed.

"You're not affected by this rancid goo?" Malimokuru asked.

"Nope." Bear applied a handful on his arms and over his clothes. "Had to use it too many times to still be bothered by it." He replaced the skin in his bag and shouldered it once again, turning to face the Mord as though facing down a formidable enemy. "I hope you're ready, because this ain't gonna be fun."

25

After several tries, Grizzled Bear finally yanked his axe free of the cruper's skull. The wolf sized animal blended well with the foliage, with its brown body and darker brown stripes. So perfect was its camouflage that even the sharp eyes of Kenyatta and Kita had missed it. Malimokuru had been the one to sense it nearby.

"Durned things'll attack almost anything," Bear said. "Even a stinkin' swamp skitter." He shoved it with his foot into the soupy water. "The Mord crocs'll eat it.

They climbed over fallen trees, hopping over patches of murky water, still reeking of the vile-smelling animal whose oil secretion they'd rubbed over themselves.

A nearby patch of large leafed plants rustled, and the group froze, hands gripping weapons. When nothing more happened they continued on.

"What're the chances we get outta dis place by nightfall?" Kenyatta asked, wiping sweat from his forehead. The heat in this place was practically liquid. He separated two long twisted locks of his hair, pulled the rest back from his face, and tied them together. He nearly sighed at the instant relief. It almost made the musty smell of the swamp bearable. He cast about, his nostrils filled with the mixed profusion of wet wood, stagnant water, and general musty air, that it was difficult to pick out any individual scents.

Grizzled Bear snorted at that. "If we sprint for it and don't stop, we'd get somewhere between halfway and the end by nightfall."

Kenyatta heard Malimokuru grumble at that, then the old man slapped his face. That had become a frequent sound—face-slapping. The mosquitoes in this swamp were big and relentless.

"If that's the case," Kita said, "we need to decide where and how we're going to sleep. I don't want to be caught on the ground." He glanced at the many branches overhead. "But what lives in the trees?"

That question brought everyone's gaze to the treetops.

"I'd gamble on the trees," Malimokuru said. "These old bones still got enough strength to get me up der." He gave his bicep a little pat. "Harder for something to attack us in dem trees," Malimokuru went on, "than to drag us off on the ground."

Kenyatta watched the old nature reader with admiration. He may indeed be older, but he was in excellent shape.

"I'm pretty sure there's several species of snakes that'd like to dispute that claim," Kita remarked.

"Think you can get up in one of those?" Malimokuru nodded at a nearby tree.

Grizzled Bear looked at it. "I'll stand my ground *on* the ground, is what I'll do. I ain't hidin' in no tree like a sloth."

Somewhere to the side, an animal plopped into the water. There was a sudden violent splash, then the surface was still again.

"I feel too exposed, sleepin' on the ground," Malimokuru said. "We should have two people keep watch."

At the head of the group, Grizzled Bear froze.

"Wonder if he spotted a swamp rat to snack on," Malimokuru muttered, but Kenyatta could tell it was a good-natured remark. The nature reader might find Grizzled Bear a little repulsive, but the man had grown on them all.

"What is it?" Kenyatta called, his hand moving to the hilt of his sword.

"Nothin'," Bear said. "That's the problem. I don't hear nothin'. No birds, frogs, lizards. Nothin'. Somethin's here, watching us. Just keep yer eyes and ears open." He hefted his large axe and continued on, Kenyatta, Kita, and Malimokuru following behind.

"I think you should take the middle." Kita recommended to Malimokuru. "Keep several feet between yourself and Ken, just in case."

"You tinking to protect dis old man, ya?"

"After what you did on our way to Tarrow's Field?" Kita laughed. "Hardly. But I can respond to danger faster with my weapon than you can access your sands—"

A soft growl slithered through the air. Everyone froze mid-step.

"What in the name of the Gods was that?" Malimokuru whispered.

Kenyatta was too busy scanning the trees to answer. The sound had come from above, and it was far too close. "Any ideas?" he asked Bear.

Still focused on the surrounding trees, the guide shook his head. "I don't know what in the five hells that was. Never heard anything like it."

"Dis a bad idea," Malimokuru said. He placed his hand on a tree wrapped with thick vines as he glanced around. "If the trees could move away, they would."

Kenyatta's eyes darted in every direction. "We're being hunted."

"I only been stupid enough to come through here once," Bear said. "Years ago. But if I remember, there's a break in the trees about a mile away. Most things in here won't attack out in the open. We can figger out what to do while we eat."

"Let's move," Kita said.

Kenyatta kept a few steps behind the guide, Malimokuru behind him, and Kita guarding the rear.

Despite the desire to hurry, the party kept a moderate, but deliberate, pace forward. Eyes scanned trees and branches, murky ponds and vines. The ensuing silence became deafening.

Kenyatta spotted the occasional bird or small monkey watching from perches high in the trees, but there were predatory eyes on him. He felt it as though it were a cloak hanging on his back.

His relief when they reached the clearing was reflected in his companions' faces as well, when one by one, they crept out of the dense foliage and into the open.

Kita moved to Kenyatta's side. "I'm not sure I like this more than the swamp. I feel even more exposed."

"Yeah, man," Malimokuru said. "But whatever come for us has to come from the ground and not on top of us from the trees."

Grizzled Bear gave a noncommittal grunt.

"Whatever come for us," Kenyatta said, "knows we gotta go back in the der." He pointed at the wall of vegetation and the dark woods beyond.

Kita half turned to see Grizzled Bear kneeling over his pack. "Hey, Bear. Still no idea what was growling at us back there?"

"Not sure," Bear replied, jowls quivering as he shook his head. "I've heard stories recently of some sort of hunting creature that stalks fools like us who pass through here. Though stories like that're usually crafted by trappers to scare others away from their hunting zones."

"I think we best hear about it anyway." Kenyatta said.

The guide gave him a skeptical look, but shrugged. "Some of

the hunters and trappers that come through Tarrow's Field talk about a thing that stalks this swamp." He dropped his axe and unstrapped his gear. "They say you never see it, but you some-times feel that it's there. And if you do see it, someone's already dead."

Kenyatta and Kita sat on opposite sides of the group, keeping vigil while they listened. Malimokuru also sat, and rummaged through his sand pouch.

"I met a trapper who used to travel to Tarrow's Field to sell skins. Lived in a cabin up in the hills. Said one time he was on the road and his horse started acting like it lost its wits. After he finally got the animal under control, he noticed everything had gone quiet. No birds chirpin', no crickets. Nothin'. He said he could practically feel death in the air, like something was watching him; waiting to take him." With a huff, Grizzled Bear set about fishing out some dried meat and cheese from his pack.

"Did he say he heard a sound like the one we heard earlier?" Kita asked.

"Nope," came the food-muffled reply. He offered everyone a piece a dried meat and a hunk of cheese. Shrugging off the hasty refusals, he shoved another piece of cheese in his mouth and bit off a mouthful of dried meat.

"Said he was on a side path that was pretty stable, so he gave the horse its head and it ran all the way to Tarrow's Field." Bear snickered, bits of meat and cheese shrapnel flying from his mouth. "Stayed in town for a week longer'n usual. He was actu-ally afraid to make the trip back home."

Kenyatta noticed Malimokuru's growing alarm. The presence of a predator could quiet an area, which wasn't unusual. But this sounded more ominous. Could it be another demon-inhabited beast like the one they'd fought earlier in their journey?

The sound of rustling bushes brought everyone to their feet. Kenyatta's sword was instantly in his hand, and Kita held his staff at the ready. Malimokuru was slower to rise, but his hand hovered over the pouch at his waist.

A four-legged creature emerged from the brush. It stood five feet tall from its heavily muscled shoulders to its massive paws. Its gaping maw opening in an ear-to-ear grin that showed two rows of knife-like teeth. Its shimmering blue coat bristled as it sized up the group.

Drool oozed from its huge mouth, and a forked tongue flicked in and out like a snake tasting the air. Slitted glowing blue eyes studied each of them while its long, barbed tail flicked back and forth. It stalked from the trees, body perfectly still while only its muscled legs moved.

Kenyatta held his sword in a white-knuckled grip. "Dat thing got a hungry look in its eyes."

Kita crouched, his staff held before him as though to ward off the menacing creature. "It's either really tough, or near to starving to think about attacking all of us."

"Ya think so?" Kenyatta replied. "It's about the size of a bear, but I'd take my chances with a bear."

"Ya wanna tell us what dat is?" Malimokuru asked their guide.

"You're the nature reader," Grizzled Bear whispered back. "I ain't seen every animal there is. You tell me."

"You just said it," Malimokuru shot back. "I'm a nature *reader*. I don't know every kinda animal in the world either. And I don't think it take a nature reader to tell you dat thing's gonna kill and eat us all." He slowly flipped open the flap of his pouch.

"Kita." Kenyatta nodded his head to the side. "Move right. I'll circle left and close it between us."

As the beast continued forward, the two warriors spread out and let it move between them, giving it a wide berth, but not too wide.

The animal noted their movements with a comprehension that sent a chill down Kenyatta's spine.

Grizzled Bear hefted his axe and shifted his weight from left to right, his thick arms pumping in and out, barrel chest heaving. "I don't know what kinda thing you are, but you come too close and I'm fer sellin' yer skin on the market. Go!" He made a pushing motion with the shaft of his axe. "Git!"

On the other side of the beast, Kita cast an incredulous look at Kenyatta who responded with a crinkled grin.

Kenyatta inched closer and behind the beast. Again, it noted his maneuver, but didn't seem to care. Kita crept in on its side while it closed in on Bear and Malimokuru. The nature reader had a hand in his pouch and Kenyatta wondered if he was going to douse the thing in fire like he had the shadow demons back at Tarrow's Field.

In the blink of an eye, the animal charged. Kenyatta made a startled sound, and sprinted after it. If he'd been in front of it and too close, it would have been on him before he realized it had even moved.

Bear and Malimokuru barely dove away from the snapping jaws, but Kenyatta was right on its tail. He brought his sword around in a tight arc, thinking to cut it across the rump.

It skidded to a stop and spun so fast, only Kenyatta's reflexes prevented him from being snapped in half by those powerful jaws. He dove sideways, came back to his feet, and skittered backward. Every step he took, the beast was there, those snapping jaws so close he could feel its breath hot in his face like an oven.

Kita moved in from behind with a downward chop of his staff. To his surprise, the beast swept its thick tail across and slapped the staff aside.

Kenyatta barely had time to marvel at the fact that this monster was fending off Kita's efforts with its tail while still focusing on him. He threw his hips back to avoid being disemboweled by a sweeping paw the size of his head, then leaned back when it snapped its jaws at his exposed face. Kenyatta swept his sword in an upward arc, but the thing hopped backward.

As it lunged in for another snap at him, Kenyatta brought his sword down. As expected, the monster recoiled, and as it did, he stabbed forward and scored a hit to its muscled neck. The creature let out a high-pitched yelp, but never slowed.

Kenyatta's shallow stab distracted it just enough for Kita to slip past that horrible barbed tail and snap his staff into its side. The impact jarred him more than the animal. The tail whipped around toward his head, and Kita dove into a sideways roll. He planted his feet, then rolled backward as the tail came crashing down. The onslaught continued, forcing Kita to continue rolling this way and that until he was out of range of those horrible barbs and that hard tail.

GRIZZLED BEAR, seeing the two warriors struggling to gain an advantage, hefted his axe again. He hesitated as he watched the beast move. It was bigger than a lion, and faster. From the size of the corded muscles in its legs and how quickly it moved, the hunter didn't doubt the thing was much stronger than all of them together.

Bear gathered his courage. In the short time they'd spent together, he'd begun to count these men as friends. He wouldn't leave them to fight this thing on their own.

Just as he was about to charge, Malimokuru put a hand on his shoulder. "Hold a minute," he whispered.

"They need me now!" Bear roared.

"Yeah, man, but not dead," the nature reader responded. "I need you to hold off long enough for me to draw its attention. If what I'm about to do works, that things gonna be charging mad at me. When it does, you need to hit it from the side."

KENYATTA SCORED another couple of cuts across the monster's

face, which cost him a nearly fatal slash across the chest, had he been but a hair slower. The wound still hurt, and despite Kenyatta's best efforts, he was slowing.

He switched to a defensive tactic and attacked only when an opening presented itself. "You got your tail, teeth, and claws," he thought aloud. "Swiping movements is all ya got. Fast swiping movements that'll remove my insides if I slip up."

His opportunity came when the animal lunged and swiped a massive paw at him. Kenyatta ducked and spun around with a downward chop that lit a wave of fiery pain in his chest. He struck true, however, and cut a gash in the animal's leg.

That got more of a reaction. The blue predator yelped and hopped sideways on three paws. The moment passed quickly, however. It settled back on four solid legs, and narrowed its eyes at him. The lips above that perpetual carnivorous smile trembled into a snarl, and it charged.

"Bombaclot!" Kenyatta backpedaled using his sword to ward off the enraged beast. Hot breath and spittle rained on him as it pressed on, hissing and barking.

Kenyatta noted movement from behind the beast and guessed Kita had seen his chance. His best friend chased after the beast and leapt into the air. He whirled the staff around and brought it down on the blue monster's back. There was a loud *whack*. The monster stumbled a bit, then rounded on Kita.

As it turned, it whipped its barbed tail at Kenyatta. The seasoned warrior had noted how the beast fought, however, and expected the attack. He hopped out of range of those deadly barbs, but kept close enough to capitalize on whatever his friend planned.

Kita whirled his staff from hand to hand, arm to arm. Kenyatta had seen him use this tactic on large predators before. The constant spinning shaft was usually confusing to an animal. But Kenyatta had seen not only intelligence in those glowing eyes, but comprehension. He wondered if it actually knew what Kita was trying to do.

THE BEAST STALKED toward Kita despite his spinning staff. It lowered its body, thick leg muscles bunching together, signaling it was prepared to spring.

Kita completed another spin of his staff, prepared to dive aside, when a sudden jolt lifted the beast from its feet. It tumbled away in a cloud of grass, blue fur, tail, and muscled limbs.

Having been too close to the animal, Kita hadn't been spared from the effects either. He dropped to a knee, gritting his teeth, willing his shaking body to still. The hairs on his trembling arms stood on end from the electricity in the air. Guessing Malimokuru as the source, he looked to the side and saw the nature reader reaching into his pouch for another handful of that mysterious sand he carried. Why didn't he just summon the fire he'd used before?

The beast convulsed on the ground momentarily and climbed back to its feet. It turned toward Malimokuru and hissed. That angry glare shot right past Kita to fall over the nature reader. He clenched his staff. Could anything bring this animal down?

The beast charged. Kita watched as the nature reader flicked another handful of electric charged sand at the creature. Once again, the assault blew the monster into the air. It twitched and spasmed on the ground but fought back to its feet and widened its stance, as though waiting out the residual shock.

"What in the five hells is this thing?" Kita stayed at the ready, but kept enough distance for the nature reader to do his work.

The beast shook its head and charged again. Malimokuru stood his ground and flicked more sand onto the charging monster. Some form of magic must have carried the granules through the air, for they flew an impossible distance in a straight line, right into the charging beast.

This time the sand erupted into thousands of tiny flares of light. They singed the blue fur, and burned the flesh underneath. Wisps of smoke trailed off its body as it tore across the ground toward Malimokuru. So deep was the monster in its rage that it didn't slow a step, didn't give any indication that it felt the burn.

Kita had hoped it was a normal predatory animal that might be deterred if it felt the odds and effort weren't worth it. But as he glanced across the two dozen feet between himself and Kenyatta, he saw the same realization on his best friend's face. They were going to have to kill it, or it would kill all of them.

Despite the sheer terror shooting down his back, Malimokuru held his ground. Mouth drawn back in a snarl as he watched the beast shred the earth beneath its razor claws as it bore down on him. Just as he was sure the plan would fail and that he'd be bitten in half, Malimokuru saw the flash of an axe.

Grizzled Bear moved several paces away from the skinny man who called himself a nature reader. Whatever that was. He didn't like the idea of leaving the man exposed, but Malimokuru had insisted. And the more they argued, the harder it was for the big man to understand the islander's accent.

As he watched the great blue beast charging, he was glad he'd listened. He'd have hated to be standing in front of the maddened animal as it bolted across the glade in such a frenzied state.

Grizzled Bear tightened his grip on his axe, gritted his teeth, and at the last possible moment, swung the weapon with all his might. The axe cleaved through flesh and bone with a sickening crack.

The force of the impact jarred the weapon from his hands and sent him spinning to the ground, but the damage had been dealt. The blue monster crashed to the grassy earth, thrashing in a death frenzy, kicking and drowning in its own blood before it finally lay still, twitching as its lifeblood poured from its body.

26

The four companions stared at the dead animal, wondering what it was. Kenyatta shook his head with regret. This wasn't like fighting a demon, or some creature that murdered for the sake of it. He'd fought those. This animal had had incredible intelligence in those fading blue eyes.

Malimokuru knelt beside the creature. As if waking from a dream, everyone came to gather around the nature reader. The bright pelt on the animal had faded to a dull blue. Malimokuru sighed, then placed a hand on the body and closed his eyes.

"What?" Bear began, but Kenyatta silenced him with a finger to his lips.

Malimokuru leaned his head back and gazed straight ahead, looking slightly above eye-level. His mouth worked silently, and he rubbed the blue pelt as though comforting it. Bear snarled in disgust and Kita frowned. Kenyatta watched the nature reader closely. It looked to him that Malimokuru was communicating with someone or something.

"What's he think he's doing?" Grizzled Bear whispered to Kita.

Kita shrugged. "Talking with the animal's spirit?"

Bear was incredulous. "Why in the hell would he want to do that? That thing would've made a meal out of us if we hadn't killed it."

Kita shrugged again. "Let's see what happens."

After some time, Malimokuru rose. Without a word, he turned and headed for the trees. The others watched him, then followed. "Does he think he knows where he's going?" Bear asked.

Kenyatta caught up to the nature reader as they navigated the vines and roots that littered their path. "What is it?"

"That thing was a mother trying to feed her cub," Malimokuru answered, not taking his eyes from the path that was becoming less and less navigable. "When we walked into that clearing, she couldn't resist. Normally, she wouldn't have tried to attack so many of us, but she and her cub were near to starving."

"You spoke to it, then," Kenyatta said, not asking. When the older man nodded, he spread his hands. "I didn't know nature readers could do that—speak to the spirit of an animal. You tink you might have done that before it attack us?"

Malimokuru glanced at the young warrior and noticed his shirt was wet with blood. He stopped to have a closer look. "Take that off."

Kenyatta waved him away. "It's not deep. I'll manage."

"Yeah, man," Malimokuru replied. He ignored Kenyatta's protests and lifted his shirt. "Till it gets infected."

"I hope you listened to me and grabbed some of that Sasha's Milk ointment," Grizzled Bear said. "The woman who concocted that stuff is long dead, hunnerds of years ago, but that stuff works on near to everything."

Malimokuru looked from Kenyatta to Grizzled Bear and back. He shook his head. "Maybe a fool bwoy don't know any better." He pulled out a jar of thick brown oil and carefully applied it over the four angry slashes on Kenyatta's chest.

Kenyatta flinched at the contact, but held still.

Malimokuru whistled through his teeth. "You'd have died in two days."

"I was going to rinse it off," Kenyatta said, "but I forget about it when you started talking to that thing."

His work finished, Malimokuru stood and turned his back on Kenyatta. "How about you, then?" he asked Kita. "Did it scratch or stick you anywhere?"

Kita ran his hands over his chest and stomach. "I don't think so. I don't feel anything."

"Yer right arm is bleeding through yer shirt," Grizzled Bear pointed out.

Kita looked at his shoulder and saw the blood. Now he felt the sting. "Ugh. Why is it you don't feel it till you know it's there?" Kita carefully rolled up his sleeve and Malimokuru went about applying the salve. Once finished, he asked Kita for his shirt, tore off a strip, then handed it back. Kita looked sadly at the torn garment. "Just bought this at the market. First day we got to Tarrow's Field."

Malimokuru tore the piece into two strips, one thin, one wide. He rinsed the material with a bit of clean water from a skin. "Your wound, your shirt." He wrapped Kita's shoulder with the thin one and did the same with the thicker one around Kenyatta's torso.

"Right, now we're done wasting time, come on."

"We need to get moving in the *right* direction," Bear said. "I don't want to get caught in the thicket in the dark. Might stumble into a bog, or some such."

"This won't take long." Malimokuru resumed his hike through the brush, carefully navigating falling logs and patches of standing water. After that last encounter, Kenyatta eyed everything around them. There was no telling what was watching.

"You think that thing back there was what made that sound earlier?" Kita asked. "Actually, I don't care. I've had enough of this swamp. We need to be out of here."

"I hope that was it," Kenyatta replied. "But I got a feelin' in my gut that it wasn't. It never made a sound like what we heard." He thumped his chest. "We got the gene of the Gods in here, but not Their luck."

"I thought I was supposed to be the guide," Bear grumbled. "Where are you takin' us, old man? This ain't the way forward."

"Not much farther." Malimokuru kept walking until finally they came upon a fallen moss-covered tree. From behind the tree, came the most eerie whimper they had ever heard.

Malimokuru stripped off his upper garments and went to his knees, shimmying into a path under the tree. "I'm not going down there," the big man stated.

"You wouldn't fit anyway," came the muffled reply. Another whimper echoed from the depths of the burrow, followed by the nature reader's soothing voice.

The group scanned the area in tense silence until Malimokuru finally emerged from the burrow underneath the fallen tree. He immediately turned and reached back in.

Kenyatta grinned, Kita's mouth fell open, and Grizzled Bear threw up his hands.

"Come, friend," Malimokuru cooed. "We must care for you in your mother's stead."

"The hell we will," Grizzled Bear roared, which set Kenyatta and Kita in a defensive crouch. The surrounding animals and birds rustled bushes and took flight, crying out in irritation at the obnoxious sound.

At a warning look from the two warriors, the guide lowered his voice. "You've seen what that thing'll grow into. It won't even get to that size before it'll eat you in one gulp."

"Yeah, man," Kenyatta said. "Fortunately for you, it won't grow that fast before we're out of here, and we'll be long on our way before it's an adult."

Malimokuru reached into his pouch and, realizing he had no meat, looked askance at Kenyatta and Kita. "I don't suppose one of you care to share a piece of that dried meat you carryin' with you? It's not the best, but it's better than starving."

Kenyatta looked carefully at the small creature next to the crouching nature reader. It might be a good animal companion if it didn't savage them in their sleep. He glanced at Kita, whose expression was even more unsure. Grizzled Bear was openly horrified.

Kenyatta reached into his pack and tossed the nature reader a hunk of meat, which Malimokuru fed to the small blue animal. It chomped a couple times before swallowing the meat whole. Kenyatta sighed. The thing was every bit the miniaturized version of its mother.

Malimokuru nodded to Kenyatta in thanks, then returned his attention to the dog-sized animal with its dim blue coat and bright, intelligent eyes. It sat on its haunches, considering Malimokuru and then the other three strangers. Its skinny barb-less tail waved back and forth while its tongue flicked in and out. It looked in the direction of the field they'd just left; the field where its mother lay dead. It whimpered again.

Malimokuru gently rubbed its head. "I'm sorry, little one. We didn't know it was your mother."

"Would it have mattered if we had?" Bear whispered to Kita.

"We have no choice," Malimokuru continued, "but she agree to let us care for you."

"Us?" Grizzled Bear muttered.

Malimokuru cast him a reproachful look, then turned back to the little blue animal. "Come little one. You travel with us, now."

Grizzled Bear turned and stalked back the way they came. "That thing is your responsibility. And if it even looks at me wrong, the cobbler will be makin' me some blue boots."

Kita cast a skeptical grin at the man's back.

Kenyatta moved beside the nature reader as they made their way back to the path, avoiding the grove where the dead beast lay.

"So whatcha wan' call it den? It's gonna grow out of you callin' it 'little one' soon enough."

Malimokuru considered the dog-sized animal padding beside them, its bright eyes darting left and right. "Nyaka."

"Nyaka," Kenyatta repeated. "I like the sound." He jerked his chin at the little animal, who looked into his eyes with startling comprehension. "I think he understand me."

"She," Malimokuru said. "And yes, she understand things better than you realize."

Grizzled Bear guided them to flatter and more solid ground wherever it could be found, all the while grumbling about the "little killer" Malimokuru had acquired. Despite the big man's complaining, Kenyatta suspected Grizzled Bear was selecting paths that were out of the way, but easier for a smaller four-legged animal to walk. He smiled inwardly at the thought, but kept it to himself.

As night crept upon the Mord and the already dark swamp grew darker and more eerie, the group reluctantly stopped to make camp. Opting to sleep on the ground instead of the trees, Grizzled Bear volunteered to take first watch and Kenyatta joined him.

For a time, neither man spoke, they just scanned the dark woods and listened to the sounds of the swamp denizens as they did whatever it was swamp creatures do.

Kenyatta glanced at the sleeping Malimokuru, Nyaka curled up a few paces away. Kita lay on his back with his fingers inter-laced atop his stomach, his staff close by.

Grizzled Bear mistook the direction of Kenyatta's gaze. "Humph. Ain't never heard of no one carin' for the offspring of something that tried to eat him." He crossed his thick arms over his chest and blew out through his beard. "Soon as that thing's big enough it's gonna devour that naive old man."

"Nah, man," Kenyatta said, patting the guide on the shoulder.

"If there's one thing I learn about him, this past month, he take no unnecessary chances with his life."

Bear responded with an unconvinced grunt. "What do you call *that*, then?" He jabbed a thumb toward the sleeping Nyaka.

"We'll see," Kenyatta replied, which brought another grunt from the burly guide.

Kenyatta grinned at the man, though Bear couldn't see it in the darkness.

27

"Hold them," Yurin Kei Daunyana called over her shoulder.

"What do you think we're doing?" Seung called back. She whirled *Vyirayoi* in an arc, bringing the blade around to crack the neck of the brown, shaggy monster. "Just hurry up, please!" *Gods forsaken mist,* she thought. They had traveled without incident for three days with little more than rain to contest their passage. Conflict arrived on the fourth day.

They'd camped in the woods and awoke immersed in soupy fog. Seung had thought it a beautiful sight, till she realized the birds and insects had gone quiet. Alurien had been the first to act, slowly rising to a crouch as he eyed the surroundings.

Then the monsters had come. Brown, shaggy horrors materialized out of the fog one by one and surrounded the camp. Wide, jagged teeth, like broken glass, littered gaping, slavering maws. More disturbing were the hungry red eyes. The group had instantly gone from groggy to fighting for their lives.

Seung skipped backward, toes barely touching the ground as she avoided a slashing claw aimed at her midsection. She moved back in, spinning her weapon around her back for momentum as she brought it around to strike the monster's exposed ribs. She ignored the sickening crack, and brought the weapon over her head and around her other side. The once-steel blade struck the creature in the side of the head. In its original form, *Vyirayoi* would have cleaved its skull in two, but this result was effective in a different way. The force of the blow snapped the monster's head to the side and it collapsed to the ground.

Seung spotted three more of the stinking, shaggy creatures moving in on her position. She'd barely turned toward the new foes when they were struck by a purple bolt of light. Seung cried out and turned her head away. When she looked back, all that remained were bits of fur and an after image from the flare. Seung gritted her teeth. If she'd had the luxury, she might have been amazed at the sight.

"Quit playing around and get over here!" Tikena shouted. She deflected a reaching claw with her spear, then ducked a slash at her head by a second monster.

"Stop whining." Seung moved in beside the unlikely elf girl. "You're the one that let them maneuver you between them." Seung brought the shaft of *Vyirayoi* up to stop a downward slash. The monster was incredibly strong, and knocked the weapon against her chest. The impact knocked her to the ground and sent her sliding on her back.

Ignoring grit and pebbles stinging her back, Seung kicked her feet over her head and rolled backward. The shaggy brute moved in as she regained her feet, and Seung spun one of *Vyirayoi's* blades around and struck it in the side of the leg.

The monster's knee buckled, and she reversed the motion and struck its other leg. Staggering, but still upright, it reached for her head, and Seung whipped *Vyirayoi* up and into a vertical spin. Wooden blade struck reaching hand with a resulting *crack*.

Seung glanced over at Tikena, spinning and hopping, twirling and sliding. *Looks like a dance,* she thought. Tikena Mojin was by far the fastest and most dexterous of the group, and her much larger enemy had no chance of following the quick elf's movements. She hopped away from attacks, only to dart back in for a stab with the tip of her spear, then jump back out of reach again. She circled her adversary for high and low attacks, smacked the side of her spear into legs, and arms, and torsos. The elf might be unlikeable, but her abilities were undeniable.

With Seung now occupying the second monster, Tikena was able to focus all of her fury on her sole enemy. The shaggy monster lunged and slashed with claws that would surely have cut the diminutive elf to pieces.

It never got close. As if seeing the attack seconds before it was launched, Tikena hopped out of reach and smacked the monster's wrist as she moved. It withdrew its claw and snapped at her, but the little elf was already on the move.

Tikena spun sideways, and as those snapping teeth flashed past, she held the spear with both hands at one end and swung it with all her strength. The spear smacked the back of the exposed head with enough force to send the beast stumbling to the ground. Tikena hopped onto its back, brought the spear up in a two-handed grip, and drove the tip into the base of the monster's skull.

Seung dispatched her last enemy just as Tikena finished hers. With no more immediate enemies, she looked in the direction of continued fighting, and her breath caught.

Alurien and Tinnoviel were a sight to behold. The elven ranger and the Daunya Warrior fought three monsters each, darting to and fro, slashing and stabbing, kicking and whirling, in a lethal dance that had their enemies stumbling and dying.

Seung watched them with admiration. She and Tae Kim had fought side by side their whole lives, and fought in a similar manner, but not like this. These two fought as though they knew each other's thoughts. They moved around each other, in some cases trading combatants or delivering a complimentary follow-up attack.

Tinnoviel brought his flat curved weapon down to break the

arm of a grabbing monster, then kicked sideways into the midsection of another. He knew such an attack would have little effect against a beast twice his size, and hadn't meant it to be. The elven warrior used the kick to propel himself sideways and out of the way of the slashing monster in front of him.

Gliding toward the third monster, Tinnoviel curled his body to avoid a sweeping claw. He hit the ground in a roll, stabbed the brute in the abdomen, then leapt straight up.

The shaggy beasts had no chance, for their quarry was too fast, too agile. Tinnoviel clenched his core muscles to remain upright as he drove the point of his weapon into the eye of the monster to his left. Still midair, he snatched the blade free the instant it pierced the monster's eye.

His left foot snapped out under the monster's chin and lifted its head. Bits of its ruined eye flew free from the socket of the brute to the left, at the same time the Daunya Warrior's foot snapped shut the mouth of the one in front of him. Part of its tongue fell from its clenched teeth to the ground with a sickening flop.

Both beasts stumbled away and Tinnoviel was already moving. He hopped backward, just as Alurien MerTana darted in. The elven ranger speared the beast on the left in the belly. Still moving, he ripped the spear sideways, disemboweling the monster. Without so much as a glance to ensure its demise, Alurien spun the weapon around and stabbed backward. The spear impaled a monster behind him. He yanked it free, dashed past the gutted beast to his left, and stabbed the big brown creature Tinnoviel had left with half a tongue.

Each stab was precise as the last, Alurien jabbed the spear into its neck again and again. The monster's growl turned into a choking gurgle. It tried to turn away from the relentless elf, but that spear was too fast, too well aimed. It half turned away and fell onto its side, blood pumping between its fingers as it grabbed at its ruined neck.

Seung watched with a growing sense of appreciation. Each knew the other so well they trusted the other with their life without hesitation.

Tinnoviel didn't look back to see if Alurien had finished the monsters behind him. Seung knew from watching them that these two had fought like this, time and again, working as one. Each was the right hand of the other, knew the other's strengths and weaknesses, speed and dexterity.

The warrior from Kyu felt a growing sense of camaraderie and family toward her new companions. She looked down at her hands clamped around the shaft of *Vyirayoi*. Kyu or Yathienel, human or elf. Were either peoples *her* people?

Tinnoviel Nai SaunyaLi killed the final monster of the six he and Alurien fought. He looked ahead to see two forms shrouded in the mist. One was small and wiry, nearly as fast as Tikena but not quite. The other stood tall and regal, as she launched a blazing stream of fire at one creature that sent it tumbling away in a ball of flame—Nuviel Titika Yurin Kei Daunyana.

Tinnoviel had never had the chance to see the Daunya Apprentice in battle. Impressive though she was, he'd expected no less from the apprentice of the mighty DaunyaSai himself.

Nuviel seemed everywhere at once. A stab here, a swinging strike there. Every blow she landed staggered her enemy enough for her to meet another trying to creep up from a different direction. Smart. They were too many and were too large for her to concentrate on dealing any real damage. She would keep them occupied until the apprentice could finish them off.

Yurin Kei Daunyana barely moved. She didn't need to, for not a single monster had gotten within ten feet without being incinerated. Together, the duo decimated the half dozen shaggy brutes they fought.

Just as Nuviel was about to pounce on the last of them, it flew away to crash into the trunk of a nearby tree. It slumped lifeless to the ground.

Nuviel crossed her arms. "I was gonna finish that, you know."

"There will be other opportunities, child." Yurin looked about the bloodied battleground. The musty, smelly beasts had either retreated, or lay dead in their own lifeblood.

"This is wrong," Yurin said. "Chimsuras are from the old world—extinct for ages. They're from before the humans' age of machines."

Now that she had time to have a good look at the things, Seung was taken back to that fateful day when her village had been attacked. More than a dozen monsters exactly like these had converged on the outskirts of Kyu. It had been a savage battle with losses that might have been worse, had not two unusual warriors arrived to help.

Seung thought of the islanders, one specifically. She wondered about the man with the odd way of talking and the long, twisted locks.

"Looks like these stinking things remind *some*one of love. Maybe she was once married to one?"

Seung snapped out of her daydream to see Tikena staring at her with a mix of humor and disgust.

"They've been back for some time now," Seung replied, ignoring the antagonistic girl. "My village was attacked by these things two years ago. It was a savage encounter."

"Two years ago?" Nuviel frowned. "How can that be possible?"

"Anything is possible," Yurin said. "The world changes like the wind."

"I suspect we'll find more than chimsuras have survived the

old age," Alurien replied. "As Yurin Daunyana says, the world is changing."

"I wonder," Nuviel said, as she tied her shoulder-length black hair back away from her face. "Maybe they didn't survive, but have somehow ... returned."

"Returned?" Tikena snorted. "What, like ghosts from the past?"

Seung, having befriended the cheerful girl, took offense. "At least it's something to consider. Do *you* have any suggestions?"

"We need to get moving," Tinnoviel said just as Tikena was opening her mouth to retort. He gathered his gear and walked between them.

Seung touched Tinnoviel's arm as everyone went about collecting their equipment. "Do you think this has anything to do with the force that's causing the tidal waves? Maybe it's tied together."

"Impressive," Tikena replied with exaggerated agreement. "And you figured that all out by yourself."

Seung eyed her. "Are you so sour because you were raised on sourgum root? Your mouth seems so big for someone barely over two feet tall."

"Hey!" The similarly sized Nuviel gave Seung a playful shove.

Tikena hissed and looked as though she would draw her weapon, but Tinnoviel stepped between them again, irritation clear on his normally smooth features. "Did I not say to dispense with the infantile bickering?"

Nuviel fidgeted and discretely stepped away.

Tinnoviel looked from one to the other as he spoke. "Tikena, you disappoint and embarrass me. Get your gear so we may be gone. And, Kiluriel, are you not a warrior of high regard in your village?"

Seung tried to repress the heat rising to her cheeks as she inclined her head to the Daunya Warrior. She went about retrieving her supplies, taking some comfort that Tikena had also been chastised.

They led the horses—the elves simply walking beside their mounts, Seung using the reins—through the mist until they reached the northbound trail. Once they finally reached open land and with better visibility, they mounted and set off.

Seung studied the posture of the other elves, and the way they interacted with their horses. She had thought of her relationship with Swiftspirit as a friendship, but she could see that their connection was rudimentary at best, and solely because of the way she interacted with the stallion. Seung vowed to change this over the coming weeks.

She reached down and patted her companion on the neck. Swiftspirit threw his head in playful response.

Twice they happened upon human travelers along the road. Each time, the humans barely noticed them and fell into some kind of daydreaming state. After the second encounter, Seung looked at Yurin, but the Daunya Apprentice looked straight ahead, her features neutral.

They came to a fork in the road where one path went northeast to a coastal town, the other continuing north.

"We've passed two towns and several villages," Seung said. "Shouldn't we stop and restock at this one before moving on?" She hadn't expected the quizzical looks she received from the others. Well, Tikena's sneer wasn't a surprise. "What?" She looked from one face to the other.

Tinnoviel cleared his throat. "We ... find it unnecessary to stop in human civilizations." His gentle tone was meant to be polite, but it didn't lessen Seung's embarrassment. "What we carry, can be restocked with what is provided around us." He pointed north. "Another few hours and we will come upon a freshwater river from which we will refill our water tubes."

Water tubes. Not waterskins like the one Seung carried, but water tubes made from the treated wood of a tree branch already fallen. The Elfinestraya never killed anything they didn't have to. They made their weapons from the bark of a special tree, then treated it to form a nearly unbreakable and beautiful creation. They ate a variety of plants and fruit and berries that grew in abundance, and cooked nothing but soup. They even said prayers of gratitude for the sacrifice of the plants. Of course the elves didn't need to stop through the town. Humans had nothing they would need.

Seung just nodded and wondered if a time would come when she didn't feel foolish around these people. She'd never felt like she totally fit in amongst humans, though she hadn't known why, but at least she didn't always feel off balance; like a baby just learning how to walk amongst graceful adults.

Nuviel nudged her horse beside Seung. "You're learning our ways, Kiluriel Sen'Mora." She offered a cheerful smile, and gave Seung a pat on the leg. "However you travel, however you fight, whatever you eat, will not be done in the shadow of our judgment. We're not here to look down on you, for you are not only friend, but family, Seung *haloren*."

Seung frowned at the foreign term. Her new companions spoke primarily in elvish, and Seung understood more every day as though remembering a forgotten tongue. "*Haloren* ... I don't know that word."

"Oh. Let me think how to explain." Nuviel rubbed her chin.

The gesture made Seung want to wrap the girl in a hug. Despite the possibility that Nuviel could be her age or twice that, Seung still found the little elf adorable.

"Hmm. There are three ways to translate it, I think."

Seung's eyes widened. "Three ways?"

Nuviel nodded. "I think so. During the times when we interacted with humans, sometimes one of our people and a human fell in love and had a child." Tikena made a disgusted sound, but Nuviel ignored her.

"Humans referred to them as a half-elf, where our term is

haloren. The literal translation is near elf. A loose translation is half-human."

"Half-human sounds odd," Seung said.

"It's because humans see themselves first, and others second," Nuviel replied. "This is why a human would call you a half-elf."

"And because elves see themselves first, you call me near elf, or half-human."

Nuviel thought on that and shrugged. "More or less."

During their continued trek north, Seung enjoyed lengthy conversations with Nuviel. She and the little elf became fast friends, a comfort Seung couldn't deny she needed, though she hated to admit it to herself.

She looked to the front of the mounted party where Tinnoviel rode. The Daunya Warrior was kind enough, but conversation with him was more ... matter of fact.

"How do you survive on nothing more than plants and fruit?" she asked Nuviel.

"How does the deer survive on grass?" Nuviel replied. "Or the lion on the meat of the gazelle? It is what we are made to eat."

"I suppose." Seung thought wistfully of the last time she'd had a meal of barbecued pork, or steamed, meat-filled buns. "I personally couldn't survive without it."

Nuviel shrugged and changed the subject. "Alurien says we should reach the docks of the human city of Pyon within the next day. I've never been to ... what do humans call it? Askata? Yes, I've never been there before. It should be exciting."

"And cold," Seung replied.

"Oh don't be such a *gloarch*."

"A *what*?" Seung stared at the giggling girl, baffled at how differently elves aged and matured in contrast to humans.

"I know that look," Nuviel said. She waggled her fingers at Seung. "You're still trying to figure out how old I am. I'll give you a hint." She gazed up at the sky as she rubbed her chin. "Let's say I've seen more than a couple decades pass by."

Seung chuckled in disbelief. "That's a lot more than a hint, Nuviel. You'd have me believe you've seen between twenty and thirty years?"

Nuviel crossed her arms and thrust her nose in the air. "Don't act so surprised. You're not *that* much older than I, you know."

Seung had been chuckling at the little elf's comical gesture, but nearly fell from the saddle. "Older?" What was the girl talking about? Seung had several years yet till her thirtieth birthday.

"Give or take twenty or thirty years," Nuviel replied with a shrug.

For what felt like the hundredth time since her visit to Yathienel, Seung once again realized her mouth was hanging open and shut it so quick her teeth clicked. Nuviel giggled, while the ever-eavesdropping Tikena laughed aloud.

How could such a thing be possible, and how could she not have known till now? And if she was somehow in her forties or fifties—she cringed at the thought—what did that mean for her life? Would it change the way she related to her dear friend, Tae Kim, or the elders of her village? Never had the mentally tough warrior from Kyu felt so off balance.

"Looks like you just broke her worldview, Nuvie," Tikena said. "Poor, poor thing."

"Stop being so mean, Tikena," Nuviel replied.

"You look troubled."

Seung was startled out of her thoughts by the deep voice of Tinnoviel. In her shock, she hadn't noticed he'd fallen back to ride beside her. Seung looked about, and saw that Nuviel now rode between Tikena and Yurin, the former chatting in her usual animated fashion.

"I've never felt as though I totally fit in, even in my own home, despite those who love me and I them. There's always been this feeling of being different. My voice, my features ..." She ran a hand over the tip of her ear, still covered by her hair due to a lifetime of habit.

"I've spent several days being told I'm not who I thought I was, and that the world isn't what I thought it was. I'm part of a race of people I never knew existed, and then there are things like what she did back there." Seung jerked her head in Yurin's direction.

Tinnoviel gave a thoughtful nod. "You've had a lot thrust upon you in a short amount of time. Under more desirable circumstances the Lady Seiyun would have taken more time with you. Perhaps you would consider returning with us when this is done, that you might further learn of your family and our ways."

Seung didn't know what she wanted. For her whole life there had been so many questions. Now that she might find answers, she wasn't sure she wanted them. "Nuviel says we'll reach Pyon soon."

"Tomorrow," came the reply. "We take our rest at Cinta Lake, then resume at dawn. By early midday tomorrow, we'll reach Pyon and book passage across the Siren Straight. The trip by sea should take two days."

"Have you ever been to Nomar?" Seung asked.

"Few of our people have ever ventured there, and I am not among them. Once, there was a time when we did go to farther lands, but that was long ago."

"And now things change," Seung said.

Tinnoviel nodded. "Now things change. The Lady Seiyun speaks of travel to different lands. Our age of isolation is waning. We must strengthen ties with the other peoples of the world once again."

"The time for *n'thresha* has ended," Tikena spat from further away.

Seung sighed and didn't bother to respond.

"I'll not hear that word from you again, Tikena." Tinnoviel spoke in a calm tone, but the weight behind it sent a chill through

Seung's skin. She'd never met someone she feared, and though she didn't fear this warrior elf, she wouldn't want to be on his bad side either. She surprised herself by removing the heat from the moment. "I was doubtful about how effective *Vyirayoi* would be without steel blades, but I'm surprised."

"A blade need not cut to be effective. The people of Yathienel have an aversion to evisceration. If conflict must happen, and loss of life unavoidable, a whole deceased enemy is preferable to one laying in parts upon the earth."

Seung chewed on that. "Interesting way to think of it."

Behind them, Tikena cursed.

"What is it?" Tinnoviel asked. His eyes darted in every direction as he took stock of their surroundings.

"There are five *n'thresha* ..." she trailed off at Tinnoviel's frown. "Five ... *humans* on the trail ahead. I smell them. The sweaty stink of human brigands."

Alurien MerTana nodded in appreciation. "You noticed them before I, Tikena."

She smirked up at him. "Well ... they *really* stink."

Soon enough they came in view of a lone figure at the top of the next hill, squatting beside a horse-driven cart.

Seung shook her head. A decoy.

The man stood by the cart, scratching his head. The thing was obviously broken, but had been so for longer than just a few moments, as this setup would indicate.

He stood and offered a hopeful smile at the six travelers. He opened his mouth to speak, but hesitated. His face screwed up in confusion, then he stared at them with a glassy-eyed expression and waved as they passed.

Seung had seen that expression before. She looked over her shoulder at Yurin. The apprentice sat erect astride her mount. She returned Seung's gaze for an instant, then looked away.

28

T he surrounding treetops shone with the golden glow of the waning sun by the time the party reached Cinta Lake. Seung removed Swiftspirit's gear and gave his forehead a rub. The beautiful stallion rubbed his head against her, then made his way to graze with the others.

"You've a loyal friend, there," Tinnoviel said.

Seung nodded. "My dear friend since the moment of his birth."

"Come with me," Tinnoviel said. "Bring your weapon."

Puzzled, Seung did as asked.

The Daunya Warrior led her halfway around the lake before stopping. He faced her and bowed. When he straightened, his weapon was in hand.

The movement was so quick and fluid Seung barely registered it. Her eyes darted to the flat wide weapon. She'd seen the elf use the strange thing to deadly effect. She snapped the halved *Vyirayoi* together and twisted the shaft, locking it in place. "Sparring?"

Tinnoviel responded with a barely perceptible grin. That grin was suddenly inches from her face when the elf launched into the fiercest offense Seung had ever encountered.

Vyirayoi was a blur in her hands as she fended off the attack. Teeth gritted, Seung held her defense. She avoided being hit by a hairsbreadth time and again.

Seung had been trained to fight since she was old enough to walk. Her ability to read an adversary's body language, the way the body moves and can't move, had served her well for her whole life. Many an opponent had she defeated by knowing the ways a type of weapon could be used, testing an opponent to judge their speed, power, endurance.

This opponent was beyond her, and they both knew it. Tinnoviel was fast; faster than anyone Seung had ever fought. He was strong, too. Each time their weapons connected, she felt the vibration through the shaft of *Vyirayoi*. She had to do something quick, for the hard impacts were numbing her hands.

Inch by inch she gave ground, using every skill at her disposal to simply keep that blur of a weapon from finding purchase.

Tinnoviel darted in with a stab, then flipped his wrist for a horizontal chop at the last instant. Seung sidestepped and spun her weapon vertically to knock the weapon low, but when the elf changed the motion, she saw the hard bark blade speeding toward her face.

She bent backwards and the weapon passed just above her face. Now she was vulnerable. Before she could recover her balance, Seung felt Tinnoviel's foot smack her heel, and her left foot flew out from under her.

Seung kicked her other foot out and threw her legs up, landing on her upper back. Bent at the waist with her legs over her face, Seung kicked her legs up and out, and threw herself back to her feet.

As soon as her feet touched the ground, she knelt, spun to the right, and whipped *Vyirayoi* around toward the elf's right leg.

Tinnoviel leapt into a backflip and Seung pursued. A grin crept across her face at the foolish—if flashy—maneuver.

Her grin disappeared.

The wide, flat weapon flashed out even as Tinnoviel was still upside down. He knocked one of *Vyirayoi's* blades aside as easily as if he'd been standing on solid ground.

Seung pressed on despite her surprise. As the elf completed his flip, not only did he fend off her attacks midair, but somehow slowed his descent.

Tinnoviel's weapon flashed left to right, diagonal, up and down, until finally his feet touched the ground.

Seung found herself fighting as if her life depended on it, and not for a simple sparing match. With every clash, she became more aware that she couldn't best the elfinestrayan warrior.

For several heartbeats, the combatants held their ground. Seung spun her weapon vertically, left to right. Then she turned and brought it around and down, kept turning and whipped it around and up. She kicked out, chopped downward, then reversed midway and brought the other blade up.

The Daunya Warrior met every attack, parried every sweep, but never once took a step backward. When her series of attacks played out, he pressed forward and once again had Seung on her heels.

Seung held strong, using every trick, every technique she had ever learned. She sank deeper into focus, not watching her opponent's movements—for her eyes could never follow the blur that was Tinnoviel—but feeling them, instinctively. He was faster, stronger, more experienced. But she was determined he wouldn't win this fight easily. Seung growled and threw every ounce of her will into one last push.

For the first time since they began, she had Tinnoviel on the defense.

Surprise lit the elf's features. "Good."

The compliment further placed Seung's adversary above

herself. She let that realization settle inside her and imagined this as an adversary who would take her life if she faltered.

Tinnoviel continued to backpedal, spun to the left, then quickly right. Seung swept low. He didn't hop over the blade as much as simply lift his feet from the ground and tuck his knees up. As the blade passed under his feet, Tinnoviel brought his weapon down in an overhead chop.

Seung predicted the counter and flicked her right hand up, left hand down. The shaft of *Vyirayoi* rotated up to knock the descending blade aside.

That mistake ended the contest.

Knees tucked against his chest, weapon knocked sideways from his target, Tinnoviel Nai SaunyaLi simply snapped his left foot out. The kick was there and gone so quickly it might never have happened. But it did, forcing the shaft of *Vyirayoi* up. Her weapon vibrating in her hands, Seung found a blade at her neck before she could bring hers around to block.

The combatants froze, Seung mid swing, Tinnoviel with his blade a hairbreadth from her neck. It wasn't lost on her how much control the elf had in stopping the blade close enough to touch her skin without doing harm.

Tinnoviel removed the blade, Seung straightened, and they bowed to each other.

"I had not anticipated your skill, Kiluriel. Impressive."

Seung blinked. "Does that mean you could have skewered me only half a dozen times before finally growing bored?"

The Daunya Warrior replaced the weapon across his lower back. "There is always more to learn, *quyo*."

Seung started after him. After a few steps, she realized that she'd understood that last word without thinking about it. *Quyo.* Young one. *He looks my age.*

Must mean he's a hundred years old.

While they were sparring, Alurien had foraged berries and

fruit, and now set up a beautiful assortment of colorful food on a large cloth. Seung's stomach growled at the sight.

"Hey, Nuvie," Tikena said. "Think if we sparred I'd beat you as badly as the beating *she* just got?" The young elf jerked her head at Seung.

"I've got a better idea," Nuviel replied. "Challenge Tinnoviel to a match and see how much better you are." The bubbly elf smiled disarmingly.

"Couldn't do worse," Tikena grumbled under her breath.

Seung smiled in thanks at Nuviel. "This looks good." She inspected a pink berry. "I've never seen this before."

"They grow from vines that only live at the tops of trees. Most ... individuals, wouldn't consider them worth the trouble, but we enjoy them."

Seung knew the ranger was trying to avoid saying most "humans" didn't pick them.

"When our mission is done," Tinnoviel said to Seung, "I'd like to train with you, Kiluriel. If you are inclined."

Both Tikena and Nuviel sucked in a quick breath at the request. Tikena cast Seung an appreciative look before she caught herself.

Seung didn't need to think hard about that humbling match to respond. "I ... would be honored. Thank you."

The Daunya Warrior nodded.

They devoured their meal mostly in silence. Through a lifetime of habit, Seung rarely spoke when in a group, as the knowledge that her voice was so different from others made her less talkative. With these companions, her tendencies weren't unusual. This group of elves rarely spoke unless there was something important to say. Seung wondered if all elves were this way, but when she thought of cheerful and talkative Nuviel Titika, she didn't think so.

"Night approaches," Tinnoviel said some time later. "We should take the reverie."

Seung watched as the five elves crossed their legs, sat erect, and closed their eyes. After several minutes of staring at the statuesque elves, she unpacked her bedroll and slipped in.

She closed her eyes just as someone spoke.

"Try not to snore too loudly in your human slumber."

THEY REACHED the outskirts of Pyon late the following morning. The elves released their horses less than a mile out, not wanting to subject them to a rocking sea voyage.

"Be safe, my friend," Seung said to Swiftspirit. "Stay with your friends until we meet again." The stallion blew through his nostrils and tossed his head. Seung rubbed his flat forehead, and he rubbed it against her arm.

"The others will guide him home," Tinnoviel said. "You need not fear for him."

"You're saying he'll be safe?" Seung asked.

"As much as can be," came the reply.

It was the most she could hope for. With a final rub on the forehead and a pat on the neck, she let him go. Swiftspirit trotted away. He swung his head around and looked back at Seung one last time, then joined the other horses.

Seung threw her saddle and reigns over her shoulder and the group started out.

Tinnoviel looked at the gear. "Do you intend to bring your belongings with you?"

"No," Seung replied. "I'll sell it in Pyon."

They reached the coastal city before midday. The elves donned traveling cloaks and lifted the cowls over their heads, while Seung arranged her hair over her ears. "You all look pretty suspicious," she remarked.

The Daunya Warrior looked the group over and grunted in agreement. He and Nuviel lowered their cowls and arranged their hair in a similar fashion as Seung's. Despite the odd looks the group received, no one bothered the party as they maneuvered the streets among the milling residents.

Parts of the city of Pyon had been rebuilt after the End of Technology. Seung couldn't imagine how long it must had taken for the people to tear down old structures and rebuild them using materials from the earth. Soft brown and white structures had only smooth, rounded edges, some standing almost as tall as the buildings of old, while most were only one or two stories high. Larger buildings still stood in spite of their rundown state.

Those in Kyu who knew the history spoke of giant buildings with skeletons of iron, so tall they reached the clouds and challenged the heavens. Seung had seen the lifeless husks of great machines lying about the major cities in some of her travels, but she still couldn't imagine anything capable of erecting such towering structures.

"Nothing but stone beneath our feet and stone all around us," Nuviel said. "Even the trees grow smaller than they should. How can humans live in such a place?"

"You would have found their age of machines overwhelming," Yurin said.

Seung found herself caught off guard whenever the apprentice spoke, so infrequently did she do so.

"We need to find our way to the docks quickly," Tinnoviel said. "There's still time to book a ship out today."

Seung smiled and waved at a passing man, who smiled back. "Please, excuse me," she said, reverting to the common human tongue of the land. "Can you tell me which way is to the docks?"

The man regarded her with amazement, then blinked and nodded his head. "Continue that way." He pointed toward a street passing between a group of brown stone buildings. "Stay on that street and it will take you to the docks. "I ..." he blushed. "You've the lovely accent of a southern neighbor, yet I've never heard a voice as beautiful as yours, pardon me for saying." He offered a half bow, and Seung returned the gesture with a smile.

"I think he liked you."

Seung turned to see Nuviel grinning at her.

They followed the man's instructions and soon smelled salt in the air. Seagulls cried out overhead as they glided across the cloud-patched sky. More of the large white birds clumped and argued over the leftovers from fishermen's daily catch.

Seung smiled and closed her eyes. She took a deep breath, enjoying the refreshingly salty air in spite of the fishy smell. She hadn't realized how tense she'd been these past days, until the sound of rippling waves lapping at the pier soothed her mind like a balm.

A man in a dark gray uniform met them halfway down the street before they reached the wharf. "What business do you have here?"

Before Seung had a chance to answer, they found themselves surrounded by the city guard. He spoke in the common human tongue of Korea, which Seung understood but the elves did not. His intent was unmistakable, however.

Seung glanced at Tinnoviel. The Daunya Warrior looked to be standing at ease, but she knew better. The street was unoccupied and far enough away from the wharf that a scuffle would go unnoticed if they were quick and quiet.

She stepped forward. If she didn't defuse this situation, the elves would have these men unconscious before they knew what had happened.

"We seek passage to Nomar, sir."

The guard gave her a skeptical look. He was a about Seung's height and solidly built, but she knew it was the silent one to his left who was more formidable. She made sure to keep him in her sight.

"Why do you dress so mysteriously?" the guard continued. "Who are you hiding from?"

"We hide from the chill, sir," Seung replied in what she hoped was an innocent tone. "We are not from the coast and we find the cool ocean air a bit frigid."

The guard's expression remained skeptical. He glanced at his silent companion who didn't blink. A warrior knows a warrior, regardless of their garb, and Seung knew the silent guard had assessed every one of them.

"You look like people with something to hide." The guard pointed at those still wearing their cowls. "Lower those. Let's see if you have faces that are wanted.

Seung held her breath as each of the group slipped their hands into their cowls and removed them. She glanced behind her to see that all of them had their hair arranged over their ears with but a slip of the hand.

The guard stared at them for several tense heartbeats, then jerked his chin toward the ships beyond. "You are strange-looking people. I've not seen before. Be on your way and gone from Pyon. Your presence makes me suspicious. You will be watched."

Seung gave the most humble smile she could stomach and led the group on, feeling the silent guard's measuring gaze on their backs. Once they were a safe distance away, she allowed herself to relax a little.

"Looks like Yurin didn't have to do her special thing this time," the ever-cheerful Nuviel said as she moved up beside Seung. "You've got a bit of special stuff of your own, don't you?"

Seung chuckled. "Not that I'm aware of."

They came to the wharf and waited while Tinnoviel assessed the ships. After a few minutes he motioned them toward a medium sized craft named *Wave Dancer*.

Noticing the six strangers studying his ship, a man spat into the ocean and jammed a rumpled cap over his balding pate. His wrinkled pants hugged his skinny legs in all the wrong places, and his stained shirt was buttoned unevenly. As he approached—rocking with every step—Tikena wrinkled her nose.

"You need a ship," the man stated.

"We do," Seung replied, taking the lead. "We wish to hire you to transport us to Nomar."

The captain eyed her. "I'm Captain So, and I normally charge thirty silver for a trip that far. What part of Nomar, then?

Thirty silver! Seung swallowed. "North Nomar. Askata," she clarified.

"Then the price just tripled," the skinny man said.

"What? Tripled?" Seung couldn't hide her shock. "We could almost *buy* a boat for that much!"

"And who would crew it, fine lady?" The captain said, looking them over. "You look a fine group, but you don't strike me as sailors." He waved a hand at the pier. "For one thing, I'm the only one who'll take you. If I'm going to risk my crew traveling through the Siren Strait, they should be paid well for it. Other thing is, I can't take you all the way to Askata. Too dangerous."

"How far can you take us, then?" Seung asked, a sinking feeling creeping into the pit of her stomach.

"Port City, Orgonin," came the answer. "No farther."

Seung shook her head. "That's too much money to drop us so far from our destination. We will give you forty silver."

"Lady," the captain replied in a patient tone, "have you ever passed through Siren Strait?" When she shook her head, he nodded as though he'd expected as much. "I could lose some of my crew on this voyage. I've been lucky to have only lost two crewmen, and I've traveled the Siren Strait more than twenty times. There are things in the ocean that live only in that stretch of water. Things that have a horrible haunting song that drive men mad or lure them overboard, or both."

He took off his hat and scratched his head, wisps of white strands floated about his sun-spotted scalp. "You'll find no other captain willing to take you across that cursed strait, though you're welcome to try." He replaced his cap, the brim stained with something Seung didn't want to think about.

"If it was anywhere else, we could talk. But I'm not bargaining on the Siren Strait. I may be sending some of that money to the family of a lost crew member. I hope not, but they understand and so do their families. It's ninety silver or no passage."

Seung was about to argue, but Tinnoviel placed a hand on her shoulder. "How soon can we depart?" she asked instead, sighing.

"Best time is in the morning, so long as the weather holds." He looked up at the clear blue sky, as though consulting the clouds above. "We should be fine to leave at dawn. Before dawn, if you can be ready."

"We will be here before dawn, Captain So," Seung agreed.

"That went badly," she said to Tinnoviel after leading them away from the pier.

"He gave us a fair deal," Tinnoviel replied.

"Why would you think that?" Seung was incredulous. "Ninety silver is nearly enough—"

"The Siren Strait is extremely dangerous," Tinnoviel interrupted. "It's home to the Sirens of the Sea, as they are called. Their song can destroy a person's mind."

"What about us?" Seung asked.

"Part of the danger of the Sirens is that they enter the person's mind and dominate their will. By our nature, we elves have certain immunities. I do not fear for you, for you have an indomitable will and a fierce spirit." He glanced sidelong at her. "Still, it wouldn't hurt for you to learn a few techniques to ease the journey."

Seung broke from the group as they made their way back toward the city. "I know you don't wish to mingle in a human civilization, but I want a bath in a tub, and maybe to have a look around. I'd also like to see if there's any news."

Tinnoviel nodded. "A good idea. We will meet you at the docks before the rising sun."

As she strode down the many streets in search of an inn,

Seung felt a sense of ease settle over her. Save for Tikena, none of the elves had shown her any judgment or dislike because of her human heritage, but she still felt different from them. If she didn't totally fit in with humans, she felt less so with the elves.

After finding a house that had been converted into an inn by a nice elderly couple, Seung sent for soap, bath oils, and hot water.

Seung lounged in the hot bath, enjoying the oils coating her skin and the steam rising over her face from the bath. She closed her eyes and reflected on this adventure she'd been swept into.

It would have been nice to have someone familiar by her side, like Tae Kim, but that was a selfish wish. Tae was needed to lead the village warriors should any more trouble arise. It would have been foolish to ask him to come for the sake of her emotional comfort.

Seung sank into the bath all the way to her chin with a contented sigh. She had a feeling this would be her last relaxing night for a while.

Kenyatta hopped over an exposed root, then leapt and grabbed hold of an overhanging branch. One hand holding onto the branch, the other his sword, he swung over a patch of mud and landed on the other side.

Ahead of him, Grizzled Bear huffed and wheezed. "Fork ... coming up ..." he panted. "Left ... path."

"Too many sandwiches, man," Kenyatta grumbled under his breath, not for the first time. "Dem sandwiches be the death of you."

The crack of snapping tree branches from behind was the only other sound in the quiet swamp, other than the guide's labored breathing.

"Sounds like it's getting closer," Kita called from up front. "Need me back there?"

"I got it, man," Kenyatta replied. "Keep going."

The last thing they needed was to leave Bear unprotected. He'd argued that he could take care of himself, but when they'd heard that ominous growl whispering in the wind, the guide offered no more argument.

Behind Kita and Grizzled Bear, ran Malimokuru. The old nature reader had surprising endurance.

More snapping branches, more soft growls. Kenyatta wondered if every living thing in this swamp capable of moving had fled. After finding the little blue animal, their passage had been uneventful. Then the insects, birds, frogs, every living thing had gone silent. Shortly after, they'd heard that growl.

Kenyatta stole a glance over his shoulder. Though he saw nothing, the sounds of pursuit were getting closer. "We're gonna need to find a spot to fight," he warned. "We not gonna outrun it."

"Don't know ... any such ... place," Bear huffed. "Gotta keep ... moving."

Kenyatta admired the man's fortitude, but it was impossible. They might have outrun this thing if it were just he and Kita. Might.

Not for the first time, Kenyatta wished he had his swords. He'd fought many a battle with them against both human and demon.

He tightened his grip on his new sword. It had held up well enough so far, but it wouldn't serve for the inevitable return to Takashaniel and the confrontation with the drek. Ever was that in the back of his mind.

Branches snapped, this time overhead. Kenyatta skidded to a stop and called out, "above!"

The others similarly slid to a stop. Malimokuru's hand was already in one of his pouches as he surveyed the trees and vines overhead. Grizzled Bear's shoulders heaved as he caught his breath, but he still drew his axe. Kita had his staff at the ready, also scanning the branches overhead.

The silence had the hairs on the back of Kenyatta's neck standing on end. He slowly drew his sword, eyes darting this way and that.

"*Grrrrrrrraaaaaaaaaaaaaah.*"

The sound drifted from on high and whipped around and

ahead of the group. Up front, Kita swore an oath and held his staff in a white-knuckled grip.

A branch snapped somewhere to the right, then another a couple dozen feet further up the trail.

Kenyatta turned as he tracked the sound. How fast was this thing moving?

The answer was swift and brutal.

Kenyatta's only warning came as a flash of movement in the periphery. He barely raised his sword in time to deflect the shaft of a heavy weapon with a lot of weight behind it.

The attack came with such power, it pressed the top of Kenyatta's sword against his chest and knocked him to the ground. He'd tensed himself against the impact, but still had the wind blasted from his lungs.

He managed no more than a glimpse of the two-legged creature standing over him as it raised a spear unlike anything he'd ever seen, and brought it down.

Weakened from the first impact, Kenyatta had not the speed nor the strength to deflect the killing blow, but then Kita was there.

Staff whirling, Kita leapt and glided over Malimokuru's head. He flicked the end of his staff sideways and the flexible shaft snapped toward his target.

The impact would have cracked its skull, but the thing simply grabbed the end with its hand and yanked Kita sideways while he was still midair. Kita held on to the weapon, but the strength of this enemy sent him flying sideways.

Kenyatta had no time to fear that his friend may have hit a tree. He stabbed up with his sword, but the attacker dodged. He'd expected as much, having already experienced its speed and power. The attack was more to buy himself the instant he needed to regain his feet.

No sooner had Kenyatta flipped back to his feet, than he heard Malimokuru shout for him to drop. He dropped to one knee and swiped his sword in a horizontal cut at the attacker's midsection. It blocked his sword with its spear, at the same time receiving a full blast of burning sand from the nature reader. The granules lit like sparks, tiny flames flaring up all over its back. It let out a horrifying scream that sounded more enraged than pained. Kenyatta slowly backed away. The two-legged creature tried in vain to slap at its back in a futile attempt to put out the flames.

Kenyatta got a good look at it as he backed away, and didn't like what he saw. He barely stood as tall as its shoulder. It was bare-chested, with skin as gray as stone, and arms and legs thick with muscle.

He stole a quick glance to the side but saw no sign of Kita. The magic of the flames started to diminish. Kenyatta tightened his grip on the sword. It must have a tough hide, as the burns on its back looked superficial. He took a deep breath and let it out in a steady stream, aware that the gene inside him remained dormant. He started to wonder if this thing, whatever it was, might be beyond them.

"It's the hunter," Grizzled Bear called from behind Malimokuru. "Got to be! We're all dead." Despite his grim procla-mation, the guide hefted his axe and trotted past Malimokuru. "At least we'll go down swingin'."

"I'm not dying here," Kenyatta said. He threw himself at the hunter with a diagonal cut toward its chest. Despite the agony of tiny flames still diminishing all over its body, it easily parried Kenyatta's attack. It continued to spin its spear in an attempt to throw him off balance, but Kenyatta recovered. He spun with the motion and brought the sword around in a horizontal cut, but again, the spear was there. Back and forth, the combatants attacked and counterattacked.

Another clash sent Kenyatta ducking and skittering backward to keep from being disemboweled and having his head taken off.

The hunter glared at him with narrowed black eyes above fangs protruding from the top and bottom of its mouth.

It was strong, too strong to clash with. Kenyatta remained defensive and used quick parries, just enough to knock an attack off course as he moved away. Despite the tactic, the constant parrying of such heavy blows required more energy to keep from being thrown off balance, or having his sword knocked from his grasp.

With a great bellow, Grizzled Bear swung his axe at the hunter's midsection. It spun its spear vertical, connecting below the axe blade and hitting the shaft. The axe was forced up, and Grizzled Bear overstepped. The hunter reversed the spear's spin, causing the other end to arc around and connect with the top of the guide's head.

Bear stretched full out and fell flat to the ground as Kita blew past, staff spinning. Kenyatta hoped the big man wasn't dead, given the power of this thing, but there was no time to think about it.

He quickly scanned their surroundings. They were in the middle of a wooded swamp with no room to maneuver the thing between them. At that thought, he realized he hadn't seen Nyaka since the attack. "No time to think about it." Kenyatta carefully moved in on the combatants as the hunter began to overwhelm Kita. When he saw an opening, he leapt to Kita's aid.

Years of fighting side by side enabled them to compliment one another's movements. With Kenyatta now by his side, Kita regained solid footing. He spun his staff vertically on his right side, then stabbed forward as Kenyatta cut horizontally from the left.

The hunter's timing was perfect. It spun its spear vertically to catch Kita's spear as it turned its body to the left, away from Kenyatta's incoming blade. It kept the spear spinning and knocked Kenyatta's sword low, then snapped the spear up again. Kenyatta threw his head back to avoid the spear tip slicing his face, but it still clipped him under the chin. He felt the very tip of that spear cut him under the chin just before the spear came back down on his head.

A heavy thump square on the top of his head knocked him sprawling to the ground. Realizing his vulnerability, Kenyatta scrambled to his feet. Or tried to. Stars danced in his vision, but he blinked a few times and forced himself upright through the dizziness.

Kita was giving ground again, but another spray of sand from Malimokuru fell over the hunter and lit it with hundreds of tiny flames.

With an ear-piercing screech, it arched its back, providing Kita the split second he needed to ram the butt of his staff into its midsection. He retracted, then snapped it up toward the hunter's face.

It grabbed Kita's staff, tucked its spear under its arm, tip facing Kita, and yanked him in.

Kenyatta thought that was the end of his friend, but Kita didn't try to resist. Instead, he pushed off, flipped his body over the spear and brought his legs down on the hunter's shoulders. Having let go of his staff, Kita crossed his ankles behind the creature's head and squeezed. He then curled up to face his adversary and unloaded a barrage of punches into its face.

The blows did nothing, but they didn't need to. As the hunter knocked Kita off with one large hand, Kenyatta drove his blade into its side. He should have been able to push the sword in to the hilt, but the thing was impossibly fast.

It screeched again, but snapped its hand down to grab the blade. Green blood oozed from the wound and its hand, which tightened around the blade. It pulled the blade out, and raised its other hand, fingers equipped with thick yellow claws.

Kenyatta was about to let go of the sword or risk being sliced to shreds, when Kita leapt at the hunter and kicked it in the chest with both feet.

It staggered back a step, just as another cloud of sand hit it mostly in the legs.

"Afreetuminos," Malimokuru bellowed, and this time the sand ignited with blue flames.

Gray skin blistered and burned. The hunter let out deafening scream and threw itself aside, right into the path of a charging Grizzled Bear on its other side. The guide let out a mighty roar and swung his axe.

Kenyatta thought the fight was ended. To his disbelief, however, the beast had enough presence of mind to snap its hand down and slap the flat of the axe blade. The hit caused the axe to miss its ribs, though it still bit into the hunter's hip.

The injury wasn't mortal, but it was enough. The monster's scream was half agony half rage. It backhanded Grizzled Bear across the head, and the big man buckled sideways on his way to the ground for the second time.

Kita regained his staff and moved in to attack. The beast snapped its spear up, to the left, then stabbed straight at Kita's face. He barely avoided being run through, but it cost him. The hunter snapped its elbow out with enough force to break every bone in Kita's face. At the last moment, Kita managed to turn his head with the blow. The grazing impact still lifted him off the ground in a spinning fall.

Kenyatta charged with what little strength remained to him, but he knew he wouldn't get there in time. The hunter stood over the barely conscious Kita and raised its spear.

A sudden loud hiss sounded from just above the hunter's head, and a patch of leaves shuffled. The thick tree branch bowed under the weight of Nyaka, who crept out of concealment. She hissed again, green eyes glowing with menace.

Kenyatta could only watch as the hunter turned its head to look at the dog-sized animal. Nyaka flicked her forked tongue in and out of her wide maw, then hissed again.

The hunter swung its spear at her with such sudden speed

that Kenyatta was sure she'd be cleaved in half. But Nyaka proved to be just as fast. She sprang from the branch at the same time the hunter swung its spear. Her sharp little teeth clamped down on the hunter's arm.

The hunter grunted as Nyaka bit down harder and held on until it swatted her with one of those large hands.

A high-pitched yelp was the last thing Kenyatta heard from her as she crashed through the brush. Without so much as a look at the beaten group, the hunter turned and leapt away.

Kenyatta watched its retreat in disbelief. Green blood dripping from what should have been grievous wounds, it leapt and grabbed hold of a branch a dozen feet above. Blood seeped between the fingers of one hand pressed to its side, but it pulled itself up and onto the branch with its other hand.

"How in the five hells dis ting still have that much strength?" Without thinking about it, Kenyatta wiped away blood trickling down his chin and winced.

The hunter swung itself onto another branch and looked down on him. High above the ground, the hunter's piercing gaze settled over Kenyatta. Their eyes locked for a heartbeat before it disappeared into the trees.

30

Surviving the fight with the hunter creature had been no small bit of luck. They might have injured it, but not mortally. It had chosen to withdraw rather than having been beaten. With that in mind, the group moved through the dank swamp with fresh urgency.

Kenyatta scanned the perpetually dim swamp. He hoped they would be free of it soon. The mosquitoes were a constant annoyance, the humidity oppressive, and the new occurrence of the cicadas' relentless droning made him wonder if he was capable of hearing anything else. Even little Nyaka seemed determined to be free of the dangers and hardships of her home. Lethal she may be, but her survival in this deadly swamp without her mother was unlikely.

For most of the day they pressed on, stopping only for a brief rest or to relieve themselves before continuing. There had been no further sign of the hunter, but the four travelers took little comfort in that.

Then there was the oppressive feeling Kenyatta couldn't shake. It had come not long after the fight with the hunter. The others felt it, too. A palpable sense of evil that crept along the trees, the vines, the murky water. It lingered everywhere; intangible yet undeniably present.

No one needed to speak the thought they all shared: If they didn't make it out of the Mord soon, they never would.

Kenyatta noticed Malimokuru's blank stare. Ever since he'd found her under the log, the nature reader occasionally reached out to her for guidance. The little blue animal had become their guide, despite Grizzled Bear's protests.

"What's it like?" Kenyatta nodded at Nyaka. "Tryin' to talk to her?"

"Same as any other animal," Malimokuru said. "Like a series of feelings and impressions. Some nearly impossible to follow, such as with small birds or rodents. Predators are easier. When ya hunt for your food, you gotta think in a more calculating way. Planning and strategy."

Grizzled Bear shook his head.

"Keep shakin' that round dome of yours all ya want, big man." Malimokuru squatted in front of Nyaka and gave her a hunk of dried meat. "We're outta dis Gods forsaken pit soon enough. You'll see."

"Yer little friend tell you that?" Grizzled Bear asked. "Don't know why you hired me if yer gonna follow some animal."

"In fact, she did tell me," Malimokuru said. "I'm not doubtin' your skills, friend. But she know dis place, and can smell from a long way off."

"What's that matter?" Bear asked.

"Fresh air," Malimokuru replied. "She can smell the direction the fresh air come from."

Her little forked tongue flicking in and out, Nyaka pushed ahead, with Kenyatta close behind. Malimokuru was next, followed by Bear and Kita. Despite Bear's grumbling, even he couldn't deny that the swamp steadily grew easier to navigate, and hints of fresh air began to pierce the thick humidity.

Kenyatta half turned to look back at the procession. Kita's

wary gaze often swept the branches overhead as well. Like everyone else, he sported his own set of bruises and scrapes.

Most disturbing was that the hunter wasn't a demon, and hadn't been inhabited by a demonic presence, either. The gene in Kenyatta and Kita hadn't activated. It was just some kind of beast that liked to hunt and kill.

Then there was that evil presence. The more time that passed, the more Kenyatta suspected the presence—whatever it might be —was following them.

"This is great," Kita said when Nyaka led them to the end of what little solid path was left.

"Well look there." Grizzled Bear put his fists on his hips. "Looks like we got solid ground over there. Only gotta cross through what looks like about thirty or forty feet of water to get to it. Water topped with a nice coat of algae, just to make it more interestin'."

The guide's words were true. The pond standing between them and solid ground on the other side looked like a green carpet, so solid was the layer of algae over it.

"I'm not wading in that," Grizzled Bear said. "Could be any manner crocs 'n' critters swimmin' around in that soup. And crupers can swim. I got no desire to tangle with one of them things in there."

"If a cruper's in the water," Kita said, "we'll see or hear it coming. The crocs are what concern me."

Kenyatta picked up a hand sized rock and tossed it into the water a few dozen feet to the side. The rock plunged in and sank, but the water remained otherwise undisturbed. "Whatever we're gonna do, do it fast." He looked over his shoulder. "That thing might still be huntin' us, and something else is out there I don't want to tangle with, either."

"So we hop in that and risk being eaten alive," Bear said.

"Or double back and risk something else catching us," Kenyatta countered.

"If you'd have let me lead the way like you hired me—" Grizzled Bear began.

"No time for this," Malimokuru interrupted. He looked down at Nyaka, and with a look that seemed far too comprehending, the little blue animal waded into the water and started swimming.

Malimokuru gingerly dipped his leg in the water and stepped in. Muttering under every step, he slowly waded after their swimming guide in the waist-deep water.

Kenyatta eased himself in behind the nature reader, and a grumbling Grizzled Bear waded in after him. Kita brought up the rear, keeping a constant watch at their backs.

The party carefully crept through the waist-deep water, trying to disturb it as little as possible. Eyes moving in all directions, Kenyatta continually scanned the surroundings, looking for so much as a ripple in the unbroken green carpet.

At the front of the procession, Nyaka continued to paddle along, keeping her head above water. Still young, the little blue animal's strokes were short and labored, but still she made her way.

Malimokuru was the first to break the silence. "Move as quickly as you can without splashing too much," he said, his tone quiet and ominous.

"Ah, fer the love of the doggone Gods," Grizzled Bear swore. "What now?"

"I don't know," Malimokuru replied. "But I do know that you won't like the answer to that question. Something's here, man. And I can't connect with it."

"Another one o' them full grown things?" Bear nodded in Nyaka's direction. "Or maybe a cruper?"

Kenyatta didn't miss the hopeful tone in the man's voice at the latter possibility. He found himself hoping the same.

"I wish," Malimokuru said. "Nah, man. Whatever it is, I don't like it. I *really* don't like it."

Grizzled Bear cast his nervous gaze about. "Damn. How many more hungry critters we gotta deal with?"

"It's not hungry, man," Malimokuru said.

That got Kenyatta's attention and he looked at the nature reader. Having strapped his sand pouches across his back, Malimokuru carefully slid the strap over his shoulder, bringing one of the pouches within easy reach.

Kenyatta slowly drew his sword, the sound of steel sliding across metal piercing the quiet of the swamp.

"Ken?" Kita asked. "Something I should know?"

When Kenyatta turned to answer, his blood froze.

Several paces behind Kita, tentacles emerged from the water. They waved in the air as if tasting it.

As Kenyatta's wide-eyed expression, Kita turned and swore.

The waving tentacles continued to rise until the solid mass they were attached to came into view. A curved mass the color of dark brown mud continued to rise out of the murky water, tentacles waving atop it.

All desire to not disturb the water forgotten, Kita half splashed half ran as he tried to get away from what was surely nothing friendly.

The sound caused Malimokuru and Grizzled Bear to turn as well, and both men's eyes widened with horror.

"What the hell dat ting is?" Malimokuru asked.

"A damned Mord special," Grizzled Bear answered. "A friggin' murgolyn!"

"A what?" Kenyatta asked.

"You got mud in yer ears, feller? Murgolyn. Native to swamps. Nasty things."

"Surely not," Kita said, looking over his shoulder in time to see a crocodile head emerge from the slimy water. Its jaws trembled as they opened, then it let out a deep raspy call, and snapped them shut.

At the head of the group, Nyaka whimpered and swam harder.

"If ever yer followin' yer little monster's lead," Grizzled Bear said, "now's the time!"

They half splashed half hopped away from the emerging murgolyn as it rose to its full height, some six feet tall. It spread its heavily muscled arms and arched its back, snapping its jaws again. The tentacles on its back writhed in the air as if in search of something to grab.

"Don't let it scratch you," Grizzled Bear yelled. "You let them webbed hands get a hold of you, it'll scratch you with its nails and you'll be dead in minutes."

"Of course," Kita muttered. The beast was nearly on him already. He stopped and turned, staff gripped on one end. "Obviously it wouldn't be much of a threat without poison-tipped nails." He flicked his staff left and right, then rolled his wrist, making the other end of the staff spin in a circle in front of the beast.

The murgolyn swiped at the annoyance, but Kita was fast. He pulled it in, then thrust straight out, careful to avoid those powerful jaws that would surely snap his staff to splinters.

Kenyatta made his way to Kita's side, sword at the ready. He eyed its long powerful arms equipped with large four-fingered hands that could easily grip his head. He specifically noted the poison-tipped nails on those fingers, and the reach of those arms.

"Only if you have to," Kita said, reading his mind.

Grizzled Bear appeared on Kita's other side, and the trio fanned out, Bear moving left and Kenyatta moving right. Malimokuru moved in beside Kita, hand gripping his pouch.

"Keep gradually movin' back and keep the end of yer staff buzzin' in its face," Grizzled Bear said. "It don't see too well out of the water and is easily confused."

Kita followed the guide's instructions and kept his staff moving, all the while steadily retreating.

Behind them, Nyaka had reached solid ground. She barked and hissed from the edge of the water, but remained on land.

"Little blue critter definitely ain't stupid," Bear remarked.

The murgolyn took a backhanded swipe at Kenyatta, who splashed water everywhere as he moved out of reach. He countered with a quick swipe of his sword, dealing the monster a superficial cut along its arm. The murgolyn responded by lunging in and snapping its crocodile jaws at his face.

Kenyatta dove aside at the same time Kita thrust his staff into the side of its neck. The resulting flinch was all Kenyatta needed. He tucked in his knees and straightened to get his feet under him. The murgolyn turned in Kenyatta's direction as it spun to face Kita, providing the perfect opening. Kenyatta got his feet back on the ground and slashed the monster across the face.

The monster recoiled and fell back a step. Malimokuru wasted no time. He flicked a small handful of sand onto its face and torso, and barked the triggering command.

The granules flared, blistering and melting the beast's moist, slimy skin.

The murgolyn's jaws opened with a terrible screech. A roaring Grizzled Bear moved in, body half turned, and brought his axe around with a mighty swing.

The blade bit deep, and he yanked with all his strength to free the weapon and retreat before it could slash him with its poisonous nails.

With the hulking beast preoccupied with its many injuries, the four men continued their gradual retreat until they finally reached land. One by one they climbed out and took defensive positions while the next person made his way.

They murgolyn swung its huge arms and slapped at the water in a fit of rage and burning pain. The four men watched until it abruptly threw itself into the water. With a great splash, it submerged, leaving algae and water plants bobbing in the rippling water in its wake.

Soaked head to toe and covered in algae, the four men backed away, heaving from the effort of running through water.

"How 'bout we get moving before it comes after us," Kita said, staff pointed toward the edge of the water.

"Nah. We're too much trouble," Grizzled Bear replied. "Though I ain't arguin' with you fer wantin' to get out of this five hells cursed swamp, but murgolyns don't usually fight to the death unless they's near to starving."

"All the same," Kenyatta said.

"Like I said, I ain't arguin'."

Their continued trek moved at a faster pace now, everyone—including Nyaka—sharing the silent desire to be out of the Mord as soon as possible.

The cicadas continued their relentless song while frogs, toads, and strange-sounding birds fought to be heard above the constant rattling sound.

"You feel it, don't you?" Malimokuru yelled over the cacophony.

Kenyatta didn't look back at the nature reader. He didn't want to take his attention from the surroundings for an instant. "Yeah, man. Been feelin' it on and off since we been in this Gods forsaken swamp."

The nature reader was referring to the evil presence, of course. The wary expression of every member of the group said that they felt it.

"I don't think it follow us out," Malimokuru continued. "It's been receding for a while, now."

"Yeah, man. Don't make me feel any better, though." Kenyatta kept his eyes moving, scanning the ground, nearby ponds, trees and vines. "If I'm hunting something, I make a move before my prey leave my domain."

Behind them, Grizzled Bear grumbled. "If that hunter or another murgolyn don't take us out, these hell-spawned bugs'll drive us insane with their noise!"

Malimokuru glanced back at the guide. Axe gripped firmly in both hands, the big man turned this way and that, teeth clenched against the incessant call of the cicadas.

"You think it's dem things we fight before?" Malimokuru asked.

Kenyatta shook his head, but said no more.

"This whole swamp is evil," Kita said from further back.

"Unpleasant though it is," Malimokuru replied, "it's not the swamp that's evil. It's what's patrolling it."

Kita grimaced. "Patrolling?"

"Yeah, man. But it won't pursue us out."

"How do you know?"

"A hunch."

The cicadas abruptly fell silent. The calls of birds and frogs fell away, and life in the Mord came to a sudden halt. The group also stopped and collectively scanned the area.

"Feels like the whole swamp is holding its breath," Kita whispered.

A gradual darkness settled over the area.

Grizzled Bear swore and looked around, then up. The tree branches overhead began to look like long clawed fingers reaching down for them. The path behind them darkened, and the way ahead stretched away as if retreating.

The guide held his axe in a white-knuckled grip. "Are my eyes tricking me?"

"If they are," Kita replied, "then it's contagious."

"Run," Malimokuru yelled. "Run!"

As if she understood the nature reader's words, Nyaka bounded ahead, the four humans close on her heels. She hopped over fallen trees and giant roots, bounded over patches of mud and stagnant water. She looked back and let out a whimper.

"Do I even want to know what she sees?" Kita asked.

"Look if ya want," Malimokuru said. The old nature reader sprinted right past Grizzled Bear and Kenyatta.

Darkness crept around the fleeing group, like long, crooked fingers of death reaching to strangle them.

Kenyatta stole a glance over his shoulder, and his heart thumped in his chest. Black as pitch, darkness pursued them like a living thing. Tendrils reached out to envelope everything it passed in a lightless void.

Malimokuru shouted something over his shoulder, but no sound came from his mouth. Kenyatta responded, or tried to, for no sound came.

The nature reader pointed past the sprinting Nyaka, where the last slivers of daylight streaked through the trees. The light was like a beacon that was both within reach and a world away.

Kenyatta tried to shout encouragement, to press forward, but his voice failed. What was happening? They ran for the light, the dark tendrils of pursing evil licking at their heels.

Grizzled Bear faltered, but Kita hoisted the big man under the arm and kept him running. The guide continued to struggle, then Kita began to slow. Then Malimokuru stumbled, and it looked as if he would stop running altogether.

Kenyatta barely had an instant to wonder what was affecting them when despair punched into his chest and squeezed his heart. He forced himself to keep moving, but the overwhelming hopelessness threatened to swallow him. His legs were lead, and all he wanted in that moment was to stop running and surrender to his fate. It wouldn't be so bad. Just a gentle surrender to oblivion. It couldn't be stopped, he couldn't avoid this fate. Better to surrender and let it end.

Kenyatta's face tightened. *Get out of my mind.* He forced one foot in front of the other, forced himself to keep moving. Though he resisted the incursion in his mind, he realized it didn't need to dominate him, only slow him down. He looked to his friends to see them enduring the same struggle as the black tendrils encircled them all. Ears pinned back against her head, Nyaka crouched beside Malimokuru, teeth bared in a soundless bark.

Kita swung his staff, but the effort was clumsy and ill coordinated. Kenyatta tried to lift his sword but it felt as though he did so underwater. Malimokuru clenched his eyes shut, his hand tucked in one of his pouches. The old man gasped and dropped to one knee. He threw his head back, mouth agape in a soundless scream, and whipped his hand out of the pouch.

White sand sprayed around them and lit in a blinding flare. Kenyatta cried out and squinted his eyes shut against the painful flash of light. After a few heartbeats, he opened them and blinked in the realization that he'd heard himself again. He looked at the others and saw them similarly squinting.

Doubled over on hands and knees, Kita heaved to catch his breath. "It's gone," he gasped. He lifted his head to look down the trail and his eyes widened. "No, not gone, waiting."

The beleaguered men looked back to see that the blackness indeed hadn't fled, but was merely waiting out the already dimming light.

"No way I'm going through that again," Kita said. "Get moving." He grabbed Grizzled Bear under the arm again and helped him to his feet. "Let's go."

Malimokuru placed a hand on his knee and pushed himself up. With a deep breath, he leaned forward into a jog toward the light penetrating the wall of vegetation. It was so close.

With one last glance back, Kenyatta similarly forced himself up and started moving. The flaring light faded and the blackness crept forward again.

They ran on—Bear half running half stumbling, Nyaka stretched out in a full run, leaping and skidding over and under roots and vines. Kita vaulted a fallen tree, then stopped and waited for Grizzled Bear to climb over. "Come on come on, big man. We're almost there."

"Moving ... as fast ... as I can." Bear looked over his shoulder and gritted his teeth. "Thing'll catch us all if you wait on me. Just go. Maybe I'll slow it down ..."

"Shut up with the heroics and get moving. You can sacrifice by cutting back on the beer and sandwiches when we get outta here."

Despite the dire situation, Grizzled Bear huffed a bit of laughter.

Kenyatta stayed at the rear, his hand firmly clenched on his sword. He doubted it would be of any use against the insubstantial enemy, but it was a small comfort.

The light was no more than a dozen strides away when despair hit them again.

Kita growled against it, slammed the butt of his staff into the ground, and pushed himself forward.

Grizzled Bear shook his head. "Argh. Keep your arse moving!"

Kenyatta didn't know if he was talking to the rest of the group or himself, but heeded the words anyway.

Their steps grew heavier, their pace gradually slowing. Black tendrils crept around them once again, while sunlight seeped tauntingly through the trees ahead.

The only member of the party unaffected, Nyaka hissed and barked at the encroaching blackness. She barked at Malimokuru and the rest of them. She snapped her jaws and bared her teeth.

She ran behind Grizzled Bear, lowered her head, and rammed into his backside. The big man stumbled forward, arms flailing as he fought not to fall face-first into the mushy earth.

"Wuhuhoa!" Bear crashed into the low growth and rolled on his side.

Sunlight blasted in through the new gap, and flooded the area.

The rage and frustration of whatever pursued them nearly paralyzed Kenyatta when it exploded into his mind. But with the warm light of the sun upon his face, it was easier to force the evil presence away.

Enveloped in warm glowing sunlight, the remaining trio dragged themselves to their feet and stumbled their way forward.

The black tendrils still pursued them, despite the burning sun. The pit of darkness continued its advance.

Though the sunlight dimmed the dark presence in his mind, Kenyatta still felt the frustration of the evil entity. It wouldn't be robbed of its prize.

But its prize would not be collected this day. The three remaining companions threw themselves through the gap and into the blessed sunlight.

Kenyatta and Kita rolled to their feet, grabbed Malimokuru and the still prone Grizzled Bear, and dragged them on. A few dozen feet into the open air they stopped and fell on their backs, heaving and exhausted, but alive.

The companions looked back to see the simmering rage of blackness swirling just inside the swamp, safely away from the burning sunlight. Though it had no eyes, they felt its murderous glare.

"That thing will be waiting for us if we ever go back in there," Kita said. He gave his head a shake. "Not that I ever intend to. I'd travel halfway 'round the world before going back in there."

"Let's move," Kenyatta said. "I don't want to find out if it can come after us when night falls."

"Not likely," Malimokuru said. "It make its home there. We're safe as long as we don't go back in."

"I'm agreeing with yer friend, there. I ain't ever goin' back in there, either." Grizzled Bear took a deep breath to settle himself, then pulled out his map. He unfolded it and tapped a sausage-like finger at a marker. "We're in Tierra Divide, right here. All we have to do is head west and we'll reach Katlan. It's not the biggest town, but we can re-supply, get a couple nights' rest and some horses. Then we make Phoenix in three days."

Noticing the silence, Grizzled Bear looked up. "What?"

"We?" Kita asked.

Bear looked at the three amused faces. Even Nyaka seemed to

give him a quizzical look. "Bah, you'd never make it without me. Or at least you'd take twice as long to get there."

Kenyatta hardly thought that traveling west across mostly flat plains was particularly difficult, but the man *had* grown on them all. Apparently, the feeling was mutual. "No problem," he said. "Didn't want you to feel obligated, is all."

"Not gonna have yer deaths on my conscience," Bear grumbled, ignoring the last comment. "Let's get moving. I know an outcropping that'll take the rest of the day to get to, but it'll provide shelter."

Though they were weary and beaten, no one was willing to camp so near the Mord, no matter the nature reader's reassurances. Despite his own words, Malimokuru was just as eager to move on.

They trekked across the flat, open plain, aware that the sun might beat them to the western horizon before they reached shelter.

Kita pointed ahead. "That your outcropping?"

They peered into the final moments of daylight as the last rays of the sun dipped below the horizon.

"Yup," Grizzled Bear said. "'Bout another hour or so and we should make it ..." he trailed off when a howl sounded in the distance. An answer came a moment later, then a third. He swore after the fourth one.

"For the love of the Gods," Malimokuru said, exasperated. "Will we get no peace?"

Another howl answered, this one closer.

Grizzled Bear swore again. "Wolves."

31

S leep. *Sleep on the fringes of wakefulness. So much pain. So much confusion. How many years had it been? How much destruction had they wrought? How much disease and famine, extinction and chaos had they caused?*

Grogginess settled in, muddling all thoughts but one: Humans. The enduring virus for which there existed a cure, yet none had utilized. So fragile they were. How had they endured for so long? How had they not destroyed themselves ages ago?

It had almost happened. The meeting of the Four had been for that very purpose: to eradicate the virus, cleanse the earth. But the decision had been unexpected, and mercy was shown to the merciless.

But they were not all so cruel. There was good in them. That goodness saved humans from extinction, though they did not know it. They could be taught. They could learn again what it was to live in harmony with the earth instead of striving to dominate it.

Burning pain and clouded thoughts. Terrible heat burned those last thoughts away until only one thought remained. Humans. The virus. The disease. A disease so fragile it could be eliminated by fire, water, or the splitting of the earth beneath them.

Endless suffering and pain they had caused for countless ages. Their time was at an end. Their fate had arrived. And the wrath of the heavens and the hells would fall upon them.

32

S eung leaned against the rail of *Wave Dancer* and gazed out at the infinite sparkling ocean. Two days into their voyage saw no more stress than the repairing of a floorboard belowdecks.

"Good day to you, lady," greeted a crew member carrying a large coil of rigging as he made his way past.

"And you," Seung replied.

She watched the sailor on his way aft. As with every other member of the crew, he offered a formal greeting to Tinnoviel, a conservative one to Alurien, and smiled fondly at Nuviel. Tikena received a disapproving scowl, like that of an adult who would have words for the parent of such a rude child. Seung chuckled under her breath at that.

Then there was Yurin. The apprentice was never unkind, but she emitted a powerful aura that one wouldn't describe as approachable. And then there were those brown, yellow-ringed eyes. The man cleared his throat and offered a nervous smile, giving Yurin a wide berth. The Daunya Apprentice acknowledged him with a barely perceptible nod.

Alurien MerTana moved toward her, his gait smooth and

sure. "Have you received any more of the contact you described to the Lady Seiyun, Kiluriel Sen'Mora?"

The ranger had begun to warm to her a bit as time progressed, even initiating conversation from time to time. She found him serious but not without a kind heart. Within his cowl, she could still make out the two solid blue stripes as wide as a thumb flowing from beneath his eyes to meet at the tip of his chin. The equally spaced white dots within each stripe drew the eye from within the shadow of the cowl.

Seung shook her head. "No. I can't say that I'm not glad, either. The experience is ... overwhelming."

"I see," came the response.

"May I ask what your markings symbolize?" she asked.

Facing her on the gently rocking ship, Alurien projected a presence that was as intimidating as it was stoic. For a while he did not speak, merely stared at her. Seung turned back to the water, figuring he had chosen not to answer.

"When an Elden comes of age," Alurien finally said, "and completes the Forging, we receive the markings of Oberon and Boraka. The Elden believe that a true warrior brings about balance, sometimes through destruction. This is why the hands of both Oberon and Boraka touch the heart of the warrior, and Elden warriors pray to both."

Seung turned back to regard him. "Are the Elden people not of Yathienel?"

"Just as there are different humans who walk upon the world, so too are there elves, and others. We are not as populous as the rapidly procreating human race, but there are different cultures of elves around the world. You will come to know this."

Seung thought about that. "Were you visiting Yathienel?" As soon as she asked the question, she knew it was wrong. She thought about how well Alurien and Tinnoviel complimented each other's movements in their battle with the shaggy monsters, days ago. "Perhaps you live there? I can't imagine your people sending you for the sole purpose of escorting me."

The ranger looked amused. "You are partially right. It is elven custom that when two kingdoms wish to strengthen ties with one another, they send an orphan child. Among our people, an orphan is cared for by all. My parents were killed when I was but a year of age. The queen of the Elden had me brought to Yathienel, where I was welcomed by Lady Seiyun. It is a great gesture for one elven nation to send an orphan child into the care of another. An act of trust."

"Were you raised in the palace?" Seung asked, intrigued.

"No," was all the elf said in response.

There was silence for a while, both Seung and Alurien MerTana gazing at the steadily growing waves. Every time a swell grew larger than a ripple, Seung held her breath.

The sun cast its orange glow on the sky as it made its western descent. Seung leaned over the rail to enjoy the mist on her face.

"Do you dislike humans?" The words came unbidden, and Seung was surprised to realize that she actually cared. She felt the beginnings of a kinship with her companions that she hoped was reciprocated. She'd even come to think of Tikena as more of a troublesome little sister than an actual enemy.

For the first time since she'd met the solemn ranger, he offered a hint of a smile. "Dislike? No. Distrust, yes." There was no insult in his tone, just a simple matter-of-fact response. "I have lived for more years than any human can claim, and have seen their triumphs and failures. Every people has them, but none so dangerous. The Lady Seiyun says that ours is a great failure in that we stepped into the shadows and allowed the world to wither around us while hiding in our protected little gardens. All children must be guided, lest the parents fail and the children grow wild."

"Is that what humans are to you? Children?"

"To all the other races of the world, they are. Humans were

the last born upon the earth." Alurien went silent for a moment. "What is interesting, is that all of the Seven hold humans, but each holds them closer at any given time. Unlike the Elfinestraya, or the Elden, who a certain one or two of The Seven hold depending on their station in life, every human is held closely by one of the Seven at any given time depending on how their spirit shifts. It has been an enduring mystery to us. Perhaps it is the shorter lifespan that leads humans to such chaotic lives. None know for sure."

Seeing her confusion, he elaborated. "Imagine Amayilah holds a human in childhood. That child may decide to begin walking the path of the warrior, and so Boraka will hold her closest. Once the child reaches the beginnings of adulthood, she may then decide to walk the path of a monk, and so Oberon will hold her. As humans are so apt to change their lives, so too does their affinity with each of the Daunyans change. And through it all, most humans are unaware of it, or that the Daunyans exist at all. Their religious dogma has ... muddled things."

Seung watched the elf as he spoke, fascinated by the outside perspective. "And what of a *haloren*, such as myself?"

Those deep green eyes bore straight into her. "An even deeper mystery. Your type are rare, as it is a difficult life. Most *halorens* choose to live away from elves, yet cannot remain in any one human civilization for long, as they outlive humans and find living among full-blooded elves undesirable. Usually, they live solitary lives, away from both."

He turned back at the ocean. "But you are not truly *haloren*, are you? Your mother was a full-blooded elf, and your father was *haloren*, if I am correct."

Seung nodded.

"That makes you more elf than human. From the last ten years to the next ten, you will begin to see the distinction in your bloodline. A *haloren* begins life looking more human than elf, but with slightly different features most humans cannot place.

Within the decade of their thirtieth year of life, the balance begins to shift, and a *haloren* starts to show more of their elven heritage. That is when the difficulties arise."

"You know a lot about this," Seung said.

Without turning his gaze from the now choppy waters, the ranger nodded. "My older brother is *haloren*." There was no mistaking the pain in his voice.

Seung opened her mouth several times to respond, but found no words. She turned back to the ocean.

The sea grew more turbulent as the day waned, and by nightfall, the wind had picked up, blowing a storm directly over the ship. *Wave Dancer* rocked with the impact of each ripple.

"The trial by sea begins."

Seung flinched before she could stop herself. Yurin Kei Daunyana's soft, silky voice practically flowed into her ear. The elven woman had moved behind them without her noticing.

Seung swallowed the desire to ask how long the apprentice had been standing there. She turned to see those haunting eyes staring from within her gray cowl.

"Tinnoviel Nai SaunyaLi would speak with you, Kiluriel Sen'Mora."

With that, Yurin turned away, gliding between two sailors who gave her twice the space she needed. They stared after her, mystified.

"That was formal," Seung remarked.

"That is her way," Alurien replied.

SEUNG ROSE from the cross-legged position she'd been sitting in for the past few hours. Her meeting with Tinnoviel had been more a session of group prayer meditation than conversation.

Tinnoviel had meditated beside her and taught her to pray to Oberon, the Daunya of Balance to whom all elven warriors prayed. She wondered if it was Oberon she'd prayed to all these years and hadn't known it.

Seung looked about the cabin, but the Daunya Warrior was gone. Haunting sounds penetrated the room, but the cabin door reduced them to a muffled—but still eerie—moan. They must have reached the Siren Straight.

After listening at the door, Seung took a deep breath and pulled it open. A wall of rain crashed into her. She leaned against the pounding spray as she pushed her way out and closed the door.

The rain was a beast, punishing *Wave Dancer* and her crew. At the helm, the captain clutched the wheel while shouting orders barely audible over the screeching voices of the sirens. The terrible song brought Seung to her knees as soon as it reached her ears. She felt the malevolence, sensed it trying to drive her insane. The captain had warned them, but he'd only understood part of it. The sirens used their song to entice males overboard or drive the stronger ones insane, as the captain had said. Females, however, were immune to the allure, so the magical voices of the sirens sought to shatter her mind.

Seung managed to cobble together enough of her thoughts to mentally thank Tinnoviel for teaching her the prayer. She then offered a silent prayer of thanks to the Oberon. As soon as she thanked the Daunyan, she felt herself wrapped within the warmth of His balancing hand. With the terrible song dulled, Seung braced herself against the wall of the cabin and stood.

Crewmen ran to and fro, manning the sails, tightening rigging here and loosening it there while rain pounded them like the fist of nature itself. A crew member ran past, and Seung noticed a clump of wax wedged in his ear.

The ship listed toward the starboard side, throwing some of the crew to the deck. They scrambled to their feet and grabbed any handhold they could find.

Fear and determination shone in their eyes, but the sirens

had done their work on some of these men. They wore haunted looks and mostly wandered about the deck, absently performing meaningless duties or simply moving toward the rails. One crewman grabbed a fellow sailor by the shoulders and gave him a violent shake, screaming in his face. The man blinked several times, then a look of fear and recognition crossed his features.

A wave crashed over the starboard side, righting the ship, but drenching the already soaked crew. Seung had been making her way toward the captain, but stopped to hold on to a nearby railing when her feet nearly slid from beneath her.

The chill night wind cut through her soaked garments and wrapped around her body in an icy caress. She sucked in her breath, forcing her mind away from the cold, and searched for the other elves who were similarly scattered across the deck. Tinnoviel was at the captain's side, and her sharp hearing afforded her some of the conversation.

"What can we do to help?" the Daunya Warrior asked, shouting to be heard over the raging storm and crashing waves. "We are able-bodied and ready to assist!"

"You can retreat to your cabins, sir," the captain yelled back. "You're not sailors, and know not the workings of a ship. Leave it to me and my crew!"

With a final nod, Tinnoviel left the man. He gathered the others and Seung, and led them toward the cabin; all but Yurin, she noticed. The Daunya Apprentice stood inconspicuously away from everyone else, eyes closed. No matter how violently the ship tipped and bucked, she never lost her footing. Seung couldn't believe her eyes as she watched the woman, standing tall and serene as though asleep on her feet, like a statue bolted to the deck.

Another wave crashed over the rails and swept a screaming sailor over the side. Several of the crew hollered in dismay as they ran to the side and looked over. Her breath caught in her throat as she watched, hoping the man might have grabbed hold of the rail and could be pulled back aboard.

She deflated when the men turned away from the rail and somberly continued their work, sliding about as they worked to obey the captain's orders.

"Port side!" the captain shouted. "Tighten the cables to the clew or they'll rip out and slap you overboard! Heng! Secure the rigging!"

Tinnoviel appeared out of the dark rainy night and pulled Seung inside the cabin. As he shut the door, she turned to see the two younger elves huddled against the far wall, soaked and shaking. Even Tikena was subdued and—Seung couldn't help but smirk inwardly—a bit green in the face.

"Are we going to leave her out there?" Seung asked Tinnoviel.

"Yurin will be fine. She buffers the song of the sirens so that the crew may work more effectively. That wax in their ears may help them from the enticement or insanity, but it would still penetrate enough to distract them and do its work in time."

Through the night, the brave crew of *Wave Dancer* battled the Siren Strait and the denizens of its namesake. And as the sailors tirelessly manned the ship, so, too, did Yurin Kei Daunyana hold her vigil against the port side of the fore cabin. A few of the crew cast her confused looks, but had little time to consider her presence.

In the silence belowdecks, Seung thought of her beloved companion, Swiftspirit. She had been heartbroken to leave him in the woods, outside Pyon city, but Nuviel had assured her that her companion would be in good company with the others, and that the animals would await their return. Seung had hesitantly agreed. As she listened to the raging storm outside and felt the ship rock back and forth against the turbulent waves, she felt relief to have spared her old friend this trial.

The ship bucked violently and tilted sideways. Everyone

scrabbled for a handhold as they slid toward the opposite wall. Then it righted itself and lifted at the fore.

Nuviel and Tikena crashed into the back wall in a tangle of arms and legs. Screams came from outside, followed by the sound of feet scrambling across the deck.

The song of the sirens raised in pitch, and Seung cringed at the intensity. "I'm going out there. I don't care what the captain says, they need us and I'm going to help."

She went for the door, expecting Tinnoviel to argue. To her surprise, he fell in step behind her. Nuviel and Tikena moved to stand, but the Tinnoviel held up a hand.

"You are too light, and would be blown away in the winds, *quyo,*" he said to them.

"You expect us to cower in here like frightened mice?" Tikena shot back, challenge in her high-pitched voice.

"I expect you to do as you are told," Tinnoviel replied. The younger elf bristled at the rebuke, and he softened. "There is a time to be brave, and a time to step aside. You would serve no purpose in being swept overboard. The wrath of nature is beyond any of us, Tikena Mojin. You will have your time, but for now, you remain here."

He nodded to Seung as Alurien MerTana joined them. Seung pointedly kept her gaze forward, not wanting to embarrass the two girls as she and the others swept out of the room.

The scene before them as they emerged from the cabin was one on the edge of disaster. The captain still manned the helm, but his pointedly stoic expression boded ill.

Tinnoviel and Alurien rushed to speak with the man, who gave them a startled look, his eyes taking in their features. Seung gasped and reached for her head. The violent winds had blown their cowls back.

After the initial shock, the captain frowned and vehemently waved them back to the cabin. After a moment of arguing, however, he relented. "Fine," he bellowed over the raging winds.

The storm had long since claimed his hat, and the few remaining strands of white hair whipped about his head. "You." he pointed at Alurien. "Man the helm."

The elven ranger was taken aback. "I not know how navigate ship," he argued in his broken and thick accented command of the Korean tongue.

"Just try and keep her straight till I get back." The captain beckoned a deckhand over; a boy in his mid-teens. "This here is Ro. He's watched me enough to know what to do, he's just not strong enough to do it yet. He'll guide you."

With a nod, Alurien took the wheel and steadied himself. The captain turned to Tinnoviel. "The ties are broken and the sails unfurled. It knocked two of my men overboard." Seung saw the hurt in the man's face, but there was no time to grieve. "We've been trying to get it back down, but the winds are too strong. No one can climb up there to unlatch it from the top of the main-mast." Tinnoviel turned away. "Hey!" Captain So exclaimed, guessing the elf's intent. "You can't climb the damn thing in this storm, you'll be swept over."

Ignoring him, Tinnoviel rushed up to Seung. "We must unlatch the sail from the top of the mainmast, and help the crew with the ropes." The wind whipped through his long black hair, revealing his pointed ears and sharp elven features. "I will deal with the mast. You must help the crew in whatever way you can."

Seung nodded and he bounded off. For a moment, she and the rest of the sailors stared as the elven warrior deftly climbed the tall mast. His cloak billowing in the violent wind, Tinnoviel scaled the mast as a hunting cat would a tree.

He grabbed hold of the first beam and swung atop it. Crouching, he held still as another gust rammed into the sail, causing the ship to lurch sideways.

The sirens continued their hideous song, and Seung saw several men go blank in the face. Most shook the effects off, but one man looked as though he was about to succumb. His nearest shipmate grabbed him by the shoulders and slapped him across the face. The afflicted crewman shuddered and blinked, then nodded his thanks.

In the same spot Seung had last seen her, Yurin Kei Daunyana continued her meditation, softening the effects of the siren's horrible song. How long could she combat those monsters beneath the waves?

Seung leapt over an overturned barrel, and maneuvered her way around the ship till she came upon two sailors hauling a thick rope around a giant metal ring. She grabbed hold and together they managed to get it coiled once again.

A blast of the sirens' song assaulted Seung's mind, and she stumbled. Were they aware of her resistance to them? How could they be? She looked out at the choppy waves, rain pelting her face, wind blowing her hair about. This had to stop. If it didn't, the storm would pull them under, and they would fall prey to the unseen monsters in the deep.

33

The elf had weathered many a storm in his life, but nothing like this. One hand holding on to the mainmast, the other tugging at the thick rope that connected the sail to the huge wooden beam, Tinnoviel used all his strength to keep the storm from carrying him off into the raging ocean below.

Something supernatural drove this storm, and the Tinnoviel wondered if it was the very thing they sought to confront. The Lady Seiyun and DaunyaSai had spoken privately with him about it. The Daunya Master had warned that he'd felt no evil from the nature of the being, but evil was present in it nonetheless. Those words led to more questions, but Tinnoviel had his own suspicions of what lay in wait for them.

Below, sailors moved about the ship, careful to stay within reach of a handhold as much as possible while concentrating on keeping the song of the sirens out of their minds. The wax balls in their ears combined with Yurin's efforts made all the difference, for this venture would have long been lost without both.

In the back of his mind, Tinnoviel considered that fact. The captain had said he'd sailed this straight several times before. Without someone with Yurin's abilities, that would be impossible.

Unless something was giving more weight to the power of the sirens this day.

He tugged at the rope with all his strength, but the sail could not be untied with one hand. The rope was soaked and firmly secured. He drew a dagger from its sheath on the side of his calf. Far below his perch, the captain shouted instructions. The man shielded his eyes and gazed up at Tinnoviel, a look of astonishment mixed with hope on his face.

Tinnoviel went to task, sawing at the thick wet rope. He'd cut halfway through the tough fibers when another gust smacked him and he lost his footing.

The elf's strength and reflexes saved him, as he put the dagger between his teeth and held on with both hands, legs dangling out behind him. The wind was relentless, and as his body stretched horizontally in the open air, all that kept the Tinnoviel from what would certainly be death beneath the surface of the raging ocean, was his iron grip.

His grip secured, Tinnoviel curled his body. He brought his legs in and wrapped them around the mast. He grabbed the dagger from his teeth, took a deep breath, and resumed his work.

SEUNG CLENCHED her jaw and pulled with all her strength. A sudden gust of wind had swept a crewman off his feet and over the rail. The only one nearby, Seung had thrown herself to the deck and grabbed his ankle. His momentum and weight slid them downward and had almost taken them both overboard.

Now she lay lengthwise atop the rail, left leg and arm curled around the bar, the screaming sailor dangling by his ankle in her right hand. Seung grunted and pulled, but the man was too heavy to lift with one arm. She concentrated on holding on to his ankle, hoping that someone had noticed them.

If not for the strain, she would have sighed in relief at hearing the cries of other sailors a heartbeat before many hands grabbed hold of her.

Seung jerked her head in the direction overboard as they pulled at her. "Get him!"

A short, stocky sailor looked over the rail and his eyes widened. He waved another crew mate over, and the taller man leaned over the rail next to Seung while the shorter one held on to him by the waist. Groaning, the tall sailor stretched over the rail, waggling his fingers to try to get a hold of the dangling man's other foot.

Seung leaned her head back and pulled with every ounce of strength left to her. She managed to lift the sailor just enough for the other man to grab hold of his ankle. Together, she and the crewman lifted him back aboard.

They'd barely gotten the man on deck, when another wave crashed against the side of the ship, punching into Seung and the other sailors and sending them sprawling and scrambling for a handhold. The wail of the sirens spiked.

Seung pulled herself to her feet and looked around. Like angry mouths of the ocean, waves opened wide and crashed shut as if to devour anything in their paths. One such wave rose before the ship, a giant maw opening wide enough to swallow *Wave Dancer*.

This is how it ends, Seung thought. The warrior from the village of Kyu stood before the massive surge, long black hair whipping about her face. If this was to be her end, she would face it squarely.

The sailors also saw the towering wall of water and dropped what they were doing to run and grab hold of anything sturdy.

It was pointless. Seung knew it, and so did they, but they had to cling to some form of hope. The surge reared high overhead and descended upon the ship. To their astonished relief, the wave crashed against some invisible force and shattered into salty rain over the confused crew. Seung couldn't believe what had just happened, but she guessed the source.

The sailors wasted no time contemplating their strange good fortune. With only a collective cry of relief, they resumed their posts.

Seung made her way across the deck and around to the front of the fore cabin. An exhausted Yurin Kei Daunyana leaned against the wall. Seung rushed to her side and helped the woman upright.

"I can hold the shield ... no longer," she breathed. "My strength has waned.

Seung looked over her shoulder. Although the wax in their ears helped to reduce the effect of the sirens' song, the crew were feeling it more.

The ship rocked to one side, throwing crewmen from their feet and sending them sliding across the deck. Seung looked up to see the sail, bulging from the wind, and high above it, she could just make out the figure of Tinnoviel. She wished she could help, but knew that she would only hinder him. Not that she could have climbed up there anyway.

The sail suddenly flapped away from the mast as the wind carried it away. Tinnoviel had succeeded.

"I'm fine," Yurin said. "Go help him."

Seung nodded and worked her way toward the mainmast, sometimes climbing, sometimes sliding downward as the ship rode the turbulent waters. She slid to a stop just as the turning pole swung in front of her, and grabbed the severed length of rope. Tinnoviel slid down the mast and together they managed to wrap it around the horizontal beam and tie it. Seung pointed at Yurin, still slumped against the cabin wall.

"The storm grows weaker," Tinnoviel said, and indeed, Seung realized the storm felt less fierce.

Tinnoviel rushed to the captain's side, and for a few moments, they stood in discussion.

Relieved of the helm, Alurien went to Yurin's side and helped her up. "The captain says we have survived the worst of the storm," the ranger said when they arrived. "We're nearly out of the sirens' reach. Even now, their poisonous song weakens." He jerked his chin at the sailors milling about. The song left them in a daze, but as it diminished, the men were better able to shake off the effects.

"He says the winds will continue for another hour, maybe two, but with the sail down, there should be no major problems." He swept Yurin in his arms and carried her belowdecks.

When the ranger left with Yurin, Tinnoviel went to speak again with the captain. A moment later, he returned with grim news. "He has lost three of his crew, and at least two more are struggling with lingering effects from the sirens."

"Then we must work in their stead," Seung replied, and he nodded.

For the rest of the night, Seung, Tinnoviel, and Alurien MerTana worked with the crew, performing any tasks assigned to them. By the time the winds died down and the ocean calmed, the sun had risen and burned away enough clouds to shine its warmth onto the ship and its battered crew.

Tinnoviel shaded his eyes as he looked to the north and east. Seung thought she would never again be as happy to see dawn as she was this day. The horrific song of the sirens finally ended, and the ship traveled upon calm waters. Their surroundings had the tinge of blue that came with dawn, and Seung wanted nothing more than to witness the sun rise to its zenith. It was at that moment exhaustion set in.

Tinnoviel and Alurien moved beside her, the Daunya Warrior putting his arm around her shoulder with a half-smile. "Well done."

Seung smiled back. "To all of us."

Captain So joined the trio, another cap upon his spotted wispy-haired head. He studied each of them while trying not to appear doing so. No doubt he was trying to decide if his eyes had played tricks on him during the storm when the elves' features had been revealed. Neither Seung nor her two companions were about to lower their cowls and offer confirmation.

"You did good last night," So said with an appreciative grin, though his tone was sober. "We surely would've been lost had the three of you not helped."

"The least we could do," Seung said, Tinnoviel nodding as she spoke. "You lost three of your crew."

A shadow of grief colored the captain's stoic expression. "Comes with the territory. Every man aboard my ship knows what it means to sail the seas. They'd rather die at sea than on the dirt." He bowed again and left to survey the damage and see to repairs, entrusting the *Wave Dancer* to his first mate. "Get some rest," he called over his shoulder. "We reach land at midday."

As if Captain So's words had brought it, fatigue attacked in earnest, and Seung found her eyelids growing heavy. When she looked at Tinnoviel and even the stoic Elden ranger, exhaustion colored their features as well.

They reached the cabin just as eight members of the crew slid oars out the side of the ship—four on each side—and started to row. They found Yurin sitting erect with her back against the wall. Seung had seen elves take the reverie enough times to know what it looked like. The apprentice was completely spent, for she rested in full sleep.

Seung felt a pang of regret that the apprentice would go unthanked for keeping the ship afloat and protecting the minds of the crew, but there was nothing to be done about it.

In the far corner of the cabin, Tikena and Nuviel talked amongst themselves, the former having returned to her normal color. "Have fun?" She sneered at Seung.

"Yes," Seung replied casually as she knelt to untie her bedroll. "You should have been there."

She slipped into the covers, far too exhausted to care that she

—and apparently Yurin—were the only ones in the room who would actually sleep.

Seung smiled to herself when she heard Tikena growling over her shoulder.

"Well," Nuviel whispered to her glowering friend. "You *did* ask."

34

Teeth bared, ears pinned back against her head, Nyaka lowered into a crouch and growled. Her hackles raised on end and her dull blue coat began to glow and pulsate.

"You wanna stop her from doing that?" Bear asked Malimokuru. Axe in a tight grip, the guide peered into the open darkness. "She's glowing like a beacon out here."

"I'm gettin' tired of being hunted," Kenyatta said. "And I'm not gonna die being eaten."

Bear spat on the ground and started off. "We're gonna have to double-time it if you want to reach that outcropping alive."

They did just that, yet not long after, it was Grizzled Bear laboring to keep up. Nyaka frequently tasted the air with her tongue, growling each time. The four travelers glanced about, but couldn't see far in the failing light. The size of the outcropping was their only indication it was there.

Another howl sounded, followed by two more. The wolves were getting closer. Another wolf howled to the right, much closer than the others.

"They're trying to herd us," Bear panted. As if in answer, a howl came from behind and to their right. "We have to keep straight."

Kenyatta felt a surge of adrenaline when he heard six more howls sounding in the distance, one after another. "There must be seven or eight of them."

"That we've heard so far," Kita added. The sun dipped below the horizon, the last of its light an afterthought as night arrived. The large silhouette of their destination lay tauntingly in front of them, but it, too, faded as the sun disappeared.

"We can make it," Kita said. He looked at Bear and Malimokuru. "Can you run any faster?"

The old man jogged beside them with relative ease, but it was the big guide, huffing loudly, that worried him.

"Don't ... know ... how long ... I can keep this up," Grizzled Bear gasped.

Four-legged shapes materialized from the darkness, loping beside them in the distance. Gradually, the wolf pack grew more visible as they closed in. Kenyatta heard a bark and glanced over his shoulder to see two wolves closing fast on Bear. He fell back and drew a dagger. "I'll buy you a couple seconds, man, but you gotta push it."

"Trying ... my best." Despite bouncing up and down nearly as much as moving forward, Grizzled Bear managed to speed up a bit.

Kenyatta moved behind the guide, turned, and let fly. He drew another dagger just as he heard the responding yelp. He drew back, ready to let fly again, but never had a chance. A snarling growl was all he heard the instant before a hundred pounds of fur, claws, and snapping jaws tackled him to the ground. Those teeth would have quickly found his neck were it not for the pack on his back.

Lying on his stomach with a full-grown wolf pinning him down, Kenyatta reversed his grip on the dagger and stabbed backwards. Again, he heard a yelp, and the weight was suddenly gone. He rolled over and scrambled to his feet as the wounded predator limped sideways away from him.

Kenyatta scanned the darkness and saw the shapes of seven circling wolves. A dagger whirled past, narrowly missing the wolf closest to him.

"Ken!" Kita called, "get over here!"

Kenyatta slowly climbed back to his feet, careful not to take his eyes off the wolves. Three stalked around to crouch between him and the rest of his party, who were surrounded by five more.

He drew his sword, but before he could make a move, a glowing blue streak bolted past him and skidded to a stop in front of the wolves separating Kenyatta from the others. He spared the little animal a glance, glad she was on his side of the conflict. Indeed, with that wide, perpetually smiling maw filled with serrated teeth, Nyaka was a fearsome sight. She widened her stance, head in line with her body, and let out a long hiss.

A short distance away, Kenyatta heard a bark from another wolf, followed by Kita whipping his staff around and the occasional yelp of from a wolf that got too close.

Fierce blue eyes glowing in the dark, Nyaka barked at the three wolves in front of her. Even her teeth seemed to shine in the dark.

One of the wolves she confronted snarled, and Nyaka responded with a hiss. The wolves crouched, bared teeth and growled, but shrank away from her.

With the wolves' continued retreat, Kenyatta dared hope that he might get out of this without a fight. His hopes died when the alpha female emerged from the darkness.

The other wolves parted, and the larger alpha stalked past them to tower over little Nyaka, who stood her ground. The alpha sized up the little blue threat, issuing a growl deep in its belly.

Kenyatta slashed at a wolf that tried to creep in too close at his side. It hopped back and barked at him. "You're the one trying to eat me, man," he yelled at the animal. It barked at him as if in response.

Kenyatta yelled in the direction of the barely visible silhouettes of his friends. "Hey, nature reader. You can tell them we just passing through and not to eat us, ya?"

"No," came the reply. "Dis nature, man. It's not personal. Dem hungry, we're food. Simple as that."

"Of course," Kenyatta muttered. He spared a glance over his shoulder at Nyaka, who stubbornly held her ground in front of a wolf twice her size. "I'm gonna feel mighty guilty if you go and get yourself killed trying to protect me."

She coughed a bark over her shoulder at him, and Kenyatta didn't know what to make of that.

The alpha ended the standoff and lunged at Nyaka, who reared back and swiped her claws across its muzzle. The wolf recoiled with a squeak and shook its head. It sniffled and shook its head again, then let out another low growl.

Kenyatta caught the exchange from the corner of his eye. This was going to be a bad fight.

At the front of the group, Kita took another swipe at passing wolf, narrowly missing, while Malimokuru rummaged through his pouches. "Hurry up, please," Kita said, warding off the hungry animals.

"I'm doing my best in the dark," Malimokuru replied.

Grizzled Bear had his axe in a two-handed grip. He yelled and shook it at the circling predators, though it did little good. "Be nice to have a skin to sell at the market, and some extra meat for the road. Yah! Come on, then!"

"You eat wolf?" Kita asked, disgusted.

"Yup," came the reply.

"Ya think there's anything he wouldn't eat?" Malimokuru muttered, pulling out a handful of sparkling sand. He threw it in the air and spoke an incantation. Light flared from the disbursing grains and lit the landscape with a thunderclap. The wolves looked to the sky in alarm and shrank away.

In that instant, Nyaka charged the alpha wolf. They rolled in a snarling mass of limbs, snapping teeth, and blue and brown fur.

The savage brawl ensued for several moments until teeth sank into flesh, followed by a yelp. Several of the wolves surrounding Kenyatta backed away as the alpha limped sideways, eyeing Nyaka.

The big wolf growled as it continued to back away to a safe distance. It stood its ground for a moment and looked as if it would attack again. It snapped its jaws, and Nyaka opened her wide maw as if yawning, and snapped it closed. She issued a long hiss and crouched so low her belly nearly touched the ground.

Kenyatta watched the little blue animal, leg muscles bunched, as she prepared to spring.

The alpha wolf must have noticed as well, for it barked and growled again, but clearly wanted no part of Nyaka. It turned and loped away with a slight limp, favoring its right foreleg.

Those nearest to the alpha followed, and the wolves surrounding Kenyatta started to back away. One wolf looked directly into his eyes, then broke off and disappeared with the others into the night.

Kenyatta let out a long, relieved breath, then cursed when he saw Nyaka. Bleeding from patches of fur missing from her torn pelt, she settled herself onto her stomach. Her long, forked tongue slid in and out as she licked her wounds.

Kita reached her first and sucked in through his teeth at the sight of her injuries. Nyaka looked up at him as he approached, but didn't get up.

Malimokuru rushed to crouch beside the animal and began inspecting her wounds. "Better hurry before the light's completely gone," Grizzled Bear said in a soft voice over Kenyatta's shoulder. He tore a strip from a spare cloth in his pack

"Staunch the blood flow for now. We'll get her patched up once we're safe. It's not much farther."

Kenyatta hid his surprise at hearing the concern in the man's voice. "Doesn't look like she'll be walking."

Malimokuru shook his head. "Someone's going to have to carry her."

Kenyatta looked at the injured creature half sitting half laying on her side. She looked to be thirty or forty pounds. Combined with the packs on their backs, that would be a heavy load, but not impossible. It would slow the carrier down considerably, though.

Grizzled Bear fished in his sack and pulled out a blanket. He twisted it on both ends and slung it diagonally across his back. "Lay her in this," he said, knotting it together across his chest. "I'll carry her the rest of the way."

Nyaka gave a pained whine as Kita gingerly scooped her in his arms.

"Mindful not to get too close to them teeth, man," Kenyatta said. "She might snap out of pain reflex."

Kita stole a glance at that terrible grinning maw filled with teeth. "You think I need you to tell me that?"

"I'll get this," Kenyatta said to Grizzled Bear, indicating the man's backpack.

The guide handed it over without a word. With Malimokuru's help, Kita gently placed the animal in the blanket where she lay as though lounging in a hammock.

Grizzled Bear started off. "Let's get moving before I think too much about what's hanging on my back."

35

Motley trio that they were, Kenyatta, Kita, and Grizzled Bear received more than a few curious looks as they weaved their way through the cobblestone streets of Katlan. Kenyatta found the place charming. The people of Katlan wore even less clothing than the residents in Fleria and it wasn't difficult to understand why. It was hot. Very hot.

Kenyatta's cheeks puffed out as he blew a sigh and looked up at the sun. "Feels like I'm in an oven." He pulled his locks back and tied them.

"Ain't you used to the heat, comin' from them islands?" Bear asked.

"Tropical heat, man. Not this skin-wrinklin' hell."

Kita fared no better. He walked nearer the clay buildings, passing through shade as often as possible. He wiped his arm across his face. "Let's find an inn and unload. This is too much." He glanced at the profusely sweating Grizzled Bear stomping beside them, ringing out his dripping shirt.

Kita swallowed. Malimokuru had gotten the better end of the deal in staying with Nyaka in the shaded outcropping outside of town.

They found an inn on the outskirts of the public square. The rates were exorbitant to say the least, but the location was perfect.

"May as well set up here," Kenyatta said. "No doubt the other places are just as expensive."

"Yeah," Kita grumbled. "Where would we go? There's no other city or town between here and Phoenix."

After securing their lodging, the three men met in the common room of the inn to discuss their plans. The place buzzed with patrons of all types, while servers whisked between tables and around chairs and stools, serving mugs of various drinks, and sizzling platters of different types of meats and roasted roots.

The now smiling Grizzled Bear ordered three mugs of the local beer, then wiped his dripping brow with his already soaked handkerchief.

"You're looking at home, here," Kenyatta remarked.

"Just call me the king o' taverns," Bear replied.

"I know we can't stay long," Kita said, "but we need the rest." He glanced sidelong at Bear, "And we need to give Nyaka a chance to recover."

"Yeah, yeah." Grizzled Bear half turned in his chair to look at the bar. "The little blue critter probably saved us."

"She definitely save me," Kenyatta agreed.

Bear patted the air with his hand. "All right, all right. I agree. And I don't want to leave the little bugger, either."

A server holding a tray of five mugs deftly wove her way through the crowded room toward their table. Her responding smile to their thanks lingered a while longer on Kita before she continued on.

Kenyatta sniggered and leaned toward his friend, who also noticed that the woman put considerably more energy in her stride as she walked away. "I think you working the magic, man." He put on his most stereotypical Jamaican accent westerners always got wrong. "Romontic voodoo mogic mon!"

Kita just shook his head and indicated for the laughing Grizzled Bear to continue.

Kenyatta pretended not to notice the frequent glances his friend spared whenever their server came near.

"We got a good look at the wounds on that thing," Grizzled Bear said. "A strip of flesh on her leg was almost ripped off, and she can't stand. You know how long it'll take for it to heal before she's fit to walk again?" He looked from one to the other, then drained his first mug and sat it down none to gently.

"I'll admit the little critter's startin' to grow on me." He wiped beer foam from the corners of his mouth with his thumb and forefinger. "But it would be hard enough travelin' with it on my back if it weren't so damned hot. It's unbearable out there with *no* load on our backs. And I don't care how much cooler it is at night, I ain't for havin' a second round with them wolves."

"We'll deal with that when it comes time," Kita said. "For now, we need to decide how we're going to keep watch over her while we're here. Surely we can't bring her into the city."

"Hah," Kenyatta barked, drawing a few stares. "That would be something; bringing that little monster into the city. We'd never make it past the city limit." He took a draw from his mug and closed his eyes for a moment, savoring the crisp cool beer. He wished this establishment had at least one kind of rum, but cold beer would do.

"So who's gonna go and relieve Malimokuru first ..." Kenyatta trailed off, mug halfway to the table.

"What's your problem?" Kita asked. When no response came, he followed Kenyatta's gaze to the other side of the establishment. At the end of the bar stood a tall figure wrapped in a green cloak with interwoven blue and purple strips of cloth. Various colored beads and shells were embroidered onto the cloak as well, spiraling from the hood to the bottom.

"Isn't it a little hot outside to be walking around in that?" Kita whispered.

"Mmm," Kenyatta said, still studying the figure and trying not to appear to. From the graceful way in which they moved, he suspected the person was female.

Grizzled Bear turned to see what the other two were looking at, then turned back to his mug.

"Crazy people everywhere. And you remember what I told you about them tall folk? Well," he jabbed a thumb over his shoulder, "there you go. There's a reason people keep their distance from them folk. Tall, silent, and weird. Who wears a hot cloak like that in the middle of this damned inferno?" He gulped down the last of his beer and held it up to signal for another.

"Yeah, man," Kenyatta replied absently. He took another sip. "Interesting folk for sure."

Kita smirked at him. "Sure. *Interesting.*"

The sarcasm was lost on Kenyatta, who sat mesmerized by the presence of the woman, easily the tallest person in the now quiet bar. Some patrons glanced at her repeatedly while others openly stared. Most studiously ignored her.

All that could be seen of the tall slender figure were the long black braids falling through the front of her hood to rest below her waist. She turned her head in Kenyatta's direction and the world slowed to a standstill as she held his gaze with those round, luminous brown eyes. The whites were so bright they shone.

Kita looked from one to the other. Kenyatta sat fixed to his seat, mug halfway between the table and his open mouth. After what must have been an eternity condensed into but a few heartbeats, the woman broke the connection. She lay her payment on the bar, drank the contents of her mug, and practically glided out of the establishment. Kenyatta blinked away the trance and looked around. Most of the patrons and even the building itself seemed to have been holding its breath. Gradually the murmur of common room chatter resumed.

"What in the five hells was that all about?" Grizzled Bear asked, indicating Kenyatta with his now full mug.

"Couldn't tell ya," Kita replied.

"Who do you suppose that was?" Kenyatta whispered.

"Trouble," said a voice from beside him. Their server removed Kita's mug and replaced it with a new one. "You're moving a little slow on this aren't ya?" She indicated Kenyatta's drink.

He shrugged sheepishly and took another draw. She leaned close to his ear and whispered, "If I were you, I'd stay away from the likes of those people. Nobody knows who they are and they never talk to anyone. Can only be trouble." When she lifted her head, she winked at Kita and left, maneuvering between tables and patrons as though it were a dance.

"I'll go and relieve Malimokuru," Kenyatta said, still gazing at the door.

Kita sighed. "Please don't find us any trouble."

"Don't worry, man." Kenyatta said, still distracted.

"Right," Kita replied.

"Don't s'pose we'll see that one for the rest of the day." Bear drained his third mug and unleashed a not-so-quiet belch.

Kenyatta barely registered the exchange as he wandered toward the door. Be it fate or foolishness that drove him toward the next step in this quest, the compulsion to find out who that person was drove him beyond any sense of caution.

KENYATTA WALKED down the street in the direction he'd seen the strange woman go through the window. Heat forgotten, he ran a hand over his tied locks and glanced around. People milled about, shopping, transporting goods, or just leaning in the shade in private conversation.

As with many cities in the land of Nomar, the population was as diverse as the environments across the land. People of various hues, shapes, and sizes crisscrossed the streets. The locals were easy to recognize, for they were the only ones not fanning them-

selves and panting with the occasional glance up at the oppressive sun.

Kenyatta sifted through the patches of milling citizens
straining to see a tall, cloaked figure standing above everyone
else. "If that stare meant anything," he muttered to himself,
"you'll find me or I'll find you."

He slowed halfway down the street when a nagging feeling
hit—someone was watching him. He turned and caught a
glimpse of the tall, feminine figure staring directly at him over
the heads of the crowd between them. Once he spied her, she
turned down a side street.

Kenyatta tried not to hurry as he weaved his way through the
throng and rounded the corner. He found her standing to one
side of the street, staring at him with those bright hypnotic eyes.
He approached slowly, doing his best to appear harmless. He
stopped a few feet away.

The silence stretched as the cloaked figure offered no
greeting.

Kenyatta cleared his throat. "I was thinkin' maybe I
know you."

"No."

In the ensuing silence, Kenyatta mentally fidgeted for something else to say. "You wanted to talk to me?" he finally asked.

She blinked at him from within her voluminous cowl.

He offered a nervous grin. "Well, if not ..."

"So reckless," she said, a hint of a roll to the "r".

She had spoken in a voice so soft, he thought she might be
speaking more to herself than him. "Pardon?" Kenyatta asked.

"You. Like a reckless child with no fear."

"can't say I haven't heard that before." Kenyatta replied, trying
to lighten the mood. It fell flat.

The tall woman closed the gap between them, all the while,
staring into his eyes. He thought he saw the whites of her eyes
glimmer for an instant, but it must have been his imagination.

She glanced at the sword strapped across his back, and he thought he saw a hint of a smile inside the dark cowl.

"*Inkosi* was right," she said, and again, he wasn't sure if she was speaking to him or herself.

"Who is In ... In ... ko ... si?"

His question pulled her from whatever thoughts she was having. "*Inkosi* is *Umkhokeli*," she stated matter-of-factly. "*Umkhokeli*, our ... leader, as you say." She continued down the street, and it was an effort for Kenyatta to match her long stride.

"Where we goin'?" he asked, scanning the streets.

"To see your *Umntwana Onomuntu*," she said. At the bewildered look on Kenyatta's face, she clarified. "Your nature child."

"You mean Malimokuru?" Kenyatta ventured, a growing sense of unease gripping his stomach. How did they know about the nature reader? And if they knew about him and what he was, what about Kenyatta and the rest of them? Was Malimokuru in danger?

She kept walking, Kenyatta following out of sheer curiosity. *Curiosity can be deadly,* he reminded himself.

36

C urled up at the nature reader's feet, Nyaka's forked tongue
flicked out and snapped the hunk of dried meat from
Malimokuru's hand.

He rubbed her dull blue coat, marveling at how much the
animal had already healed. "That was my last, greedy girl. Unless
dem cotton-headed bwoys bring more."

Malimokuru looked toward the mouth of their rocky shelter,
and the bright and blazing hot day beyond.

The big odoriferous man had known what he was about. The
outcropping had a recess in the middle, similar to a cave,
providing a much cooler shelter. A bit dark but cool.

He rubbed her rough blue pelt again, and Nyaka twitched her
tail. He smiled and gave her a pat, careful to avoid the tender pink
scars, all that remained of the gashes inflicted by the wolf. How
formidable a species she must belong to, that her body had
already knitted large open wounds together overnight. Even her
strength was coming back. The more he looked at her, he
wondered if she might even have grown since he'd found her in
the Mord.

"How big you gonna get, little one?" he asked the snoozing

animal. Her ears perked and swiveled toward the opening in the outcropping. She raised her head and growled deep in her throat. Nyaka slowly rose, still staring at entrance.

Malimokuru watched her for a moment, growing more nervous by the moment. "What do you hear?" he whispered. Another growl. Malimokuru opened himself to her and was immediately awash with feelings of wariness and threat. Someone, or something, was coming.

He let his senses leave the wary beast and sent them out to any other inhabitants they shared the rocks with. He connected with a carrion crow perched just outside the opening to their camp, about to give up the wait for one of them to perish.

His amusement was cut short by the image of several bipedal animals converging on their location. Their movements were light and deliberate, like predators. Of course, the bird could not relay a numerical count, but there were several of them.

Malimokuru rubbed Nyaka's back again. Only one of the three who'd left was supposed to come and relieve him. Whomever these people were, he didn't want to take a chance on whether or not they were friendly.

He searched for somewhere to hide, but they'd chosen this spot specifically because there were no places for anything to hide. Cursing this lack of forethought, he looked over at Nyaka. She crouched low, growling softly, ears pinned back.

"Nyaka," Malimokuru whispered, "hide, girl." He sent his intentions to her and was barely able to penetrate the wall of survival instinct that had taken over her thoughts. *"Hurry, my friend."* He told her. *"Better to wait and watch before they see us."*

That caught her attention, and she moved closer to him. He moved toward the entrance of the camp and hid in the shadows to the side. To his surprise, the blue animal went to the other side of the cave, further away. His breath caught in his throat as he watched her color shift from blue to black. Even as he watched her, Nyaka blended with the dark.

He opened his senses to her and received what felt like the animal equivalent of smugness. Malimokuru sighed and sent his awareness out of the cave. He flinched. Something stopped him so abruptly it was like he'd crashed into a wall. He had no time to react before his senses were thrown back and shut away.

Malimokuru went rigid. Whatever he'd just encountered knew he was there and knew how to block him.

Before he could consider the implications, something sharp gently poked him on the top of the head. The blood froze in his veins as Malimokuru slowly craned his neck to stare up into two glimmering orbs. He saw nothing else until a gleaming row of white teeth curled upward underneath them. The smile disappeared at the sound of a half-hiss, half-growl coming from somewhere to the side.

Malimokuru backed away, and after a few moments, a figure materialized from the shadows just in front of him, Nyaka on its heels.

Malimokuru stared in disbelief. The tall slender figure looked to have seen no more than fifteen years of life, just between boyhood and manhood. In the dim light of the camp, the boy's features were indistinct, save those constantly glimmering orbs, and that shining smile that returned.

"Who are you?" the nature reader demanded.

"Who are *you*?" came an accented reply from behind, a slight roll to the "r". "How did they get in here without being seen?"

He was careful to move slowly as he looked over his shoulder. Nothing. Behind his only visible guest, Nyaka hissed again.

"Calm your friend," a disembodied voice declared. "We do not wish her harm."

Malimokuru tried to reach Nyaka and failed. "I would if ya didn't have me blocked—"

"Now you can," the voice interrupted.

The nature reader hesitantly opened his senses and found he was indeed no longer blocked. He connected with Nyaka immediately. She had not known the others had entered the cave either, and was panicked and ready to attack the boy in front of her.

He pushed through a cloud of fear and anger, fought against her instinctive reaction to tear the boy apart. He finally reached Nyaka and coaxed her to calm down. She remained crouched, but stopped hissing.

With Nyaka guarding the boy, Malimokuru felt safe enough to turn and face the speaker. He looked around the barely lit campsite and found nothing. How was this possible? The darkest part of their cave was to the side of the entrance where no light shined. Although not bright, there were few shadows, and most of the place was at least touched by the sun.

His heart skipped when three figures materialized from both sides and directly in front of him. Their skin had changed color to blend with the darkness. Each held a spear like the boy, tips pointed up. The whites of their eyes also shone in the darkness.

They wore only brown loincloths, and Malimokuru had to wonder what he and his companions had done to bring these men out into the open desert to find him.

"My name is Malimokuru," he began, "and I am just traveling through these lands ..."

"With *umzingeli unwabu*," the man—Malimokuru guessed to be the leader—interrupted.

"I'm not sure I understand what that is," he responded. He followed the other man's gaze until they rested on the crouching Nyaka.

Malimokuru looked back to the man who had spoken, a cold lump settling in his stomach. "Dis my friend, Nyaka. I was compelled to help her or she would have died where I found her. She is no threat."

The man looked at him incredulously. "Only *Umntwana Onomuntu* would think so." He walked past the nature reader, and the two men at his sides relaxed. Malimokuru turned to regard the tall man who now stood looking at Nyaka.

"In your common tongue of this land, *umzingeli unwabu* is called goar cat." He looked over his shoulder. "It can kill an animal three times its size when fully grown." He turned back and looked Nyaka directly in the eyes. The two stared at each other for several heartbeats, and to Malimokuru's surprise, she relaxed.

"Are you a nature reader?" Malimokuru asked.

The man squatted beside the goar cat and rubbed her behind her jaw. "They like when you rub them here," he said. "They use their jaws a lot for hunting, it is massage to them." He looked back to Malimokuru. "What you call reading nature, Amahle call linking. When we link, we hear and see."

Nyaka swished her tail side to side and the man tilted his head at her. "If she were but a few months older, you would not be friends."

"What do you mean?" Malimokuru put his hands on his hips. For more years than this boy had been alive, he'd prided himself on being able to communicate with nature, had never failed at connecting with an animal that wasn't desperate with hunger or diseased in the mind.

The man stared at him innocently. "Be not offended. *Umzingeli unwabu* are difficult to make friends with after they become juvenile. Even our most powerful *Umuntu Onomuntu* cannot always communicate with an adult."

Malimokuru made a mental note to ask questions later if this continued to be a friendly visit. "Why ya come surround me in my camp, man? Have I entered your territory?"

"We live here," the leader answered, "but the land belongs to no one but *umDali.*"

"Of course," Malimokuru agreed, guessing that *umDali* was likely some divine entity. "Why ya come here?" he asked again. "I don't think I've done anything wrong."

"You travel with *umzingeli unwabu*." The other man pounded the butt of his spear to the ground. "They are dangerous animal. Only fool would not investigate."

Malimokuru conceded the point with nod. They looked to the opening when another tall cloaked person that Malimokuru guessed was female, strode into the campsite. Despite the concealment of her cloak, she cut a regal figure.

Right on her heels entered the fool child Kenyatta. Malimokuru wondered if any of this had to do with him. He huffed. Of course it did.

The woman stared with disapproval at each of the four men, who shared uncertain glances between them. She spoke in urgent, annoyed tones in their native language, and the others looked guilty.

She approached Malimokuru, and he resisted the urge to take a step back. She was tall; easily over seven feet. "I am sorry my people bring welcome to you at the tip of a spear. It is not our way."

"They travel with *umzingeli unwabu*," the man Malimokuru had first thought was the leader responded. He pointed at Nyaka. "Should we not have been careful, *Inkosazana*?" He bowed his head respectfully after he spoke.

At the mention of the blue creature sitting behind the young warrior at the entrance, the woman turned and sucked air in through her teeth. She whirled on Kenyatta, and Malimokuru didn't envy the man at that moment.

"You travel with *umzingeli unwabu*?" she hissed. "Goar cat?"

Kenyatta held up his hands defensively. "We were forced to kill her mother. She would have died if we hadn't brought her with us."

Malimokuru gave Kenyatta an appreciative nod for sharing the blame. "It was my decision to bring the animal, *In ... kho ... sazana.*" He bowed his head as the other man had done at the mention of what he believed to be her title. He was rewarded with an appraising look before she turned back to Kenyatta.

"He your father?"

"Um, no." Kenyatta's body shook with repressed laughter. "No, just some guy who wouldn't leave us alone."

The woman's eyes glimmered, then darkened. "Have respect for *Umntwana Onomuntu*."

Kenyatta flinched at the rebuke. "Just joking, man," he said. "He's our good friend and a very wise man. Him save us too many times already just to get here."

Every one of the men surrounding them bristled. "You would dare call *Inkosazana* a man?"

Malimokuru gritted his teeth. Things were deteriorating. "He wasn't calling her a man, friends. That is the way we talk in our land. He meant no disrespect."

The woman seemed amused by this. "Be calm, Jabu. They are not like us. We must be understanding."

"Of course, *Inkosazana*," the man named Jabu bowed in obeisance.

She looked back, or rather, down to Malimokuru and offered a smile. "*Umntwana Onomuntu*." She lowered her cowl, held her hands out, and offered a half bow. "I am Naiyala, *Inkosazana* of the desert Amahle."

Naiyala indicated with an open hand the man who'd spoken earlier. "This is Jabulani, Elder Hunter of our village." She nodded toward the two flanking the nature reader. "Ayanda and Sakhile. And the one praying to *umDali* that your *umzingeli unwabu* friend does not eat him, is Akana." Shooting a glance at Nyaka still sitting behind him, Akana cast him that same—albeit nervous—grin from when they'd first met.

Malimokuru did his best to hide his shock. The woman was obviously female, but not obviously human. In the dimly lit camp inside the outcropping, he could barely make out her features. The perfect white of her eyes contrasted with her brown irises, but even more so with her smooth black skin, the color of perfectly polished onyx.

"I ... am Malimokuru," he said, returning her gesture. He tried —and suspected he failed—to not be too obvious at taking in her foreign features. The tips of her ears ended in a slight point, her teeth, as white as the whites in her eyes, were like a flickering light whenever she spoke.

When the unusually tall woman grinned at him, he realized he'd been staring for too long. "Ahem." He waved a hand to the side. "And you've already met my cotton-headed friend, Kenyatta."

"Funny man," Kenyatta muttered.

"Our little friend there is Nyaka." Malimokuru smiled at the goar cat. She sat on her haunches, tongue flicking in and out, ears pivoting in every direction. Her bright blue eyes had fixed on the nature reader when he'd spoken her name.

"Malimokuru." Naiyala's smile grew. "I ask that you come to our home and meet my father *Inkosi Lwazi*."

Malimokuru noticed the intense scrutiny of the other men in the cave. From the grave looks on their faces, he guessed it would be a tremendous insult to refuse, so he quickly accepted.

"We would be honored, of course, if your father would see us."

The elder hunter, Jabulani, went stiff. He spoke to Naiyala in what sounded like a question in their native tongue.

"I hear you," Naiyala replied. "And we will speak common western tongue of humans. It is rude to talk of them in words they do not understand, is it not?"

The elder hunter bowed respectfully to her, then to Malimokuru and Kenyatta in turn. "Is this wise, *Inkosazana*? To bring *abantu* ... humans, before *Inkosi*?"

"There is no malevolence in their hearts, Jabu." Naiyala responded.

The elder hunter frowned. *"Abantu dernage mwantu gersh, au ihansi derange awasha."*

Naiyala laughed and patted the sour-looking Jabu on the shoulder. She turned away, beckoning for the others to follow.

One and all they left the cave. Kenyatta turned a questioning expression on Malimokuru as they fell in behind the others. The nature reader shrugged.

Nyaka padded silently behind them, apparently at ease with their new acquaintances.

Naiyala waved Malimokuru and Kenyatta beside her. "Only once before has my father met *Umntwana Onomuntu*. When I was child, he tell me the story. All these years have passed and you, another *Umntwana Onomuntu* cross these lands. And with *umzingeli unwabu*." She shook her braided head. "This must have meaning. One hundred and twenty years, it has been."

"How many years?" Kenyatta asked in a strangled voice.

Naiyala winked at the astonished islander. "Your people are most short-lived in the world."

Again, Kenyatta turned a questioning expression on Malimokuru, who held out his hands. "You think I'm knowin' any more than you?" He addressed Naiyala. "*Inkosazana*. We should tell our friends where we're going, or they'll worry."

"They will meet us at the home of the Amahle." Naiyala said. "I sent message to them."

"I didn't see that," Kenyatta said.

"No?" was the only reply.

"May I ask you a question, Naiyala *Inkosazana*?" Malimokuru said.

She smiled. "*Inkosazana* means princess. You can use my given name: Naiyala. In answer to your question, I hear you."

Malimokuru smiled back. "Thank you, Naiyala. What was it that the elder hunter said that made you laugh?"

Her features crinkled with amusement. "Humans find trouble, as geese find water."

Kenyatta snorted, and Malimokuru spared him a dry expression. "Can't deny that."

Malimokuru studied their new companions as discretely as he could. These Amahle were the most unusual people Malimokuru had ever seen, and the fact that they repeatedly referred to he and Kenyatta as a separate species made him nervous. What had they stumbled upon?

37

The docks of the sprawling Port City of Orgonin smelled much the same as that of Pyon—fish and salty air. Being from inland, Seung never tired of the fresh ocean air mixed with the cry of the gulls and the ringing bells at the wharf.

"I've traveled great distances from our homeland, but never have I crossed the ocean." Beneath his cowl, Tinnoviel's expression was obscured, but the appreciation of their new surroundings was reflected in his tone. "Our people have remained withdrawn from the world for too long. It's time more of us venture forth once again."

A short distance away, the remainder of their party spoke amongst themselves about the alien surroundings. Well, three of them spoke. Yurin Kei Daunyana silently watched everything and everyone.

Captain So made his way toward them. "As agreed, you owe me forty-five silvers, the remaining balance from the half you already paid." Captain So seemed to have aged since they'd set out. Seung didn't envy him the grim task of having to inform the families of the lost sailors. She translated to Tinnoviel, and the elf handed over the payment.

The captain's eyes looked like they would pop out of his head. He stared at the coins in his hand, then at Tinnoviel, and back again. His mouth bobbed several times before sound finally came. "B ... b ... but. This isn't forty-five silvers, it's forty-five *gold*."

Seung had to swallow to keep from blurting out something embarrassing. Forty-five gold? She'd never even seen that much money at one time. She looked at the Daunya Warrior and tried not to gawk at all the gold coins in the captain's cupped hands. Were all elves so rich?

"Is least I do," the elf replied, then spoke in elvish to Seung.

"Lives cannot be measured in coin, good captain," Seung translated. "Regrettably we can only offer you this addition to our fare to help in some small way for the loss of your crew members, and the loss to their families. We trust you will deliver their share of this on your honor?"

The captain nodded through every word. He looked into Seung and Tinnoviel's eyes, tears threatening to spill down his cheeks. "I will. I will only take what is mine, and the families of those good men will live in comfort for many years, thanks to you."

Seung studied the man. He meant what he said. She looked at Tinnoviel and saw the elf draw the same conclusion.

Captain So squinted at them. "You know. I've never seen anybody that looks and sounds like you people. I suspect that's why you keep those hoods up all the time. When the wind blew them off, I saw, begging your pardon." He bowed. "I don't know where you come from, but as long as you're not wanting to pass through that cursed Siren Strait again, you're always welcome aboard *Wave Dancer*."

Seung inclined her head. "Our thanks, good captain."

So thanked them again and returned to his ship.

Seung watched him go. "We've made friends," she said. Tinnoviel turned to the ship, where every sailor in view waved to them from the deck. They had lost comrades on this voyage, but the elves had fought beside them against the Siren Strait and the storm. Seung and her companions had earned their respect.

"You know," Seung said as she and Tinnoviel walked toward the group. "He can buy a new ship, pay his crew handsomely, and every one of those three men's families can buy homes on a farm or ranch and still have money left over."

"I do not take lightly the sacrifice of those men," Tinnoviel replied. "But the currency of humans has little value to us. Ever since they came to value shiny metals and minerals, we've learned to produce them and trade in secret. In her wisdom, Seiyun knew dealings with humans would be unavoidable."

"Have you mined every bit of gold and silver in the region?" Seung asked.

Tinnoviel shrugged. "Since we rarely interact with humans long enough to spend it, the metals and gems accumulate. And even if it did carry value for us, I would still have given that captain as much as was possible to help with their loss, caused in part, by our need to cross the strait."

"Look at the structures," Nuviel exclaimed as they approached. "They're so high. As high as the red trees!"

"There is a name for these things, naïve one," Tikena said. "It's called arrogance. Humans seek to outdo the Daunyans Themselves."

"That is true, Tikena," Tinnoviel said. "But not always. There are many humans that build as a labor of love, for the art of building. If you look upon their creations, sometimes you can see what is created out of love, or greed, or arrogance as you put it." The caustic elf responded with an irritated shrug.

"Have you not seen anything like this, Kiluriel?" Nuviel asked.

"I haven't," Seung admitted. "Near my village, there are the remnants of tall structures that humans once lived and worked in, but nature has reclaimed it. The stunted and decaying husks of those buildings remain to provide shelter for animals and a place for plants to grow."

Buildings tall and short dominated the surroundings, ancient remnants of an age long past. Mostly, the smaller buildings were used for the demands of this current age, while taller buildings were either occupied as homes, or left to be reclaimed by nature.

They passed through a section of town where the buildings of old once dominated the skyline, but had been torn down in favor of more practical structures. Seung hadn't known how large these buildings reached during the Age of Technology, but she wouldn't have believed they could be so tall if she hadn't looked upon them with her own eyes.

While Nuviel found the giant brick and mortar buildings with endless panes of dirty glass fascinating, the charm quickly faded. "It's all so unnatural. No insult to the human craftsmanship—"

"Which is ugly and clunky," Tikena interjected.

"—but everything is so big," Nuviel went on. "So much glass and steel. And the roads are so ... so *hard*. They hurt to walk upon."

Tinnoviel smiled and placed a hand on the girl's shoulder. "According to human history, *quyo*, this was once a thick, liquid-like substance, mixed and then spread upon the earth and left to solidify. In but hours, it hardened into what is now beneath our feet."

"But why?" Nuviel asked. "Why create this substance when it hurts to walk on?" She waved her hands to encompass the area. "And the trees. Where are all the trees? I see only saplings and growth-stunted dwarfs here. They sound so unhappy. So solemn."

Seung's heart broke to look upon the usually happy-go-lucky elf, who looked near to tears.

"So much stone and rock, glass and steel," Nuviel whispered. "How long must we remain here?"

"Not long, little one." Tinnoviel patted her shoulder and gave it a squeeze. "We must find our way out of this labyrinth of steel and glass, and continue north."

Alurien shaded his eyes. "Once we reach the border where fewer of these stone giants hold sway, I will be able to find our best path." He looked toward the ocean. "The sun tips that way, so our path lies straight ahead. The trees whisper little, here. It'll be easier once we've left."

Seung would have liked to stay at least for a day to explore the massive city, but the others were right. She thought of Kyu, of her best friend Tae Kim, and the refugees whose island home had been destroyed. How much time remained? Was Kyu already underwater? Had its residents—her friends, her aunt—escaped further inland? Or were they at the bottom of the ocean, the sea having risen up too quickly for them to escape? Was she too late?

"All is not lost, Kiluriel." Seung was startled out of her grim daydream, not by Nuviel or the Daunya Warrior, but Yurin. The apprentice was watching her with those haunting eyes. "Do not let your mind betray your resolve. If you received news at this moment that everyone you loved had perished, would you stop now?"

Just the thought of such a possibility threatened to break her heart, but Seung shook her head. "No." She forced herself to look into Yurin's eyes as the other woman studied her.

Yurin gave a subtle nod. "Very well." She looked away. "I suspect your village and your people yet live."

"How can you know that?"

Several heartbeats passed before the answer came. "To be in connection with the Daunyans is to feel a connection with creation itself. To the degree our physical bodies can endure, that is. If such a massive loss of life had happened, I would have felt it as surely as DaunyaSai himself. Even across the great distance between us, he would have contacted me, should such a tragedy have befallen your home."

"Did you feel what happened to the people of Ulleung?"

"I am not familiar with that name, but there have been two such misfortunes recently. This Ulleung you speak of would be one, and there is another. Farther away. Many souls left this world to return to the Daunyans. An island of many proud and festive, happy souls."

That sent Seung's thoughts again to the man she'd met over two years ago. Festive and happy—a description that easily fit the man whose name she struggled to remember only because it was so difficult to pronounce. Key ... atta?

An hour after their arrival, dark clouds rolled in and released their burden. Soaked in short order, the elves pushed onward. As quickly as the rain had come, it abated.

Tikena glared at the sky, her upper lip curled. "Even nature hates these stinking humans. The rain comes in just long enough to soak everything, then leaves.

"So sour," Seung said under her breath.

Tikena glanced in her direction but didn't respond.

Seung caught part of a conversation between Tinnoviel and Yurin. The apprentice argued of the wastefulness of using the gift of the Daunyans for the meager task of air-drying their cloaks. Tinnoviel insisted, however that it was either dry their cloaks, or bear the breezy streets of the city weighed down with cold, damp, and heavy garments.

"I sense predatory curiosity," Yurin said. Despite the urgency of her words, the apprentice might have been discussing the weather.

From the corner of her eye, Seung noticed Nuviel. The girl was unusually subdued. The towering buildings must be pressing in on her.

Tinnoviel's mouth moved but no sound came. After a moment, Yurin's did the same. Seung watched this silent exchange with more than a little confusion, until Tinnoviel's voice entered her mind. It was an effort not to jump.

"This is called the whisper," Tinnoviel's voice said.

She heard no sound. Not from his lips, anyway. But his words were as clear in her as if he'd spoken them aloud. Was she hearing with her ears, or her mind?

"All elves have several extra vocal cords which afford us this form of communication. It enables us to speak at a different frequency to the ears of only those we wish to hear us. Can you hear me?" Seung responded with a shaky nod.

"Good. Perhaps you can be taught to use it later. For now, listen. The guards watching us"—he indicated with his chin toward the end of the street ahead—*"they lie in wait up there, and behind. We've been watched since we left the docks. Our cloaked appearance has garnered the very attention we sought to avoid. If we are questioned, you must speak for us. Can you speak the common human tongue of the western lands?"*

Seung tipped her hand left and right to show that she could speak enough to get by.

"It will have to do. We must avoid confrontation. Humans are not yet ready to know with whom they share this world. I don't intend us to be the ambassadors of such an event this day."

Seung couldn't have agreed more.

Four sets of footfalls sounded from behind, though their pursuers probably thought they were being quiet. As the elves reached the end of the alleyway, four more men stepped out of concealment.

"Afternoon," one of the guards said, a large and squarely built man with a broad chin creased by a dimple. He looked them over with icy blue "no nonsense" eyes.

"You six don't look like you're from here. Where're you going?"

Seung didn't know the laws of this western land, but she wondered if he had a right to question them in such a way.

"Sorry," she replied, selecting her words with care. "We are not from here." The man looked at her as if that were obvious.

"We go that way." She pointed to the east, away from their true destination to the north.

The man didn't move. The three men behind Seung's party stood with their hands on the handles of long slender black clubs.

Seung attempted a disarming smile. "We go east. Have long way to travel."

The man looked skeptical. He turned his head to converse with one of the men behind him, never taking his eyes from the group. The exchange was too quick for Seung to catch it all, and after one of the others responded, the man addressed her again.

"Before you lie to me, I'm going to tell you this: You were seen leaving the docks and hurrying in this direction as if you were fleeing something. The ship you left behind was beaten and battered. You must have made some friends, because the crew would only tell us that you paid fairly and were good passengers. I surmise that for a ship to have taken that much of a beating, you must have crossed the Siren Strait, which is as near to suicide as any seagoing person could come.

"You've taken every quiet street you could find, which looks to me like you're trying to avoid being noticed. By someone like us, maybe."

A few of the other men chortled at that, and he silenced them with an upraised hand. "Why the large cloaks? You look suspicious, and suspicious is a bad thing. So, I'll ask you one more time, and only one more time: Who are you, why are you here, and where are you going?"

The man spoke so quickly Seung was only able to follow a portion of the dialogue, but it was enough to understand that their situation was on the decline. She decided on the truth, or a portion of it, at least. "We go west first, to meet friends. Then north to Askata." It sounded contrived even to her own ears, but she was thinking on the spot.

Her statement drew incredulous looks. The man with the

cold eyes stared at her. "We come here because captain only come this far. That is why we here. We do not cause trouble, only wish to continue travel."

The men—officers? Some sort of patrolmen without uniforms?—looked at each other.

The one who spoke for them pointed at the others behind Seung. "Why don't they talk?"

"They do not understand," she answered.

"Do you carry weapons?"

He was fishing for an excuse to detain them. He'd also backed her into a corner, for there was no way she could lie. "Yes."

"Why?"

The young warrior kept her temper in check. "Thieves on the road. We must be safe." The guard clearly didn't believe her and he motioned for the others to surround them. "I'm not sure I believe you, lady, and I am charged with keeping order here. You are strangers dressed mysteriously and it is my duty to preserve the peace. Slowly lay down your arms and be escorted to the central hub where you will be further questioned."

"Lay down arms?" Seung frowned at her arms, then back at the man. He wanted them to lay down their arms?

"Your weapons," he snapped.

Seung looked at Tinnoviel. She barely made out the subtle movements of his lips. He was *whispering*, but she didn't know to whom.

The tone of the conversation had been easy enough to follow, for he spread his arms, revealing the exotic wooden blade at his side. The guards frowned. Even the large, stern man in front of Seung looked puzzled by the odd weapon.

"Place them on the ground," the guard commanded.

Showing by example, Seung reached around her back and brought *Vyirayoi* in front of her. Still keeping her movements slow, she placed the halved weapon on the ground and stepped back. The others followed suit, all except Yurin, who stood with her hands tucked in her sleeves.

"What about her?" the guard asked.

"She carries no weapon," Seung replied. It was more or less true.

"Tell her to remove her cloak, then."

Seung translated to Yurin, and the apprentice nodded. She stepped forward and turned sideways.

"Be ready," Tinnoviel *whispered* to Seung.

In a movement so fast Seung barely registered it, Yurin whipped her arms out in an arc.

A powerful gust of air blasted Seung off her feet and down the alley. Keeping her wits about her, she managed to somersault backwards and land on all fours, skidding to a stop. The guards also flipped end over end in the air, but didn't land so well.

One flew past her and crashed into a large metal bin with a slanted top. The others slid and rolled in every direction. They lay squirming on the ground holding knees and elbows, or slumped unconscious against building walls where they'd been flung. Seung retrieved *Vyirayoi* as the other elves recovered their weapons.

"Couldn't you have just manipulated them like you did those thieves on the road?" Seung asked.

"That only works on the weak-minded," Yurin replied. "It would have worked on some of those men, but not all, and not their leader." She looked over her shoulder at Tinnoviel. "My apologies, Daunya Warrior. There was no way for me to get far enough away for everyone not to be affected."

"All is well," Tinnoviel replied.

"They'd disagree," Seung said, indicating one guard lying on his back with his legs curled against a wall.

Tikena giggled, then caught herself. She spun on her heel, pretending to look around for any other dropped possessions.

Was that an actual positive response? Seung wondered if she might yet make friends with the girl.

DUSK SAW the elves many miles outside Port City. Once the guards—assuming they were guards—regained consciousness, a citywide search would ensue, possibly even extending to the surrounding lands. As soon as they were outside the city limits, the elves made straight for the trees and didn't stop until they were in the thick of the forest.

Nuviel closed her eyes and took a deep breath. She held it for a few heartbeats, then let it out with a contented hum. She stretched out her arms and spun a circle, giggling.

The others showed the same—if less energetic—relief. To her surprise, Seung found herself more relaxed as well. A lot of that could be on account of them eluding the city guards, but she couldn't deny how at peace she felt in this rainforest, like it was part of her. The place buzzed with energy and joy. When she mentioned this to Tinnoviel, he nodded. "Away from human civilization, the trees grow tall and thrive. They speak to each other and to those who have the ears to listen."

"I never knew the lands of Nomar had such beautiful forests," Nuviel said. The young elf danced around the group, giggling and hugging any tree she came near.

"It's been long since this forest has seen an elf of any kind," Alurien said. "They live farther north and east, in the mountains."

"How do you know?" Seung asked.

"*Nyet'alo,*" a smug Tikena muttered, taking a draw from her water tube. Seung sighed. So much for that progress she was hoping for. She didn't know how much more she could endure of the girl.

"When you listen," Alurien said, "the forest will speak to you. And you can speak to it, if you know how."

The ranger placed his hand on a redwood tree and looked up at it, his black hair falling back to reveal his pointed ears, slightly longer than the elfinestrayans.

"This large one is over seven hundred years old," the ranger said. "The last time an elf passed through this forest was about half that time." He turned to the others. "Our path leads first north, then west and north again. We can move through the cover of the forest for about eight hundred leagues before we encounter the mountains. We must then turn west to travel around them, then north again, which will take us into the rain forests of Simarin. That's just under a week of travel by foot, unless we find horse friends willing to bear us."

Seung wondered if she'd ever stop being amazed in the presence of these companions. The ranger had never traveled these lands, yet knew all of this? Surely he hadn't had such a lengthy conversation with the trees.

After a lunch of fruit, roots, and water, they made their way through the forests of Orgonin, running on land, and occasionally taking to the trees when that route was more easily traveled.

To her surprise and delight, Seung found that she was not only able to keep up, but enjoyed moving through the dense foliage and among the many thick branches and vines. She'd never known herself to be capable of such feats, but it was as though the other part of her heritage had taken over, and her body remembered what had been dormant for most of her life.

They set camp at a placid lake that so perfectly reflected the surrounding evergreen trees, it might have been an enormous sheet of polished glass.

Tinnoviel watched as Seung prepared her bedroll. "I can teach you to more fully take the reverie, if you wish."

Seung thought it over. "I'd like that, but perhaps tomorrow?

The past few days have left me weary to the bone, and longing for regular sleep."

The elf nodded. "That would be best. It wouldn't do for you to attempt it when near exhaustion. You would fall asleep anyway." He turned away. "Sleep well, Kiluriel Sen'Mora."

Seung thought about the offer long after Tinnoviel had gone. With every day that passed, she connected more with her elfinestrayan heritage, yet knew not what it meant for her future. Would she become more elven, and less human? After a lifetime of feeling different, but not knowing how or why, Seung had finally begun to uncover parts of herself long hidden.

She watched the Daunya Warrior move away, his every step a graceful expression of nature itself. "Sleep well, Tinnoviel Nai SaunyaLi."

38

A s Naiyala had promised, Kita and Grizzled Bear had been informed—to their discomfort—of their friends' meeting with their strange new companions. In short order they had arrived to meet Kenyatta and Malimokuru armed with plenty of questions. Now, the four friends, joined with Naiyala and her band, turned their sights west. To Grizzled Bear's delight, they'd procured horses at Katlan and now rode at a brisk pace. The pace didn't seem so brisk to the Amahle, however, for they ran with little difficulty beside the animals.

Kenyatta shook his head as he watched the Amahle princess, jogging beside his cantering mount. "Don't you ever get tired?"

The stable from where they'd purchased their mounts had more than enough to spare, yet these desert Amahle had refused when Kenyatta offered to go back and acquire more.

He gave the Amahle princess a sidelong glance. *Dem probably not have horses tall enough for these folk anyway.*

"We do not ride horses," Naiyala replied, as if it were a well-known fact. "No need. We only ask for their aid for larger burdens than we ourselves can bear."

Kenyatta looked beyond Naiyala at the other three Amahle,

jogging and chatting idly amongst themselves while the cantering horses huffed each breath. The mounts would likely tire long before their new companions.

He whistled through his teeth, making a mental note to stay in the good graces of these people.

They rested the horses at the base of a mountain covered in boulders, and took to the shade.

Sakhile frowned as he gazed into the distance. "With permission, *Inkosazana,* I will scout ahead."

Naiyala gave a sharp nod, and the scout bounded off into the scorching heat.

"Does it leave a bitter taste in your mouth as well, that we were able to outrun any horse like them?" Kita asked.

Kenyatta offered water to his gray mare. "Yeah, man. Maybe when we're close to our destination, we will."

"I don't think a demon lies at the end of this journey, Ken." Kita shaded his eyes and looked out at the expansive desert, as though seeing their destination from afar.

"Still don't know that," Kenyatta replied.

Kita lowered his hand from his brow and looked at his friend. The remark might have been offhanded, but Kenyatta's tone seemed to lighten and darken at a whim, these days.

He felt helpless watching his best friend's mood shift at the slightest stimuli. The loss of Jamaica weighed heavily on him.

When Kita thought of the Philippines, and if the same fate had befallen his beloved homeland, he would surely be in a similar state. "Guess we'll know when we get there," he replied, not knowing what else to say.

"A demon at the end of all this is the best we could hope for," Kenyatta said. "That is, assuming we find a way to get these *weapons,* if you can call 'em that, charged to kill a demon." He looked at his sword with a sour expression. "Otherwise it's a long trip to a quick death."

Kita watched his friend closely. Kenyatta never spoke so

darkly. True though his words might be, Ken always found a way to lighten any situation; even one that involved the possibility of imminent death.

"I can think of better things to hope for than encountering a demon as the cause of all this."

"For once the cotton-head bwoy is right." Malimokuru climbed atop a small bolder and sat down with a contented groan. "At least if it's a demon, you two got dem augmented abilities to battle the thing. If it's a normal monster, that could be a bigger problem. Think about what you fought in the ocean."

Kita couldn't disagree with that line of thought. The possibility of engaging a monster on the same scale as what they'd fought in the ocean, without their augmented abilities? It was a terrible thought.

The sound of Jabulani speaking in hurried tones to Naiyala interrupted their conversation. The elder hunter pointed out into the desert where a lone cloaked figure approached.

Kenyatta and the others strained to see in the direction he pointed. The cloaked figure walked toward them from the middle of the desert where only small bushes and cacti dared grow.

"How is that possible?" Kita said. "There's nothing out there; no civilization on our maps from that direction."

"Don't take a stretch to imagine a civilization of these people not being on your maps," Malimokuru said.

"Amata Daunyana," Naiyala said, her voice heavy with awe.

Kenyatta squinted across the distance, then shook his head. "Dem must have sharp eyesight to know who that is from so far away."

The distant figure walked without urgency, yet each step brought her closer as though she ran. In the span of several heartbeats, the woman named Amata Daunyana stood before Naiyala. The three male Amahle bowed deeply.

With hands as black as onyx, the regal figure removed her

cowl. She inclined her head, long beaded braids clicking as they fell over her face. "*Inkosazana*." She spread her arms.

To the humans' surprise, Naiyala returned the gesture. Did this woman rank higher than the princess of these Amahle people? Was she an older sister or family member?"

After a short exchange in their native tongue, Naiyala looked to the four humans. She spread her arm in welcome.

"These are our *abantu* friends," Naiyala said, and she introduced each of them in turn. "You are in the presence of Amata Daunyana. Apprentice to the Seer of the Daunyans."

They bowed in respect, but when Kenyatta looked up again, the newly arrived woman had moved to stand in front of Malimokuru.

"You are *Umntwana Onomuntu*. Almost two hundred years it has been, since last we've seen you."

Malimokuru huffed. "Beggin' your pardon, Miss Amata Daunyana. I may be old and dusty, but I'm not that old."

Despite her powerful presence, the towering woman smiled warmly. "My words are not precise in your tongue. It has been almost two hundred years since last we saw a nature child. There was a time when *abantu* lived so long, but that was long ago."

She looked up from the nature reader to the other Amahle. "Seer has sent me to you, *Inkosazana*."

Kenyatta watched Naiyala's face, saw trepidation there. Was this Seer some kind of clairvoyant? And what of the new arrival? The term, or title, 'Daunyana' was not lost on him. Was this woman somehow tied to the Daunyan Gods?

Naiyala steeled herself. "What has the Sight shown her, Daunyana?"

Amata tilted her head and touched Naiyala's cheek, as though inspecting the other woman's face. "Death."

The other Amahle went rigid. From the corner of his eye, Kenyatta saw the muscles in Jabulani's arms bulge when he clenched his spear.

Amata Daunyana spared a quick glance at the elder hunter, then back to Naiyala. "Do you understand the purpose of these humans, *Inkosazana*? Do you understand their quest truly, that you would join them?"

"They travel with *Umntwana Onomuntu*, and make friends with *umzingeli unwabu*."

Amata responded with a barely perceptible nod. "To see a nature child after so long is a sign of change in this world, finally. The appearance of nature child and *umzingeli unwabu* together is significant. The human that makes friends with the beast who cannot be befriended." She looked the four humans over. "Great adversity hangs over your shoulders. You've walked a path that ends with cliff." She indicated the Amahle band. "Fate brought you all together, yet even so, the cliff waits."

Amata Daunyana stared into Naiyala's eyes, held her fixed to the spot where she stood. As imposing as the Amahle princess had felt to Kenyatta when first he'd met her, this woman's presence could cast shade on a mountain.

"You were going to bring these *abantu* home." It wasn't a question.

Naiyala inclined her head. "Do you not agree that this mix of *abantu* is a sign that the king and queen must see, Daunyana?"

"They are a sign you do not understand, *Inkosazana*. A sign deeper than you, the king and queen, in all your collective wisdom can foresee. You would bring them to our clan, and depart with them to the frozen lands of Askasha."

Askasha, or Askata? Kenyatta wondered. Perhaps these people knew the place by a different name?

"The frozen land?" It was Jabulani who spoke. He bowed respectfully to the two women. "Please excuse me, *Daunyana, Inkosazana*."

"We hear you, Elder Hunter," Naiyala said, never taking her eyes from the other woman.

"Askasha is frigid and dangerous. Why would we travel to

such a hostile place where even nature itself demands we avoid it?"

"Those who inhabit the lands of Askasha would speak the same of our desert home, Jabulani Elder Hunter," Amata replied. "The answer to your question, and the one in your own mind, *Inkosazana*, is beyond my sight, and that of Seer, herself."

That drew a gasp from all the Amahle. "What could be beyond the sight of Seer?" Naiyala asked, her voice barely a whisper."

"Something waiting to swallow every one of your *abantu* friends, and every one of you," Amata replied.

Grizzled Bear elbowed Kita, who flinched. "I'll be apologizin' now, but not on my own hairy arse am I goin' anywhere to be swallowed whole."

The big man's "eloquent" statement practically echoed in the ensuing silence following Amata's words. The Seer's Apprentice arched an eyebrow at the guide.

"Seer has sent you to retrieve us," Naiyala said.

"No, *Inkosazana*. Seer has already foreseen your return home. She sends me because there is no time for that. She entrusts me with the task of preventing your death." She swept her gaze over the assembled. "All of your deaths."

39

Crouched atop a boulder overlooking the sprawling city of Phoenix, the words of the Seer's Apprentice still dominated Kenyatta's thoughts. He and Kita had faced death countless times in their adventures. Kenyatta had always found a way to laugh through it, even smile in the face of an enemy he thought might well be more skilled than he.

He'd even won a battle that way. His sudden smile while facing a combatant who was surely on the verge of ending his life, had bought him that moment of hesitation to give him an edge. Brighten life's grimmest moments; that was how he lived.

Then had come Jamaica's destruction. He thought about the aftermath of those enormous and unnatural tsunamis. Buildings collapsed and washed away like piles of matches. People dead or displaced, animals killed, land destroyed. He'd been convinced it was a major demon, one that had somehow escaped its fate in the battle of Takashaniel, or even one newly summoned by the creature, Brit.

Now he wasn't sure, and that was the worst of it. It was easier to battle evil. Well, emotionally, anyway. Were it a demon waiting at the end of their quest, Kenyatta would launch himself into that battle without hesitation, laugh in the face of injury, dealt or received. He would take great pleasure in eviscerating the abysmal creature in retribution for the suffering, death, and damage it had caused.

But if it wasn't a demon, what was it? A human? He sighed at the thought. Humans were ever complex, and that was the most frustrating thing. Humans could be purely evil, but most were some variation of good, if chaotic. Humans could kill countless members of their own or other species in the misguided belief that they're saving the world from one great catastrophe or another.

He rested his head in his hand. What if such a man or woman waited at the end of this quest? How could Kenyatta take joy in ending the life of such a person, no matter how much damage they'd wrought? He made a frustrated sound, and rapped the butt of his sword on a rock.

When Kenyatta noticed Kita looking at him with a worried expression, he smirked. "Wah gwan, man? "What's up?"

Kita returned the smirk, but the concern in his eyes didn't waver. "I'm good, brother. Are you?"

Kenyatta sighed heavily and looked back out at the city stretching for miles below. "Yeah, mon. Just thinkin', is all."

Kita blinked. "Mon? You thinking about Jamaica? I'm ... I'm sorry, Ken. I really don't know what to say."

"Neither do I, man," Kenyatta replied, reverting back to the general way he pronounced the 'mon' outside his homeland.

Kita looked as if he was about to say more, but changed his mind.

A dozen feet away, Malimokuru stretched his legs. "Unless you thinking some wave come washing across the land and over all that"—he waved a hand in the direction of the city—"I say let's get down there and get resupplied. I don't wanna chance our new friends leaving us behind to get 'swallowed whole' by whatever's waiting for us in the cold lands."

The city Phoenix seemed to stretch into the infinite. Kenyatta, Kita, and Malimokuru passed through the wide streets and avenues, marveling at the endless number of structures of every size and type. They stepped over large iron bars sitting atop evenly spaced thick wooden beams. The bars stretched as far as the eye could see in either direction.

Like Jamaica, Fleria, and many of the big cities of this new world, Phoenix was a paradox. In the centuries following the End of Technology, nature had wasted no time in reclaiming the earth. Vines grew over unkempt buildings and many types of animals and birds had claimed them in the absence of humans.

The elements, in concert with plant growth, had eroded the structures in short order, leaving only pieces of what were formerly great buildings. The hard roads that had once borne self-propelled carriages—Kenyatta couldn't remember what they were really called—lay cracked, rusted, and broken. Yet despite the decay of an age long passed, life thrived.

In contrast to Kenyatta and Kita's amazement, the two older members of the group were less affected. Grizzled Bear, while not as old as Malimokuru, had done a fair bit of travel and had seen such cities as a child. Malimokuru had also done a bit of travel, as was necessary in his studies to become a nature reader.

Grizzled Bear fanned himself. "Gotta admit, I've seen my share of big cities, and this is a big'un. Never been to Phoenix, though, and now I'm knowin why; I'm sweatin' like a pig."

"Pigs don't sweat," Malimokuru said. He gave the guide a once-over. "Not ... that much."

Grizzled Bear eyed the nature reader, then laughed and gave the old man a slap on the back. "Look at these streets. They're so wide you couldn't even spit across 'em."

Malimokuru actually chuckled at that. "Charming."

"According to the directions I got," Kita said, "there should be a shop to replenish our supplies, and a Travel Master shop not farther that way." He pointed down a wide street with white

markings one either side. "They should have more detailed information, since this Phoenix is closer to our destination."

Kita's directions had proven correct, but not quite to scale.
They had indeed soon found several shops to replenish their
supplies and replace gear, but the Travel Master shop was far
enough away that an entire village could be placed between
them.

"Why would anyone want to live in a place so big?" Kita said.
"Does anyone even know anyone else, here?"

They continued their trek across town, walking under
massive bridges made of stone, and Grizzled Bear walking in any
shadow he could find.

"This twice cursed place is gonna be the death of me, I'm
tellin' you." Bear pulled at his sweaty shirt, which clung to him
like a second skin. "Ain't nobody supposed to live in this
kinda heat."

The shadows began their flight to the east as the sun
descended upon the western horizon when the nature reader
froze.

They'd gone several steps before realizing Malimokuru had
stopped. Kenyatta hurried to his side. The old man's eyes darted
left to right, as though he were afraid to move.

"Something huge is bearing down on us," Malimokuru
whispered.

"What?" Kita's staff was instantly in his hands, and on the
nature reader's other side, Kenyatta drew his sword.

Grizzled Bear unstrapped his axe. "Where? I see no one
comin' at us."

"I don't know how to explain it, but something or someone is
watching us. It's overwhelming. We're not safe."

"Then we're outta of here," Kenyatta said.

"I can *feel* him, man" Malimokuru went on. "I normally can't
read much from people, but this is something so primal I can feel
him. He may as well be thirty feet tall. Fifty."

"Him?" Kenyatta and Kita repeated in unison.

Grizzled Bear growled. "I seen more danger in my days travelin' with you three than my whole life up to this point."

"I remember something about us telling you that you could leave whenever you wanted," Kita replied, glancing up and down the street. The surrounding buildings suddenly felt as though they were leaning in to glare down at them.

"Ain't about to leave now," Bear replied. He shook his axe in both hands. "I'm seein' this through."

They started back the way they came, expecting a concealed enemy to jump out at any moment. The hidden predator never appeared, and when they were out in the open again, everyone breathed a sigh of relief.

Kenyatta saw Kita peering at the sky and knew what he was thinking. The sun sat low in the west and they were in danger of being caught in this unfamiliar city at night.

"We'll come back and look for a Travel Master shop tomorrow. One not in that direction." Kita pointed toward the ominous street they'd left. "We either find our way out now while it's still light, or we'll end up in an inn."

"Where we'd never get a fair rate," Malimokuru added. "These big city folk know foreigners when they see 'em. We'd be charged a premium."

They wove through the many avenues, passing unfamiliar buildings and shops. After turning down several such streets, they stopped.

"Where did we turn wrong?" Kenyatta asked.

"That's what's bothering me," the nature reader said. "We went exactly the way we came."

They rounded another corner and stopped. An empty street stretched out before them. Kenyatta leaned back and looked down the street they'd just left. Multicolored buildings from orange to yellow to red towered over a bustling crowd, vendors, and parents pulling distracted children along.

"Why did we turn here?" Kenyatta asked in a low voice. The hairs on the back of his neck stood on end. Kita's staff was in his hands again.

Grizzled Bear held his axe in a white-knuckled grip. "I almost wish we didn't have to leave yer little blue monster back with them weird tall folk," he said, nervously looking up and down the street.

Kenyatta barely heard him. The more he thought about it, the more he realized that they'd taken the streets they had without making any conscious decision. "Something's wrong. Why'd we come this way?"

"Because I would speak with you away from inquiring eyes and ears," a deep voice replied.

Grizzled Bear made a startled sound and spun. Kenyatta and Kita also turned the instant they heard the voice.

The most imposing man any of them had ever seen leaned against a nearby wall. He stood halfway between six feet and seven, yet seemed as though he could be ten feet tall. Within his inconspicuous brown cloak were thick crisscrossed bands of cloth wrapped around a heavily muscled torso. He wore a flowing black half-robe like garment with loose fitting trousers underneath, and worn black boots.

A faint red color radiated from within his fair skin. A half-smile distorted the perfectly groomed inky black goatee that matched his long hair, which was tied into a tight ponytail. Dark eyes regarded them with amusement.

The expression gave Kenyatta the impression of a cat toying with a cornered mouse, and he was the mouse.

"You may put away your weapons, good travelers. I'm not here with malicious intent."

"I like holding my weapon," Grizzled Bear said. "Makes me feel warm and comfortable."

The stranger's responding laugh echoed in Kenyatta's ears and vibrated in his chest. What were they dealing with?

"I must insist that you be at ease." To their mutual astonishment, Kita and Bear were compelled to put their weapons away. Kenyatta fought against the compulsion, but only managed to stand paralyzed until he finally complied.

"Come," the man said. He strode between them and walked further down the vacant street. No invisible force urged them to follow, but the four men did as told. What could they do, in any case?

"Tell me," the man said as they walked. "Why do you seek me?"

"Who said anything about us looking for you?" Kita replied.

More quiet laughter. "No one ventures so close to my domain, yet the four of you stroll right through, blithely pushing through the energy I've set to ... encourage, people to avoid my space."

"We don't know whatcha talkin' 'bout, man," Kenyatta said. "We come look for a travel master. Just passing through."

The grin never faltered. "Ah, Jamaican. I haven't ventured out of my home in too many years, it seems. How refreshing to hear the accent of a land I often enjoyed visiting." The man's grin disappeared when he saw the shadow passed across Kenyatta's face.

"Apparently I've struck a painful cord." He stopped, the others stopping with him. His eyes never left Kenyatta's. "You've made it apparent that something has befallen your island home. I would hear of it."

Kenyatta looked up at the man standing over him, all memory of the powerful force surrounding him forgotten. "We don't come here to tell stories. We come lookin' for a travel master and be on our way ..."

The stranger's words cut right through. "I ask you once more while offering a bit of council. It is advisable that you share the tale of your homeland with me."

Kenyatta's palms started to sweat. This man exuded a power he couldn't place. He might have thought the man was inhabited by some malevolent being, like the monster in the ocean he and Kita had battled. But the gene of the Daunyans remained dormant.

Kenyatta studied him. There was a heaviness there, as though a much larger being had condensed itself into a tiny form. Whether the gene was active or not, Kenyatta wasn't sure he wanted a fight with this one.

He told of the demise of most of the Jamaican island, of their travels to Carrabisha and ultimately to this continent, leaving out only their battles with the demons and water elementals.

"Hmm." The man looked into Kenyatta's eyes, and he thought he saw a flicker of red pass across them. "You have a strong will. To tell me so much of your story, yet leave out that which you wish me not to hear." He nodded in approval. "Admirable." He looked at Grizzled Bear, Malimokuru, and Kita.

"All brave men to have faced such adversity. And you," he regarded Kita. "Your features speak of ancestry from the Philippines. A similar fate has not befallen your homeland, has it?" He tilted his head. "I've slept for too many years. It *is* still called the Philippines, correct? So much has changed since the age of machines ended."

"It's still the Philippines, Kita said. "And no tsunami has taken my homeland that I'm aware of."

"We didn't mean to disturb you," Malimokuru said, "and would gladly take our leave and not inconvenience you further."

The man leaned against the wall and crossed his arms and ankles. "How kind of you, yet I still haven't heard the whole story. Two completely random tsunamis destroy most of a major island, gigantic waves just ... appear, without any kind of warning, yet you fail to tell me the whole of it. Surely there was some sound preceding the wave?" He shrugged. "Some ... odd sound, like the intake of breath, a sound as though half the world itself exhaled? A powerful force bearing down on the land?"

Kenyatta went still, his blood gone cold. Was he reading their minds, or was it something worse? Beside him, Kita's hand tightened around his staff. Was this "man", the force behind the tsunamis? How could that be possible? Kenyatta's mind raced. If this was the enemy, they would need to figure out a way around his abilities. He remembered the compulsion to cooperate. Could he resist that force and still fight? He didn't think so.

"Did you battle not one creature of the ocean during your adventure?" the man asked. "Did you not encounter a single monster born of water on your voyage?"

"Who are you?" Kita asked.

"Someone with few manners, I fear." Once again, the grin returned. "I am Darius. I've lived in this lovely city of Phoenix for many years. Too many, it seems. From your story, it sounds like I've missed a great deal."

"You seem to know a great deal about our story, man," Kenyatta said.

"Suspicion," Darius said. "You must have seen some rather ... extraordinary things in your adventures to even suspect a single man capable of the mass destruction you've described." He looked from Kita to Kenyatta. "What horrors have you seen, young warrior? What reawakened evils have surfaced?"

"I don't know a thing about any 'ancient evils,' but there's plenty of horrors." Kenyatta decided to take the leap. "Which are you?"

Darius thought on that, and with each silent heartbeat, Kenyatta's grip on his sword tightened. How he wished he had his two enchanted swords instead of this inferior blade.

On the other side of Kita, Grizzled Bear stared intently at the man named Darius. Kenyatta knew the guide would fight with them, despite his trepidation.

"Some might consider me one of those horrors, but the same could be said for almost anything in this world."

"I don't see how so," Kita replied.

"Does the insect not think the bird a horrific monster? Does the gazelle not flee the terrible lion that would feed on it? Does the rabbit not scamper in terror away from death's talons, descending from the sky?"

Malimokuru held his hands up. "Poetic. So let's just go with you being a kindly fellow, ya? We didn't mean to bother you. We can be on our way without wasting any more of your time."

"You need not worry about my inconvenience. If that were the case, I would have left you to go on your way. I brought you here because you piqued my interest."

Malimokuru spread his hands. "You've got our story, Darius. I don't know anything more we'd be tellin' ya."

"Daunyarka," Darius said, more to himself than anyone else. "Could it be that after all this time, one awakes?" The four men glanced at each other, not sure what to think. "Perhaps I will be of assistance," he said at length. "I've given you my name, yet …"

Kenyatta gave his name before he could stop himself, and the others did likewise.

"I don't think we need your assistance, sir," Kita said. "Our road is a long and … uncomfortable one."

Darius arched an eyebrow at him. "I believe I'll manage well enough."

"Truly, we aren't in need—"

"I insist."

The weight of those two words evaporated any further argument. Kenyatta's heart pounded in his chest.

"We don't have much coin, sir," Kita said. "We cannot pay what your aid would doubtlessly warrant."

Darius waved the notion away. "My pursuit of monetary gems and baubles ended long ago. I've little need of that now."

"Then what would you want from us?" Kenyatta asked. "We have little else."

"Not so, young warrior," came the baritone answer. "You have time and an adventure at your disposal. You can share both with me in return for my aid." Darius looked from face to face, chuckling at the alarm coloring the features of each of them.

Malimokuru sighed in resignation. "We'll need to leave to gather our supplies. On our honor, we'll return to you after we've gathered our gear. Can you procure a horse? It's a little far for a walk."

Darius watched the nature reader through every word. "Your concern for your friends is admirable."

Malimokuru's mouth fell open. "Whatcha mean—"

"They aren't here, so you would warn them to stay hidden in the event things did not go as planned with me? I applaud your loyalty. As I would applaud theirs, when they finally decided to enter the city looking for you when you did not return to them. I would applaud them personally when they came upon me." His voice grew deeper, and the street darkened with each word. After a moment however, the darkness lifted.

"Of course," Darius continued, his tone lightening once more. "All of that is unnecessary. I would be honored to meet your friends and join you on your most courageous journey to battle the greatest challenge of your lives."

Kenyatta didn't recall ever wanting to run away from anything. Now he wanted nothing more than to be as far away from this man as possible. "How would ya know this is our greatest challenge?"

Darius smiled at him as one would a naïve child. "Return to your friends this night. I will join you on the morrow. It will be fun."

They nodded in agreement, for what choice did they have? Grizzled Bear, having been silent through the entire exchange, just stood there, staring at the man.

"Do not worry about returning," Darius assured them despite their not volunteering to. "I will find you."

40

True to his word, Darius found their camp outside the city.

Sakhile had awoken the camp quietly, but in the short time he'd known the scout, Kenyatta had never seen him so unnerved. When he spotted a statuesque figure standing a couple dozen feet from camp, he understood.

"After the *abantu* warned us, I kept careful watch, *Inkosazana*," the normally stoic scout explained. "There was nothing, then he was standing there, watching."

Kenyatta looked about the camp, but there was no sign of Nyaka. Probably out hunting, as she sometimes did while they slept.

"Be at ease, Sakhile," Naiyala said. "No eyes are sharper than yours. If you did not see him, none would."

The mysterious man named Darius waited until the camp was fully alert and waiting for him before approaching. He stopped a dozen feet from camp and offered that slanted smile, his black goatee stretching to one side.

"My name is Darius. I hope that your friends have spoken of me before now. May I enter your camp?"

"Be welcome, Darius," Naiyala said.

After introductions were made, conversation ensued about their best route to the lands of Askata. Ever full of surprises, Darius also knew the distant land in the same name as the Amahle: Askasha.

"Hope this guy doesn't turn out to be a snag in the arsehair," Bear grumbled as Darius engaged in dialogue with Naiyala and Amata Daunyana.

Malimokuru ran his hand across his face at that. "Eloquently put."

The three men went to join the others, leaving Bear to gather his gear.

"... and so you see, I feel that I have much to offer your little band," Darius said. "The Amahle are an old people, like the others of the Four. You understand that there are things waking up in the world, yes?"

"The Four?" Kita looked to Kenyatta, who shrugged.

"You wish to accompany us with no expectation of payment?" Naiyala asked.

Darius shrugged. "It's been too long since I've ventured beyond the borders of Phoenix. I would see what has become of the world."

"You carry no weapon," Jabulani said.

The red flicker passed across Darius's eyes again. "There are other ways."

KENYATTA DIDN'T KNOW what astonished him more, the fact that their Amahle companions had visibly lightened several shades in complexion right before his eyes, or Darius's lack of reaction.

They'd been traveling for a week, only stopping at villages so the four men could replenish their supplies.

Darius rarely accompanied them into civilization. In fact, he rarely ate or drank, but when he did—usually every third or fourth day—it was enough to give even the hearty Grizzled Bear a stomach ache.

It had been a somber morning. They'd been forced to entrust their mounts with a local farmer, as the horses wouldn't be able to traverse the mountainous terrain that lay ahead. The farmer, a family man of six, had been generous, and exchanged dried meat and cheese and any other supplies they needed, as well as a hearty meal for the day that would last into the next. Not long after they'd entered a wooded area, Nyaka appeared and shadowed their progress, easily traversing the uneven terrain. The land grew more harsh in the forested mountainside, yet the sun less punishing.

"How do you do that?" Kenyatta asked Jabulani as they climbed around a group of trees. Having passed through the desert flatlands of Phoenix, they traveled over the northwestern mountains.

"A bird could no easier explain how it ruffles its feathers," came the response. "You could no easier tell me how you grow hair upon your head."

Kenyatta conceded that point with a nod. "How about this: *Why* do you lighten your complexion?"

"Mostly camouflage," the elder hunter said, as though it should be obvious. "But in this case, we need not block the sun as much."

"So you're able to lighten or darken your skin to adjust to the sun or to camouflage?" Kenyatta whistled through his teeth. "Wouldn't mind being able to do that. Handy."

"Mostly," Jabulani replied. "Our hue doesn't have a great deal of range, but it helps. There are other Amahle who live in the jungles. You would easier spot a chameleon.

"Sounds nice," Kenyatta responded, not knowing what else to say.

"Desert Amahle have a different advantage." Jabulani winked at him. "Be happy we fight side by side, *abantu*."

The hike grew progressively steeper until they were more often climbing from tree to tree than hiking on the ground.

The Amahle leapt from branch to branch, and sometimes leapt to the nearly vertical mountainside to spring to a higher perch atop a leaning tree. Kenyatta watched in admiration and envious disgust.

"I'm so glad we got them tall, lanky folk to show off how it's done," Grizzled Bear grumbled as he scrabbled over a boulder, using the branch of a nearby tree to pull himself up.

"Might be that some of that formidable belly is not suited for this terrain," Jabulani said, patting the big man on the stomach as he passed. "Take that path, round friend Grizzle. You'll find it easier."

"Friend Grizzle," Bear grumbled, "*round* friend Grizzle, yet somehow they can't remember it's Grizzled Bear."

Kenyatta chuckled.

The elder hunter fell back to the rear of the group with Amata Daunyana, while Sakhile and Naiyala took the front, pointing out the safest routes for their human companions as well as scouting ahead for any possible danger. Jabulani and Amata would frequently sit and wait till their human companions put a sizable distance between them before bounding up the mountain to wait again.

Beside the laboring nature reader, Nyaka practically walked up the mountainside, her razor-sharp claws creating a foothold where none existed.

Darius seemed to climb just for the sake of climbing. With inhuman ease, he leapt and grabbed a tree limb with one hand, hoisting himself atop it and continuing up.

The scout's call from ahead told them that Sakhile and Naiyala had reached the top of the slope. No sooner had the scout called down, when the rest of the party heard a terrible roar.

Kenyatta looked uphill in the direction of the sound, then at

Kita whose concern mirrored his own. That sound had come from the same area Sakhile would have been.

Jabulani and Amata Daunyana leaped the distance between themselves and the human climbers. Once they caught up, they looked ahead, then back at Kenyatta and Kita.

"You will be okay, friends Kenyatta and Kita?" the elder hunter asked.

"Go!" Kita told them. "We're not that far from the top, it's no problem."

The elder hunter glanced at the laboring Grizzled Bear, and cast him a skeptical look.

"We look after the big man," Kenyatta assured him.

Jabulani responded with a nod, and he and Amata bounded up the mountain, leaping atop jutting rocks and tree limbs, grabbing handholds and catapulting themselves upward. They reached the top in but several heartbeats and disappeared over the edge.

Several roars split the air and rumbled down the slope, one after the other.

"We won't make it up there in time to help, Kita said, glancing down at Grizzled Bear and Malimokuru. The old man was strong and had stamina, but this was a challenging climb.

"Perhaps I can assist," Darius called from above. He was standing on a leaning tree, cloak swirling about him in the canyon breeze. Without waiting for a response, he stepped off the tree and fell.

Kenyatta and Kita watched as the man fell past them, but they needn't have been concerned. With impossible ease, Darius landed in a crouch atop a boulder protruding from the mountain, several paces to the side of Bear and Malimokuru.

Nyaka growled, but didn't hiss. Ever since she'd returned to the group, the goar cat had been wary of the man, yet hesitant to attack him.

"It seems our friends above have met with danger," Darius

said, smiling at the goar cat. If we are to help we must make haste."

"Thanks for telling me to make haste," Malimokuru breathed. "If I could make haste, I would. But if I make haste, it will undoubtedly be in the opposite direction, and I've still got a few years in this old body I'd like to enjoy."

Darius grinned. "Of course, good nature reader. I should have spoken more clearly. I will assist you up the mountain."

"And how in all the hells combined you gonna manage that?" the nature reader asked.

Kenyatta's mouth twitched. Malimokuru probably didn't want to know the answer to that.

Darius positioned himself beside Malimokuru. "Grab hold, please."

"What? I'm not trusting you to—"

"Grab *hold*, please." With more than a little trepidation, Malimokuru swung onto Darius's back. To the amazement of the three remaining men, Darius bounded up the mountain with much the same speed as the Amahle. In the time it took Grizzled Bear to mumble a curse under his breath, Darius and Malimokuru were up and over the top, a barking Nyaka hot on their heels. After a moment, Darius descended, similarly collecting an arguing Grizzled Bear.

"Hey now! I'm not string and bones like that crow you just hoisted!"

"I will manage, good man," Darius replied.

No longer having to worry about the other two men, Kita and Kenyatta doubled their efforts. Though not as fast as the Amahle, they moved with the speed and strength of a lifetime of training. In short order Darius—with a hollering Grizzled Bear on his back—whipped by. "We'll be there soon," Kita called after them.

"Yeah, man," Kenyatta huffed, as the two went over the side. "Not sure how I feel about help from that one," he said to Kita, who nodded in agreement.

Nothing could have prepared the two warriors for what they saw when they finally reached the top.

Two four-legged horrors crouched in front of their companions. Each stood as tall as an ox, but twice as wide. Bulging muscles flexed in thick legs as one of the hulking beasts dug its black claws into the ground. One of three sets of eyes settled its gaze on Kenyatta.

"C'mon, man." He drew his sword. "How much strangeness can we find on this quest?"

"Don't even ask that question," Kita said, whipping his staff out.

The cerberus half-turned to face the two newcomers, angling its body so that the head on one side faced Kita and Kenyatta, while the other side faced Sakhile and Naiyala. Darius crossed his arms and leaned against a nearby a tree.

Kita snarled at the amused expression on his face.

Malimokuru and Amata Daunyana faced the other monster not far away. The nature reader had a hand in his pouch, his lips moving silently. Amata slowly moved away from him, eyes fixed on the center head as it tracked her movement.

"What are you planning to do?" Malimokuru asked the apprentice.

"Kill it," came the reply.

"Oh good," Malimokuru muttered under his breath. "Hadn't figured on that."

THE HEAD FACING Naiyala and Sakhile barked. The Amahle princess hissed in response, whirling her spear over her head and tucking it under her right arm as she advanced.

As Sakhile circled around behind it, the cerberus turned, its heads swiveling this way and that as it tried to keep them both in sight.

Naiyala watched it closely. It was deciding which one of them to attack first. She jabbed at it with her spear, knowing the scout would do the same. After several rounds of jabbing and retreating, the beast bled freely from many wounds.

Those wounds did little to slow the beast, however. As if unaware of its wounds, the beast crouched low to the ground, ready to spring.

Sakhile waited till it was just about to leap, and hopped onto its back. Once, twice, thrice, his arms pumped as he stabbed it behind the shoulder three times in the span of a heartbeat, then hopped off.

The cerberus grunted and spun around to face the scout, but the movement was a clumsy limp.

A streak of blue shot out of the brush and landed atop the three-headed animal. It roared, turning and bucking, but Nyaka dug her claws deep into its flesh.

Naiyala seized the opportunity and darted in close to score several stabs to its left flank before retreating again.

The cerberus barked again and charged, then stumbled when Nyaka clamped down on the neck of the middle head. With the same wide ear-to-ear grinning maw as her mother, Nyaka bit down on the neck of her foe, a beast more than five times her size.

She twisted, pulled, and yanked at the monster's neck. The cerberus stumbled sideways, then widened its stance. The other two heads barked and tried to bite at the goar cat, but Naiyala and Sakhile stabbed them every time they tried.

Nyaka bit down on the monster's middle neck twice more. The cerberus shuddered. The two heads on either side arched their necks with a dog like squeal, while the third head hung limp.

It fell flat to the ground and Nyaka hopped off and circled, sizing up her kill. The two Amahle left for the second cerberus as the goar cat started to feed.

KITA AND KENYATTA looked at each other, both cursing their luck as they circled the bigger and more aggressive cerberus. In the instant Naiyala, Sakhile, and Nyaka attacked the other monster, this bigger one went on the offensive. Kenyatta dove right at the same time Kita dove left.

Kenyatta rolled to his feet and whipped his sword out in a horizontal arc. The beast recoiled out of reach then lunged again, forcing Kenyatta to hop back on his toes.

Kita spun his staff around and struck the beast in the side of the leg with as much force as he could bring. He hadn't expected to do anything more than draw its attention; he succeeded.

The cerberus rounded on him with the swipe of a razor-clawed forepaw. Kita felt the swoosh in front of his face as he narrowly avoided a paw that was twice the size of his head.

Kenyatta thought to rush in, but its thick tail swatted him in the arm and sent him rolling again. "Bomba*clot*," he growled, rubbing his arm. If he hadn't curled it in at the last moment and braced himself, his arm would surely be broken.

The beast charged and Kita retreated. He sprinted for the nearest tree and just as the middle head lunged out to snap at him, he jumped forward, pushed off the tree, and sprang backward and over the three heads. Holding the staff at one end, he chopped downward. The staff crashed down on the right head with enough force to shatter a human skull.

The blow dazed the monster long enough for a recovered Kenyatta to drive his sword through the side of the head on the left. If demon dogs existed, surely their squeal would sound like this. The three-headed horror shuddered when Kenyatta pulled his sword free. Blood dribbled from the slack-jawed head, and with one last coughing bark, it hung limp.

A roar came from beside the beast, and Grizzled Bear brought his axe down in an overhead chop. In the midst of shaking off Kita's blow, the right head hadn't seen the guide run up beside it.

The axe fell, and the blade sank into flesh and bone. The beast staggered and dropped to the ground, struggling to rise only to fall again. Grizzled Bear hacked at the thick neck until the head dropped to the ground in a pool of blood.

To their surprise, the monster regained its feet despite so much blood flowing from the stump where its right head had been.

It turned toward Malimokuru and barked, but it was a weak threat. The nature reader whipped his hand out of his pouch and spread a cloud of black dust into the eyes of the remaining head. Its bark turned into a howl as it stumbled backward into a sitting position, then howled again and slashed at empty air.

"Its eyes are burned," Malimokuru yelled. "Finish it!"

He'd barely spoken the words when it burst into blue flames. Now its howl was one of anguish as the flames devoured its thick hide. The shrieks were deafening, and Kenyatta wanted nothing more than to put the thing out of its agony. An arrow, nearly the size of his arm, whizzed past him to bury itself in the mouth of the middle head. It finally fell onto its side, gave one last shudder, then went still.

Kenyatta looked over his shoulder to see Jabulani lower a half-drawn arrow and replace it in the quiver over his shoulder. "Good shot, man."

The elder hunter responded with a grim nod.

"This is wrong." The flames dissipated the instant Amata Daunyana knelt beside the felled monster. "Cerberus spawn are from the ancient world. More than ten millennia have passed since one walked the earth."

She turned to Naiyala. "They aren't native to these lands. That they return after so many ages is significant. And that we find them here is a mystery."

"Or they never left," the Amahle princess mused.

"Could they have hibernated for so long?" Jabulani asked, standing over the charred remains.

"Maybe we find answers to this, too, when we reach Askasha," Sakhile said.

Kenyatta watched the Amahle as they spoke about the smoking monstrosity they had just killed. "Spawn," he said to Amata. "Whatcha mean, spawn?"

"I meant what I said, friend Kenyatta. Cerberus does not reside in this world, but its spawn sometimes roam the lands far away and across the oceans."

Kenyatta pointed his sword at the smoking beast. "And that?"

"I would like to know that myself," Darius's deep voice rumbled from behind.

Kita glared at the man as he approached. "Our thanks for your help."

Darius shrugged as if he hadn't noticed the venom in Kita's voice. "Do you suggest four formidable Amahle warriors, an almost juvenile goar cat, two seasoned warriors, a nature reader and"—he glanced at Bear in appraisal—"an armed guide, needed my assistance against two cerberus?" He blinked lazily at them. "You do yourself and your comrades a disservice."

Kita opened and closed his mouth several times to argue, then just turned his back.

"You're not surprised to see these beasts," Naiyala said.

Darius looked down at the dead cerberus. "As the Daunyana says, they are from the ancient world."

"You aren't surprised they exist," Naiyala clarified. "To humans, these animals lived only in ancient mythology."

Darius responded with a slanted smile. "As far as humans are aware, yes. For my part, I've seen a few things in my time."

Kenyatta watched the exchange with more than a little confusion. Whatever it meant, Naiyala's expression said she didn't like Darius's answer.

A few dozen feet away, Nyaka crunched on a neck bone. The sound sent a tremor down Kenyatta's spine.

Grizzled Bear made a disgusted face when Nyaka turned her blood-stained grinning maw in his direction. She licked her chops a few times, then returned to her meal.

"Impressive," Darius said. "Cerberus bone is easily as hard as steel, yet she crunches through it with minimal effort."

"*Umzingeli unwabu* has the right idea," Jabulani said. "You would like to take some meat from the animal? You need not hunt for many days." At the horrified expressions he received, the elder hunter opened his hands in question. "You eat the meat of animals, yes? I have seen you."

"It's a giant three headed dog ... thing," Kita said, his tone thick with revulsion. The four Amahle looked as confused as the men were horrified.

"Some humans are selective in what types of animals they eat," Darius explained. He walked over to the larger cerberus and knelt beside it. After running a hand along its side, he stopped at a spot where its ribs would be.

"Ah." He looked up at Sakhile and indicated a dagger strapped to his leg. "May I?"

After a glance at Naiyala, the scout handed over the blade.

Darius took great care in cutting through the hide. "This one wasn't fully matured," he said. "But the hide is still tough. You can break a blade if you cut wrong."

He pulled back a strip of bloody flesh to reveal several rows of rib bones. Then, to Kenyatta and Kita's mutual confusion, the man climbed on top of the dead cerberus and began cutting into its back.

"Mind tellin' us what ya on about, strange man?" Malimokuru asked.

Darius grinned at the nature reader, then looked past him at Kita.

Kenyatta found he didn't like when Darius's focus was on him, so he imagined his best friend felt similarly.

"This will be, messy." Darius drew his arm back and curled his fingers.

"Ya can't be serious ..." Kenyatta flinched away as the man drove his hand into the middle of the cerberus's shoulders. The sound of flesh ripping, and bone crunching made his stomach lurch.

Satisfied he had a good handhold, Darius pulled.

"Can't say that ain't useful," Grizzle Bear said. "Wish I was strong enough to do that. Make skinnin' a fresh kill much easier."

Darius hopped off of the monster. "Amata Daunyana. Might I ask your assistance?"

Amata moved to stand over the kneeling Darius. "What do you need of me?"

"You wielded the fire of Boraka. There is no hotter fire. I require but a flicker of those flames from you." He held up the long, grisly object swinging in his grasp.

Amata's hand lit with blue fire, and she cast it upon the spine, burning away the blood and gore.

Darius looked over his shoulder at Kita and tilted his head. After appraising the man, he snapped off a small piece of the spine, then held it up. He looked it up and down, then glanced at Kita again, and nodded. "Raging winds, violent waters, burning fires. The destructive power of nature. The fingers of Boraka." He held the spine straight, then looked expectantly at Amata.

The seer's apprentice cast blue fire.

"Careful, my powerful friend. Careful. Just enough to make it durable, but remain malleable."

"Your hands," Amata said.

"I will not be harmed," Darius replied.

That brought an uncertain look from the apprentice, but she continued her work. With the tiny bit of blue fire, and Darius stroking and molding the spine, twisting and compressing, it soon stiffened. At his bidding, Amata released the fire.

Darius bent the staff several times. "Durable yet flexible." He looked at the end of the staff that was once the tailbone of the cerberus. That end was now as sharp as a spear tip. "Sufficient." He looked up. "Daunyana. Do you wield the power of Oberon?"

"I am able."

"I bid you, cast His power upon it."

Amata's hands lit with a green glow. With Darius's guidance, she moved her hands up and down the spine, hovering over the transforming bone. When she was done, Darius tossed the item to Kita.

Before he could stop himself, Kita's hands snapped up and caught it. His eyes widened. Despite its grotesque origin, Darius had crafted the spine into a beautiful staff, black as polished lacquer. Tiny green runes appeared from the top of the staff and spiraled down its length to the spear tip.

"Oberon, Daunyana of Balance," Darius said. "There are stories of His propensity to change form to mingle with mortal life-forms of this world; birds, squirrels, eagles, humans. Any life that Amayilah sang into existence, Oberon has existed among them." He nodded at the staff. "It is attuned to you. Though not even a flicker of Oberon's power is present in it, your weapon possesses the idea of that power. You will discover its properties in time."

"I can't begin to understand what you just said," Kita replied, still staring at the newly crafted weapon. "But it's magnificent.

"Of course it is," Darius said. He looked to Kenyatta. "You wield your sword with either hand interchangeably. It surprises me you don't wield two."

"They were lost to me," Kenyatta said. He looked at Kita, who took a practice swing with his new weapon.

Darius looked back to the dead cerberus's exposed ribs. "You could break your sword upon these bones, warrior. Imagine wielding such bones as incredible weapons? Lighter than a sword, but stronger, more durable."

Kenyatta was horror-stricken. "I'm not holdin' three-head dog bones in my hands."

"Do you not trust me?"

"No."

Darius conceded that with a chuckle. "Then I will let you choose whether or not to accept my gift."

"A gift for what?"

"Allowing me to accompany you on your adventure."

Kenyatta though back to their first encounter. "Allow" wasn't quite the word he'd have used to describe Darius's inclusion to their party.

Darius looked again to Amata Daunyana. "I will remove the needed bones. I would ask your aid again in molding them."

"I am not a blacksmith, strange man Darius."

"This one last time, I ask. I'll guide you hand as before."

The seer's apprentice considered him for a few heartbeats, then nodded.

Darius cleared away more charred flesh and gore from two long rib bones. With the spine removed, it took little effort to remove them. He inspected the two ribs, gave Kenyatta an appraising look, then moved to a nearby boulder.

With one more head-to-toe look over Kenyatta, then his bared katana, Darius positioned an end of the bone over the boulder. With minimal effort, he struck it with the butt of his hand, and the length of bone snapped off. He placed it over the second bone and repeated the process.

Satisfied, Darius nodded to Amata Daunyana. "This looks thick enough." He sat one end of the bone on the ground, holding it upright. "With the tip of your finger, Daunyana. Press it to the tip and summon the fire.

Amata did as he asked.

"Less than a flicker of a flicker," Darius reminded. He held his hand over hers. "May I?"

Amata Daunyana looked into his eyes, then nodded.

Darius placed his hand over hers and guided her finger as the fire of Boraka bore into the length of bone.

Once finished, Darius turned it upside down and charred remains fell out. He held it up and looked inside. "Perfect." He sat it aside and turned to the second rib bone.

Kenyatta started to ask what in the five hells he planned to do with it, but looked again at the undeniably formidable weapon Kita now held. He wished he wasn't feeling more than a flicker of hopefulness when looking at that staff, then the rib bone in Darius's hands.

"Daunyana, if you would summon the fire of Boraka once again?"

Amata Daunyana's onyx black hands lit with blue fire once more, and she touched the bone.

"Now," Darius breathed. "Run your hand along its length."

As she complied, Darius ran his hand behind hers. With some effort, he straightened the bone ever so slightly.

The muscles in his arm flexed as he worked the bone, careful to apply just enough pressure to mold it. When his efforts were done, the bone had less curve than a rib, but retained enough to resemble that of a katana.

Darius looked to Kenyatta. "You do not trust me." He led Kenyatta's gaze to Kita's rune-covered staff. "But if the weapon in your friend's hand lends me any credibility, I ask that you extend me some small bit of your confidence. The blade you carry is formidable so long as your fight is restricted to clashing with another human blade. For your task ahead, it will fail you."

Kenyatta considered the man's words. There was no doubt to the truth of them, but Darius's very presence didn't inspire much in the way of trust. But the man could have done harm to them countless times already. Whatever his motives, there was that.

"Yeah, man. Whatcha need from me?"

"Your sword."

Kenyatta almost refused on pure reflex. Instead he asked, "Why?"

"The same answer I've given your friend."

Kenyatta handed over the sword before he could think twice about it and stepped away.

Darius turned the sword over in his hands, considering the hilt. He looked up at Kenyatta. "You've been lucky. Your hilt is not of the best quality, but with reinforcement, it will be strong enough."

"For what?" Kenyatta asked.

"Patience," Darius said. "Patience and a little trust."

"You givin' me a bad feelin', man."

"Relax, warrior." Darius gripped the blade at the base of the hilt with one hand, and the hilt with the other. He snapped it in two.

Kenyatta blinked helplessly, while beside him, Kita flinched. The gathered Amahle, for their part, gave no overt reaction.

"Trust," Darius repeated. He looked to Amata. "Touch here." He pointed at the base of the hilt, and the embedded length of broken blade. "Just a tiny flicker of a flicker of the fire."

Amata Daunyana focused her energy on the target while the blue flames engulfing her hand receded to the tip of her finger. She touched the indicated spot until Darius motioned for her to move away.

Despite what must be incredibly hot steel, Darius gingerly slid the metal free of the hilt. He dropped the useless piece aside and lifted the bone. With Amata's aid, he reshaped and shaved away the jagged edges where he'd broken it until it slid snugly into the slot. As before, Amata touched the same area until Darius was satisfied, then moved away.

After a few test swipes, Darius nodded in satisfaction. He held the bone sword so that the curved end faced upward, then looked to Amata.

The apprentice's hand lit in blue flame again, and she wrapped her fingers around the bone and slid them down.

Darius pressed his thumb, middle, and forefinger on the bone and slid downward along its length. After several passes, repositioning his fingers each time, the bone resembled a sword.

"Run your finger along this edge," he said to the apprentice.

Again, Amata complied, and he ran his finger along behind hers. They repeated the process, Amata running her finger up and down the rib while Darius ran his finger behind hers.

After more than twenty passes, the bone sword split perfectly in two, right down and through the hilt.

Kenyatta's mouth fell open.

"And lastly ..." Darius held the two halves of the sword up and turned them in his hands. He winked at Amata. "The forefinger of Boraka, the lightening of the endless storm."

Amata inhaled deeply, and the blue fire covering her hand winked out. She exhaled a long and slow breath, then inhaled again.

She balled her hand into a fist, then opened it, fingers curled, and blew the breath out in a huff. Tendrils of electricity sparked between her fingers, and with Darius's instruction, she passed her hand between the two halves of the blade. Each time her hand passed between, Darius looked to exert more effort at keeping them apart.

After her last pass, Amata moved her hand away, and Darius closed his eyes. A long low hum rumbled in his throat as he ran his hand along one half, then the other. He lay both halves of the blade on the rock and waited. Several tense moments passed, then without warning, the two halves snapped together as one.

Darius held up the sword with a grin of satisfaction. "You will find this a formidable weapon." He offered the sword.

Kenyatta gingerly wrapped his fingers around the hilt. When

Darius released it, Kenyatta felt a jolt of energy coarse through his body. For a flicker of an instant, it felt as though another presence had acknowledged him.

He took a practice swing. It was lighter than his old sword, but when he inspected the edge, it looked just as sharp.

Kenyatta picked up a fallen tree branch, tossed it in the air, and swiped downward. The bone blade passed through the branch as though it were made of butter.

"Yeah, man." Kenyatta gripped the hilt with both hands.

"That will require little energy," Darius said. "The sword was crafted with a flick of power from a Daunyan. As with Kita's staff, this is your weapon and now attuned to you. Will it, and it'll divide, or combine."

Kenyatta nodded, and held the sword in both hands. "Two swords."

The weapon divided in his hands. He stared in amazement at both swords. To his further amazement, Darius and Amata had somehow fashioned it in such that the halved hilts weren't awkward in his hands. He did a few practice twirls and swipes, then brought the blades together. They linked as one.

"I hope you're not going to say 'two swords' every time you do that," Kita said.

"Just to annoy you," Kenyatta quipped.

Darius stood. His gaze fell upon the remains of the cerberus. "Two mighty weapons for the effort of one kill. Very good."

Kita moved beside Kenyatta and stared at the sword. "Not even a hint of a seam linking them. Don't lose this one, Ken."

Kenyatta looked up and down the sword, still barely able to believe what he'd witnessed. "My thanks to you, Darius." He slipped the sword into its bone sheath with a satisfying *click*.

"My many thanks."

Darius grinned.

41

From her position high in the trees, Seung watched the struggling wagon's side-to-side wobble with increasing resignation. Up to this point, her turn at watch had been uneventful, but she had a feeling that was about to change.

Her rain soaked hair hung limp and heavy, plastered to the side of her head and face. She had found Orgonin to be a beautiful and wondrous place, full of lush plant life as small as a patch of moss on the trunk of a giant maple, to the great evergreens and redwood trees that were the forest's skyline.

And the smells. So many different scents and aromas of the various flora of the rainforest. Fresh, crisp, earthy. Heavenly.

Only a day into their arrival she'd learned why the trees grew so tall. Rainforest. And being such, it rained. Constantly. In the three days they had traveled through Orgonin, the rain had ranged from a misty dew to a deluge. Today was decidedly aggressive.

Perched high above the road, she'd heard the sloshing *clip clop* of horses' hooves long before she saw them. Now Seung just shook her head as she watched the lone driver guide the team down the sodden and slippery road. Who would travel in weather like this? They were many miles from the next city, so the roads were not as well kept.

As these thoughts passed through her mind, the wagon bogged down in a soft patch of road. The driver whipped the struggling team as they pulled the stupid man's wagon out of the rut. *He's the one that should be whipped,* she thought. The horses hadn't made the decision to travel in this rain.

Seung wished she could pull her gaze from the approaching wagon. She wished that if she did not look at it, the inevitable wouldn't happen and the man and his wagon would pass safely out of sight. She closed her eyes and sighed at the sound of cracking wood and whinnying horses. She opened her eyes and shook her head in disgust.

There sat the wagon, leaning to one side, one of the large round wheels sunk in a rut and broken in two places. *Of course,* she thought. She knew what would come next. The man was either a trader or had a family in that wagon. It would have been too easy had he been a trader.

When a woman emerged from the wagon, motioning for someone else to stay inside, Seung laughed under her breath, though she felt little mirth in it.

Nature decided the situation wasn't challenging enough, so the rain intensified. In short order the couple was as soaked as Seung. More than anything, she wanted to retreat back into the woods. She knew that a warm campfire in the middle of a canopy of trees on dry ground awaited her. How easy it would be to leave this fool to the rain and his wife's wrath.

Seung wouldn't do that, of course. She sighed again and made her way to the ground, then moved along the tree line, just out of view alongside the road. The deluge roared in her ears and pelted the arguing couple. Unfortunately, Seung could hear them.

"... told you we shouldn't have come out now. What are we

going to do?" Fists on her hips, the sturdy woman looked not at all affected by the rain as she berated her husband.

"We didn't have a choice," the man said. "I've told you that four times already. Just go back in the wagon and I'll figure something out."

"Like what?" the woman replied. "What are you going to do in this?" She waved her hand out, indicating the torrent soaking them both. "You gonna fix the wheel with wet wood, in the mud, in the rain?"

The man looked as though he was grinding his teeth.

Seung had seen enough. She stepped out of the trees and waited. After a moment, the lady spotted her and cried out. After her initial shock, the woman balled her hands into fists and shook them in challenge. "Hey now!"

The husband whirled, also with his fists up. "What's this, now?"

Seung glanced from one to the other, figuring the wife to be the bigger threat. Her mouth crinkled with repressed laughter. She held her hands out at her sides, showing them she was unarmed, or at least, not holding her weapon. Seung was rarely unarmed.

"What do you want?" the man yelled over the rain. "We got nothing for you here."

Seung raised a hand and beckoned to them. "You come with me." Her command of the western tongue was stiff, but strong enough. "Come and be dry for the night."

"We're fine. We don't need no help, thanks all the same."

"You cannot stay in rain," Seung pressed. "Come and be dry. I can help." The man started to argue while the wife gave Seung a long, appraising look. While the husband continued to banter on about them being fine, his wife grabbed him by the arm and pulled him to the side of the wagon. Animated arm waving and finger pointing ensued.

Her husband sufficiently cowed, the woman ducked into the

wagon and came out with a few sacks over her shoulder. A girl and boy, looking to have passed no more than ten or twelve years each followed her out with their own packs. The husband reached into the wagon and produced a couple more sacks that he hoisted over his broad shoulder, then they gathered and waited.

Seung looked them over and resisted the urge to shake her head again. She tried to ignore the arguing couple, but they were making enough noise to wake a hibernating bear. The children followed in silence, doubled over under the weight of their packs. Seung brought the group to a halt a safe distance from the hidden camp.

"You wait here," she said. "I will be back in short time."

"You're gonna leave us here?" The husband said. The wife looked concerned, her eyes darting around at the surrounding woods. The couple were afraid she was leading them into a trap. They thought she might be a thief. Seung didn't blame them that. This circumstance was perfect for highwaymen.

"Nothing to hurt you here," Seung said over her shoulder. "I will be back in a few minutes." The couple looked suspicious, but remained where they were.

Seung returned to the camp to find the others alert and gathering their things. Questioning looks greeted her arrival.

"There was a family on the road," she said, easily reverting back to the elven tongue. After weeks of travel with the elves, it felt as though she had spoken it her whole life. "Their wagon broke and they have nowhere to go. They have two children with them." Five sets of eyes bore into her after she finished explaining the situation.

"We heard them coming," Tinnoviel said. "We wondered how a group of humans that noisy could have slipped past you."

"*Some* of us wondered," Tikena muttered, dropping her pack to the ground and staring at Seung. "Let me guess. You want to bring a family of soaked *N'thresha* here to eat our food and stink up our camp."

"We have no food that they would want," Yurin responded.

Seung was taken aback at what sounded like a sarcasm-laced comment from the apprentice.

"Go get them," Tinnoviel said. "Our thanks for warning us first."

Seung inclined her head to the Daunya Warrior, glanced at the others, then left. She returned to find the family where she'd left them; soaked, shaking, and clutching their packs. They looked like a family of trapped deer.

"Come," she said. They followed without comment.

Seung winced at the sound of feet crunching on twigs and branches. Once, she heard the man slide a machete out of his pack and raise it to clear away some of the foliage. Seung half turned and gave him a warning look, staring him in the eyes, then glaring at the machete until he put it away.

"Hope you're not planning something," the man threatened. "I know how to use this." He patted the machete strapped to his pack.

"I'm sure," Seung replied. "My camp is not far. I have friends but they will not harm you."

Soon enough the group came upon the camp and the seated figures on the other side of the fire.

Like Seung, they wore their hair close to the sides of their heads in an attempt to hide their elven features. Seung turned to see concerned looks on the faces of the family as they surveyed the group. "You be safe and dry here." She offered a conservative smile, hoping her human features were enough to comfort them.

The couple and their children scanned the camp. The sight of the young-looking Tikena and Nuviel likely set the family more at ease.

"You want food?" Seung indicated fruit and vegetables in bowls near the campfire.

"Ah, no, thank you." It was the wife who spoke. "But I would be happy to fix something for you all for sharing your camp with us." she offered a firm smile to hide her nervousness.

Seung heard Tikena snort from across the campfire. She leveled a glare at the young elf before returning her attention to the woman.

"Thank you, but no, we are fine. Please be welcome and comfortable. My name is Seung and these are my companions." She spread her hand to indicate the elves, now rising and approaching the group. The family shrank away from Yurin and Alurien, likely due to the apprentice's unnerving eyes and the ranger's facial tattoos.

The father held out his palm and looked up. "It's dry in here." He turned his attention back to Seung "Why are you in these woods like this? Seems strange to me." He dropped his hand in an attempt to place it inconspicuously near his machete.

Yurin stepped closer and, to Seung's surprise, inclined her head. Her hair fell forward, revealing the tips of her ears. The four humans gasped.

"Who ... *what* are you?" the woman asked.

"She's beautiful!" the little girl said. Seung turned an amused look on the girl while her brother bobbed his head excitedly. "She looks like something outta the stories, doesn't she, mamma?" the girl squeaked.

"This can't be real," the father said, staring into the Daunya Apprentice's eyes. He never blinked. Beside him his wife stared, equally bewitched.

"To you," Yurin said, "we are not real."

Seung felt a subtle power resonating in Yurin Kei Daunyana's voice.

Tinnoviel and Alurien stepped behind the mother and father, so entranced that they were unaware of anything beyond the gaze of those pulsating yellow-ringed orbs.

Seung watched with growing tension. What was the apprentice doing to them?

Once the two males were in place, Amata blinked and the husband and wife collapsed into their waiting arms.

"What did you do?" the children wailed.

"You killed Mamma and Papa," the girl cried.

"Not so, little one." Nuviel Titika, so like a child herself, hopped up before the frightened children. "Yurin is mean. All business." Seung watched as the little elf searched for the right words in her broken grasp of the western tongue. "Mamma and Papa ... they sleep. Only sleep."

The girl had begun to cry. "Just ... sleep?" Her shoulders bobbed and she hiccupped.

"Elf's honor!" Nuviel said brightly, holding up a slender hand next to her shoulder and tilting her head sideways. The mention of "elf" brought the children around. Nuviel giggled.

"Why did they have to put Mamma and Papa to sleep?" the boy asked.

"Because they wouldn't understand," Nuviel said. Her singsong voice brightened the entire camp. She grabbed the children by the hands and led them around the campfire from the others. "Your parents be just fine when they awake tomorrow, 'kay?"

The little girl hiccupped again, but nodded.

"But why did you put them to sleep and not us?" the boy asked.

In the light of the campfire, Seung saw that the boy was a few years older than the girl, and protective of the family. She smiled in approval. Now that the father was down, the boy would protect his sister.

"Because you can keep a secret," Nuviel answered. Whether through some form of magic or her very nature, Nuviel's voice was filled with excitement and wonder.

"You're an elf?" the little girl asked. She looked at Nuviel with a mixture of hope and excitement.

"So I am." Nuviel spread her hands to indicate the others. "Humans don't know about us. Only children can know elves. Not adult humans. Not now. That is why my friend not fog your mind." Nuviel mocked a glare at the apprentice who returned it with sincerity.

"Are there a lot of you?" the boy asked, unable to contain his curiosity any longer.

With a devious grin, Nuviel leaned in close. "Can you keep secret?"

Both heads bobbed with excitement, and Seung giggled before she could stop herself.

"There are lots of us. Lots and lots!" Nuviel spread her arms wide. "In the trees and forests, in the mountains and hills."

"Anywhere there are no humans," Tikena muttered. Nuviel flashed her a dangerous look that cowed the sour girl.

The exchange was so quick the children missed it, but not Seung. She glanced at Tikena sitting by the fire studying the flames, then back at Nuviel. She dazzled the human children with her animated gestures and wild elven stories. Seung watched with growing certainty that there was more to that one than what shone on the surface.

"Are you going to make us forget?" the girl asked. "I don't wanna forget you."

The boy managed to keep his wits enough to watch Tinnoviel and Alurien gently lay his parents by the fire on their bedrolls. Not until they joined Yurin and Tikena did the boy turn his focus back to the elf that seemed more sprite-like to Seung at that moment.

"Not if you promise not to tell," Nuviel chirped.

"You sound like you're singing when you talk," the girl said, giggling.

Nuviel winked at her. "Because there is much to sing about."

She hopped and twirled, letting her head fall back and her arms spread out. "Look around you. The trees, the plants, the *life*. Everything around you is so alive! Doesn't it make you want to sing, too?"

The siblings looked around, then back at the exuberant elf. Nuviel danced back to them and grabbed their hands. She whirled the children in a circle and they giggled all the louder.

Yurin and Tinnoviel cleared a space between them as Seung approached. "You going to wipe them clean like the parents?" she asked the Daunya Apprentice as they watched Nuviel dazzle the children.

Yurin shrugged. "I don't think it's necessary."

Seung didn't hide her surprise. "You would trust humans with your ... our, identity?"

Yurin nodded. "Children are in many ways similar to us until their parents destroy them."

"Destroy sounds a little harsh, does it not?"

"What would you call it?" Yurin countered. "Children can commune with nature and even the world of the Daunyans, at least on a rudimentary level, until they become adults. They are strongly linked to the higher planes of existence. They see and hear things that most human adults do not.

"They are strongly connected to the Daunyans during their first seven years of life. After that their world tears the magic out of them. They are taught that none of it is real and they should stop behaving strangely." The Daunya Apprentice again glanced at Seung. "I don't insinuate that human parents maliciously destroy their children's spirit, but out of detached ignorance, they inhibit their children's growth. The world humans have created for themselves limits their potential. It is a baffling irony."

Seung's lips pressed together. "Your contempt for humanity is a little strong."

"Can you blame us, *haloren* child?" Yurin replied. Her tone held no hostility, but carefully controlled passion. "We have cared for and danced these forests for countless centuries. The Four had stewarded the world together, loving and nurturing all that the Daunyans blessed us with. And what happened?"

Yurin swept a hand in the direction of the sleeping adults. "Humans turned away from the light. They chose to rule the lands instead of sharing them. *They* chose to have more and take more without giving back. Why? Was this not enough?"

She spread her hands to encompass the forest. "Was there not enough food and land? Were their homes not strong enough? Large enough? Did the Daunyans no longer speak to them? Why did they turn their backs, break the world, forget us?"

The uncharacteristic reply left Seung reeling. She stared into the campfire, having no answers. Nothing she could say felt adequate. Of course, Yurin was right, but was every human to be held responsible for the failings of some? Many?

Not all humans knew the full history preceding the End of Technology. She thought back to the forest just outside Port City, and remembered how subdued it felt. She compared that to the forest they now sat in, miles from the nearest village, many scores of miles from the nearest major city. This forest was more alive, more vibrant.

She thought of Nuviel, still playing with the children. How depressed the bubbly elf had been as they passed through the forest north of Port City. Now she was more alive, more her cheerful self. Seung realized Yurin Kei Daunyana had gone silent. She looked to her side to see the apprentice studying her.

"Forgive me, Kiluriel Sen'Mora," Yurin said. "I did not intend to speak harshly."

Seung held up her hand. "You needn't apologize. You're right. It's just hard to hear."

Tinnoviel lay a hand on her shoulder. "It is a tender wound to us Kiluriel. Not only because of what humans have brought the world to, but because we let it happen. Some of our anger is guilt. Humans may have acted misguidedly, but we elves, and the other two of the Four should have acted on behalf of our world."

"Who are these Four you speak of?" Seung asked.

"You already know of two," Tinnoviel replied, never moving his gaze from the diminishing fire.

Seung frowned at that. "Who else could it be?"

"You'll not find answers from me," Tinnoviel said. "The world is for you to discover, not for me to hand to you."

Tikena stood and practically stomped over to join them. "If we can pry Nuviel from the baby vermin, we should be away before the parents awake."

Tinnoviel regarded her with amusement. "And when would you have us depart?" It was a question asked in the tone of a lesser to a superior, but it had the desired reverse affect.

Tikena shrank in on herself. "I just thought ..." she looked at Seung and stiffened. "I meant no disrespect, SaunyaLi." She executed a precise bow. With another angry glance at Seung, Tikena returned to her place by the fire, away from everyone else.

SEUNG WATCHED TIKENA, who sat staring daggers at the oblivious campfire. "What in all the world is her problem? I can handle her hatred of me, though I know not its source. Surely she cannot hate me so much simply because I am partly human."

Tinnoviel regarded the girl with sympathy, then gazed into the dancing flames as though seeing events much farther away. "Tikena and her parents and sister are all that remain of her family. When she was but a child, she came to learn the fate of her grandparents, and the rest of her family."

Through the forest canopy, light flickered in the dark sky followed several moments later by the distant crackle of thunder.

"Though Tikena's distaste would indicate otherwise," Tinnoviel said, "her parents' parents were among the most tolerant of humans. They always spoke in favor of stepping out from the forests and living openly with them to help rebuild their world for the betterment of all."

Night insects and frogs sang to one another, a chorus complimenting the life-giving water that fell from the sky.

"Time and again, their pleas fell upon deaf ears," Tinnoviel continued. "This frustrated them to no end, but in her wisdom Lady Seiyun understood that they were both right and wrong. It is true that the Elfinestraya should find a way to help humans rehabilitate, but it should be done from a position of anonymity, not direct contact. Not yet."

Tinnoviel looked past the fire at the small figure of Tikena. "Her parent's parents sought audience with the monarchs of one of the central provinces of Nomar; Arrydia. This was some ten years prior to the human machine cataclysm. They sought to explain that machines had been eliminated as gently as possible for the good of the world." The Daunya Warrior sighed with regret. "It was too soon. Humans had not begun to settle within their new lot in the world. At first, the couple were tolerated as one would tolerate a slow-witted person. It wasn't until they revealed their true nature in the midst of an audience, that they received a reaction. Chaos erupted in the court and they were imprisoned and interrogated."

"Why didn't they escape?" Seung asked, for surely they could have.

"I'd personally gone to bring them home, but they refused. They were convinced that if they allowed themselves to be held and posed no threat, the monarchs would permit them to speak." Tinnoviel's face hardened. In the light of the campfire, it was an intimidating sight. "Before their captivity, Tikena's grandparents had mentioned that they lived in the forest. Within days, the monarchs mustered their forces. We found axes, swords, and fire directed at our homeland. In their outrage and indignation at the loss of their way of life, and the struggle it had brought, our silent intervention was viewed as an attack.

"The rest of Tikena's family came together to free the imprisoned family members, first by diplomatic means, then by rescue. Her parents weren't so optimistic, and begged the family to quietly rescue their parents and leave. In their naïveté, the family insisted there was a diplomatic way to solve the problem. The result was the death of every one of them."

Seung shook her head. What must it have been like to learn such a fate of one's family? "You must know that not all humans are so irrational?" Seung stole a glance at Tikena, saddened by the girl's past.

"Of course not," he agreed. "If we did feel that all humans were like the royalty of Arrydia, we would have long ago eliminated them." He held up a hand at the look of outrage fixing on Seung's features. "Would you stay your hand if the urcha multiplied in numbers and threatened the world?"

Seung softened at the mention of those vile creatures that would have killed her and Swiftspirit, had Tinnoviel not come when he did.

"We did not, and do not believe humans are inherently evil, *quyo*. But you must understand, three of the Four have shared this world and watched in discontent as the human children break it. All hold out hope for human redemption, otherwise we would have long ago risen against them."

"How can this be?" Seung stared at the elven warrior in bewilderment. The implications of Tinnoviel's words washed over her. "What you're telling me is that humankind came close to a war with every other people of this world?"

Tinnoviel responded with a grim nod. "You barely understand how tenuous humanity's position was, and still is. There are others who felt differently. It was by our intervention, as well as one of the other Four, who convinced them to stay their hand."

Seung felt as though she had been punched in the stomach. "Why did you decide not to fight?"

"The Meeting of the Masters," Tinnoviel answered. "A rare and sacred meeting of Daunya Masters representing each of The Four."

"I wish you would say who the other two of these mysterious Four are that you keep mentioning."

"There is no mystery about this," Tinnoviel replied. "But you must discover these things on your own. Trust me when I tell you that despite what you have already seen, there are still things you would not believe."

Seung couldn't imagine what else in the world could stretch her sensibilities any more than what she'd already seen. "I want to hear more about this Meeting of the Masters."

"Another time," Tinnoviel said. "We've gone off track from our original conversation."

Seung glanced at the brooding Tikena. The girl hadn't moved, although she did cast irritated glances at Nuviel and the children. "I can't recall ever seeing someone so angry."

"She is only so intense when she is near humans, Kiluriel. She blames them wholly for the death of her family, and every problem in the world."

"From what you tell me," Seung replied, "that sounds like the truth. I suppose humans are lucky elves are so rational."

"Our rational nature is sullied by an inherent stubbornness." Tinnoviel looked around Seung at Tikena. "Although some are more stubborn than others. As you spend more time among us, you will find that we can be a stubborn and sometimes haughty people."

"I appreciate the warning," Seung said, remembering the reception she'd received from some of the elves during the banquet.

Tinnoviel smiled when Nuviel came to sit between them. "You have fun?"

"Yup," came the cheerful response. "Good children. Their parents should be proud." She looked at the sleeping parents, then back at the children. "I wonder what they will grow to be like."

"Looks like they're off to a good start to me," Seung said as she stood. "Do I assume correctly that we *will* be gone when they wake up?"

Tinnoviel nodded.

"Then good night."

"Good night." Nuviel waved.

Seung smiled. The elf girl was the second person she'd met when first she awoke in the Wood, and the first to treat her as a friend.

"Should I call you Seung?" Nuviel asked when she turned away. "Or your *real* name?" Nuviel smiled in exaggerated innocence.

"I've always known my name to be Seung, but I find Kiluriel to be quite beautiful. I think I need some time to fit into it."

Nuviel's grin broadened. "Seung is a beautiful name as well, but when Omalah defined you, Kiluriel was His choice."

Seung stared at her. "How do you know that?"

"Silly. You were born in Yathienel, remember?"

"I suppose so." Seung untied her bedroll.

"You really need to learn to take the reverie, one day," Nuviel called back. "I don't think human sleep is good for *you*."

Seung rolled her eyes, ignoring the heat rising in her face at having that fact broadcast across the camp. "Nuviel, humans have been sleeping for thousands of years, have they not?"

The elf nodded. "I didn't say humans were wrong to sleep, I said I don't think human sleep is good for *you*." She skipped over to sit cross-legged at the base of a tree, the others picking out their own trees to do the same.

Seung watched her travel companions, these five elves who were part of a life newly discovered. She looked at the man and woman on the other end of the campsite, wrapped within the coma-like sleep Yurin had placed them in.

She couldn't imagine the atrocities the elves insisted humans had committed. Having fought in only a few skirmishes over land or property, with the occasional fight against bands of marauders, Seung had glimpsed some of the worst human beings were capable of. She'd seen it in herself.

But there was good as well. When a young raider had been captured and pleaded for his life, Tae Kim had stayed his hand and put the boy to work. And he'd changed, becoming part of the village.

Seung thought of that boy as she lay to rest on her bedroll. The boy hadn't even had a name. He'd been hungry and was taken in by a band of raiders, told that if he fought hard, he'd have food and clothes. They'd simply called him Jek.

Had she been the one standing over him, *Vyirayoi* poised to deliver the final blow, would Seung have relented? Would the young man's pleas cooled the fire in her blood she'd felt that day at watching several homes being put to the torch, villagers injured, and three dead? That Jek hadn't killed anyone didn't excuse his actions, but would Seung have given him the opportunity to change his life as Tae Kim had done?

Seung closed her eyes, truly not sure she would have. Humans. Capable of incredible goodness and unspeakable evil, and everything in between. She couldn't fathom the thought of other races of beings rising up against them. If Tinnoviel's words were true, humans of the old world had been such a threat that the elves and two other peoples had been near to aligning and wiping them out.

She remembered something her aunt had told her. Much of humanity's recorded history had been destroyed in the chaos of the End of Technology. Some knowledge had survived, however, and it was said that the ancient humans who lived thousands of years before the Age of Technology had little in common with their descendants, who were more closely related to those in the age immediately preceding and following the technology age. They were a more peaceful and patient people, much like the Elfinestraya. What had happened? What had caused such a dramatic change?

The warrior from Kyu Village let out a heavy sigh. Questions for another day. She lay down, and before long, had dreams that brought more questions.

42

Seung's thoughts were far away from the thick green forest she and the elves traversed. It had been a week since they'd slipped out of the camp in Orgonin, leaving the human family in the safety of their campsite and continuing north. Yesterday they had crossed into the Rainlands, known as Semerest by humans.

Luck traveled with them for the better part of two days. The season had begun to turn, and the cold had little bite and less rain. Luck fled on the third day.

The rain might not have been torrential, but it fell in an unrelenting sheet between mist and downpour. Seung looked up from under her cowl at the treetops, thankful the towering sentries broke the bone-chilling winds that sought to caress their bodies like the icy hands of a frozen lover.

Not for the first, or third, or fifth, time, Seung reflected on her conversation with Tinnoviel a week earlier. As a seasoned warrior, she was certain what the outcome would have been if such a catastrophe as a war between humans and the other three of this mysterious Four would have occurred. She could practically see it in her mind.

Technology suddenly dying, mass confusion and chaos, then

magic wielders and amazing warriors converging on hapless populations. Seung had learned something of the types of weapons human militaries had used at the height of technology, but none of that would have worked. Only weapons that didn't require some form of power source could have been deployed.

Humans might have had a chance, if they'd known what to expect. Seung couldn't imagine that being so. With only the old weapons called "guns" the historians mentioned, what could even the most well trained force do when confronted by beings they'd never seen before, wielding power they'd never known existed? It would have been a slaughter, humans may well have gone extinct, and Seung might never have been born.

But that hadn't happened, and for whatever reason, it was determined that for every destructive and inconsiderate human, there was another who cared for and loved the world.

And so, this was, no doubt, the dilemma that faced the Four. A dilemma that prompted the Meeting of the Masters Tinnoviel had spoken of.

A flock of chattering birds suddenly took wing, shattering her thoughts. Seung looked around. The forest had gone quiet. The rain increased, and in moments they were soaked.

"Something approaches," Alurien MerTana said, his voice low and urgent. "Take cover."

In the weeks they had traveled together, Seung hadn't once seen the ranger unsettled. Seeing it now made her uneasy.

Tikena pointed to a fallen redwood. "There!" They followed her lead, scrambling to take cover against the trunk. Rain pounded the forest, battering through the thick canopy of leaves and branches to punish the flora and fauna below.

Plants and trees swayed in the suddenly violent wind. The elves shielded their faces with their arms against raindrops that felt like pebbles crashing into their faces.

Seung peered up at the bits of gray sky through the cracks of the forest ceiling. The torrent had come without warning. No rumbling in the sky, no gradual increase, just rain one moment, then an instant deluge.

"I still feel exposed," Seung yelled over the tempest.

"Yurin'll take care of it."

To Seung's surprise, it was Tikena who'd spoken. There was no hostility in her voice. The young elf must have realized this as well, for she quickly looked away, muttering so that no one could hear. Seung also looked away, but to hide her smile. *Adversity breeds closeness.*

Yurin Kei Daunyana stood tall and still, her mouth moving around the words of some silent chant. As the moments passed, her words grew more audible, and her voice flowed softly on the wind, like a hint. A promise.

The air around the apprentice warped, pulsated, then expanded until it finally engulfed the party.

"Whatever is upon us," Tinnoviel said, answering the question in Seung's expression, "is of an elemental nature. Yurin has summoned its like to protect us. Not an actual elemental; they are too unpredictable to summon without preparation."

"I think I've seen something like this before," Seung said, thinking of her attackers on the road to Little Seoul. "Monsters made of water."

Tinnoviel tilted his head. "You've seen one?"

"Several," Seung replied. "They attacked me a mile or two outside of a city."

Crouched beside Seung, Tinnoviel looked up at the Daunya Apprentice, who had also been listening.

"You're sure?" Yurin asked.

"Not something I could mistake," Seung replied. "The blade of my weapon passed through them as though I was cutting through a body of water. When Swiftspirit crashed into them to help me, he blasted them apart."

Yurin looked to Tinnoviel. "There is more to this. Elementals are linked to one species."

"One of the Four?" Seung asked.

Yurin shook her head. "Far beyond anything of the Four. They were the first ..."

An oak split in half with a resounding *crack* that broke through the cacophony.

The howl of the wind rose to a scream. Seung peeked over the fallen trunk, then hurriedly ducked back. Leaves and branches, grass and dirt flew toward them in a funnel that crashed into their fallen tree shelter. The earth groaned.

The assault continued for what felt like hours, then, as abruptly as it began, it stopped.

Seung slid her disheveled hair out of her face and blinked. She held out a hand. No rain. Not even a drizzle. No howling wind or blowing leaves and dirt. Nothing. "I don't understand."

"That was a water elemental trying to take shape," Nuviel said. It was only the second time Seung had seen her so serious.

"Whatever is causing the destruction from the ocean is affecting everything to do with water. If more elementals become active"—she turned a sober look on Seung—"it won't be good."

"And it's only going to get worse as time passes," Tinnoviel said.

"For us," Alurien said, "it will get worse regardless, the closer we draw to our destination."

"We must be gone from this place," Yurin said. "I kept its energy scattered enough to not focus on forming together. It will try again."

As the hours passed, the elves encountered no more oddities of nature, but that did little to lessen Seung's anxiety.

Her companions were similarly ill at ease. Alurien continually scanned the environment as though he expected attack at any moment. Tikena wore a sour look, but that was not unusual for her. Yurin seemed the least concerned of the party. The apprentice strode confidently in the middle of the group, her gaze never faltering from the path ahead.

Nuviel seemed at ease, but her mood remained as subdued as the forest. Every elf Seung had met was highly attuned to the forest, but Nuviel more so. Seung wondered if she was a different kind of elf, or perhaps it was nothing more than one person being naturally better at certain things than another.

They maintained a swift pace, with Alurien MerTana leading the group. Seung looked over her shoulder at Tinnoviel, bringing up the rear. Having sparred with him, Seung had firsthand experience of his capabilities. Thinking back on all that had happened since her time in Yathienel, she had to admit to herself that she might not have made it even this far without the Daunya Warrior, or the others.

"Master Ranger Alurien MerTana," Tinnoviel said. "How near are we to the end of the forest?"

"About half a league, Daunya Warrior Tinnoviel Nai Saun-yaLi," the ranger replied.

Seung sped up till she was beside the ranger. "Why the formalities?"

Alurien kept his gaze forward. "We revert to our formal titles for the benefit of those monitoring our progress. We are in the forest of the Myzelli."

Seung's heart skipped a beat. No one had ever been able to sneak up on her without her knowledge. Her hand instinctively drifted behind her back toward the shaft of *Vyirayoi*.

"Be at ease," the ranger said. "Your movements denote aggression."

Seung made an effort to relax. "Myzelli?"

Alurien nodded. "Myzelli elves. I know not the human name for this forest, but it has been known to elves as the Myzelli Forest for as long as we can remember, and the Myzelli elves have lived here for just as long."

"Will they confront us?" Seung asked.

"Only if they believe we are a threat," Alurien replied. "For now, they will watch. If we do not disturb the forest, we will pass unmolested."

Seung studied the surroundings but found nothing. "How many are there?"

"We are surrounded to the point that their numbers matter not."

Seung kept her features neutral, hoping no one could hear her heart pounding in her chest. "I've never felt so vulnerable."

The ranger finally turned those bright green eyes on her. They glowed in stark contrast to the blue with white dotted tattoos that flowed from beneath his eyes to his chin. His expression was a stone attempting to show kindness.

"All is well, Kiluriel. The Myzelli can blend into the forest better than any elf you will ever meet. They are a reclusive people, and for them, stealth is inherent. In the forest, they are invisible." He turned his gaze to the surrounding woods. "But even the Myzelli are visible if you have the eyes to see."

Less than an hour later, the group passed through the forest of the Myzelli elves without incident. Alurien pointed to a range of mountains in the distance. "The Sleeping Titans. We are entering the land of the Okanagan. During the human age of machines, the Okanagan border sat farther north and east. In these times, the borders have extended farther south and west, all the way to the coast."

Day had given way to dusk when the companions finally stood before the rocky green mountain range, which stretched from east to west, horizon to horizon.

"The Sleeping Titans." Seung gazed at them for a time, imagining the enormous range of mountains to be a group of titans sleeping head to foot for as far as she could see in either direction. "It's going to take a lot of time and effort to climb over that."

"It would," Tinnoviel said. He nodded at Alurien, and the ranger joined the rest of the elves, standing a discreet distance away. "But we'll not be traveling over the mountains. We will pass *through* them."

Seung offered only a nod as she watched Alurien move toward the rest of the party. *What now?* Whenever the others stood away from her and Tinnoviel, it meant the Daunya Warrior was about to share some elven ability or knowledge she did not possess.

Seeing her lack of comprehension, he continued. "Have you ever traveled through a mountain or cave?"

Seung shook her head. "Never had a reason to. I seldom traveled far from my village."

"By the Daunyans." Tinnoviel stared at her for several heartbeats, his expression a conservative mixture of concern and bewilderment. "It's fortunate you've allowed us to join you in this errand, *quyo*. Accomplishing your task alone would have proven ... difficult."

Seung wanted to be offended by the remark, but it was true. "Seems that way."

"I ... meant no offense," Tinnoviel replied, hearing the stiffness of her voice. "But there are things that sleep inside the mountains that are best left undisturbed."

The unspoken words hung in the air. Her hands grew clammy and her mouth went dry. "I ... I have no intention of disturbing anything."

"Of course," he said, dropping his voice. "Your abilities cannot be doubted, but there is no light where we must travel. You may not possess the heatsense of dark travel." He held up a hand as she was about to speak. "Heatsense is how we see in darkness. In the light, I see you as you are; a young woman teetering between apprehension and irritation at me."

Seung wrinkled her lips at that.

"In the darkness," Tinnoviel said, "I would see you by the heat your body emits. The hotter something is, the brighter it shines. All other objects that emit no heat are more or less outlines."

"And you aren't sure I have this, heatsense?"

"If you were a true *haloren*, you would not have the innate ability. But enough elfinestrayan blood flows through you that it's possible. If you can't see in the dark, we'll have to change our path."

Seung had come too far to succumb to the creeping feeling of inadequacy. "I understand. Whatever I can or can't do, I'll improvise. There's always a way."

Tinnoviel gripped her shoulder and gave a firm nod. "The Daunyans set you on this journey. You will write its conclusion."

***

"I'VE FOUND THE ENTRANCE." Tinnoviel ran his hand along the rocky wall of the mountain.

"Do you always engage in unnecessary practices, Daunya Warrior?" Yurin asked.

"I know you could have found the entrance faster than I, but I would feel the energy that shrouds it for myself before it's opened." He stepped aside to allow her access to what looked to Seung like solid rock.

Yurin arched an eyebrow at him as she drifted by. For a time she said nothing, just stood with her eyes closed, head lowered. She raised her hands and silently mouthed what Seung could only guess was an incantation of some sort.

The Daunya Apprentice raised a fist in front of her face, and one by one, extended her fingers. In unison with each finger, a green rune glowed to life. Once all of her fingers were fully extended, she moved her hand sideways in a sliding motion.

Rock crumbled and ground against itself, falling away in a cloud of dust. As before, in unison with Yurin's motion, a large piece of the rock wall around the glowing runes trembled and

slowly moved aside to reveal a tunnel. Once finished, she opened
her eyes and looked at Tinnoviel.

Seung shouldered her pack and moved to stand with the rest
of the group.

"No turning back now," she said, eyeing the darkness.

"You thought to turn back?" Alurien asked, incredulous.

"No, no," Seung shook her head. "It's just a saying. It means
the path is set from this point."

Alurien looked confused. "It has been set since the Lady
Seiyun decreed it."

"Never mind," Seung replied with a sigh.

Tinnoviel stepped just inside the entryway, paused for a few
heartbeats, then disappeared into the darkness. One by one, the
others did the same, pausing for a few heartbeats just inside
before entering.

Figuring they were letting their eyes adjust to the dark,
Seung imitated the process. Standing just inside the opening, she peered into the wall of blackness. Nothing. She
squinted, straining for something to happen, but still
nothing.

"Are you well, Kiluriel?" Tinnoviel asked from somewhere
inside.

"Humans can't see in the dark, TinTin," Tikena's teasing voice
answered. There was a high-pitched titter in response and Seung
couldn't help but feel betrayed at the sound of Nuviel
suppressing her laughter. Seung cursed Tinnoviel for not *whispering* to her.

"I'm fine," she said crisply. "I was waiting for the door to close
so no one follows us in."

"Oh yes, because there are so many humans stumbling
around this forest at this time of night at the base of this
mountain."

More of Tikena's endless sarcasm. Seung wished she could
throttle the irritating girl.

Yurin's voice floated out of the blackness. "Once you pass through, the wall will seal behind you."

Oh good. Seung took a deep breath and stepped inside. With a sense of dread, she turned to watch the last bit of light from the outside world grow more narrow as the wall slid shut. She might have been standing in a void. She saw no up or down, held her hand right in front of her nose and saw nothing.

She shut her eyes and took measured breaths. The darkness was so complete, it closed in on her. Seung opened her eyes again, though there was no difference. She continued to breathe, steadying her nerves against the feeling of vulnerability.

She looked in the direction of footsteps coming toward her. "Tinnoviel?"

"Uh, no. It is Alurien MerTana. Master Tinnoviel warned me that you may not see in the darkness. I am here to guide you."

Seung appreciated the ranger choosing to speak quietly. "The others are already down the tunnel?"

"Yes, they are a bit ahead. Tinnoviel did not want to call attention to your disadvantage."

"I appreciate it, but I'll not be a burden. I'll find a way." Her mind conjured the image of Alurien nodding his head stoically.

"We can ask no more, and I am sure you will. Come."

With the ranger's guidance, they soon caught up to the others. For a while, they walked in silence. Seung thought her imagination had run wild. The pitch darkness was as oppressive as anything she'd ever felt, but her mind was also visualizing her surroundings. It was as if she actually saw the group just ahead, easily making their way down the pathway.

She imagined Alurien just in front her. Impossible as it seemed, she felt the presence of small animals scurrying in and out of the cracks in the walls ahead and behind them. What could live down here? "Who made these passages?" she asked.

"Informally, we call them Ground Forgers. They craft wares from the earth and live within its depths, surfacing infrequently and only when it suits them." The ranger's voice was tinged with distaste. "They're a gruff and often unreasonable lot, but still a goodly people."

"One of the Four?" Seung asked. Her mind visualized him absently nodding.

"Yes." He went silent for a few moments, then, "the stonework is odd in this place."

Seung frowned. "How can you see the stonework with heatsense?"

"The rock in the depths of the earth holds heat, Kiluriel," the ranger said. "Although it does not shine brightly to us, it shines enough that we can decipher shapes or impressions."

Seung's mind conjured the image of the ranger running his hands along a piece of rock larger than himself.

"This stonework. Why would they fashion it in the image of ..."

"A two-legged scorpion?" Seung blurted out before she thought about it. Why would she think that? But she couldn't help it. She practically heard the images in her mind, and saw them through the sound.

"You see it?" Alurien sounded surprised.

"You're telling me that's what it is?" Seung's mouth fell open. "Somehow I saw it in my mind. It's as though I hear the image in my head and see it without eyes. I can't explain it any better than that. Is it a statue of a scorpion you see?"

"Fascinating," the ranger said. "Perhaps this is a varied manifestation of your dual heritage ..."

Seung nearly jumped when Tinnoviel's commanding voice *whispered* to her, *"Be silent, we're not alone."*

43

The gene of the Daunyans faded into dormancy once more. All about the calming warrior, heaps of demons dissolved, fading back into their abysmal dimension. Colors, once vibrant and practically glowing, faded back to normal.

Kenyatta held his newly acquired swords in front of his face. He discovered that when the gene was active, they felt like nothing. Now, though they were still light, he felt their weight.

He looked across the field of dissolving fiends to see Kita similarly surveying his work, likely also feeling the effects of the gene of the Daunyans fading.

"Well done, friend Kenyatta." Jabulani gave him a pat on the back. The Amahle hunter had to reach down to do it, for the top of Kenyatta's head didn't come close to his shoulder. "The power of the Daunyans burns within you."

Kenyatta responded with a rather nervous smirk. "Feels like we all surprised each other, today."

Jabulani laughed at that, and moved toward the others. Kenyatta watched the elder hunter as he strode away, his skin gradually reverting back to its normal onyx black color.

Kenyatta had enjoyed the satisfaction of seeing the surprised looks on the Amahle faces when he and Kita went to work. The two friends had blazed a savage trail through the demons, cutting down and eviscerating everything that came within reach. Demon arms and heads fell, rolling upon the ground before dissolving back to the abysmal realm.

Then their tall friends had entered the battle.

Kenyatta and Kita had turned to work their way back toward the others and had almost attacked their allies. Having expected to see their onyx-skinned friends, the two warriors instead saw four horrors with skin as red as blood rip through the fiends in the grip of battle rage. Somewhere in that rage, their intellect remained, for the tall folk fought with a combination of efficiency and brutal grace.

When Naiyala pounced on a demon from behind, Kenyatta had seen the recognition in her blazing red eyes right before she thrust her spear into its back and through its chest.

Kenyatta gave his head a shake at the memory of the sound she'd made. Something like a half growl, half gasp, similar to the thing that hunted them back in the Mord. Despite being charged with the power of the Daunyans, his blood had curdled at that sound.

"You look like I feel," Kita said.

The green runes on his staff pulsated, and Kenyatta wondered if the power within the staff was reacting to the demonic presence. Was it a product of the nature of the cerberus it was crafted from? Or some kind of magic from Amata and Darius's efforts? Both?

Grizzled Bear raised his axe in an overhead chop and brought it down into the skull of a demon that looked to be too slow in dematerializing. He chopped again and again until nothing remained of the fiend but a dematerializing mess. The guide stood over the dissolving remains, shoulders heaving.

A short distance away, Kenyatta watched the man. Bear's initial terror at the sight of the abysmal creatures had given way to pure survival instinct, to which Kenyatta was glad. Still, he hoped the man didn't have a mental breakdown because of what he'd witnessed this day.

Beside Kenyatta, Kita chuckled. Jabulani had thought it best to pair the big man with Amata Daunyana, and the two had worked well together. Bear put his now enchanted axe to effective use while the Seer's Apprentice called upon the powers of the Daunyans.

Another impressive revelation about these tall folk—they adjusted quickly. The moment the fiends appeared, Amata Daunyana enchanted the Amahle's weapons, including Grizzled Bear's.

"I almost feel sorry for the demons," Kita joked, jerking his chin in the direction of Naiyala.

The princess bared her elongated canine teeth as she grabbed one unfortunate demon by the throat, lifted it, and impaled it with her spear. She slung the fiend over her shoulder in search of more enemies to dispatch.

The battle clearly over, she straightened and closed her eyes. When she opened them again, they'd reverted from the blazing red of her battle rage back to their normal dark brown color. Her skin also began to shift back to its normal hue.

Kenyatta whistled through his teeth. "That's ... pretty terrifying."

Malimokuru and Nyaka appeared just then. Today had been the day to discover how frightening their friends were. Malimokuru had used his sands to deadly effect, burning fiends to ashes and causing some to simply dissolve as though showered with acid. Nyaka, frightening sharp-toothed grin dripping with saliva, had leapt atop a demon and bit down on its neck with a horrible crunch. She'd ripped its head off and slung it aside, then went after another. The damage she'd dealt might have been temporary, but Malimokuru had been there to finish it off.

Her tongue flicked in and out as she tasted the air. Kenyatta stared at those teeth in her "smiling" maw. Young or not, the goar cat was lethal.

"Does it seem strange to anyone else," Kita waved a hand at the numerous dissolving carcasses, "that a random horde of demons sat in wait for us? And out in the open?"

Sakhile used his foot to kick a dissolving demon aside and stepped in front of them. "While we fought, I saw a pair of identical winged Dark Ones, up there." He pointed to a distant range of hills. "I've felt eyes on us for three days, but I couldn't place it." He continued to stare at the hills as if they held the answer. "If you believe this was planned, I agree. I think they were sent here to die."

Kenyatta and Kita nodded through the whole explanation.

"At Takashaniel," Kita said, "we fought a horde of demons many times larger than this, and the weakest one was tougher than anything here." He shook his head at the memory. "And even *then*, when the battle was done, it hadn't felt like it. It felt more like whoever summoned them had been testing us."

"These are not demons," Amata Daunyana said as she, Grizzled Bear, and Naiyala joined them. "A demon leaves a distinct mark upon the earth where it is defeated. The mark is like a poisoned wound that doesn't heal until it is dissolved by one capable of wielding Daunyanic power." The apprentice indicated a blackened stain on the ground. "This is a similar 'wound', but it will fade in little time. The creatures who leave such a stain are, in your language, called demonites."

"Demon*ites*?" Kita said.

"One of the lowest forms of dung excreted by any of the hells." Darius, ever illusive when conflict arose, came striding up behind Bear.

"We missed you," Kita said. "Didn't see you during the fight."

"They are indeed demonites," Darius said, ignoring the sarcasm. "In the higher levels of the abyss, they rank above imps and familiars. Although dangerous to the average human, they are practically harmless in comparison to a true demon."

"So what now?" Bear asked. The man still looked somewhere between panic and paranoia. "Suren we don't have the time to figger out what this is about, and I don't need to run into another crowd of them things."

Kenyatta didn't need to see Kita's expression to know they were having the same thought: The battle at Takashaniel might have been finished, but with no real conclusion.

In addition to the missing drek who'd summoned them, there was a monstrous demon general named Kabriza who had commanded the fiends. Kenyatta's suspicions immediately went to whatever awaited them in the frozen tundra that was their destination. Was the drek planning another strike at Takashaniel as they traveled long and far to deal with a problem he himself created? Was this his plan from the beginning?

Kenyatta's jaw tightened. There couldn't be a worse time for this problem to surface. When this was done, he had business with their unseen enemy.

"We must go," Naiyala said. "There is still a long way to travel."

The non-Amahle travelers found their horses still tethered in the spot they'd left them.

"Considering Sakhile thinks we're being watched," Kita said, "it's a miracle our horses are alive." He patted his mount on the neck and rubbed its nose. "Why *are* they alive?"

"More fun to have with the eight of us is my guess," Kenyatta said. "Dem slaughter our mounts after we're dead, is my guess."

Holding his own mount's reins, Kenyatta stared at the distant hills rimming the field, and thought he saw two winged figures standing at the highest point, just before they disappeared from view.

44

Cold and soaked to the bone, Kita looked ahead with relief at the distant mountain range known as the Sleeping Titans. They'd traveled for two weeks since their battle with the demonites. Having acquired fresh mounts to traverse the flat lands and valleys that lay between them and their destination, the group hadn't encountered any more abyss-spawned challenges. In place of that, however, nature saw need to test their mettle.

Stoic and uncomplaining, the Amahle ran beside the cantering horses. Despite the toughness of every member of the party, the merciless rainstorm slowed their travel. More than once, they'd been forced to find shelter until nature's fury calmed long enough for them to see more than a dozen feet in any direction.

They'd crossed out of Phoenix and headed northwest into Damar, the Mountain Lands. From there, they continued northwest, passing through the lands of Narfel and heading further north and west toward the coast of Semerest.

Near dusk, the sodden travelers had entered the Okanagan and finally arrived at the base of the mountain range. In short order, Sakhile found a shallow cave suitable to camp for the night.

The roaring campfire was a welcome comfort to the weary party.

Kenyatta looked across the fire where Darius sat with his back against the wall, away from everyone else. The man obviously had some use of magic; the newly crafted weapon at his side was proof enough of that. But *what* was he?

"I wouldn't let him catch me studying him like that, if I were you." Despite his words, Kita also watched the man. "That one makes me uneasy."

"Ya mean how come he doesn't feel the wet cold, and doesn't need the campfire to warm up?" Kenyatta shook his head.

"More than that," Kita replied. "There's something beneath the surface I can't place, and I'm not sure I want to."

"One way to find out."

Kita watched him stand. "You're crazy."

"I feel like him dispatch us a long time ago if he wanted," Kenyatta said.

Darius watched Kenyatta's approach. When his gaze flicked past, Kenyatta knew Kita was behind him.

"In the mood for conversation?" the mysterious man asked.

"You seem the knowledgeable type," Kenyatta said. He waited until Darius indicated they should sit.

"I didn't realize I exuded a scholarly aura," came the response.

Kita chuckled at that.

"You showed no surprise at the sight of the cerberus or demons," Kenyatta said, stepping around the mention of the power the man had wielded over them back in Phoenix. Darius raised an eyebrow at that, and Kenyatta wondered if the man suspected as much.

"The world is an old place, and there are things living upon it that are just as old. The history of creation is long in the telling for such a fleeting time as we have." Darius looked around the cave; at Jabulani and Sakhile standing guard at the entrance. He looked at Amata Daunyana and Malimokuru, meditating in front of the fire, then at the lump that was Grizzled Bear, snoring at the back of the cave. "The Four, the Tribe, and Boraka's Guardians."

"What?" Kita said.

Darius blinked, as though waking from a trance. "Humans have found their history to be somewhat elusive, even before the death of the Unnatural Age."

"The unnatural Age?" Kita and Kenyatta asked in unison.

"What humans refer to as the Age of Technology, others refer to as the Unnatural Age."

Kenyatta thought back to the events preceding and during the battle at Takashaniel, then considered their Amahle companions. He and Kita had met many nonhumans during the last couple years of their travels. It was all so unbelievable and yet undeniable.

"Human history," Darius continued, "is riddled with holes and mysteries. Although they managed to discover their origins, there are centuries of gaps that exist. The wisest among humans have known this for generations, and have been tolerated as superstitious storytellers. But these wise humans knew the truth, or rather, a small piece of it."

"Let's go back," Kita said. "You mentioned something about the Four, the Tribe, and the Daunyans. We know who the Daunyans are, but who are these others?"

Darius thought on that. "I mentioned Boraka's Guardians, specifically, but I suppose it matters not. This is an answer I cannot give fully." He smirked at their dissatisfied look. "Understand"—he looked toward the Amahle again—"those whom humans share this world with have kept themselves hidden for thousands of years. Tens of thousands of years, and more. When, or rather if, their presence is revealed, it will be of their choosing."

"What does it matter, man?" Kenyatta asked. "You think we go to every city from here across the ocean shouting about it? We've already seen demons, elementals, all kinds of crazy things people wouldn't believe.

Darius conceded the point with a nod. "True words, yes. But there was an agreement, long ago, that when the other three of the Four stepped back into the world of humans, it would be of a time of their choosing. All respect this pact." He waved a hand at the Amahle. "You've met one of them already, and you have but to look at yourselves to see another."

"So ... Amahle and humans are members of the Four?" Kita asked, to which Darius nodded.

Despite the fascinating conversation and Darius's apparently vast knowledge, Kenyatta couldn't shake the wariness he felt. The man continually referred to humans as something apart from himself.

OUTSIDE THE SHELTER of their warm, dry cave, wind howled like the bellow of a great beast. Trees swayed and bowed under the force of the storm, some were torn from the ground and carried off into the night. The nervous whickering of the horses echoed through the cave, the whites of their eyes showing as they shuffled about.

"I'm thinking this storm will pick the mountain up and chuck it the last miles we need to go," Kenyatta said. "Or dis thing we go to meet has got a serious case of the winds."

If Naiyala understood the joke, she gave no indication. "Friend Kenyatta, whatever has the ability to cause such destruction from so far away would simply level the mountain."

Kenyatta forced himself to laugh. "That sounds like ..." he trailed off at her sober expression. "Truth?"

"Truth," Naiyala replied.

"And we're gonna pay one of dem things a visit?"

"Whatever it is, yes."

Kenyatta ran a hand through his locks. "Fun times."

"I do not think the confrontation will be fun, friend Kenyatta."

Not long ago Kenyatta might have laughed at the misunderstanding and tried to explain it. Now he stared out at the angry storm.

"Ironic," he said. "The thing that destroy my home have me feeling like this storm."

"This storm is yet another expression of the thing that destroyed your home, friend Kenyatta." The Amahle princess lay a hand on his shoulder. "Don't forget who you are."

"Yeah, man," Kenyatta replied. "But you barely know me."

Naiyala's gaze into his eyes was difficult to meet. "I see your heart."

His responding laugh was without the usual lightheartedness. "I always find a way to make the best of it, ya know. See the lighter side of the dark. But Jamaica, mon. When dis ting, whatever it is, take Jamaican from us, it take something inside me. All I can think about is how much I want to kill it."

"And what if you can't, friend Kenyatta? What if this enemy is beyond you?"

A lifetime of blood, conflict, and death passed before his eyes. He thought of the demon horrors he and Kita had faced. "Then it's my time, ya?"

He stared out at the violent rainstorm, hardly seeing any of it. "Two years ago, we're sitting in front of Takashaniel, still standing because of us and an army of mortal and magical beings. I wonder to myself if the demons we fought were as bad as humans. I don't have much experience with 'em, but I know what humans are capable of."

Naiyala's responding smile down at him, thawed Kenyatta's mood. "Demons are worse, friend Kenyatta. They are not capable of good. Not even the potential is there."

Something that sounded between a howl and a shriek cut through the roar of the storm, and all eyes turned to the mouth of the cave.

"Nyaka." Malimokuru said. The goar cat had gone out hunting, despite the violent weather. Another howling shriek. By then, everyone had risen to their feet, readying weapons and taking positions.

"She flees," Jabulani said. "In all my years of life I have never known anything to make a goar cat run away." He looked to Naiyala. "*Inkosazana*, we must keep whatever pursues her out of here."

"Planned on doing that anyway," Kita thought aloud.

"Your pardon, friend Kita?" Jabulani said.

Kita waved a hand. "Nothing."

Side by side, Malimokuru and Amata Daunyana approached the mouth of the cave, passing by the ever-apathetic Darius. Surprisingly, even he watched with interest.

"Move away from the entrance," Amata commanded. The apprentice stopped just inside the cave, her colorful robes and waist-length braided hair whipping in the violent winds.

Kenyatta flexed his fingers around the hilt of his sword, not sure what to do. Darius leaned against the wall with his arms crossed, while the snoring, shadowy lump that was Grizzled Bear challenged the storm with each breath.

A dark blue blur shot past them and skidded to a stop at the back of the cave, spraying Bear with dirt. The sputtering guide rolled over and clambered to his feet in a tangle of dust, coughing, and oath swearing.

"All right then," he yelled. "What're you about?"

"Quiet please, friend Grizzle," Jabulani said. "Danger approaches.

Bear started to grumble at Nyaka, but seeing the goar cat, crouched in the middle of the cave, fur bristling and tail whipping back and forth, he thought better of it.

Nyaka became almost indistinguishable from the cave walls as her color shifted. Kenyatta held back his snicker as Grizzled Bear watched the goar cat blend with her surroundings. When she hissed, the guide's hand drifted to his axe.

As soon as Nyaka had entered the cave, Amata Daunyana stepped in front of the entrance. With raised hand, she began a soft chant that grew louder with each word. She repeated the words over and over, each time her voice growing louder, stronger in cadence.

Amata Daunyana's voice echoed through the cave, penetrating the cacophony of the raging tempest. The storm stopped at the mouth of the cave as though it collided into an invisible wall.

Through it all, Kenyatta stood frozen where he was. Amata's voice penetrated his being and caressed his soul. It was lovely and terrifying at once.

"I don't understand your language," he said to Sakhile, "but that doesn't sound like it."

"It is a language known only to servants of the Daunyans," the scout replied. "And for her to speak it means that something dangerous is out there. "No *Ibun* Daunyana, 'conduit of the Daunyans' in your language, would speak those words unless there was no other choice."

"Isn't it just a violent storm?" Kita asked.

Jabulani was shaking his head before Kita finished speaking. "Do you not feel it, my *abantu* friend? Something is out there. Look at *umzingeli unwabu*." He pointed at the crouching goar cat.

She was hissing, her tongue flicking in and out. Every muscle in the goar cat's body clenched together as she stared at the mouth of the cave. Her claws extended and pierced the ground.

For a while, nothing happened. The seer's apprentice stood tall and strong, one arm extended, fingers spread, palm facing out.

Malimokuru fished into one of his waist pouches. "What now?"

Amata Daunyana kept her concentration on the storm outside. "It comes."

She'd barely spoken the words when an unseen force struck. Amata leaned forward against the invisible assault, sliding backward even as she struggled to remain upright. She pressed her eyes shut and resumed her chant as she pushed back.

The winds swirled and coalesced as they pushed against Amata's barrier. The outline of a humanoid figure hovered in front of her and pounded the barrier again. It looked on the Amahle apprentice with angry yellow eyes.

"I seen those eyes before." Kenyatta looked at Malimokuru, who watched the struggle with a mix of trepidation and awe. "They look the same as what I seen when I touch the ocean."

"That can't be what's causing all this," Kita said. He held his forearm over his eyes against bits of dirt and debris that slipped past the barrier.

Inch by inch Amata gave ground while the air creature grew in size. It grew until it looked Amata in the eyes, close to eight feet tall.

Kenyatta drew his sword, and Kita gripped his staff in both hands.

"Remain where you are."

To their surprise, it was Darius who spoke. He moved to stand beside them. He watched the struggle with interest now, his expression no longer apathetic. "This is her battle alone, and there is nothing you can do to help."

Amata narrowed her eyes. In the face of the still growing air creature, she held strong, her words of power reverberating through the cave. Her voice rode it the storm, swirled through the camp and outside of it. Words of power. Words of the Daunyans.

Now Amata Daunyana stood a little taller as the power flowed through her, while the elemental creature began to shrink.

"What the durned hell is happening?" Grizzled Bear shielded his eyes. "I fall asleep and wake up in some corner of hell?"

"Hm hm hm hm." Darius eyed the man from across the cave. "Careful the questions you ask, my friend."

DESPITE HAVING similar abilities to communicate with animals as Jabulani, Malimokuru had remained close to Amata Daunyana since first she'd appeared in the desert and joined their party. Now, as he stood nearer to the Seer's Apprentice than anyone else, Malimokuru watched the confrontation in what was becoming a frequent sense of amazement.

The power radiating through the woman crackled around them, filled the air with electric energy. The others felt it, he could see it in their faces. But they only felt a small bit.

Malimokuru focused on the confrontation with the benefit of newly acquired knowledge. This wasn't some earthly creature, some monster come to devour them. It was a force of nature; an elemental expression.

Amata Daunyana had agreed to school Malimokuru in some of the ways of a Daunya Apprentice. She was the Seer's Apprentice of the desert Amahle, which afforded her a degree of future sight. To channel the power of the Daunyans, however, one must be chosen before birth for the honor. Such was how one became a Daunya Apprentice, and later, a Daunya Master.

The past weeks had shown the old nature reader the truth of his skills and abilities. He'd thought that his skills had been passed down through the generations of his family, much like a blacksmith or a farmer. Amata Daunyana taught him differently. The power of the Shaldun sands couldn't be activated by just anyone trained to know the words. It was Omalah, the Daunyan of Spirit, who'd blessed Malimokuru with the power to breathe His essence into the special sands. It was then, depending on the need of the conduit, that the power of the other Daunyans were used to transmute the nature of an object.

Omalah had blessed him with this ability, allowing him to channel His essence into the sands he used. To learn that it was the Daunyans who'd blessed Malimokuru's family with their abilities, had been a pleasant surprise.

He squeezed his hand inside the pouch, feeling the sand slide through his fingers. He now knew it had been Boraka, the Daunyan of Destruction, who'd blessed him to use the sands as he had when fighting beside Kita and Kenyatta.

As he watched the confrontation, he now realized it was the power of the Mystic, Quel'yar, that Amata channeled.

The apprentice stood tall and powerful, as regal a presence as even Princess Naiyala.

The nature reader watched the woman with no small degree of awe and disbelief. Amata Daunyana was many years older than Malimokuru, yet to her people, she was considered as young as she seemed to him.

Amata's voice shook the cavern and her adversary shrank with an agonized wail. The Daunyana towered over her rapidly diminishing foe. With a final phrase of power, she swept her hand out, blasting it away as she would a pile of leaves.

The elemental burst apart in a final screech of defiance, taking the raging tempest with it.

With a great sigh, Amata Daunyana dropped her hand to her side. She made her way to the glowing embers that remained of the campfire. She breathed a single word and passed her hand over the smoking logs.

The glowing embers sparked back to life and flames licked their way over the logs until a warm fire crackled once more.

45

The *whispered* words of Tinnoviel froze Seung mid-step. She held her breath, not wanting to risk even that being heard.

Alurien must have received the same message, for he had gone silent as well. She heard him ready his spear, and did likewise, drawing forth *Vyirayoi,* and slowly, carefully snapped the shaft together.

Seung willed her rapidly beating heart to slow, and steadied her nerves. Crouched in the darkness, she heard scrabbling from further down the corridor and overhead. She heard the other companions shifting into a defensive formation, which she saw in her mind.

All around, the scrabbling intensified, and it was an effort to keep her imagination under control. Seung wished she had never come into this pitch-black grave. No, she mustn't let fear take hold or this mountain would become her tomb.

In her mind, images of dog-sized creatures with eight legs, two pincers, and tails curled over their backs scuttled toward them. "Scorpions," she breathed.

"You see them," Alurien responded.

"The sound is making me think of scorpions. I see them in my mind."

"We're surrounded," the ranger replied. "I count ten, and they're big."

"How is that possible?" Seung replied. "They don't grow this big.

"Cave Scorpions," Alurien clarified.

Seung didn't have time to consider this, as she heard one crawling on the ceiling directly above. She thrust *Vyirayoi* upward, impaling the giant arachnid. As it squirmed on the enchanted wooden blade, she spun the weapon and dislodged it. From the sound of things, the fight was on in earnest around her. Seung listened and allowed the images to take form in her mind.

Tinnoviel held off two scorpions with his wide and flat curved weapon. With a twist of his wrist, he slashed a scorpion across the face several times before it could attack. As it fell away, a second scorpion hopped at him from the side. The Daunya Warrior dropped to one knee and thrust his weapon up and out, impaling the monster. The corded muscles in his arm tensed, and he turned as he yanked backward. He continued the turn as the dead scorpion crumpled to the ground, and slashed a third across the face, then twisted his wrist and brought the weapon around and down on its back. The resulting crunch signified another dead enemy.

Nuviel took her position near Yurin. Her hand spears whirred as she spun them in her hands, batting a poison-tipped tail aside and darting in for a quick stab. Like the weapons of every other Elfinestrayan, hers were made from the bark of the *Kakaya* tree. With speed and dexterity her enemies had no hope of following, the little elf avoided every snapping pincer, sidestepped every stabbing tail, while delivering deadly counterattacks.

Still not sure if she was seeing or imagining what was going on around her, Seung's attention was pulled to two more scorpions descending from above. She whirled *Vyirayoi* and knocked the creatures away. That made up her mind. Whatever this strange ability was, it had twice saved her already.

The two scorpions she'd swept aside twisted and squirmed until they righted themselves. Their efforts succeeded too late. Seung spun *Vyirayoi* in a vertical arc and brought one of the blades down on the back of the first scorpion, then reversed the spin and chopped down on the second. More scrabbling came from every direction.

"Everyone to me," Tinnoviel called. "We must break through or we'll be swarmed."

Seung turned with each swing of her weapon, using the momentum to carry her strokes while preventing attack from the side or behind.

The group beat back one giant scorpion after another as they made their way down the cavern. The sound of scuttling legs on stone filled Seung's ears, but she forced herself to remain calm and heed the images in her mind.

Those with longer weapons guarded against descending attacks while the others held the front and back.

Yurin Kei Daunyana mostly used objects like rocks or bones and sent them speeding through the air to collide with one or sometimes multiple scorpions at a time. The enchanted missiles left a glowing tail of light in their wake that lit the pathway just enough for Seung to see that they were in trouble. Two horse-sized scorpions were approaching from the front. If one of those pincers managed to grab hold, it would snap them in half.

"Are we even in the same world?" she thought aloud as she struck another scorpion dropping from above. Given the numbers of the vile creatures, it was fortunate they weren't very smart. "The two big ones up front are closing fast."

"I will handle them," Yurin declared. She moved to the front of the party. A moment later, hundreds of shards of ice ripped into the two giant scorpions. They fell over dead under the barrage, and for the moment, nothing came from that direction. The group broke off the fight and sprinted down the path.

Seung used the sound of their footsteps to judge the distance between herself and the person ahead. When Yurin fell back, Seung thought to help. The sight of the glowing yellow ring that surrounded the woman's irises persuaded Seung against it.

"Stay to the front," the apprentice said. Her voice radiated power. "I will deliver them with fire."

Deliver them? Seung thought. Whatever her choice of words, Seung was glad for Yurin's decision to launch that fire from the rear. What would have been blinding from the front, lit their path from behind.

The light revealed an opening at the end of the tunnel about the size of the village square back in Kyu. Before the light faded away, Seung caught glimpses of scorpion statues. In the middle of the opening was a humanoid scorpion standing upright. She would have been horrified if she'd had time to think about it, but Tikena's screaming voice drew her attention.

"No!" the elf girl shrieked. "We've stumbled upon a Flesh Forge!"

"A what?" Seung asked. How could things possibly get worse? She didn't have to wonder for long.

"Flesh Forge," Nuviel breathed as the firelight faded to be replaced by darkness once more. "It's said that in order to pass, a sacrifice of flesh and blood must be made. In exchange, the traveler may continue with their strength rejuvenated."

As soon as the first person entered, orange flames lit each of the four corners of the chamber. The light wasn't bright, but Seung's eyes were able to adjust. She looked back the way they had come. Their pursuers did not enter the room, but crowded at the threshold. They wouldn't be going back that way.

"Please tell me you did that," Seung said to Yurin.

The Daunya Apprentice stood frozen to the spot as she

nervously scanned the chamber. "I did not. Our presence has awakened the sleeping evil here."

"Of course," Seung said, still eyeing the giant scorpions blocking their only means of exit.

"There's another corridor on the far side," Alurien said.

Seung looked where the ranger pointed. "We can easily make it to the other side before the scorpions catch us." She looked from face to face, and saw that everyone's attention was fixed to the wall where another statue of a two-legged scorpion stood. A bloodstained platform sat at the base of the statue.

The stench of long lingering death hit her then, and Seung suddenly wished for the stale and stuffy air of the mountain corridors behind them.

"Am I not understanding something?" Seung asked, moving beside Tinnoviel. "We can make the other side and be out of here."

Without looking at her, he replied, "If you try to leave without a sacrifice being accepted, you will die. The malevolent magic permeating this chamber is too strong."

Magic. Seung had only ever experienced magic when Yurin wielded it to their benefit. It hadn't occurred that it might be used against them.

"So, we need to give some blood?" she asked hopefully. "Cut ourselves and drip some blood into a goblet or something?"

Tinnoviel wrenched his gaze from the altar to look at her. "Do you think those ancient stains upon the altar are from a cut? No. Someone must die."

Seung felt her blood turn to ice.

Tinnoviel continued, "In the unlikely instance that someone were to make it here alone, they would have the option of dying quickly at the altar, or they could challenge the lord of the chamber. Should they defeat it, its flesh provides the sacrifice. If not, the challenger is devoured. Slowly.

Seung felt the sinking in her stomach with each word he spoke. "And since there are more than one of us?"

"One sacrifices themselves for the rest, or all take the risk and challenge the lord of the chamber."

The blood in Seung's veins turned from ice to fire. "In other words, there's no decision to make."

Tinnoviel responded with a nod.

Beside Yurin, Nuviel trembled. Seung moved beside her and placed a comforting hand on the young elf's shoulder.

Nuviel rested her hand on top of Seung's. "I've never seen a Flesh Forge, but I've heard of them. They're horrible." She looked up into Seung's eyes. "I don't fear death, but I wouldn't want to die in a place like this."

"Then let us die elsewhere," Seung replied, "and a long time from now." The little elf nodded.

"Shed the blood of one... and the rest ... may pass." The sinister voice came from everywhere, as though the chamber itself had spoken.

"Ugh," Tikena said. "It felt like that voice touched me."

Tinnoviel stood tall. When he spoke, power vibrated from his voice. "Blood will not be given, this day."

"The Scorpion Lord will decide."

Tension hung in the air during the silence following the declaration. Then the sound of rock grinding against rock echoed through the chamber, and a section of the wall near the statue shook as it slid aside.

From within the recess emerged a scorpion resembling the giant statue. It straightened to its full eight-foot height and flexed its arms, all four of them.

The pincers of its two lower arms snapped at the air, while the claws of the upper arms flexed and trembled. Its poison-tipped tail waved side to side behind its back. Its milky white skin shimmered, as did the white pupils of its eyes.

The ground vibrated in protest of each step as the Scorpion

Lord stalked toward them. The six warriors silently spread out as it drew near.

"I have a feeling that door on the other side has never been used," Seung remarked.

"Probably not," Tikena replied. "But it'll be used this day. Try not to die here, *Nyet'alo*. Even you don't deserve such a fate."

"Thanks," Seung replied dryly.

The warriors formed an arc, Tinnoviel and Alurien facing the approaching monstrosity, with Yurin and Nuviel to one side, and Seung and Tikena on the other. It turned a head littered with tiny horns from side to side, noting their positions. When it turned that milky white gaze on Seung, she thought she might vomit.

On came the beast, claws reaching for the nearest target while the lower pincers snapped.

Tinnoviel Nai SaunyaLi slapped the claw aside with his weapon and executed a one-handed chop as he spun. The blade struck the side of the creature's neck, and it turned its milky white gaze on him even as one of its pincers snapped at Nuviel on the other side.

The Daunya Warrior was fast, but Nuviel was faster. She hopped back, then darted in close for a flurry of stabs in the creature's side before rolling safely out of range.

To both their surprise, Tikena and Seung played well off of each other's natural abilities. While she might be fast, Seung couldn't approach the speed of Tikena Mojin. The little elf—only a bit slower than Nuviel—launched herself into a blur of movement as she dashed to and fro, scoring multiple hits every time she came close enough.

Seung whirled *Vyirayoi* with deadly force. Slower but by far stronger, Seung struck powerful blows every time Tikena forced an opening.

Alurien MerTana sliced the monster with each turn of his spinning staff. Any normal animal would have been cut to ribbons, and while clear liquid oozed from every wound, the Scorpion Lord gave no indication it was hurt.

Yurin Kei Daunyana circled behind and hurled a focused barrage of ice shards slicing through the air. Streaks of blue light lit and faded as the shards zipped across the space and stabbed into the Scorpion Lord's back.

That got its attention. With speed that should have been impossible for its hulking size, the Scorpion Lord whipped its tail out wide. The massive scaled tail swept Alurien, Seung, and Nuviel into the air like children's dolls.

The tail was heavier than it looked. The impact blasted the wind from Seung, and she and Alurien hit the ground hard, but managed to roll into a crouch. Seung took deep measured breaths as she rubbed her side. *Not broken, but I can't take another hit like that.* She looked to the ranger. Similarly winded, Alurien knelt doubled over as he, too, tried to catch his breath. Across the cavern Nuviel lay unmoving on the ground near the altar.

The sight of the unconscious girl near that evil place sent a stab of fear through Seung's chest. She forced herself to her feet. She didn't know what would happen, if anything, but she had to get her friend away from that horrible altar.

TINNOVIEL AND TIKENA managed to avoid the sweeping tail but were still forced to keep their distance as it whipped from side to side. Tinnoviel stole a glance at Yurin and saw the horrified look on her face. When he followed her gaze, he understood her dread. Nuviel lay unconscious near the blood-stained altar while Seung struggled to put one foot in front of the other to reach her.

Tinnoviel looked back at the Daunya Apprentice. Only magic users, or those who wielded the power of the Daunyans could see magical auras. From her expression, he guessed that Yurin saw an evil aura descending upon Nuviel Titika while at the same time it inhibited Seung's efforts to reach her.

He returned his attention to the monster just as Yurin blasted it again with ice and fire. Her efforts did little more than anger the Scorpion Lord. It rounded on her, and Yurin dove aside, barely avoiding being disemboweled by a sweeping pincer.

Tikena growled and darted forward. She dodged left and right, rolled sideways then leapt forward. As soon as her feet touched the ground, she leapt sideways so quickly, she might not have ever been on the spot.

The little elf came in at an angle, easily avoiding the poison-tipped tail. She sprinted forward as the tail curled back, poison tip aimed straight for her chest. It came straight for her, and Tikena dropped to her back, sliding underneath the stabbing tail. She turned onto her stomach just as she slid between its legs. With all her strength, she ran the spear tip of her staff into the back of its leg.

For the first time, the Scorpion Lord showed pain. Its angry screech shook the chamber, dislodging pieces of rock and stone from the cavern and statues.

"Yurin," Tinnoviel called. "We'll deal with it. Get Nuviel!"

BEFORE THE DAUNYA Warrior finished speaking, Yurin launched a final stream of fire into the side of the Scorpion Lord's head. She didn't wait to see if the distraction worked, but bolted in the direction of the altar and the unconscious Nuviel.

Yurin didn't need the flickering light of the flames about the chamber to see the force gathering around the girl. The presence that permeated this place was evil—old evil. From the moment it had emerged, she knew that the Scorpion Lord was no more than an expression of the malevolence that dominated this chamber.

She skidded to a stop in front of the aura of evil energy and sank within herself. The apprentice called upon the Daunyans. She felt their presence building within her, flooding her with love and light until she could no longer contain it. She crossed her hands in front of her chest, palms facing opposite directions, and released the power straining to be free. Blinding white fire erupted from the erect form of Yurin Kei Daunyana and collided with the wall of evil.

With every ounce of her will, Yurin Kei Daunyana channeled the power of the Daunyans through her body, focusing it upon the darkness. Sweat trickled down the side of her face but she held firm. The evil force pushed against the white flame, testing a muscle against a weight. Through the struggle, Yurin could feel the other's thoughts. She sensed amusement, as though whatever she fought found her struggle a rare treat.

As soon as Nuviel awoke, she knew she was in trouble. The last thing she remembered was being batted aside by that thick tail. Now, trying to clear the fuzziness from her head, she saw that she lay at the base of the altar of sacrifice. She was no cleric, but the evil gathering around her was so heavy, so intense, she could feel it.

Claws of fear gripped her heart, for she knew that if she died in this place, her soul would be torn asunder and devoured by the evil that lived here. She felt the hunger, the unseen jaws, closing around her. As despair closed in and wrapped around her, a bright white light pierced part of the darkness.

Yurin Kei Daunyana, tall and powerful, channeled the light of the Daunyans. The light filled the Daunya Apprentice and flowed through her, then out of her, colliding with the evil vacuum of light. It wasn't enough.

Yurin Kei Daunyana threw the whole of her will against the

malevolence of which the Scorpion Lord was merely a tool, and expression.

Nuviel watched with growing dread as her dear friend threw every bit of the power of the Daunyans her body could channel against the closing jaws. Her foe was too powerful. The apprentice could not defeat it.

SEUNG WATCHED in helpless despair as Nuviel finally came awake and struggled to her feet. Her powerless friend could only watch as well, Yurin's struggle against the malign presence gradually overpowering her. The Daunya Apprentice looked as though she would fall over at any moment.

Seung fought against the invisible force restraining her, dragged herself step by step toward Nuviel. Tears fell down her cheeks to see her friend's face, always so bright and cheerful, twisted with anguish and fear as she watched the battle to decide her fate.

Step by laborious step, Seung struggled toward Nuviel until she suddenly stumbled forward. Whatever had held her back had simply released its grip. Seung broke into a run, fighting back her desperation to keep a clear head.

Tikena tackled Seung to the ground before she reached the altar. "No! You mustn't! There's a wall of evil there. If you touch it, you'll die."

"Then what do we do?" Seung yelled.

"Nothing. The only one of us with a chance of saving her is there." Tikena pointed at the faltering Yurin.

Seung felt helpless. She looked from Yurin to Tinnoviel and Alurien battling the Scorpion Lord. As before, the two warriors complimented each other's actions flawlessly. They'd managed to disable both pincers, which hung limp and bleeding, and the monster's movements had noticeably slowed.

Alurien swatted aside a reaching claw and spun his spear around to stab the monster in its exposed side. Tinnoviel slashed down on its tail with two rapid strokes. The shell of the tail broke under the quick and heavy blows. The elven warrior ran up the Scorpion Lord's back and kicked off of its shoulder. He twisted mid-air and chopped his weapon down on the head. In the hands of the powerful Daunya Warrior, the weapon cut a line from the top of the Scorpion Lord's face down its torso.

The Scorpion Lord staggered backward and draped one arm across its midsection while lifting its other arm to protect its injured face.

With a guttural cry, Alurien drove his spear through its arm, and into its throat. Because of the awkward angle in which it stood, the Scorpion Lord slashed harmlessly at the ranger with its free arm, while Alurien held its impaled arm pinned to its oozing throat.

The fearsome Tinnoviel went on the offense once more. His weapon spun and struck, swept and stabbed. The sound of rapidly cracking carapace echoed throughout the chamber.

Clear white lifeblood flowing from its throat, its midsection pulverized, the two-legged scorpion brute sagged to the ground.

Tinnoviel aided its descent. He pummeled the dying Scorpion Lord all the way to the cavern floor. Bits of shattered carapace sprayed through the air. Tinnoviel Nai SaunyaLi, helpless to save his little friend, brought his full rage down upon the pure evil creature. It convulsed in death even as the elf further destroyed its body.

As the Scorpion Lord finally hit the ground, Tinnoviel's curved fan-shaped weapon descended with it. The hulking body thumped to the ground as the blade struck true. The horned head broke apart under the thunderous blow.

Tinnoviel turned to the struggle between Yurin Kei Daunyana and the true essence evil of this chamber, and his heart sank.

NUVIEL WATCHED the apprentice sink to her knees. She watched as her friend gave everything she had to save her. She watched the tears stream down Yurin's cheeks with the realization she could not win.

Yurin's scream echoed through the chamber. She collapsed to the floor just as Tinnoviel rushed to her side. It was then that the evil fell upon Nuviel.

A darkness she never imagined possible enveloped her and tore at her soul. It stripped every happy memory from her, snatched away every positive sensation and experience, erased every moment of love she'd ever had; she might have never been happy in her life.

Her body lifted from the ground and the evil passed through her over and over again, snatching and tearing at her spirit and blotting out her inner light. Tears welled in her eyes as the potent evil of the true Scorpion Lord sought to rip her soul asunder.

As the endless evil pressed down on her, crushing her under its enormous weight, a voice penetrated Nuviel's torment. A playful yet powerful voice that the poor elf girl desperately grabbed hold of.

"Speak my name, child. Upon your lips, within your mind, your heart, within your very soul. It matters not. Speak my name."

"Nakiya?" Nuviel breathed. "Nakiya!" Nuviel Titika, at the end of her life, saw the light and love of The Redeemer as it flooded into her. It blasted away the dark evil that tried to tear her apart like black leaves in a gust of wind.

Light. The brilliant light of love flooded into Nuviel in torrents until she thought she would burst. Strength replaced pain, joy burned away sorrow, love burned away her torture.

The brilliant light of the Redeemer filled Nuviel until every sliver of darkness was gone. It built within her, gathered inside her tiny little body, then exploded.

The sinister voice that had once demanded their sacrifice, now shrieked in enraged agony as the blessed light burned the evil of the Scorpion Lord away. The Redeemer absorbed the Scorpion Lord into her divine light and obliterated it.

The Scorpion Lord's final scream shook the chamber. Every one of the hideous statues toppled over and broke apart. The wall of giant scorpions at the chamber's entrance exploded into a mass of milky white ichor.

Nuviel rose from the ground, the love of Nakiya still flowing through her. She looked about the chamber to see the evil darkness fading away. She spied the destroyed altar, a dozen cracks spider webbing across its ruined surface. The stone effigies of the Scorpion Lord were reduced to rubble. The evil that had sustained the chamber had been eradicated.

The sound of quiet sobbing drew Nuviel's attention to her five friends gathered around ... her body. Her *body*. A shadow cast over the joy that Nuviel felt, but only for an instant. She heard the voice of Nakiya again, and felt the Daunyan fill her spirit with love.

"*You're not dead, silly,*" the childlike voice said. "*The Scorpion Lord is destroyed, but you, my love, you, my sweet, beautiful, perfect child, are* alive. *So alive!*"

"*What of my friends?*" Nuviel asked.

"*They will survive because of you, little sprite. Many spirits are freed because of you. The evil that lived here has been destroyed and this place is cleansed. Come.*"

Nuviel watched Seung kneel beside her body, cradling her head in her lap and sobbing over her face. Tikena knelt to her other side, head lowered, tears falling from her closed eyes. Yurin, Alurien, and Tinnoviel hovered over them, solemn.

Nuviel felt warmth and sympathy surround her, and she heard Nakiya's voice again.

"*My dear sweet child. I will wait.*"

SEUNG CRIED over the lifeless body of the first friend she had met when she awoke in Yathienel, what seemed a lifetime ago. Nuviel's eyes were closed, her beautiful little face peaceful in death. It was so wrong. She was little more than a child, whatever her age in human years might have been. Across from her, Tikena sat grieving in silence, tears streaming down her cheeks.

The cold agony of grief began to melt away to be replaced by the familiar warmth of Nuviel. A surge of love, joy, and playfulness filled Seung to bursting. She felt insubstantial arms wrap around her in a crushing hug that embraced her soul. Seung looked up at the others and saw every one of them wearing the same startled look of awe.

"Don't cry for me, my family. My time here is finished and I am alive now."

Love like nothing Seung had ever felt flooded through her and the others. Even the stoic Tinnoviel and Alurien MerTana were brought to tears.

"I'm sorry, little one," Yurin said in barely a whisper. "I was not strong enough." After a moment, the apprentice raised her head. A hint of a smile stretched her lips and tears flowed down her cheeks. "Thank you, my friend," she whispered. "Thank you."

Seung wondered what Nuviel's spirit had said to the apprentice, but that was a private matter.

Slowly, hesitantly, the warming love that filled the five companions receded and with it, the essence of Nuviel Titika. As if in one final comforting "goodbye", they heard the far away sound of cheerful laughter.

46

Rain clouds gave way to sun, only to return again by midday. It had become an all too familiar sight to the party, now into their second day of climbing.

The slopes of the western edge of the Sleeping Titans were not treacherous so much as awkward. A carpet of trees covered the mountains, which provided some relief from the rain and wind, but also softened the angled ground, making travel slower at times. Then there was the cold.

Kenyatta flexed his cold fingers, not bothering to look back at the sound of yet another splash and growling curse—Grizzled Bear. The man had the most difficulty navigating the sloping terrain of any of them.

A running stream flowed down the latest ravine they'd had to hop over. While Kenyatta, Kita, and the Amahle were able to jump across it from the top, Malimokuru had climbed down nearer to the bottom and hopped across, then climbed back up.

Being larger and less able to lift off the ground, Grizzled Bear had taken the nature reader's method, but tried to step across, straddling the running water while trying to grab hold of a root, or hanging branch to pull himself over. "Thrice damned ravines," the man grumbled. "Ground's too soft to climb. Gotta be a better way."

"Some are made for jumping, and some for climbing, friend Grizzle," Naiyala said.

A shadow passed overhead, and the refreshing damp smell of moisture in the air signaled another round of rain.

Kita cupped his hands over his mouth and blew to warm them. "Uh, oh." He shoved his hands back into his gloves and looking to the sky. "Looks like we're getting wet again."

Malimokuru held a hand out and looked at the sky. "Wonderful. I suppose the chill up here get lonely punishin' us by itself."

Punish them the weather did. The windy cold found every space in their warm garments to pass through. Despite the layers of clothes they wore against the cold, the Amahle fared no better than their human companions. The desert folk wrapped their arms about themselves, bent forward, and marched uphill. The cold wrapped around their hands and wrists, caressed their faces, stiffened their limbs.

"This cold is a terrible thing," Jabulani said. His long, braided hair slithered about his head in the wind.

"It's only gonna get worse the higher we climb," Kita replied.

"Hopefully the mountain don't try to slip out from under us again," Kenyatta said, referring to the near disaster that struck the previous day.

Near the top of a steep incline, the party had just crested a particular difficult slope when the mountain shuddered beneath them. Trees fell over, and boulders dislodged and tumbled down. If they'd been but seconds later ...

"I still say that was some kinda angry scream we heard," Grizzled Bear said. "Like the whole damned mountain was mad at us for climbin' it."

"That wasn't the mountain, friend Grizzle," Amata Daunyana said. "Something ancient and unfriendly made that sound. We are fortunate not to have encountered it."

Nyaka took the lead. The goar cat could have easily run up the mountain and waited for them at the top. Instead she revealed the best routes for her laboring companions to follow.

Kenyatta looked up the hill at the animal. She'd grown half her size again since they'd found her. "You ask her to help us out?"

Malimokuru nodded.

Three days later saw them over the other mountains and beyond the borders of the Rainlands. Evergreen trees, moss, and soft, sloping soil gave way to the frozen tundra and snowstorms of Askata. The smell of green foliage, tree sap, and forest soil became freezing air that stung the lungs to breathe.

Only a few hours into the cold lands, the first snowstorm blew in.

"Wish the damned beasts could've climbed the mountains," Bear grumbled. "Could've used 'em now, in this hell sent snow."

Not for the first or second, or even third time, Kita rolled his eyes at the absurd complaint. Unfortunate though it had been to have to sell their mounts, it would have been impossible to get them over the mountains. And even if they had, the horses would have perished in this environment.

Kenyatta scanned the white barren landscape that stretched as far as he could see—which wasn't far in this storm—and realized how much he missed the company of their new friends. With visibility so poor, the Amahle frequently ventured off, scouting the front, rear, and flanks. Even when close by, they were nearly invisible, having taken on a hue light enough to provide a small measure of camouflage in the snow. Their clothing gave them away, but with so much snow blowing in the air, it clung to their garments, making them nearly indistinguishable from the environment.

But even the chameleon-like attributes of the Amahle paled in comparison to Nyaka's. The young goar cat was starting to grow into her innate abilities, and shifted her color to blend perfectly with the pure white environment.

"You'd think that damn monster was the same as them tall folk out there, the way it turns colors like 'em." Grizzled Bear patted at his shaggy beard where snow had collected and frozen to ice.

Kita tightened his cloak around his body and threw an annoyed glance at the complaining guide.

Despite his grumbling, Grizzled Bear fared better in the cold than any of them, save Nyaka, who seemed not to be affected by any weather type.

"Wish I knew *his* secret," Kenyatta said, watching Darius.

Their mysterious travel companion moved easily in the shin deep snow, his cloak billowing behind him. He walked with the same ease in this blizzard as he had on solid ground, and the cold bothered him not at all.

Kita squinted against the flurries assaulting his face. "Why don't you ask him?"

Kenyatta laughed, then regretted it. Even with his cloak wrapped over his mouth, the frozen air was harsh. "Not sure I'd want to know even if he agreed to tell me."

"I wish I could see farther than a few yards away," Malimokuru said, his voice muffled behind his scarf.

Small comfort though it was, the blizzard tapered off. Still, the wind pelted them in the face with snow and sometimes tiny bits of hail, frequently shifting direction at the whims of the wind.

"Argh!"

Kenyatta and Kita turned, weapons ready. Grizzled Bear picked himself up from the ground. "Damn beast scared me off my feet, appearin' next to me like that."

Kita squinted at the spot a few feet away from the grumbling man and barely made out the figure of Nyaka. "I swear, if I didn't know any better I'd say she looks like she's smirking at him."

Malimokuru snickered at the remark. "Maybe if ya quit callin' her a monster, she play nice."

"Don't want the damn thing to play at *all*," came the retort.

"Visibility is too bad to see how much further we have to go," Kita said, deflecting the inevitable argument. He shielded his eyes with his hand and tried to peer into the distance. "We could be a day or two away and not know it. Or we could be wandering in the wrong direction."

"We are not far, friend Kita." It was Sakhile who spoke.

Kita nearly whirled his weapon around at the sudden appearance of the scout. He looked to the side to see the same startled expression on Kenyatta's face, though he hid it by adjusting the straps on his pack.

"You can't see from here," Sakhile continued, "but we are less than a league from the Sentinels."

Darius threw back his head and laughed.

"What do you know?" Kita demanded. Malimokuru shot him a warning glance but he didn't care. "You know more about this than you let on."

Darius turned an amused expression on the young warrior. "I'd only begun to suspect our destination once we neared these frozen lands." He started walking again, and the others following.

"Now that I do know, I can tell you that if our errand takes us beyond or atop that mountain range, we will be waiting till summer." He winked at them. "You won't enjoy that wait, I assure you. If our path lies within the mountain, this will be more ... interesting than I had anticipated."

"There is more," Sakhile said before Kita could respond to the ever-cryptic Darius. "Others have passed through these lands recently."

Bear looked at the scout in disbelief. "How could you know that? An ox-driven snowplow could have passed through here and we couldn't know in this storm." He spread his hands to indicate the white, featureless landscape. "Ain't nothing to be seen with this damnable snow blowin' over everything."

"Sakhile has the gift of being able to feel the subtlest indentations in the ground." Naiyala appeared from behind. Like Sakhile, her skin had lightened considerably. While not as white as the snow, she still blended in well.

"It was luck that I crossed it," Sakhile said. "The ground felt different so I tried to follow it. Eventually I felt an indentation in the earth that was the size and shape a human foot."

"can't say I can imagine why anyone would be wanting to travel through all this," Malimokuru said.

"We are," Kita responded.

"What's strange," Sakhile continued, "is that the tracks indicated there was only one. I searched but found only one set of tracks.

Kita raised his eyebrows. "So, one person is trekking through all this?"

"Maybe single file to hide their numbers," Grizzled Bear suggested.

"From who?" Kenyatta asked. "Who in the five hells come here? Anything hardy enough to live out in this don't care about numbers, man."

"They're moving toward the Sentinels," Sakhile said.

That got everyone's attention. Even Darius perked up at that.

"In line with our destination," Malimokuru said. "What does it mean?"

Amata and Jabulani caught up by then. "We must move faster," the elder hunter said. "This storm will not relent soon."

At those words, the party started forward again.

"Who would be out here?" Malimokuru continued. "In the middle of nowhere?"

The tracker shook his head. "I do not know these lands. It's possible that they're inhabited, but it seems unlikely."

Nyaka's low growl caught everyone's attention. The goar cat

crouched low to the ground, forked tongue flicking in and out as she tasted the air. She backed away from her position, glowing eyes narrowed at the icy ground.

Kenyatta's sword was instantly in his hand. He scanned the area, but saw nothing about. He looked at Nyaka again. The goar cat hissed at the ground. "We're not gonna like this."

"Damned pup gettin' spooked by the winds," Grizzled Bear remarked, but he didn't sound like he believed his own words.

"Jabu," Naiyala said. "Do you sense any animals about? You said there was nothing here."

"I've sensed nothing, *Inkosazana*," Jabulani replied.

Kenyatta saw the elder hunter look at Nyaka, who was now pawing at the snow.

Jabulani gripped his spear with his other hand and slowly circled around to the side of the goar cat's position. "Not above gr—"

Frozen earth exploded in a shower of snow.

Kenyatta shielded his eyes against the debris. When he lowered his arm, it was to see a massive whale-sized animal climbing out of the hole.

"What the five hells is that?" Kenyatta said as he backed away. "Looks like a cross between a walrus and a ground mole."

"Never seen a walrus or a ground mole that big," Kita replied.

With clawed flippers, it pulled itself free of the earth and turned a hungry gaze on its intended prey.

Kenyatta backed away. "What in the abyss *is* that?"

"And how did I or Jabulani not sense it?" Malimokuru added.

"ICEMASTER!" Grizzled Bear answered. "Digs far underground and is too stupid fer you to talk to." He wiped his mouth with his forearm as he backed away. "If that thing gets a hold of you the best a friend can do is kill you before it starts to eat you ..."

"Save the details," Kenyatta said. "Can we outrun it?"

"In this snow? No way."

The icemaster brought a flipper crashing to the ground just in front of Kita. The force of the impact sent him flying backward. He threw himself into a roll as soon as he landed, and shook off the freezing snow.

Kenyatta had no time to worry for his friend, as the beast turned its attention to him. He saw its four black eyes, little bigger than a human's, look down on him. It opened its blubbery mouth to reveal three rows of small peg-like teeth.

Grizzled Bear tackled Kenyatta aside just as the beast vomited a thick yellow substance his way. The disgusting goo sizzled in the snow.

"If it opens its mouth get outta the way," Bear shouted. "Or you'll be melted to death so it can get you down its gullet."

"Thanks for that." Kenyatta scrambled to his feet and swore an oath. The icemaster was nearly on top of them. He grabbed Grizzled Bear by his coat and pulled him to his feet. "Move!"

A red streak descended on the monster. It wailed and twisted its fleshy, gray body to get at Naiyala, who stabbed it repeatedly with her spear.

She leapt away just as Jabulani appeared at its side and drove his spear through thick, folded hide and into the soft flesh underneath. He growled and yanked his spear free, then retreated. The icemaster turned to face him, but the elder hunter was already long out of reach. It wouldn't have mattered anyway.

Spear in a two-handed grip, Sakhile glided through the air, descending on the huge walrus-like body. As soon as his feet hit its back, Sakhile drove his spear deep into its neck. The resulting spray of blood coated the scout's clothes, indistinguishable from his bright red skin. The icemaster moaned and tumbled sideways, dislodging the tracker. Sakhile rolled into the snow and came to his feet in a full run.

Bleeding red ichor from its wounds, the blubbery animal thrashed and moaned as it fought to right itself.

Kenyatta saw his opening. He raced toward the icemaster and

scrambled atop its back, even as it turned itself over. The icemaster folded itself almost in half and tucked its head to the ground.

Kenyatta lost his hold and started to slide off. He reversed the grip on his sword and drove it into the thick hide all the way to the hilt. He knew what was coming next, and held on for his life as the icemaster wobbled and swayed.

Out of the corner of his eye he saw a whirling black staff.

Kita crashed into the side of the giant slug-like body in a flurry. His staff spun as he pounded at the thick blubbery hide. It seemed as though his efforts yielded no fruit, but Kita didn't let up. The icemaster tried to wobble around to face Kita, but he easily moved with it, battering the same area repeatedly. When the hide began to turn black and blue, Kita doubled his efforts.

Kenyatta curled his body up and braced his feet against the monster's side. He pushed with his legs, and pulled with his arms. His sword was firmly embedded. Corded muscles in his arms and legs bulged as the warrior threw every ounce of his strength into pulling the sword free. The icemaster moaned and wobbled its body left to right, but still Kenyatta pulled. He clenched his teeth, threw his head back, and pulled. Inch by inch, the blade moved. Kenyatta growled and gave a final tug. The blade came free and he launched away.

The icemaster turned just as he pulled the weapon loose, and Kenyatta found himself ten feet in the air and falling backwards. He threw the top half of his body back while bringing his feet up and over his head to execute a backflip. Though he landed feet first, Kenyatta fell knee deep into a patch of snow the icemaster hadn't swept away. Realizing his vulnerability, he hopped up and back before the thing could roll over him.

He needn't have bothered, for the monster was occupied on all sides. A grievous wound to the lower part of its body had slowed it enough for the bellowing Grizzled Bear to rush in and bring his axe down on the tail. The thick, pointed piece of tail flopped into the blood-soaked snow.

When the moaning beast swung what remained of its tail at him, Bear held his axe in a two-handed grip and whacked it as it came around. The blow was true, but the force of the impact still sent him spinning backwards.

Grizzled Bear hit the snow and sank in just as a hissing Nyaka appeared out of the snowstorm and bounded past him. She sprang onto the icemaster's back and dug her razor claws into its hide. In short order, the goar cat ran up to its head and drove her foreclaws into the top two sets of eyes. When the icemaster reared, she bit down on its nose with a sickening *squish*. Nyaka held her grip on the ruined nose, braced her forelegs, and pulled. With the icemaster's head arched back, she began tearing at the back of its neck with her rear claws.

With its full attention on Nyaka, Kita leapt back in and punished the same area he'd been working on. The blubbery hide had turned black, and the beast began favoring that side whenever it moved. He looked up to see Nyaka savaging the thing in a horrific spray of blood.

Kenyatta moved around the agonized beast, searching for a place to enter the fray. He looked up at what looked like the sky raining red. The crimson rain wasn't blood, however, but three battle-enraged Amahle. As one, Naiyala, Jabulani, and Sakhile landed with spears piercing the humped back.

Amata Daunyana clapped her glowing hands together and blue fire funneled from her fingertips into the side of the beast.

All of these things happened in less than two heartbeats, and the Amahle were airborne once again, having leapt from the monster's back as Amata burned it. Kenyatta watched in amazement as the three warriors blended with the snow before they touched the ground.

Nyaka ceased her attack as the icemaster erupted in flame, and leapt away just as a blanket of yellow sand drifted through the air. It settled over the icemaster's body and Malimokuru shouted a word.

"Afreetuminos!" Every grain of sand ignited in violent flames.

Kenyatta almost felt sorry for the thing, for it seemed overkill.

The huge walrus-like monster squirmed and thrashed under the burn of the nature reader's flames as well as the Daunyanic fire unleashed by Amata. It swatted at the ground with its clawed flippers, moaning as its scorched hide blistered and smoked under the torturous fire. It finally managed to roll over back onto a patch of snow-covered ground.

Kita covered his nose against the horrible stench.

The flames were extinguished as the icemaster rolled in the snow. Kenyatta looked at the apprentice. The blue glow of Bora-ka's fire winked out from her hands. Surely the flames of a God couldn't be so easily put out.

"What the hell more we do to kill this thing?" Kenyatta yelled.

"Whatever we must," Sakhile growled.

Kenyatta gave a little shudder at the sight of the fearsome scout. His skin shone red once again, an outward expression of his rage. He snarled, revealing four elongated canine teeth. Kenyatta backed away.

Burned all over its body, its nose crushed, the back of its neck ruined, and two of its four eyes destroyed, any normal animal would have long given up and retreated. But the icemaster opened its mouth and coughed more yellow liquid. The grotesque fluid sizzled in the snow, but didn't get near anyone.

Kenyatta began circling behind when a large object streaked past him and across the front of the icemaster.

Darius skidded to a stop several yards away. He flicked bits of blood from his hand, not bothering to look back at the dying animal as its insides spilled out of the wide cut across its neck. The icemaster flopped forward and lay dead in its rapidly pooling lifeblood.

Darius looked his hand over and gave a lazy grunt.

Fixed to the spot, Kita watched the man walk away to retrieve his dropped pack. He looked around at the others to see similar reactions. Even the Amahle looked impressed. Wary, but impressed.

Kenyatta moved beside Kita and cleaned his sword in the snow. "Show off."

"That man makes me uneasy."

His sword cleaned, Kenyatta sheathed it and strapped it across his back. "Yeah, man. Like hunting with a lion you don't know." He started away. "As long as he's helping, I'm good with him. Let's move before another one shows up."

Kita looked back at the huge dead mass of cut and burned blubber that was the icemaster. "Another one?"

WITH THE DEAD icemaster well behind them, the party continued their laborious trek across the brutal tundra. Bent forward against the shifting winds of the unrelenting blizzard, conversation remained limited.

After a time, the weather relented, just a bit, and the faces of the various members of the party reflected the conservative hope that the storm might finally have played itself out.

"How ya know what that thing was back there?" Malimokuru asked Grizzle Bear, his breath misting in the frozen air.

"All guides have stories," Grizzled Bear responded. He patted at a new layer of snow in the process of freezing in his beard. "I met a guy who lived farther north than we are now. Group of eight hunters he was guidin' had a run-in with one of them nasty things. They weren't warriors like you all, just hunters and guides, like me." Bear turned aside and spat. "Damned thing wiped out all but three of them, and they barely got away. One lost an arm and the other two were only a little better off. Worst story I ever heard."

"Sounds awful," Malimokuru said, and Bear nodded. "You know anything about them?" Malimokuru pointed to the barely visible silhouette of the mountain range.

"The Sentinels," came the reply. "Like our scary, tall scout called 'em. Every guide worth his arse has heard of 'em, though. They're called the Sentinels because those three peaks there"— he pointed to each peak respectively, reaching high into the clouded sky—"loom above all around them. It's like they's watching you from on high. Some say that mountain range is so treacherous that no man has ever crossed over 'em, and that they guard a beautiful land on the other side."

Bear's gaze lifted to their ominous destination drawing nearer with each step. "The Sentinels. Guardians to mysterious lands beyond." He hawked and spat in the snow again, drawing a disgusted wince from Malimokuru.

"I s'pose one day somebody'll make it over. Who knows, maybe somebody already has."

"Maybe," Malimokuru replied.

Under the canopy of endless white clouds and blowing snow, no one could tell what time of day it was. It hardly mattered, however, for their destination finally came into view. The beleaguered companions didn't know whether to sigh in relief or trepidation at the sight of the Sentinels, their destination, glaring down on them.

47

S eung sat in the dark silence of the tunnels beneath the mountain range Tinnoviel called The Sentinels. The trek north from the Sleeping Titans had been full of nothing but rain for many miles.

They'd passed near a large human city that sat nestled between the mountains and the ocean, and Seung had gone in just long enough to replenish supplies.

They'd passed forests of towering redwood trees, while beneath them, their smaller moss covered kin grew thick and squat beneath the leafy canopy. When the rain finally let up, the beleaguered travelers had sighed with relief. Then the snow had come.

In the weeks following their battle with the Scorpion Lord and the subsequent loss of Nuviel, the party had fallen into a solemn mood.

Seung had known Nuviel for only a short time, yet the world felt a less happy place without her cheerful friend. Sitting in the darkness of their camp, Seung would have appreciated that cheer now. Even Tikena was subdued. In her need to be alone with her grief, Seung had wandered away from camp and nearly stumbled upon the silently weeping elf, who'd done the same.

Seung tried not to think of how Nuviel would still be alive if she hadn't come on this errand. She reminded herself that she'd led men and women to death in battle. That brought little comfort.

Now they sat in the impenetrable darkness of mountain tunnels once again. The oppressive blackness and endless walls of stone tempered the thrill of discovering abilities she hadn't known she had.

Seung looked around their camp in vain. How she wished she could see with her own eyes what was around her. No matter how much she'd come to rely on her other senses, it still took an effort to keep her nerves in check.

She'd asked Yurin why she didn't produce some sort of light, like she had back in chamber of the Scorpion Lord. The response had been rather embarrassing.

"You, a warrior, would suggest such a thing?" Yurin had said. "To have whatever lurks in these depths be made aware of us long before we reach them? That would be a poor decision, Kiluriel."

Of course it would be. Seung took a deep breath and blew it out in a steady stream. These dark, dank tunnels were getting to her, affecting her judgement. It was the stale, musty air, the stone beneath her feet, and on all sides. It was the notion of a mile of rock sitting above her head, sitting between her and the glorious sky.

Seung had found some small comfort in that Alurien found her ability to be an odd but useful surprise. "Perhaps it is a manifestation of your *haloren* heritage," he'd said.

Perhaps.

She turned her head in the direction of the ranger's footsteps, though of course she couldn't see him.

"There is a lava pit ahead, about a hundred yards."

In the perfect silence, the elven ranger's voice echoed down the tunnel like a shout. Seung wondered why Alurien didn't use the *whisper*. Perhaps he knew that Seung couldn't respond in kind. Yet another hindrance making her a liability.

"The path is straightforward for as far as I went," Alurien continued.

"That's good news," Tinnoviel said.

She stood when she heard the others rise.

"That isn't all," the ranger said.

Seung felt a sinking feeling in her stomach that was becoming too familiar.

"Something is down there?" Tinnoviel asked.

"There is."

"Of course there is," Seung replied dryly. "Of course."

"What is it?" Tinnoviel asked.

"I'm not certain, but judging from the size of the two tunnels high in the walls, I would guess at least two fire basilisks live in there."

Tikena groaned.

"Two what?" Seung asked. She took another deep breath to keep her heart from pounding out of her chest. Men, she'd fought. Even monsters that lived in the wild outside her village. These past few weeks had shown her more horrors in the world than she would have believed possible.

"Fire basilisks," the ranger repeated. "Four-legged reptiles from the old world when the great lizards roamed the earth. Some basilisks are giant snakes, while others, like the fire basilisk, walk on four feet. These types are attracted to intense heat, such as the lava bed."

Yurin Kei Daunyana started down the tunnel. "What we seek may be here."

"That doesn't make me feel any better," Seung muttered.

"It shouldn't," Tikena said.

Minutes later, the group arrived at the lava pit Alurien had spoken of. The intense light and heat stung Seung's eyes at first, but it was good to see again. After three days of traveling underground, the darkness had taken a toll.

Lava oozed through the circular pit into some tunnels the Gods only knew where they led to. Massive boulders lay strewn about the oval chamber, in the walls, and even the ceiling.

Seung wiped away a stream of sweat trickling down her face. The heat was unbearable. She looked up at the two ominous holes in the wall Alurien spoke of, and wished she could stuff a boulder into each of them.

The heat grew so overwhelming, Seung was about to suggest they find another way, when suddenly it grew cooler. Well, not cooler, but not deathly hot.

Puzzled, Seung looked around until her eyes settled on Yurin Kei Daunyana. Soft purple light outlined her body. The power of the Daunyan Oberon. Seung remembered Him to be the God of Balance. Perhaps the apprentice used His power to balance the heat with cooler air?

They made their way around the pit, watching the holes in the wall as they passed underneath the first one.

"You know what I don't like about this?" Seung said to Tinnoviel, using a normal whisper.

As they neared the exiting tunnel, a three-toed claw the size of her body gripped the rim of the hole closest to the exit. A forked tongue flicked in and out.

"Those holes are wide enough apart to trap us between them," Tinnoviel answered aloud, the need for silence gone.

As soon as she saw that claw, Seung backed away. Another claw gripped the rim of the first hole just as the basilisk near the exit emerged. Seung recognized the danger even as Tinnoviel had spoken of it. She skittered backward and dove past the first hole.

The two massive reptiles climbed down the wall, trapping the party between them. The rear lizard hadn't noticed that Seung had slipped behind it yet, so she backed farther away in hopes it wouldn't smell her right away.

"We cannot win this fight," Alurien said. "Neither steel nor *Kakaya* will penetrate their armored hides.

Tinnoviel leapt sideways when the closest lizard snapped at him. "Their armor can be pierced, but we wouldn't live long enough to break through it and make a difference."

Seung's old teacher had once told her of the great lizards of Komodo whose saliva could kill. To Seung's eyes, these lizards looked like the ones her master had described, only five times larger.

She watched the giant reptile. Its thick hide reminded her of boiled leather, only tougher and covered with plate scales. Given enough time she could work through it, but she didn't think it would sit still for that.

The fire basilisks hissed as they converged on their trapped prey.

Seung slowly closed in on the giant lizard. She waited until it was about to lunge at Tinnoviel again, and hopped on its back. As fast as her arms could pump, she smashed one of the ends of *Vyirayoi* against the beast's right eye. The animal's dexterity caught Seung off guard when it recoiled with surprising speed. She tried to jump away, but got clipped on the shoulder by its swinging tail. The impact sent her spinning into the wall, and she lost her grip on *Vyirayoi*.

Seung tried to blink through the stars in her vision as she climbed to her feet on wobbly legs. The hissing grew louder as the basilisk closed. Seung took a step back and her legs buckled. She fell back and scooted away from the reptile, and away from her weapon.

The basilisk was nearly on top of her when it suddenly stopped and half turned to snap at the tiny form of Tikena who danced in and out of reach of those deadly teeth. The thought of those jaws closing on the diminutive elf helped bring Seung out of her daze. She climbed back to her knees and blinked, then forced herself up and staggered forward. She finally reached Vyirayoi and snatched the weapon up.

Seung watched as she waded into the fight. Her legs grew stronger with each step and, with it, her confidence. She moved into position, watching the back and forth conflict between the giant reptile and the elf. She planted her feet, spun Vyirayoi in a vertical arc, and moved in to strike in rhythm with the faster Tikena.

Yurin Kei Daunyana watched for her opportunity as Tinnoviel and Alurien fought as one against the second basilisk. As soon as an opening presented itself, she hurled razor-like ice shards which glanced off the scaly body armor of the giant lizards. Try as she might, she couldn't find a weakness. Neither electricity nor ice had any effect; the hide was too thick.

The basilisk made a choking sound and started convulsing. Alurien watched the oddity for only a heartbeat before instincts took over and he dove to the side. The basilisk vomited a thick brown substance that sizzled when it hit the ground where the ranger had been standing.

Yurin silently called to the Daunyans for guidance, and sent a blast of electricity at the eyes of the lizard. The beast flinched its head away, then hissed at her. Alurien forgotten, it plodded toward Yurin, swinging its legs with every step. Its long snake-like tongue flicked in and out, and when it drew near, its scaly lips parted as it prepared to snap.

The opening was narrow, but it was enough. Yurin aimed a stream of freezing air and ice shards into its mouth. The fire basilisk went into a fit of coughing and gasping as the cold air entered its hot lungs.

The lizard swung its head left and right, but Yurin waited

patiently. Every time it coughed, she sent another gust of freezing air or ice shards into its mouth until the pain outweighed its hunger. After another round of coughing, stinging cold and cutting ice, the basilisk finally lost its desire to fight. It turned away and labored up the wall and back into its hole.

WITH ONE OF the basilisks gone, the others rushed to aid Seung and Tikena, who were having a hard time simply not being killed.

Alurien smacked it in the rear leg to draw its attention. As it turned, Seung struck it in the other rear leg, to no affect. Back and forth they antagonized the basilisk, hoping that like the other, it would simply deem them not worth the trouble. Yurin moved around the lizard, looking for a good angle.

Tikena darted in and slashed it across the face several times and was back out of reach before the basilisk could retaliate. As soon as it tried, Seung struck it across its side. When it reacted to her, the others attacked.

And so the dance continued, none gaining advantage or giving way until finally, the basilisk decided to focus on one target. It rounded on Tinnoviel and opened its mouth wide enough to swallow him whole. Yurin immediately she sent a stream of ice shards slicing into its throat. The beast gagged and backed away. It went into a pained fit of coughing, and its long thick tail flicked sideways. It happened so fast, Alurien didn't have time to react. The tail struck him in the side, sending him tumbling over the ledge.

Tinnoviel cried out and dove headlong after him.

Wide-eyed with horror, Seung watched the two elves go over the edge where the pool of molten lava waited.

Yurin cried out in dismay, the most overt emotion Seung had ever seen from the apprentice. That instant of shock cost her. The basilisk's tail flicked back the other way and hit Yurin as well. The Daunya Apprentice had been preparing another icy assault when Tinnoviel and Alurien had fallen. The energy had still been built up when the tip of the tail clipped her in the shoulder. The impact sent her flying, and the built up energy exploded from her hands.

The released power zigzagged in every direction, blasting into the walls and ceiling. A section of wall above the entry tunnel collapsed and sealed off any hope of returning the way they'd come. Rocks large and small fell everywhere, breaking off chunks of the walkway to tumble into the lava bed.

Seung realized she was beginning to feel the unbearable heat of the chamber again, and looked for Yurin. The apprentice knelt several feet away from the angry lizard, dazed, but not unconscious. If the basilisk got hold of her, everyone was dead.

Tikena had been in the midst of springing back in for another stab when the beast turned. Unable to reverse her direction or even alter it, she crashed head-on into its shoulder and bounced off.

Seung saw the impact as the little elf rebounded off of the solid animal. Now Tikena slid helplessly toward the lava bed.

"Not again." Seung sprinted past the snapping jaws of the angry lizard and dove for her. She dropped *Vyirayoi* and drew a dagger from her hip, then stabbed it into the ground just as her fingers closed around Tikena's ankle.

With half her body hanging over the pool of lava, holding onto the dangling elf, Seung saw to her relief and desperation that Tinnoviel and Alurien were in a similar situation.

"Ugh," Tikena moaned. Her head fell back, then her eyes widened when she realized she was hanging upside down over a lava pool. "Don't you dare let go of me or you're in trouble."

"Lucky for both of us you're little more than a slip of a thing, girl," Seung retorted. She clenched her teeth and slowly pulled the little elf up, praying to all the Daunyans that her dagger did not slip out. She finally lifted Tikena high enough for the girl to scrabble for a handhold. Once she climbed over, Tikena dropped to her stomach and grabbed Seung's hand. The girl was stronger than she looked, and helped pull Seung over the edge to solid ground.

Seung immediately looked for the basilisk. She sighed in relief when she saw it had gone back into its hole. Her relief was short-lived when more large rocks were dislodged and plummeted from the ceiling. She heard Tinnoviel's voice and swore an oath. She and Tikena raced for the ledge and looked over.

Tinnoviel and Alurien were too far down for them to help. All they could do was watch helplessly as Tinnoviel held on to his best friend.

"You can't hold us both," Alurien said. The ranger's voice was calm, a stark contrast to the desperate situation.

"By the Daunyans," Tinnoviel growled, "if you let go, Boraka Himself won't be able to protect you from me!" The Daunya Warrior hurriedly spoke an incantation that Seung couldn't understand, but the result was easy enough to see.

Suddenly imbued with incredible strength, Tinnoviel bellowed to the heavens and hoisted Alurien over his head.

Seung saw the ranger ascending and reached out for him. Once their hands locked, Seung pulled with all her strength. The ranger was too heavy, but Tikena reached over the side, fingers wiggling as she stretched as far as she could. Her little hand grabbed hold of Alurien's forearm below Seung's hand, and together they lifted the ranger up.

"Hold on, TinTin!" Lying on her belly, gazing over the side, Tikena searched frantically for some kind of handhold, some way to get to the dangling warrior.

"GET BACK!"

Despite the warning, Seung peeked over the edge to see Tinnoviel hanging by one hand over the pool of lava below. His eyes were closed and a blue aura surrounded his body.

His eyes snapped open, and the power Seung saw there had her scrabbling away from the ledge. The Daunya Warrior launched himself over the edge, over her head, and landed behind her. He hit the ground with a heavy thud, and rolled to his hands and knees, gasping.

"You okay?" she asked.

"Yes," he responded between gasps. "I'll be fine."

"You couldn't have used that power before now?" Seung asked, thinking of their confrontation with the Scorpion Lord and the loss of Nuviel.

The Daunya Warrior still didn't look up. "There are many dangers ... Kiluriel," he responded between breaths. "My abilities differ from Yurin's. When two powers collide, the results can be ... unpredictable. I know of what you're thinking. I would have used my power if I could have been sure I wouldn't have killed us all."

"She's alive!" Tikena crouched beside Yurin, who lay propped against the wall near the exit.

Seung helped Tinnoviel to his feet and they started toward the others. They'd gone only a few steps when the entire chamber groaned. They froze.

"What now?" Seung thought aloud.

Alurien looked up. "I hear something."

Seung strained to listen. "It sounds like fighting." She looked from Alurien to Tinnoviel. "Who else would be in this hell?"

Another groan. The chamber shook more violently. A boulder fell from the ceiling of the cave and splashed into the lava pool.

"Why is this place still shaking?" Seung yelled as they reached the exit tunnel. "There was only one blast from Yurin, and it wasn't that bad."

"No time," Tinnoviel said. "We need to get out..."

The chamber groaned again just as they entered the tunnel. The ground collapsed beneath them, and Seung had just enough time to turn in alarm to see her longtime weapon, *Vyirayoi*, laying on the ground out of reach as she and the others slid down the tunnel.

They ricocheted off walls and boulders in an uncontrollable descent. Another section of the ground collapsed beneath them and they fell into darkness.

48

Kita tried to keep the giant badger-like animal's attention on him while Grizzled Bear maneuvered for a better attack position. The man was strong, but not quick. He'd already been pummeled several times by its quilled tail, and now bled in multiple places. Despite his injuries, the man continued to fight beside Kita. He admired the guide's courage, but feared for his life.

"Wait till it lunges at me, then take a swing at it."

"Aye," Grizzled Bear huffed. "If you can just keep the durned thing busy."

Kita skittered backward to avoid a downward swiping claw. *What do you think I'm doing?* "I'll work on that," he replied as he smashed the creature in the side of its wide flat head.

The force of the impact should have broken its skull. Instead, the animal grew angry. It charged head first into Kita, who leapt away and arched his back, his staff held over his head. As he came back down, he hammered the shaft down onto the flat skull with all his strength. It stumbled forward and fell onto its fore legs. Kita didn't waste any time. While the vicious animal struggled to rise, he continued pounding it over the head.

Grizzled Bear charged in with a roar and swung his axe in a two-handed grip. The curved blade bit deep in the furry hide. The beast craned its neck with a wheezing growl and sprang sideways, away from the guide, and tore the axe from his grasp.

The badger monster wasn't out of the fight yet. It swept a paw equipped with long sharp claws across his chest and sent the Bear tumbling to the ground.

It had happened so fast, Kita hadn't time to intervene. Now his friend lay on his side, blood staining his heavy shirt.

With a roar of his own, Kita leveled the end of his staff and drove the bladed tip into the animal's eye. The big black orb exploded, spraying Kita with its sickening contents. Without thinking about what he was doing, Kita pulled the staff free, twisted the shaft, and separated it into three parts.

He gripped the shaft in the middle, the two sections hanging limp, and set the weapon spinning. With the two shafts bending independently, Kita whacked the animal on top of its hard skull repeatedly. He spun to the side, tossed the weapon and caught the two separated shafts, and stabbed the spear end into its neck.

He hopped back and stood ready, once again spinning the weapon by its middle shaft, the two ends connected by the suddenly loose, chain-like vertebrae of the cerberus from which it was crafted.

The injury to its neck must have hurt, for the beast didn't pursue. Kita stopped the spin and grabbed it by the two ends again, letting the middle hang between them. The angry warrior moved in close and battered the short, wide beast with both ends of his transformed weapon. He pounded it on the head, the face, its neck, smacked it in the nose, and stabbed it repeatedly with the spear tip.

Grizzled Bear pulled himself up from the ground and made his way to his axe, still imbedded in the monster's side. He growled and cursed through the pain in his chest as he tugged and yanked at the weapon. One final tug wrenched the axe free.

He used that momentum and swung the axe around and up. The big man clenched his teeth as he brought the axe down with all his strength. The axe crunched down through the animal's ribcage, and it let out a terrible howl. Bear threw himself into a backward rolled just in time to avoid a feeble kick from large hind claws.

Kita saw the brave guide fighting through obvious pain, and he redoubled his efforts to keep the animal distracted. The ox-sized badger monster moved much slower now, its lifeblood flowing from the gaping cut in its ribs. It wheezed, but still labored toward him.

No normal animal would keep going, Kita thought.

Grizzled Bear waded back in, turned a circled, and swung his axe around with all his weight behind it. The axe bit through thick hide and bone, and severed the monster's rear leg.

The beast dropped onto its stomach. With one last effort, it swung its spiked tail around.

Again, Grizzled Bear wasn't fast enough, and the tail caught him fully in the arm and hip, burying several long quills into his skin. His body jerked once, then the axe fell from his grasp as he toppled over.

It all seemed to happen in slow motion, yet Kita wasn't fast enough to stop it. When he saw Grizzled Bear fall, his world shifted. Sound muffled, colors faded, fatigue dissipated, and the severely wounded beast became his sole focus.

Despite its grievous wound, the monster lifted itself up with its forelegs and snapped at him. Kita sidestepped and smashed it across the nose again. It recoiled, and the motion cost it another blow to the throat. It reflexively tucked its head in, and Kita pounded its skull with one-two blows, left-right left-right, hammering it to the ground.

He tossed the three-shafted weapon and caught it in the middle and spun it vertically, swinging it alongside his body from left to right. With each spin, a hard tip of one end pounded the flat skull while the spear tip sliced it.

Over and over, the beast struggled to rise only to be hammered back down by the end of that brutal staff.

Left and right Kita spun the shaft, beating the badger monster until he heard a voice penetrate his focused rage.

"Kita! It's dead, man! *It's dead!*"

The voice of his friend, his brother, pierced the void. Kita blinked the world back into focus. He looked down to see the bloody mess that had been the monster's head. The flat-bodied beast lay still in death, no longer a threat. He turned to see a cautious Kenyatta, standing several feet away, watching him.

"You all right, man?"

"Bear," Kita panted.

"Amata is tending him now," Kenyatta said. "We're okay for the moment, but we can't stay here long." His gaze lowered to the altered weapon in Kita's hands.

"I couldn't explain it if I tried," Kita said.

"Later," Kenyatta replied, and Kita nodded.

They rushed to Bear's side just as the apprentice finished cleaning and dressing the deep wounds. Beside him lay a handful of the long quills the apprentice had extracted from Bear's side.

"He was pierced in many places and the cuts across his front are deep and feverish." She poured some water from a skin onto a rag and cleaned the last cut.

"He'll make it," Kita half asked, half told her. Amata's lips pressed together and he saw the uncertainty in her eyes. "I've done what I can with what I have and what the Daunyans have given me. It may be time for him to join Them. Or not. I cannot know."

Kita looked down at Grizzled Bear. He still breathed, but it was shallow. The crude man had become a friend to them all.

Malimokuru and the rest of the Amahle trotted up from

further down the tunnel and stopped at the sight of the trio gathered around Bear.

"Dammit." Malimokuru knelt beside the man. Nyaka flicked her tongue several times across the big man's face and rumbled deep in her chest. Bear's eyes fluttered open.

"Told you that thing's been wantin' to eat me," he mumbled.

Malimokuru sighed and ran his hand along the goar cat's back.

Bear's eyes focused on the nature reader. "Who's gonna protect you when I can't? I still think yer too feeble for all this adventurin'."

"I don't know what ya talking about," Malimokuru retorted, feigning indignation. "You're too disgusting to die, so just lie there for a while. I'm sure your own stench will rouse you soon enough."

The big man chuckled at that, then winced, causing the nature reader to lay a concerned hand on his shoulder. "Gotcha," Bear wheezed. "I know you didn't mean all that. Well, you did, but still ... I know you don't mind if'n I call you friend." He reached out a large hand and Malimokuru grabbed it in a firm grip.

"You honor me, my friend," the nature reader whispered.

Grizzled Bear fell into a fit of coughing and Amata Daunyana placed a hand on his forehead. She spoke a word and his eyes closed. With a final sigh, he sagged against the wall.

Amata studied his wounds one last time, then his face. "The body heals with rest. If he wakes, he will live."

"We must keep going, and quickly," Jabulani said. "More of those flat-bodied animals were coming our way when we left the tunnels back there." The Elder Hunter had scratches and gashes all over his body, and bled from many superficial wounds.

"What about him?" Kenyatta said, indicating the guide. "We all leave, or none of us leaves."

"I will bear him," Darius said, his baritone voice echoing

through the tunnel. "He will witness this quest's conclusion with us in body, or in spirit."

A thunderclap shook the wide corridor. All around, rocks crumbled from the walls and ceiling.

"That was an impact," Sakhile said. "Sounded like it came from there." He pointed further down the tunnel where red light shone from around the corner. "We must move."

With little effort, Darius gently lifted the rotund Grizzled Bear and held him cradled in his arms as though he were no more than a child. Kita stood and looked into those powerful eyes. He nodded, and Darius returned the gesture. The chamber gave another violent shudder as the group hurried down the corridor.

"LIGHT UP AHEAD," Kita called.

All around them, rocks large and small fell from the walls and ceiling. Stalactites snapped and crashed into the ground, others shook loosely in the cavern ceiling, threatening to impale the fleeing party.

"There's a lava pit ahead," Darius called. The man showed no signs of exertion as he carried well near three hundred pounds of Grizzled Bear in his arms while keeping pace with the rest of them.

"How do you know that?" Kenyatta yelled over his shoulder.

"Do you not feel the heat?" Darius replied. "Only a lava pit could generate such."

His reasoning proved sound. Soon the group entered a chamber with a walkway that split around the molten pool a few dozen feet below, and met at the other end at yet another tunnel.

Kenyatta held his arm over his face against the unbearable heat. "Too hot. I bet even the walls and floor are too hot in there."

Amata Daunyana's hands glowed purple, and she waved them

to encompass the party. "We are shielded from the worst of it for a time," she said. "Hurry."

The chamber shuddered again, nearly lifting them off their feet.

"Is it just me," Kenyatta said, "or did this entire room just buck like an animal?"

No one disagreed, but there was no time to consider it. Carefully, they trotted along the wall, keeping as far from the ledge—and the molten pool below—as possible. Several times Nyaka growled at the two large circular tunnels high in the wall on the other side of the lava bed. Kenyatta didn't want to think about what might live in there.

"Looks like the ground collapsed down there," Jabulani said, leaning into the dark corridor. Amata uttered a word and waved her hand toward the darkness ahead. A dull light shined from her hand and streamed down the descending tunnel.

"Nowhere to go but forward," Kita said. He took hold of the nearest stalagmite and eased his way down.

Something caught Kenyatta's eye as he turned to follow the others down. He looked back to the far end of the broken walkway and squinted against the heat.

A long-shafted weapon, each end equipped with a strange blade—flat on one side with a sharp tip in the middle, and a crescent curved cutting edge on the other—lay on the ground.

"Whatcha doing, fool bwoy?" Malimokuru called as Kenyatta crept along the wall toward the weapon. "Forget that and get back here before you kill yourself."

Ignoring him, Kenyatta kept low to the ground and moved along the wall. Much of the walkway was gone, but there was just enough for him to ease his way across. The room shuddered again and this time, he could have sworn he heard an inhuman roar. It must have been the part of the caves collapsing or shifting.

Finally, he reached the weapon. It was finely made, and beautiful. He had seen a weapon like this before, two years ago. This one was somewhat different. The shaft was the same, yet the blades, instead of metal, were made of some kind of hard wood. How hadn't it caught fire, or at least warped from the intense heat?

The shaft had a circular metal piece in the middle. *Impossible,* he thought. Remembering that time, two years ago, he gave the shaft a little squeeze and twist, and it separated in half, held together by a metal latch.

The chamber shook yet again, and Kenyatta waved his arms to keep his balance. He stumbled against the wall, taking one quick glance down at the waiting pool of lava. The walkway suddenly felt much too narrow. He noticed the heat of the room and the wall at his back growing more intense, and looked back toward the exit. Amata must have ventured too far away.

"What in the five hells are you doing, bwoy?" Malimokuru screamed. "Get back here!"

Kenyatta used the attached strap to tie the weapon to his back, then crept along the wall, making his way back across the narrow walkway back to the exiting tunnel. Rocks beneath his feet shifted and fell from the ledge. He gave the two holes above a wary glance, and hoped whatever made them stayed in there.

Once he reached Malimokuru, the nature reader gave him an exasperated look and started down the tunnel. With one last glance back at the lava chamber, Kenyatta climbed down. He hoped his suspicion was wrong.

49

Seung ricocheted off of stalagmites, tumbling sideways and head over heels down the sloping tunnel. She tried to push her arms out to right herself and get her feet under her, but succeeded only in seeing a stalagmite rushing toward her. The painful impact sent her spinning, and she hit a bump in the ground that set her to rolling. Disoriented, bruised, and scuffed and cut in more places than she could think of, Seung tried again to push her arms and legs out to steady herself.

The grunts and gasps further down indicated that the others were having no better luck. The tunnel shook again, and Seung bounced into the air. She instinctively curled into a ball just before crashing mid-air into another stalagmite. With only the view of her feet and the ground and ceiling spinning into one vertical jumble, Seung could only grit her teeth and endure the uncontrollable descent. She heard a large piece of the ceiling collapse from behind, and the rubble came tumbling after them.

Great, she thought. "Rubble coming from behind!"

A section of the ground below fell away, and bright light followed by oppressive heat rushed into the dark cavern as they slid down. She saw the others fall through the opening an instant before she dropped through.

As her life flashed before her eyes, Seung prepared for her death. Well over a hundred feet below waited a bed of lava more than three times the size of the one in the chamber they'd just escaped.

Suddenly, her descent slowed. She looked below and saw the glowing form of Yurin Kei Daunyana, straining from the effort of not only slowing their fall, but also guiding them to safe ground on the other side of the huge chamber.

Seung said every prayer she could think of to give the Daunya Apprentice the strength to carry them past that molten pool of death. Whether through her prayers or the other woman's endurance, they barely cleared the lava pool when Yurin's strength gave out and they crashed to the ground.

Everyone lay where they fell, struggling for breath. All eyes turned to Yurin with the unspoken hope the apprentice could once again save them from the unbearable heat.

Yurin lifted herself to hands and knees, gasped the words of an incantation, and waved a hand in three large circles. She touched herself, then thrust her hand out toward the rest of the companions.

Seung blinked. She still felt the heat, but as before, enough of it fell away that she was able to endure it.

One by one the companions struggled to their feet and took in their surroundings. The portion of ceiling that wasn't broken was littered with stalactites. Their way out was impossibly high, and over the far wall of the lake-sized lava pool that dominated the circular chamber.

Waves of heat rose from the pool, and they would surely have died from the heat if not for Yurin Kei Daunyana's efforts.

"You wouldn't be able to levitate us out of here, would you?" Seung asked.

Yurin shook her head. "I don't have that kind of skill. Master DaunyaSai would have been able to do it."

"Master DaunyaSai was unable to accompany us," Tinnoviel said, still scanning the room for a way out. "So he sent his most capable apprentice in his stead." He walked over and put his hands on her shoulders. "You have done a fine job at that, Yurin Kei Daunyana. I'll have no regret from you."

The Daunya Apprentice gave a weary nod of thanks.

"We'll have to figure out a way to climb the walls if we're going to get out of here," Tikena said. Her eyes darted nervously around the room. "And I wouldn't mind if we got out of here as soon as possible, TinTin. Something isn't right about this chamber."

Seung had the same feeling.

A waterfall of rubble fell through the opening in the ceiling where they'd fallen. The elves watched the heavy rocks splash into the lava bed with a stream of thick *plops*.

In the blink of an eye, Tinnoviel's weapon was in his hand and he backed away. No one questioned the Daunya Warrior's actions. They drew their weapons and did the same.

Seung had no time to lament the loss of her *Vyirayoi*. She whipped out her dagger. "What is it?"

"Something moves in there," Tinnoviel said, pointing at the lava.

Seung cast an incredulous look at the molten pool, then back at the slowly retreating elf. She looked back at the lava pool again and saw row after row of ripples flowing across it. Toward them.

Seung backed away faster until her back touched the wall, not nearly far enough away.

An enormous curved surface, resembling a turtle shell, slowly emerged from the molten bath and floated across the pool. It drifted through the magma to the edge and stopped.

Not sure what to make of it, Seung glanced at the others and received similar looks of wary confusion.

Bubbles burst around the front of the giant shell closest to their position. Seung stared unblinkingly at the curved surface. She clenched her dagger in a white-knuckled grip.

Two long multi jointed appendages slithered out of the lava and waved above the giant shell. Each appendage was as big around as her body and ended in a hard, pointed tip.

Seung glanced at the suddenly insignificant dagger in her hand.

"What in the abyss is that thing?" Tikena whispered.

"Assume we'll not be happy when it reveals itself," Tinnoviel said.

The front of the shell lifted just enough to reveal a head the size of an elephant. The long, angry-looking head ended in a wolfish snout, but instead of snarling canine fangs, it was filled with finger-length teeth.

Streams of molten liquid flowed down the angled red face. It focused its glowing red eyes on the gathered elves, and blew steam through flat breathing holes.

"What in the name of Boraka the Destroyer?" Tikena swore.

"Do not attack," Tinnoviel commanded. "Let's hope it's curious. If it does attack, be quick. Study its movements."

As Seung watched it, she realized something wasn't right about this thing. It practically sat atop the lava, and those spider leg-looking appendages were coming from under the surface.

It spat a stream of molten saliva at Tikena, who hopped out of the way. The ground melted where she'd stood an instant earlier. It raised its right appendage and brought it down toward Yurin. She dove out of the way, sliding on her stomach. Still lying on the ground, she stretched out a hand and sent streams of ice shards sizzling through the air into the face of the monster. It gurgled in displeasure and raised its appendage for a second strike.

Seung didn't know what to do. She might as well have no weapon, for all the use her dagger would be.

Tinnoviel call upon Boraka, his voice dropping into its

echoing baritone. He slashed his fan-like weapon downward, sending what looked like a blue slash of light racing at the tentacle. The Daunyanic wave of power sliced clean through the tip.

The monster recoiled, and the sudden movement sent ripples of lava splashing over the edge in front of the retreating elves.

Seung saw those angry red eyes boring into all of them, then her eyes rose as the already massive beast lifted its bulk out of the lava.

Yurin raced past the others as it rose up before them. She slid to a stop in front of the companions, waved her arms in a circle, and spoke an incantation.

The Daunya Apprentice's beautiful melodic voice resounded through the chamber. She spoke the final word and placed the heels of her hands together, palms facing out. She thrust her hands forward just as the monster slapped itself down into the magma.

Seung cried out and reflexively threw her arms up as a wave of lava washed over them. When she realized she hadn't been incinerated, Seung looked overhead in awe at the lava sliding down an invisible dome.

As soon as the danger passed, Tikena sprinted forward and slashed the injured appendage resting on the ground. The attack did little more than make it move away, whereupon she drew a belt dagger and let fly. Her aim was true, and the dagger punched into the bloody stump.

The monster jerked the appendage away with a screech that had the companions pressing their hands to their ears.

Alurien snatched his own dagger from his belt and sent it spinning to imbed itself between the two breathing holes in the lava monster's face. Its responding wail shook the chamber and dislodged stalactites.

Everyone scattered and dove in different directions as the stone spears fell from the ceiling and shattered. The lava monster thrust its uninjured appendage forward, dealing Tinnoviel a glancing blow. The impact sent him flying sideways to crash against the wall. He hit the ground hard, but immediately struggled to his feet.

Alurien leapt atop the appendage and drove his spear between one of the joints. He held tight as the monster recoiled and, pulling his weapon free, leapt onto the flat part of its head and stabbed it at the base of its skull. It should have been a killing blow, but the monster was too big, its neck too thick. It pitched forward, launching the ranger into the far wall, a dozen feet away from the kneeling Tinnoviel.

He crumbled to the ground in a heap, the impact blasting the air from his lungs. Alurien coughed and wheezed as he struggled to catch his breath, but he pushed himself upright on shaky legs. He looked up just as the sharp end of the monster's appendage impaled him to the wall. He spat blood on it and grabbed hold in a futile attempt to dislodge himself.

Tinnoviel's face twisted with rage. He regained his feet and released a roar that could have come from a titan. The Daunya Warrior unleashed such power it shook the cavern.

"HaaaaaAAAAAAAHHHH!"

Seung lowered herself as the entire cavern rumbled. She looked at the elven warrior with a mix of awe and trepidation. This must be what he meant when they spoke about his power.

The bellow was an enormous shockwave that threw the monster sideways. The enraged Daunya Warrior sprinted across its path and cut a deep gash across its face. Once clear, he skidded to a stop, spun, and reached deep within himself again. "YeeeaaaaAAAAAAAAAAA!"

The chamber rumbled again under the power of the elf's voice.

Seung glanced nervously about the cavern, hoping the furious Tinnoviel wasn't about to bring the whole mountain down on them.

The invisible force slammed into the beast again, knocking it in the opposite direction. It withdrew its snake-like appendage and thrust it repeatedly toward Tinnoviel.

One after another, the elf met those stabs, not parrying, but fully blocking each blow. Seung didn't know how he was able to withstand the strength behind those massive tentacles, but Tinnoviel Nai SaunyaLi met each one with the strength of one many times his size.

Seung saw Alurien slump sideways, and her blood lit afire. She picked up a piece of shattered stalactite and threw it like a spear. It broke apart in the monster's face, and it recoiled and slid its stump sideways across the ground. Expecting the attack, Seung jumped over the sweeping tentacle and sprinted past it to draw its attention.

As she'd hoped, Tikena Mojin read her intentions. The quick little elf raced forward and climbed up the injured tentacle. As Alurien had done, she found a joint and drove her belt dagger to the hilt into the vulnerable flesh and hopped off.

As it rotated toward Tikena, Yurin launched another stream of ice into its face.

Stung, and with a dagger imbedded in its joint, the monster swatted its uninjured appendage on the ground and slid it sideways, trying to scrape the elves into the lava.

They leapt over it, each watching for an opportunity to counter.

"What now?" Seung heard Yurin say. She followed the Daunya Apprentice's gaze to the opening in the ceiling.

Four humanoid figures with skin as red as the lava beneath them fell from the opening.

Seung skittered backward while watching with no small amount of wariness, as one of the four figures glowed in the same manner Yurin had done, and guided them over the lava monster.

The mouths of the descending figures opened wide, revealing elongated canine teeth.

As one, they landed on the shell of the monster and sprinted along the top. One after the other, they stabbed it at the base of the head and leapt off.

The elves backed away, watching these new horrors as they landed and spun to face the lava beast. The three women glanced at each other, uncertain what to make of these tall red creatures who didn't seem concerned with them at all.

The battle began anew, and though they kept a wary eye on their unexpected allies, the elves were grateful for the aid.

THE FOG *of hatred for everything in the world thinned, just a bit. The haze parted like a window covered in dirty film, providing a glimpse, a tiny glimpse, of clarity.*

It turned toward that window, however clouded it may be. The claws holding its mind slipped, its grip weakened. In that instant of clarity, that tiny pinprick of light piercing the fog infecting its mind, it became aware.

It flexed its awareness; tried to push the fog further away.

The fog clamped down again, the insubstantial claws tightening their hold. Only one such presence, parasitic to its kind, could keep such a hold on its mind. If only it could focus its thought on it. It could fight back, break free. If only it could lift the fog and remember.

TINNOVIEL RUSHED to Alurien's side, inspecting the wide hole in his torso. Blood bubbled from between his lips and Tinnoviel sighed, amazed the ranger was still alive. "Alurien, my friend."

Behind him, Seung, Yurin, and Tikena continued to battle the beast, but Tinnoviel hardly noticed.

"My road is at it end, brother," the dying elf whispered. "I go to the Daunyans, where my family awaits." He looked past Tinnoviel, his eyes moving as he looked around the chamber at things the Daunya Warrior couldn't see. "As my life drains, the veil thins. There is more, my friend. Much more."

The ground shuddered with the impact of the lava monster's appendage swatting the ground.

Tinnoviel swallowed his grief. "Then go, my brother. Bathe in the light of the Daunyans." He eased his friend onto his back and closed his eyes.

Tears streamed down Tinnoviel's cheeks. He rose and turned to face his enemy, only to see four unnerving creatures, the shortest still over seven feet tall. They fought as allies.

When his gaze settled on the lava monster, anger welled within him. It swept its appendage again, and the newcomers leapt over it.

Tinnoviel stalked forward, and the appendage slid toward him. With the power of Boraka the Destroyer blazing inside, Tinnoviel brought his blade down with enough force to shatter a piece of the sectioned armor. With a gurgling wail, the monster withdrew the limb.

And stood up.

He craned his neck, following its ascent all the way to the ceiling of the chamber. A long slender torso raised out of the lava to support the upper half of the body. The shell was actually just protective armor that covered the upper part of its back to the base of its head. It stood up like a cobra, hunched under its shell.

The furious lava beast made a sound like metal grinding on metal as it repeatedly rammed its shelled back into the ceiling. Stalactites and large chunks of rock dislodged and fell to the ground and into the lava. The warriors dove aside as the beast slammed its appendage at them. The impact crumbled the cave floor, and lava oozed the surface.

The beast surveyed them from on high, then rammed its back into the stone ceiling again and again. A chunk of the ceiling above Yurin collapsed and fell. With a call to the Daunyans, she raised her hand and deflected the descending chunk of rock into the lower half of the monster's body. The impact knocked it off balance.

The beast reared and slammed its back into the ceiling again, playing out its endless rage. One of the newly arrived red creatures ran forward just as the monster slammed its appendage on the ground. It hopped atop the slithering tentacle and held on as it lifted into the air.

The red humanoid jabbed the tentacle repeatedly where the armor was cracked, then climbed higher, unaffected as the appendage twisted and shook in an attempt to dislodge it. The red creature leapt atop the shell and slid forward. With a mighty stroke, it plunged its spear deep into the back of the monster's head.

The lava monster screeched and twisted, turning and crashing sideways into the wall. It straightened and thrusted itself upward, ramming its back into the ceiling again. The red humanoid lost its hold and fell.

One of the red creatures standing in front of the elves screamed as the monster caught their companion between its teeth. The red creature was strong, and held the jaws apart for a time. But the lava monster was too big, too strong, and finally snapped its jaws closed with a horrible crunch.

SEUNG WATCHED as one of the tall red "allies" launched some kind of magical assault into the monster's midsection. When it bent forward, another one leapt forward so quickly it looked as though he glided. The red creature thrust his spear into one of the nose holes, then planted his feet and kicked off.

The monster shrieked and swatted him out of the air. The red ally rolled toward the crumbled ground and exposed lava. He skidded in a sprawl, then screamed when his leg passed over the lava. Seung winced at the horrible sound and smell of sizzling skin.

The monster made that metal-grinding screech again, twitching its bleeding nose hole.

Seung saw her chance and sprinted past the weaving appendage and leapt atop its head. She held on to a piece of broken shell and stabbed the monster repeatedly in the back of the neck. Blood spurted with each thrust.

"No, no, no." He would not allow the *haloren* girl to die here. Tinnoviel raced forward and launched a dagger at the lava monster's face. The elves had the best aim of the Four, and his aim was true. The dagger imbedded itself completely inside the uninjured breathing hole.

The monster let out an agonized shriek and jerked its body up, launching Seung from its head with such force, she flew through the hole in the ceiling. The last the group heard of her was her surprised scream as she hurtled out of the chamber.

50

From their perch, high above the confrontation, Kita, Kenyatta, and Malimokuru watched in awe at the battle beneath them. The two warriors had wanted to fight, but Naiyala and Malimokuru had reasoned with them against it.

"Amata Daunyana cannot shelter all of us against the heat, friends Kenyatta and Kita," the Amahle princess had said.

Despite the gene of the Daunyans burning inside them, Kenyatta and Kita couldn't deny the truth of her words. Surrounded by the molten liquid and towering over its enemies, the terrible creature the Amahle called a lava leach would have been tough enough to handle with Amata's protection. Without it, the heat would surely kill them.

Grizzled Bear lay unconscious against the far wall, Nyaka lying beside him. The young goar cat had become fiercely protective of the man since he'd fallen.

"How do those others down there stand the heat?" Kita wondered.

"Wish I knew how they come to be down there in the first place," Kenyatta replied. "If they slid down this corridor, they should have landed straight in that lava opposite of where they are now."

"Hardly matters," Kita said. "I'm more interested in how they're going to kill that thing and then get out."

The beast began ramming its shelled upper back into the ceiling of the chamber again. The impact lifted the three men off the ground. Nyaka crouched against the wall and growled, her tongue flicking in and out as she tasted the air for a potential threat.

"What in the abyss is that damn thing doing?" the nature reader exclaimed, holding on to a nearby stalagmite. "It's going to bring the whole mountain down on us."

"By the Gods," Kita breathed. "Is that the thing we came here to find?"

"I can't think of anything worse," Kenyatta said. "But no, that's not it. What we come to fight has to do with water, not lava."

Moments passed and the three men watched as the eight figures below fought off the huge monster that dwelled within that molten pool of lava.

"I wish the scary man would get back soon," Kenyatta said. "I got a bad feeling 'bout this thing."

"Oh, no," Malimokuru said. "Look." He pointed at one of the Amahle who'd leapt on the beast and began stabbing it in the back of its head. "That look like Jabulani."

The Elder Hunter drove his spear in again and again to brutal effect, but it wasn't enough.

After a fit of swaying and twisting, the lava leech managed to dislodge him. Luck was not on the elder hunter's side. The moment he lost his grip, the huge monster swung its head around and caught Jabulani between its teeth. For a moment, it looked like the Amahle hunter would hold those jaws open long enough to escape. But his amazing strength faltered, and the jaws clamped down.

Kenyatta and Kita cried out in frustrated rage. Kenyatta had to remind himself of the pool of lava below, or he would have thrown himself down there.

The other three Amahle launched their throwing spears into the beast, and it reared and dropped the body of their fallen comrade into the lava.

Kenyatta closed his eyes, then opened them again.

"Better to go back to the earth through fire, than be eaten." Kita said through clenched teeth.

Kenyatta looked at him and saw the same barely controlled anger he felt.

"Don't you have something in that sack of yours you can help with?" Kita asked Malimokuru. The nature reader just shook his head, looking as helpless as they felt.

They looked back to the battle and saw that a woman had managed to get onto the lava leech's head.

"Has she lost her mind?" Kita said, for surely she'd seen how poor Jabulani had just met his end. He looked at Kenyatta, but his friend stared intently at the woman who valiantly rode and stabbed the beast in the head.

"What happens?" Darius came trotting up the slope of the collapsed tunnel, on the far side of the hole from the others.

"We found some people trapped down there with some monster," Kita replied. "Naiyala and the others went to help."

Darius moved to their side. He looked down into the molten chamber and swore in a language they did not understand. It was the first time he had ever expressed any emotion. "Lava leech," he said. "Temperamental and destructive. The more they injure it, the more enraged it will become." As if to prove his point, the lava leech rammed its shelled back against the ceiling several times again. The whole corridor bucked.

Darius hopped over the hole and went to collect Grizzled Bear. Nyaka watched him but made no move. Gathering the unconscious guide in his arms, he strode to the opening in the ground and leaped back over. "About a hundred feet down, the tunnel forks." He gently lay the guide down and pointed over his shoulder. "The right corridor looks to be the way out but I turned back when the disruption started.

"What about the left tunnel?" Kita asked. "We came here for a purpose."

"You will have come here for your own burial if you remain," Darius replied. He opened his mouth to say more, but a scream cut him off.

Impossible as it seemed, a woman flew through the opening. Darius ducked and the woman passed over his head. He looked in the direction she'd flown, then back at the two men with a surprised smirk.

The ground shook again.

Darius stood and looked down into the chamber. "Do not linger. The ground beneath us will collapse and you have the injured man to attend to. I will deal with this."

The three men looked at him with disbelief, but Darius's hardened visage did not encourage argument.

Darius's physical body may not have grown, but his presence did. Kenyatta felt that he was looking at a giant more than a man.

MALIMOKURU HAD BACKED away from the intimidating man until his back pressed against the wall. He watched as Darius studied the lava leech below, stood, and without hesitation, dropped through the opening.

51

The raging monster reared up to its full height and pounded its back against the ceiling repeatedly. The molten chamber shuddered, and lava splattered on the ground in front of the trapped warriors.

One of the elves spoke an incantation and waved her hand over Sakhile's leg. He sighed in relief as the burning stopped, but he would forever bear the scar; a small price to pay if he survived this. The scout nodded his head in thanks and groaned as he tried to stand. Naiyala hurried over and wrapped his leg. Sakhile growled through clenched teeth. The intensity of the pain overtook his battle rage, and his elongated fangs retracted as he reverted to his normal onyx black pigment.

THE HUMANS WERE brave but had no idea what they'd stumbled into. Not even the Gene of the Daunyans would help them with what lay at the end of the tunnel on the left.

Darius had indeed traveled all the way down that side, where a shallow wall of rock had collapsed. It would have been easy enough to push through the thin wall of rubble, but he hadn't needed to. He could feel what waited on the other side and had no desire to confront it.

The source of the disasters in the ocean, the restlessness of the wind elementals. He had suspected it from the start, but they'd slept for tens of thousands of years.

In the many centuries of their hibernation, the Four had not forgotten them, though humans thought of them as nothing more than legend.

The mighty Daunyarka.

He turned his attention back to the lava leech. They were little more than gigantic parasites. The restlessness of the thing behind the rubble wall made sense. The toxic presence of the lava leech combined with the sickness and disease inflicted on the world for so many years would undoubtedly have taken its toll. But there was more to it, an otherworldly evil permeating its very presence. Darius wondered how many others would be affected.

He stepped over the edge.

Darius gathered the power born unto his kind, channeled it into his feet and hands as he descended upon the massive lava leech. The instant he landed on its shell, Darius punched a tiny explosion of built up power into it.

The force of the impact drove the monster down into the lava with Darius atop it. He punched through the hard, protective shell as though it were no more than brittle clay, and held on as the lava leech submerged.

Instead of being consumed by the molten liquid, it invigorated him. Too many years had it been since he'd felt such heat, such energy. It felt like an eternity had passed since Darius had felt so alive.

Though he hadn't much time to revel in the experience, he would enjoy every moment it took him to destroy this monster.

Malimokuru watched in disbelief at the sight below. Darius might have been no more than a sparrow in size compared to the massive lava leech. Apparently size mattered not at all, for as soon as Darius landed on its armored back, the lava leech went under.

He sucked air through his teeth at the apparent death of the man, for surely he'd been burned to nothing. His shock gave way to amazement when the lava leech surfaced again with Darius ripping away pieces of shell and flesh from its back.

"Definitely want to stay on that man's good side," the nature reader thought aloud.

Having hopped to the other side of the opening to continue her guard over the unconscious guide, Nyaka barked as if in agreement.

Malimokuru looked across the opening at Grizzled Bear. "And how in the five hells me gettin' you outta here, big man?"

He returned his attention to the fight below. If his friends and the others down there didn't kill it and find a way out, he'd have to find a way to get the guide out on his own. Upon remembering the brutal tundra awaiting his exit, the nature reader thought it might be better to just throw Grizzled Bear and himself headfirst into the lava, should their friends fall.

As soon as the injured creature's skin reverted to its onyx hue, recognition washed over Tinnoviel. These were Amahle! The tall folk had come to help them. Why? How? But the questions would have to wait, assuming anyone lived to ask them.

The monster rammed its shelled back into the ceiling again, dislodging more chunks of rock and stalactites from the ceiling of the trembling chamber.

Its body gave a sudden jerk downward, as though something had struck it from above. Tinnoviel watched, puzzled as it simply fell into the lava pool.

Everyone scrambled out of the way as the ripple of molten liquid rushed toward them. The wave crashed against the edge, and washed over the side.

The beast splashed out of the molten bed, mouth agape in an ear-piercing shriek, and turned its focus on Tinnoviel.

Rage still burned in the Daunya Warrior from the loss of Alurien. "Is it time to wake from the dream?" he whispered to Omalah. "If I am to die here, grant me the strength to send this thing into oblivion first."

"No!" Tikena screamed. "You can't die. Don't you dare give up and leave me. Fight. Go get it, TinTin!"

The words of Tikena, so like a little sister to him, cut through Tinnoviel's dark thoughts. He readied himself. Whether he died here or not, he would make sure it didn't harm her or the rest of his friends.

The lava monster swayed violently and wailed again. Something was on its back. The distraction finally passed and the monster came toward him, jaws agape.

Just as Tinnoviel prepared himself for the incoming teeth, it reared back again. When it straightened, he saw the shaft of a spear protruding from its right eye. He looked to see Alurien MerTana, on one knee and clutching his midsection. With a final half smile at his childhood friend, the ranger toppled over, the life finally leaving his body.

"Your final gift to me, my brother," Tinnoviel whispered. "It will not be in vain."

The lava monster gurgled and shrieked, thrashing from side to side. Blood exploded from the protective shell on its back, and it careened into the opposite wall of the chamber where it slid into the lava. For a heartbeat, they thought it was over, till it splashed out again, lava gushing to the ceiling fifty feet above.

Something flew from its back, twisted in the air, and landed kneeling with its back to the monster. It was a man, almost as tall as the Amahle, though his presence was far more imposing than his near seven feet of height. He straightened, and Tinnoviel saw that he was holding two large chunks of the monster's shell.

"What in the name of the Daunyans?" Tinnoviel thought aloud. The man stood unburned despite plunging into the lava. Even his clothes, though sizzling, were unaffected.

———

CHUNKS OF CEILING and stalactites crashed around them. Darius stood to one side, away from the group. It was interesting to find a band of elves in here.

He returned his attention to the lava leech. "I thought your kind were extinct. I shall have to correct that."

He tossed the two chunks of shell to the ground just as the lava leech swung an appendage at him. He caught the tentacle under his arm and skidded sideways. Darius bared his teeth, gave a vicious twist, and snapped it off. The screaming monster threw itself back.

Darius picked up a man-sized stalactite with one hand and sent it rocketing toward the lava leech. The missile penetrated its torso and the force of the impact knocked it back into the far wall.

The lava leech swayed and started falling. Darius ran towards it and rammed his shoulder into the flat end of the stalactite. It stabbed through flesh and broke through bone until it punched through the shelled back.

The power behind Darius's assault knocked the lava leech back against the far wall again. This time, instead of falling forward, it slid lifelessly into the lava. The dead monster lay half submerged surrounded by huge sections of the ceiling it had destroyed.

That final impact brought down a sizable piece of the ceiling.

Amata and one of the elves Darius took to be another Daunya Apprentice formed an overhead barrier that shielded everyone from the falling rock. He chuckled when the two looked at each other in surprise.

They guided the mass of rock and gently lay it in the pool around the dead lava leech.

Darius looked from the apprentices to the male elf struggling with his fallen comrade. When Darius approached, the elf looked into his eyes, then gave a nod and stepped aside.

He gathered the body in his arms, and together everyone hurriedly picked their way over the rock and atop the shell of the dead lava leech until they reached the far wall of the chamber. With both Daunya Apprentices' efforts, the survivors were able to touch the hot surface and climb their way out. Sakhile and Tinnoviel were the last to climb over the edge when the ground shook beneath them, and more chunks of ceiling collapsed into the chamber.

Together, the survivors hurried down the sloping tunnel as the lair of the lava leech collapsed in on itself, and became its tomb.

52

Through the tattered shards of his broken slumber, sounds and tremors came. And with them, his anger. He'd slept through countless ages, content to let the youngest of the Four, or indeed *all* of them, annihilate each other. Now the vermin had come here. Now the rodents brought their stench and endless problems to his lair.

He came awake. If these insects had come to kill him, to destroy his home, he would raise the pits of the abyss and bring the heavens themselves down upon them such that Boraka the Destroyer Himself would take notice. And so, he waited; a simmering cauldron of rage.

53

Seung tried to curl her body tight to brace for impact. Her body glanced off the wall and she lost control, bouncing and skipping painfully across the ground like a stone across a pond.

With the tunnel rotating, rising, and falling to her disorientated eyes, Seung thought she saw a split in the path. She barely had time to register it as she tumbled downward, collided with the side of the tunnel, and crashed through a thin wall of rubble. The impact made her teeth rattle. Every part of her body must be bruised.

Her relief was brief when she no longer ricocheted off the walls at the realization that she was now falling. Seung managed to look down just before she plunged into water.

The impact stung, and she had to fight not to open her mouth to gasp at the shock of the cold water. When she opened her eyes, it was to little more than darkness. Above, a dull haze of light beckoned her to the surface.

With what little air remained in her lungs, Seung righted herself and swam for the light. She broke the surface with a wheezing intake of sweet air.

She tread in place, turning this way and that in search of solid ground. She spotted a rocky shore and swam for it. Each stroke brought a wave of pain, and Seung figured she must have cracked a rib or two. She forced the pain away and focused on reaching the shore. So close.

After what seemed forever, her feet finally touched ground. Doubled over and holding her side Seung dragged herself ashore. Her teeth chattered from the cold water, but the air in this massive cave was, surprisingly, not cold. Well, chilly, but not freezing.

A groan escaped her clenched teeth as she forced herself upright to have a look around. Hundreds of stalactites hung from the ceiling like the teeth of a great beast. At the sight of the lake from which she'd just emerged, Seung closed her eyes and thanked the Daunyans she'd fallen into water and not a molten death.

Before she could finish her prayer, the middle of the lake erupted in a geyser of water that shot straight to the ceiling.

Seung turned away from the wave of water as it fell over her. Drenched all over again, she barely heard the violent splashes. She did feel the ground rumble beneath her.

Thud thud, thud thud thud. Thud thud.

Seung stumbled backward from the lake, but before she could make sense of what was happening, a wall suddenly appeared just inches from her face.

Seung stood frozen and confused as she stared at the rocky, blue wall, rivulets of water flowing down its many grooves and protruding stones.

As the water thinned to a trickle, the wall rose, until two giant holes the size of Seung's body hovered in front of her. No, not holes. Nostrils.

The nostrils took in a breath and puffed it out in an exhale that blew her off her feet.

Seung landed on her backside and winced. Rocks.

The large nostrils turned away to be replaced by an even

larger blue eye. Its gaze moved down until it was directly in front of her, and she sat transfixed by the cold blue stare. The eye lifted away to afford Seung a view she wished she didn't have.

Towering high above her was the thing she sought.

Through skirmishes and raids, through battle and death, she had led the warriors of Kyu. Seung had fought monsters the people of the larger cities would not believe existed. Many times had Seung faced death stoically and prepared for its inevitable embrace. She'd fought water elementals, an abandoned town of hideous green monsters, traveled across harsh lands and waters inhabited by creatures whose song could destroy the mind.

None of it mattered. Nothing could have prepared her for this. She had once overheard the elves mentioning creatures from an age long gone. Creatures called Daunyarka.

At the time, she hadn't known what it meant. Now she knew. Though humans did not believe they existed, the marvelous and terrible creatures lived immortal through legends and folk tales. For humans knew them not as Daunyarka, but as dragons.

Seung Yoon, warrior of the village of Kyu. Kiluriel Sen'Mora, great grandchild of Seiyun, the Lady of the Wood and Queen of the Elfinestraya of Yathienel, stood before a dragon. And for the first time since she was a child, she knew real fear.

IT TOOK every bit of her will for Seung to stand and not cower before the awesome presence of the dragon. A dragon. Despite her sensibilities screaming at her of the impossibility, that this was just some delusion resulting from a hit on the head, she couldn't deny it.

It rose up to its full height and flexed its wings, for they could not fully extend despite the great size of the cavern. Though it looked down on her, Seung could not will herself to meet its eyes.

Instead she saw her own terrified visage reflected in the shimmering, ocean-blue plate scales covering its massive body.

It fixed her with an angry blue glare, and she saw her death in those eyes. It took one step forward and the resulting tremor lifted Seung from her feet. She fell back on the painful rocks again, but quickly scrambled to her feet. A huge, three-toed claw sank into the earth before her. Black talons, as long as she was tall, dug into the ground.

Seung scanned the cavern, looking for a way out. Even if there was, how would she get to it before being stomped into the ground? She wished she had *Vyirayoi*, but even if she'd had the weapon, what use would it be against this godlike creature?

The scaly blue head lowered in front of her again, two spiraling horns protruding from the back of its armor-plated skull.

"Why are you here?"

The words entered her mind, not her ears. The sensation felt similar to the *whisper* the elves used, only infinitely more powerful. Her body shook with the impact of the question. Seung felt it could dash her mind to the winds with but a word, a twitch of inflection.

"Speak."

Seung fell over and scrambled upright again. The simple word, a calm, yet forceful demand, made her knees buckle. She knew beyond doubt that if it shouted into her mind, she'd be destroyed.

"I ... I have come to this place seeking—" Seeking what? To find the source of the disasters and stop them? What could she say to this terrifying beast that wouldn't result in her immediate death?

"Seeking what, little rodent? Adventure? Amusement? Or do you seek me? Of course you do. Why else would you traverse lands uninhabitable to your infectious kind, only to find my mountain and come tunneling through it like a mole?"

She felt its amusement, like one would feel toward a particularly resourceful ant.

"*Of course you seek me, but the question—one I'll not ask again —is why?*"

"I ... there have been disasters. Island destroying waves, violent and unnatural storms." Seung started to feel more steady as she talked. "Destruction ... as though nature is angry." She thought she saw a crimson glimmer pass across its eyes. "I was guided ..."

"*Do you know why you are not spread across my lair from one end to the other, little pest?*"

Seung felt her legs wobble. She shook her head.

"*Because I would have to smell your disgusting remains. And I would not think of eating such a disgusting creature.*"

Seung didn't know whether or not she should feel relieved.

"*You come here because nature has turned against you,*" the tone was coated in sarcasm. "*Insignificant nature, no more relevant than a passing thought to you. Now that it causes you displeasure, you embark on a mighty quest to solve the problem. Or in this case, slay the beast.*" Seung's heart fluttered in her chest. "*You look ill prepared for your grand adventure. Where is your gleaming lance and shield?*"

"I have come here to slay no one, only to understand what has happened and see if I may do something to end it."

This time the dragon chuckled audibly. The sound sent tremors through her body. She squinted her eyes shut and concentrated on not letting her body shake apart.

"*You've found the* source *of your displeasure, brave warrior.*" It tilted its great scaly head at her. "*So what now? Now that I awaken, I tell you that I am indeed the source of these disasters as you call them. They are the result of my restless sleep; disturbed for countless centuries. The winds and oceans are my province, and sometimes they manifest my contentment or displeasure. Now that I am fully awake, what shall I do with you?*"

"I came not knowing what I was searching for. I wished to ..."

"*Speak no more,*" the voice commanded. "*You are less than a child. You are the youngest of the Four, the children of the world. You have been here the shortest time and have tried to tear the world asunder. It is through the grace and compassion of the Daunyans that your entire species still exists. DEMONS have created less havoc.*"

The dragon's temper was rising. She needed to slow it down or she was doomed. "There are many who seek to right these wrongs, mighty Daunyarka."

That stopped the tirade. For several tense heartbeats, the dragon looked as though it waged some inner battle with its thoughts. Despite her fear, Seung saw its indecision.

It looked closely at her. "*Long has it been since I've heard that word.*" It lowered its head in front of her again. "*The stench of human blood hangs about you like a pall, but I smell the blood of the star people within you as well. Perhaps there is a chance you will survive this day.*"

Seung kept her features neutral despite the surge of hope growing within her. She didn't quite understand the dragon's hatred for humans, but maybe her elven blood would save her.

The red glimmer she'd seen before flickered across its eyes again. "*Or perhaps not.*"

Seung felt her hope fade. It was toying with her. She looked about the cave again. There must be an exit.

The dragon chuckled, and the ground rumbled beneath her. "*Even if you found a way out, vermin, you'd not make it three steps.*"

It was right, of course. So Seung stood tall. If this was to be her death, she would meet it without fear. She forced herself to look up into those cold, blue orbs. Again she saw that crimson flicker. What was that?

As soon as the thought entered her mind, something came to life inside her; a tiny spark ignited deep within. She glanced down at her chest, then looked back up at the dragon. All of her senses were suddenly sharpened. The dragon's scales shone brighter, her hearing was more acute. She smelled the tiny forms of life deep in the lake behind the dragon. And she felt stronger. Far stronger. What was happening to her?

A WIDE-EYED KENYATTA and Kita watched the exchange from their crouched position in the opening of the tunnel. To their disbelief, it was indeed Seung down there. That would have been shock enough, but the presence of legend come to life overshadowed their elation. In all their adventures, never had they felt so overwhelmed.

A dragon.

The demon horde two years ago might have been little more than an inconvenient day by comparison.

Despite the gene of the Daunyans burning inside them, neither men made a move. What could they do? The sword at Kenyatta's back and the staff in Kita's hands felt like little more than harmless twigs.

They watched in confusion as some dialogue took place, but the only person talking was Seung.

"What should we do?" Kita whispered.

"Whatever it is, we'd better do it fast." Kenyatta ran a hand through his locks. "I still feel the gene inside, but is it because of that thing back there?" he jabbed a finger over his shoulder, "or *that* down there?"

"Both?" Kita whispered.

"Let's hope they kill it quick and get down here. We'll need all the help we can get."

"You think this is the cause of all the destruction?"

Kenyatta stared at the dragon's back from on high and hoped not. "If it is, it's going to pay."

"How?" Kita asked. "Indigestion?"

SEUNG DIDN'T KNOW the source of this newfound power building inside. Perhaps it was her elven lineage? She clenched her fist, once again wishing she had *Vyirayoi*.

"*Your friends have found you.*" Quiet rumbling laughter; an ominous sound.

Seung felt a surge of hope. It didn't like humans, but perhaps it would be more friendly toward her elven friends.

"*They will suffer your fate. No human will enter my home and leave, only to bring more for me to exterminate.*"

Humans? For a moment, Seung forgot her situation and gave the dragon a quizzical look. "I know of no humans here."

"*Oh?*" The dragon flicked out its left wing and struck the wall just under the tunnel Seung had fallen through. To her surprise, two men tumbled out and splashed into the water. With surprising agility, the dragon lowered its wing and scooped them out. With another flick, it launched the two humans in her direction. Seung hurried out of the way as the pair skidded across the water and tumbled in a ball of grunts and pained curses across the rocky surface.

Her mouth fell open at the sight of the two wandering warriors who had come to her village's aid what seemed a lifetime ago.

"Keyatta?" she breathed stumbling over the dark islander's name as she had two years ago. "Kita?"

"*And so the allies are revealed,*" the voice remarked in a lazy tone. "*And so you die.*"

The two islanders were instantly on their feet and on the move.

Kenyatta reached behind his back. "You lost something!"

Seung felt a surge of excitement at the sight of *Vyirayoi*. The islander tossed it toward her and Seung snatched it out of the air and snapped the shaft in place with a twist.

KENYATTA'S LEGS PUMPED, the gene of the Daunyans augmenting his speed. He saw the long, plated tail rise out of the water and curl toward them as soon as he and Kita hit the ground.

It shot straight for him like an arrow. At the last possible instant Kenyatta skidded to a stop and spun aside. With inhuman speed, Kenyatta drew his sword and brought it down on the armored tail as it passed.

The dragon pulled its tail out of reach and stared at him. It looked ... amused.

Kenyatta stole a glance over his shoulder at the hole in the rocky wall behind him. A better description would have been incision. The tip of the dragon's tail had sliced into the rock like a knife through fresh butter.

The tail came again and again, thrusting in and out. Kenyatta separated his sword into two and dodged, every time countering with solid strokes that would have ruined the tail of a lesser beast.

But this was a dragon.

When the assault ceased, Kenyatta stole a glance at his friends. They fought valiantly, but to no better effect. He looked back at the mighty creature. Did it even feel anything?

He settled into a low stance and waited. He knew it was unlikely he could kill a dragon. Then he thought of his destroyed homeland, of the many dead and displaced he'd left behind for this very confrontation. Live or die, this was why he came. Why they'd all come.

The indestructible tail hovered in front of him.

So be it.

54

Never had *Vyirayoi* been so mighty. Never had Seung been so deadly.

The dragon struck with surprising speed. A stab and sweep at the other two warriors and it was back quick enough to block or deflect her weapon. But still she fought. The power burning inside her flared with each stroke. *Vyirayoi* disappeared in her hands, so fast did she whirl it.

The tail struck at the man named Kita, who leapt aside and struck it with a powerful downward stroke of his staff. Unaffected, the tail curled back to turn Seung's attack aside. The force of the impact knocked her backward, but Seung somersaulted in the air. As soon as her feet touched the ground, she launched herself forward.

The dragon had whipped its tail around to stab at Kenyatta again, and Seung dealt it an endless flurry of slices along its fore-leg. Its leg should have fallen apart under her assault. Instead, she heard rumbling laughter in her mind. It lifted its foot, Seung leapt away, and it stomped the ground. The tremor of the dragon's stomp might have shaken the world. Despite the incredible power burning in her, this dragon was beyond her.

Seung thought of the people of Ulleung. She thought of the lost family and friends of the survivors, now without a home. She thought of her beloved Kyu.

With a lazy flap of its wing, the dragon created a wind more powerful than any storm. It swept Seung off the ground with ease and sent her hurtling toward the cavern wall.

Seung tucked *Vyirayoi* under her arm and twisted her body in the air. In the span of a heartbeat she hit the wall in a crouch and launched herself forward. An arrow speeding toward her mighty foe, Seung curled her body in at the last moment. She landed on the side of the dragon's neck in much the same manner as the wall. She landed many blows—once, twice, thrice —before gravity claimed her once again. Seung continued her assault on the dragon even during her descent. Any normal creature would have been reduced to ribbons. But each blow slid along those beautiful, plated scales like a stick against a mountain.

She landed and immediately launched herself backward. Her instincts saved her life. The dragon raked the ground where she'd landed, leaving long scars in the ground deep enough for her to stand in.

The warrior from Kyu landed ready. She studied the dragon as it fought the other two. No, not fought—toyed. She realized then that this was not a fight they could win. This mighty beast was far beyond them, and they were likely no more than a rare novelty to a long-slumbering, godlike creature who would eventually grow bored.

She again thought of her homeland. She set *Vyirayoi* spinning. She threw herself back into the fight.

THE INSTANT the dragon struck at his friend, Kita entered the fray. Together they met each thrust of that massive tale with everything they had, but the futility of their situation was clearly evident.

The dragon was toying with them. The more they fought, the more obvious it became. Kita hadn't spoken much about his concerns for his own homeland because the grief of his friend was so great.

But now they had found their greatest foe. This beast had destroyed half of Jamaica without even being there. He imagined the woman fighting beside them was here for a similar reason.

Kita whirled his staff. The dragon was fast, and had not the gene of the Daunyans burned inside them, the fight would have long been over.

But something wasn't right.

How many blows had he landed? How many from Kenyatta? The gene burned inside them, which meant this dragon was some sort of demonkind. Their weapons held the power to banish demonkind back to the abyss, yet the dragon seemed not to notice at all. To it, this was fun.

The dragon sat comfortably in the water, content with thrusting its tail in and out, swatting at Seung whenever she got too close. When it turned its amused expression on Kita, he saw a red flicker in its eyes. For a fleeting moment his mind went back to their battle with the monster in the sea. He'd seen no such thing in its eyes, but he remembered the evil cloud of blackness that had taken shape when they'd dealt too much damage to the monster. That cloud had taken shape just long enough to open its mouth in an outraged scream, then dissipated. Could this be a similar situation?

He dodged the tail again and struck hard and fast before it retracted. He hurried out of the way when the bulk of the dragon's tail sped toward him even as the spear-like tip thrust at Kenyatta. This wasn't working.

"Not sure how to feel about it ending like this," Kita yelled to

Kenyatta. "I mean, dying in a fight with a dragon tops anything I've ever imagined."

He dove away from the crashing tail and shielded his eyes against the flying dirt. He leapt forward and struck the tail with an overhead chop. "But dragon or not, the thought of death while being toyed with is a little embarrassing."

Kenyatta scored several hits on the armored tail again. After a flurry of slices on the impenetrable armor, the tail slowly—lazily —eased away.

Kita watched the exchange with growing hopelessness. The dragon had actually kept its tail there long enough for Kenyatta to finish his attacks.

One of its wings uncurled from its side.

Kenyatta and Kita looked at each other and braced themselves. Whatever it was about to do, Kita doubted they'd like it.

He was right.

With one mighty flap, the dragon blew a gust of wind that sent them all flying back into the wall. Kita and Kenyatta fell to the ground in a heap, but Seung hit the wall in a crouch and threw herself back at the dragon.

Kita groaned off the pain. The rocky wall was hard and sharp in places. He turned his attention back to the fight and watched with growing bewilderment. The woman moved with swiftness and power that easily matched their own. She rushed in and out, each time dealing what should have been a lot of massive damage. He wondered if she too fought with the burning gene inside.

Kita whipped his staff in an arc and tucked it under his arm. He crouched, preparing to launch himself again at this great enemy. He blinked. The dragon's scales still shone magnificently, but less so. His body, while still strong and fast, felt ... diminished. His senses dulled, and with it, his confidence. The gene had fallen dormant.

"I THANK YOU FOR THIS ENTERTAINMENT."

Kenyatta clamped his hands to his head against the painful rumble of the dragon's voice inside his head.

"But I can tolerate your scent no longer. I will deliver you to the Daunyans and let them decide your eternal fate."

Kenyatta didn't have time to ponder why a creature of demonkind would speak of the Gods, nor why the gene of the Daunyans winked out at that moment. Death had finally arrived for them.

Two figures dropped from the tunnel behind the now standing dragon and glided across the water. They passed right under the dragon as it rose up and arched its neck back.

"Pray you, vermin, that you are delivered into Se'lir's mercy."

The three mortals stood paralyzed, for what could they do? The sound of the dragon's long, deep intake of breath filled the chamber.

From the corner of his eye, Kenyatta saw Amata Daunyana skim the surface of the water holding another woman by the wrist. They skidded to a stop in front of the three trapped warriors, turned, and together shouted an incantation just as the dragon breathed upon them.

Burning cold washed over them. The two women leaned forward and braced against the force of the assault.

Kenyatta, Kita, and Seung stood in helpless amazement as the dragon's icy breath broke around an invisible barrier like a river water around a boulder.

Despite the protective shield, the three warriors wrapped their arms about themselves against the terrible cold. Surely they would be dead were it not for the two women who slid back, inch by inch, as they struggled against the power of the dragon's breath.

Many heartbeats passed before the dragon finally relented.

Amata Daunyana and the other woman dropped to their hands and knees, exhausted.

The warriors started toward the struggling women, but the dragon's snort stopped them cold.

The look of disbelief in the great blue beast's eyes changed to curiosity.

Kenyatta gritted his teeth against the laughter rattling in his mind. So offhand yet so powerful, it brought all of them to their knees.

"Impressive. How much strength have you left, my new visitors?"

The tail raised again as if to strike, then something odd happened. First, the dragon shook its head and blinked. When it turned its gaze on them again, it was one of confusion. *"What is this?"*

Before Kenyatta or the others could begin to understand this new development, the dragon stumbled backward, causing splashes and waves from the lake to crash on the shore.

It whipped its head around and followed a solitary figure as it ran along its scaled back and leapt a great distance across the water to the shore.

"After all these centuries, could it actually be the legendary Khairon the Blue?" Darius smiled and opened his arms as if to embrace the incredulous dragon. "I hadn't thought to ever see any of the mighty Blues upon this world again."

The dragon looked the tiny figures over. In his face, confusion gave way to anger.

"ONE OF THE RED TRIBE ENTERS MY LAIR?"

Everyone, save Darius, dropped to their knees, hands clamped over their heads as the dragon roared in their minds.

Kenyatta pressed his eyes shut, willing his head not to explode.

"Come now, Khairon," Darius said. "You'll kill them all if you yell so."

Khairon threw his head back and audibly roared. Stalactites fell from the ceiling and shattered against the dragon's impenetrable hide; pieces of the ceiling and wall crumbled away to splash in the lake.

Darius stood with his arms crossed, waiting for the dragon's rage to play out. "If you are quite finished?"

Khairon thrust his tail at the man with such speed, Kenyatta knew beyond doubt that the dragon had indeed been toying with them earlier.

With a two-handed slap, Darius deflected the tail aside.

"What in the five hells is he?" Kita asked.

Kenyatta had no answer. He looked down at the swords in his hands. Despite the power imbued by Amata Daunyana, they seemed as insignificant as he felt.

Khairon growled deep in his throat, scaly lips parting to reveal teeth as long as Darius was tall. The dragon inhaled a long deep breath, then thrust his head forward and breathed icy death.

The bellow that erupted from deep in Darius's core tossed the five watching mortals to the ground. His body ignited in flames that matched the blue dragon's icy breath. He threw his head back, arms extended, surrounded by a blazing inferno.

When Khairon finally relented, the flames surrounding Darius flickered out as well. For the first time since they'd met him, the "man" looked visibly taxed.

Khairon's outraged roar shook the chamber again.

On the far side of the shore, everyone slowly retreated until their backs pressed against the wall. Kenyatta realized he was holding his breath. When he glanced at the others he saw the same reaction. No one wanted to so much as breathe.

"A red drojan comes to kill me in my own lair!"

"Clear your thoughts, Khairon," Darius yelled. "Even if that were true, what good would it have done to bring ..."

The blue dragon lunged forward and Darius jumped back just as giant teeth snapped at the spot where he'd been. Darius set his feet and leaned into a right-handed punch, just as the jaws snapped shut.

The dragon let out a sound that could only have been described as a squeal. Khairon recoiled and looked down at the man in shock. He tilted his head with a quizzical expression.

"You are strong, drojan. Even for your kind."

Darius drew himself to his full height. "The blood of Asclepius burns in my veins."

"Asclepius The Red." Khairon raised his head in appreciation. *"That explains much."*

Just then, Tinnoviel and Naiyala appeared at the edge of the crumbled tunnel. As the others had, they fell back in shock. Khairon swung his head over his shoulder, then looked back to the others.

"More of your friends, I presume?"

"More or less," Darius replied. The dragon snorted in irritation.

"I have never met a Red that could speak in straight lines." He considered the party. *"My home is becoming as crowded as my mind."*

"But your mountain has been cleared of a great nuisance, mighty Khairon," Darius replied. "We've cleansed the filth of the lava leech from your home, and with it, banished a powerful demon essence".

The dragon perked up at that. *"A lava leech? All these years, my slumber was disturbed because of that filth?"*

Darius tilted his head at that. "You didn't know?"

"I did not," Khairon replied. He regarded the five mortals pressed against the rocky wall, a good distance from the solitary Darius. *"Am I to assume you played a part in its removal?"*

The only answer the dragon received were glances at Darius.

"One and all," the man said. "And this is despite the unfortunate event of you destroying their homeland."

Khairon's resulting snort wasn't derisive, but puzzled. "In my restless dreams I killed a great evil that would have destroyed the land upon which they walked. The everlasting poisoning and destruction of all that lived upon it ended by my power."

"You kill countless people living peacefully on our island home." Kenyatta yelled, and Khairon whipped his head around to face him. Kenyatta swallowed, but pushed on. "I don't know a thing 'bout evil poisoning my homeland. We live in peace till you send death on us all."

"My dreams do not lie, human. Speak your next words carefully."

Kenyatta forced himself to look into those enormous blue eyes. Creation itself stared back at him. "I swear by the gene of the Daunyans that burn in my chest when demons are near, that no evil you speak of torture and poison my beloved Jamaica. They're dead. Dead and displaced because of you." There. He'd said it. If the dragon killed him, so be it.

Khairon didn't kill him. In fact, the great blue dragon looked on him with confusion bordering on remorse. *"I feel no lie in your words, yet my dreams do not lie. How can this be?"*

"Your dreams were caused by the presence of the lava leech in your mountain, and the demon spirit occupying it, great Khairon." Darius's tone held a sympathetic note that Kenyatta felt directed at both of them. "Though doubtless humans have done much damage to this world, that ended hundreds of years ago. Their age of machines has long been dead."

"And now demons roam the land," Khairon said.

"We fought them at Takashaniel," Kita spoke up. "A being with great power summons them from the five hells. The battle ended undecided, but the final conflict approaches."

"The weakening of the barrier to the abyss provides a small tear between our dimensions," Darius added. "Enough for a demon spirit to inhabit a host. Such as a corruptible human or any of the long dormant ancient evils deep in the earth ... such as a lava leech."

Khairon regarded each of them as they spoke, comprehension and regret lined his scaled features. *"Humans chosen by the Daunyans to decide the fate of this world. Humans who travel beside elves, Amahle, and a drojan."* He cast a side eye at Darius. *"It seems I have committed a great misdeed in my prolonged slumber. And in the thrall of a demon-inhabited lava leech, no less."* The dragon gave a great cavernous sigh.

The anger Kenyatta felt toward the object of so much suffering and death dimmed at the sight of the dragon's regret.

"We, the Daunyarka were once the protectors of this world, as well as guardians of the realm of the Daunyans. How far have I fallen to have committed such an act?"

Kenyatta wanted to be angry at the dragon. He wanted to strike him down for what he'd done, make him bear witness to the destruction, suffering, and death that he'd wrought. But the anger slipped through his fingers like sand, no matter how hard he fought to hold onto it.

Kenyatta looked away from the dragon. His emotions were still too close to the surface, the pain too raw.

Khairon gave another great sigh. *"It seems I owe a moral debt I can never repay."* He looked back at the two stunned figures in the tunnel opening and extended his wing.

Tinnoviel and Naiyala stared at the wing until the dragon grunted at them. With more than a little hesitance, they hopped onto the giant blue wing and Khairon transported them to the edge of the shore.

"Three of the Four have come to my lair. How many atrocities have I inflicted to create such an unlikely unity?"

And so, the two groups told their tales in turn, finally coming to the point where their separate adventures overlapped.

Khairon settled down for the tale, occasionally interrupting to ask for more news of the outside world. *"Long has it been since I've walked the world. Perhaps the time is coming when we the Daunyarka will walk it again."*

"I, too, have slept for many years, great Khairon," Darius responded. "I believe humans still need time. What I've seen in my few waking years prior to meeting this unusual band has shown me such." His typical smirk returned. "But then, what is time to Daunyarka, hmm?"

The blue dragon looked directly at Kenyatta. *"I see the sorrow and rage in your eyes. You see before you the one who has destroyed your homeland and many of your people. There are no words I can speak that will bring comfort, for I barely comprehend what has happened. But I will attempt to explain.*

"You see, when we the Daunyarka sleep, nature can become physical expressions of our minds. Though it has been hundreds of years since your advanced age met its end, the poisons I have felt within the oceans and the air had caused my slumber to become fitful. To learn of a demon-possessed lava leech, and demons roaming the land ..." Khairon made a regretful huff. *"I can think of no other recompense for this tragedy than to offer myself to you, little warrior."* Khairon rammed a huge claw into the wall and tore free a patch of mineral rock. With barely a thought, the dragon clenched his claw and crushed the rock to bits. What remained was a jagged stone the size of Kenyatta's head.

Khairon gently breathed his icy breath onto it, eroding it down to its core shape. When the dragon lowered his giant claw to Kenyatta, what remained was a stone as smooth as if it were taken from the bottom of a river.

"I've imbued this stone with a flake of my power. Should you hold it and project your thoughts into it, I will know."

Tears fell from Kenyatta's eyes as he looked at the perfect, glistening stone. Anger and vengeance had carried him from the ruins of Jamaica across the ocean, a continent, and the harsh tundras of Askata to this moment. He'd come here to confront the demon who'd unleashed death and ruin on his homeland, only to discover it was a majestic creature out of legend, manipulated in his sleep by an evil monster inhabited by an even worse evil.

He looked at the stone in his hand. Primal energy pulsated inside of it. Deep within himself, Kenyatta felt not only his own despair, but that of Khairon's as well.

The mighty blue dragon looked them over before stopping at Darius again.

"I would name you friends, if you would have my friendship. After what I've done ..." the dragon looked past them, his gaze far away. *"If ever you find yourself near my home again, know that I will receive you kindly. I offer you transport from my home and the icy lands beyond."* Khairon looked at the still emotional Kenyatta. *"My gesture does not begin to make amends, but I hope it can be a beginning."*

Kenyatta looked up into those huge blue eyes. His voice came out in a whisper. "Yeah, man. It's a beginning."

THE COMPANIONS MET with Khairon outside the mountain, where the snowstorms still raged.

Gathered in a crook where the wind couldn't reach, they made a proper farewell for their fallen friends. They lay Alurien's body to rest in the ground at the base of the mountain, and although Jabulani had fallen into the lava, and Nuviel had been buried back in the Rainlands, they were all honored side by side.

After words had been spoken, the ground trembled as Khairon strode solemnly to the place where the Elden elf was interred. He lowered his head and, with a rumbling in his throat, breathed gently upon the ground. The air above the frozen burial site gathered and crystalized. It built upon itself, rising, like water flowing upward. The dragon repeated the process until three beautiful ice sculptures adorned the head of each grave.

Above where Alurien lay, stood a six-foot ice replica of the great tree of Yathienel, So'orya. Beside it was an equally marvelous sculpture of the desert tree of the Amahle, the *Oyala*. The third sculpture was the dancing form of what looked like a stunning blend of the Daunyan Nakiya, and Nuviel.

The surviving companions marveled at the sculptures with a mixture of awe and grief.

"They're beautiful." Tikena's shoulders shuddered as she choked out the words.

Seung looked at the emotional elven girl. It was the first time she'd heard the elf speak with kindness.

"You honor us and our fallen friends," Tinnoviel Nai Saun-yaLi said.

Khairon raised his head and looked to the sky. *"Fallen, Daunya Warrior? You, as well as I, know they have ascended beyond this world to join the Daunyans."*

Tinnoviel bowed.

And so more words were said and memories shared, then it was time to leave.

"You would be wise to guard yourselves and your friends against the cold, Daunya Apprentices," Khairon warned. *"To avoid the sight of humans I must fly very high. The cold will freeze you."*

After Amata and Yurin had done their work, Khairon opened one of his gigantic claws. They climbed in, one at a time. Kenyatta ran his hand over the blue shimmering claw. The surface felt harder than any manmade steel.

Darius had a different idea. "I would ask a boon, great Khairon." He executed a perfect bow. "Although the scales of your back would slice my friends to pieces, I am a little more ... durable. I would ride on your back if you would have me."

"I am no beast of burden, drojan."

"Of course not, mighty Khairon," Darius replied. "But I would stand atop a mountain not in conquest, but in awe of its magnificence."

The dragon snorted. *"Then find a mountain to climb."*

"There is no mountain in the world comparable to your splendor."

Khairon stared at Darius, then blew out through his nostrils in a sarcastic huff. *"Honeycoated words from a red drojan."* He lowered himself and dropped his wing to the ground. *"Spare me any more of your charm and climb onto my back, that we may be gone."*

After Darius found a favorable position, Khairon crouched and the muscles in his legs bunched as the dragon prepared to take off. With a great leap and flap of his wings, Khairon the Blue lifted into the air and the ground quickly fell away.

The dragon held them loosely in his partially enclosed claw, so as not to crush his diminutive passengers. Some of the riders climbed up his scaled claw to peek over the side, thrilled at the speed and height at which they traveled. Others sat in nervous silence.

Kenyatta watched as Malimokuru stroked the whimpering Nyaka behind her ears. It had taken some coaxing to get the goar cat to allow herself to be wrapped in the claws of an infinitely larger and more dominant predator to begin with. This was more than the poor animal could bear.

So high did Khairon fly that they passed above the clouds. Despite the protective barriers created by Amata and Yurin, tears still streamed from their eyes from the cold wind.

The dragon glided for hours across Askata and the northern Rainlands. He passed high above mountains, lakes, and forests until finally coming to a remote valley of equal distance from the coast and the Amahle village.

Kenyatta watched Seung walk up to Khairon. She looked surprised at herself for being sad at seeing the dragon go, after having come close to being killed by him.

"Lament not at our parting, for I have not the stomach for it. You know where I dwell, and the years are slower for you."

With no further words, Khairon the Blue spread his wings. With another great leap and a flap of his wings, he launched into the air. The companions crouched low, bracing themselves against force of his takeoff.

Seung watched the shimmering blue figure recede into the distant sky.

"Natsuninu lei al tamu."

55

K enyatta, Kita, and Seung leaned on the rail of *The Ocean Goddess*, silently gazing at the rippling waves and gentle swells of the sparkling ocean.

Kenyatta took a deep breath and reveled in the smell of fresh salty air. No one needed to say it, for they all felt the same. After the trials endured and the losses they'd experienced, this uneventful voyage was welcome, if bittersweet.

Though their journey had been both physically and emotionally exhausting, it had taken little prodding for Kenyatta and Kita to accept Seung's offer to travel with her back to Kyu.

Unsurprisingly, Malimokuru and the slowly recovering Grizzled Bear had opted to travel with the tall folk. To their relief, the guide had finally awoken hours after the ship left port, but was in no condition to travel all the way back to Tarrow's Field.

Parting ways with the Amahle had been a more emotional affair than the two friends anticipated.

"Do not forget me or my people," Naiyala had said.

"Impossible," Kita had replied.

"You give so much to help us," Kenyatta had said, tears

welling in his eyes. "We never forget the sacrifice of Elder Hunter Jabulani."

"He lives on with the Daunyans and in our memories," Sakhile replied.

And so, they'd parted ways, each with hesitant yet heartfelt goodbyes, and promises of a reunion.

The ocean continued its soothing melody while gulls glided overhead adding to the serenade. They closed their eyes and basked in the sun and salty mist on their faces.

After a while Kita excused himself, claiming a desire to get to know the elves better.

Now alone, the two weary warriors gazed out at the endless ocean, content to simply enjoy each other's company.

To Seung, who'd traveled for days in the dark tunnels of the Sleeping Titans and then into the depths of the Sentinels, it was a welcome sensation to feel the fresh, crisp ocean air caressing her face. From the corner of her eye she saw Kenyatta pretending not to steal glances at her.

"What do you think will happen now?" she asked. Her grasp of the western tongue had improved considerably since last they'd met.

"Don't know," Kenyatta responded. "I seen a lot of things these past couple years that make me think this is just the beginning."

Seung nodded. "After what we've seen, nothing can surprise me." She saw the flicker of doubt in the man's expression at her words. What else had he seen in his travels?

She looked into his brown eyes, so full of kindness and pain. There was more there as well, and what she saw filled Seung with warmth.

Kenyatta took her hand in his, and she felt tiny jolts of electricity shoot through her stomach. A nervous smile twitched the side of her mouth, and she gave his hand a welcoming squeeze. "Thank you."

Kenyatta arched an eyebrow. "For what?"

"For bringing *Vyirayoi* back to me. It is," she searched for the right word, "special ... to me."

Kenyatta nodded and began talking too much. "Yeah, man. I see it in dat chamber way back and thinkin' ..."

She wrapped her arms around him and crushed her body to his. He smelled like salt. She was sure she did, too.

Still holding each other, Seung leaned away, just a bit, and tilted her head to the side. For the first time in her life, she let another human see her pointed ears. Despite his already meeting and marveling at the elves, she hadn't revealed her secret to him. Now she waited nervously for his reaction.

Kenyatta's mouth fell open. He reached up and gently ran a finger over the tip of her ear. Then he moved her hair from the other ear and did the same. His brown eyes held wonder and, to her relief, affection. "Wish I'd never left your village," he said.

"No you don't," Seung replied. "But I'm glad we're here, now." He was studying her round pink lips, and she gave him a half smile. "How long will you stand there, imagining how soft they are?"

"That's enough," came the reply, and he pressed his lips to hers. She wrapped him in a tight embrace, crushing her body to his once again.

Seung opened herself fully to the experience. Ever had she been focused on her role as the leader of the warriors of her village. Always so immersed in the responsibilities of her station that she rarely allowed herself to feel affection beyond friendship.

In feeling so different from everyone around her, Seung had grown up keeping herself guarded. Since she was old enough to remember, Seung's life had been a mystery, not only to those around her, but to herself. How could she love someone when she scarcely knew who she herself was? And now she realized that she'd fallen in love with a man she had only just met for the second time. Perhaps infatuation from her lack of experience?

As quickly as the thoughts entered her mind she knew they were untrue. She knew that she had fallen in love with this man she barely knew, yet felt as though she'd known him all her life.

All of those thoughts passed through her mind as the kiss endured, until they finally broke away, gasping for air.

Kenyatta opened his mouth to speak, and she kissed him again, deeper this time. His tongue found hers and her body radiated with heat. The sound of someone clearing his throat shattered the moment and they broke apart like children caught in mischief.

Tinnoviel stood with his arms crossed, tapping a finger on his arm with an upraised eyebrow. "I thought you'd like to know the captain says we should make land in a few hours." He turned to leave, saying over his shoulder, "I suspect I was wrong."

Seung felt heat rising to her cheeks, but Kenyatta laughed and wrapped his arm around her. She stepped in close and pressed her body to his, feeling his warmth mingle with hers.

"This is going to be complicated," Seung said as they turned and faced the ocean once more. "My people, my *other* people, will not be as accepting of you, or us. Humans have something of a bad reputation."

He tightened his arm around her, the iron-like muscles made her feel—oddly enough—content.

"Then I'll have to help change that," he said.

"What if they refuse to accept you?" Seung asked.

He turned soft brown eyes on her and her heart leapt at the love she saw there. "You mean more to me than all the people you would have me meet."

She rested her head on his shoulder, staring out at the sea. The sun peeked through the clouds, casting its rays upon the water. "We meet the future together," she said. His simple response brought a smile to her face.

"Yeah, man."

ABOUT THE AUTHOR

Ramón Terrell is an author and actor who instantly fell in love with fantasy the day he opened R. A. Salvatore's: The Crystal Shard. Years (and many devoured books) later he decided to put pen to paper for his first novel. After a bout with aching carpals, he decided to try the keyboard instead, and the words began to flow.

As an actor, he has appeared in the hit television shows Supernatural, izombie, Arrow, and Minority Report, as well as the hit comedy web series Single and Dating in Vancouver. He also appears as one of Robin Hood's Merry Men in Once Upon a Time, as well as an Ark Guard on the hit TV show The 100. When not writing, or acting, he enjoys reading, video games, hiking, and long walks with his wife around Stanley Park in Vancouver BC.

ALSO BY RAMÓN TERRELL

World of a Broken Age:

Echoes of a Shattered Age

Legends of a Shattered Age

Heroes of a Broken Age (forthcoming)

Saga of Ruination:

Unleashed

Hunter's Moon:

Running from the Night

Hunter's Moon

Darkness of Day

Revenire (Forthcoming)

The Fairies:

Out of Ordure